JACOB MOON

A NOVEL
LETTER 26

JACOB
MOON
PUBLISHING

JACOB
MOON
PUBLISHING

Copyright © 2024 by Jacob Moon

All rights reserved.

Paperback ISBN: 978-1-7361642-8-0
Hardcover ISBN: 978-1-7361642-9-7
eBook: 979-8-9913032-0-0
Audiobook: 979-8-9913032-1-7

First Edition

Library of Congress Control Number: 2024916480. Published in the U.S.A.

Also by Jacob Moon

Furlough

Dead Reckoning

For Jordan
A great son, and even better man

CHAPTER 1

The elephant on her chest made it difficult to breathe. From her position on her living room's plush, oversized couch, her laptop balanced on the crook of her leg, Abby Carlson felt that familiar tightness press upon her as it often did during times like this—expected conversations about her childhood. It had been two months since the elephant had made its last appearance, when she'd been notified about her stepfather. Brain cancer. Three months, maybe six with treatment. Abby had handled the news well enough, telling herself that although her plan to finally visit him in prison and confront him about what he'd done to her as a little girl would now be expedited, it needn't be immediate. But all that had changed two days ago when she'd heard that the three to six months he had left was now mere weeks, if not days. More tumors had been found. Soon, his cognition would be severely reduced, followed by unconsciousness, then the end quickly thereafter. She'd had five years and every opportunity to visit him, but here she was, about to speak with her counselor over Zoom instead of heading to the prison; because rushing something like this didn't just bring the elephant back, it invited the whole herd.

Her computer clock read 4:29 p.m. The virtual therapy

session she'd scheduled two days ago would start in another minute. Her cat Thomas Magnum lay curled beside her on the couch, oblivious to his master's growing anxiety. A familiar mix of sadness and happiness came to Abby when she settled her gaze on him; sadness that the tabby she'd adopted from the local cat café would never get the chance to experience human emotion, and happiness for the same reason. When the clock turned to 4:30, she exhaled a deep sigh then moved the cursor over the "Connect" tab and clicked on it. The throbber whirled for several seconds before the connection was made, then her screen changed to the live-camera image of a smallish man seated in a wheelchair behind a desk.

She'd chosen the man on purpose. Not so much due to his gender, or Abby's self-professed reluctance to spill her guts to another woman, but because the man's profile had included a photo of his undersized body hunched over in a wheelchair, his equally undersized head twisting upward in what appeared to be a painful attempt to face the camera. If Abby was going to endure emotional pain, she figured the counselor she would choose might have more sympathy for her if he was enduring some physical pain of his own. While making sense to her, the thought had made her feel guilty at the same time, which was even worse now as she sat watching him shift uncomfortably in his electric wheelchair. His under-developed arms lay like a child's on the chair's armrests. The dark blanket he wore like a shawl couldn't hide the melon-sized hump on his right shoulder. In college, Abby had known someone with a similar-looking disability; the woman had been prone to getting cold, even in warm months, and had always worn a blanket.

Abby eyed the counselor's pale expression and guessed he didn't see much sunlight. No surprise there. Other than his obvious disability, he had the expected counselor appearance: readers perched low on his nose, an Oxford/sweater vest combo, and a wisp of gray hair swept across his balding head.

"Good afternoon, Ms. Carlson," he said, his voice surprisingly deep for his size.

"Good afternoon to you, sir," Abby said, managing a smile. He waved one of his smallish hands. "Please—no 'sirs' around here. Call me Harlon."

"Okay. And you can call me Abby. It's Abigail, technically, but only my mother called me that."

"Abby it is."

They locked eyes through their camera connections momentarily, an awkward silence filling the net-provided space between them, until Harlon shifted in his wheelchair and said something that surprised her. "Before we begin, I'd like to disclose something about myself. I am by no means required to discuss it with patients, but I choose to anyway since it tends to clear the air and offer some perspective." He motioned toward his child-sized, twisted body, no more than three feet long from head to foot, and barely fifty pounds, from the look of him. "I was born with an obvious birth defect that, well…can be disquieting to some people. I've even been compared to a hunchback." He indicated his disproportionately-sized upper back and the sizable hump on his right shoulder, under the blanket. "Congenital scoliosis gave me this hump, and microcephaly gave me my head and limbs."

He manipulated a control on the chair's armrest and reversed the chair away from the desk to quickly reveal parts of his undersized legs. The blanket lay bunched around them and fell to the floor. He shivered, then touched a control and moved the chair back to where it had been. "The doctors said the odds of a child having both these conditions is one in several million," he said. "The odds of that child surviving to adolescence is even rarer. But others are much less fortunate than me, so I try not to complain." He smiled and pushed up the glasses on his nose.

"It must be difficult for you, going out in public," Abby said, surprised the session was beginning with her expressing empathy for the man who was supposed to be showing it to her.

"It was much more difficult as a child, emotionally speaking. My condition has worsened as I've aged, but it's something I've learned to live with. On a slightly different subject, have you heard of the fictional character Quasimodo?"

"Wasn't he the Hunchback of Notre Dame?"

"Yes!" the counselor said, his face lighting up. "Most people don't know that. He happens to be my favorite fictional character, so I take it as a compliment when someone calls me that." His smile broadened as he reached forward as far as he could and rotated his laptop ninety degrees to show a large bookcase against the wall. He zoomed the camera shot for her to read the titles more easily. "There it is on the top shelf, in the middle—quite a read if you have the time. I feel that I've always shared a commonality with Hugo," he said off-camera.

Abby stared at the book, wide-eyed. "Talk about a doorstop."

The counselor laughed and rotated the laptop back to face him, adjusting the zoom back to normal. "Indeed. Publishers balk at longer works these days. I mention it to give you an example of taking something good from a bad situation. From an early age, I knew that I would never play sports or even take a single step on my own. Instead of self-pity, I directed my life toward doing this." He spread his hands and looked around the office before settling his gaze back onto his computer screen. He appeared to be reading something off of it. "Let's see...your written application states you're thirty-one, single, and that you wish to focus on your childhood sexual abuse, correct?"

"Yes."

"Specifically, you're wanting to speak to your abuser before he is expected to pass away soon?"

Abby's stomach fluttered. "Um...yes. I guess I need some advice on how to handle it."

"Okay. We'll begin in a moment. And no worries, we'll still have our full hour once we get through these formalities. Before we start, I wanted to let you know that I like to challenge my clients to accept their past and understand that although they cannot change it, it makes them who they are today. Like Quasimodo, we must all look past our ugliness and find contentedness. For him, it was looking down on Paris from the tower and ringing the bell. The question is, where will you find yours?"

Abby, taken in by the man's surprising insight, felt her previous anxiousness begin to melt away. She was already feeling her body relax into the couch's plushness. "I'll try my best."

They began where he suggested, her childhood. After describing her earliest years, which had been filled with mostly pleasant, albeit fleeting, memories of both her birth parents, she moved on to the years following her father's sudden death and her mother's second marriage. Immediately, the mood of the conversation changed. She took a breath and let the information come out without trying to sugarcoat it.

"He molested me, my stepfather. From age six to about ten. It started with touching, then progressed into other things. It happened a long time ago, but sometimes it feels like yesterday, if that makes any sense." She looked into the man's eyes. "It's weird, but sometimes I feel like it happened to someone else."

A curious expression passed before the counselor's eyes. Abby noticed it and wondered if it'd been caused by a fleeting personal memory, perhaps. "It's common for victims of abuse to become disassociated from their trauma. I encourage you to treat your child-self and adult-self like travelers on a long voyage. You will never be the same person once you reach each signpost in life because each experience and every person you meet along the way will imprint upon you. Make sense?"

"I guess," she said. She turned to gaze out her living room window onto Lyndale Avenue, two stories below. The busy Uptown thoroughfare was especially so today, with weekday rush-hour traffic clogging the street, and pedestrians strolling along the sidewalk. Separating her hands and shoving them beneath her thighs, Abby shifted her gaze back onto the counselor. "Part of me hates myself for not resisting him more. It wouldn't have stopped him, but it's always made me feel like a coward for not trying anyway."

The counselor's eyebrows arched from behind his glasses. "That's a common feeling for people in your position. As for when you plan to visit him in prison and speak with him about the abuse...I'm assuming that's why he's there?"

"He only has a few weeks to live at most. I have a visit scheduled for Monday, but he might not be in any condition to talk. And no, he's there for dealing drugs. He'll never serve a day for what he did to me."

The counselor nodded. "I see. What do you plan on saying to him?"

She prepared to say something she'd thought of many times before, a line that said if what had happened to her had taught her anything, it was that she'd die fighting rather than be subjected to anything like that again. To prove that he hadn't truly defeated her. But instead of that, she said something that surprised her. "I'd tell him I feel sorry for him. It must have been agonizing waking up every day, wondering if that would be the day my mom found out."

"Did she?"

"No, I never told."

"What do you think she would have done if you had?"

Abby huffed. "She would've waited until he passed out, then poured gasoline on him and lit it. Like the movie *The Burning Bed*."

"And now that you're an adult?"

Abby shrugged. "I'll never know. She died two years ago. A year after my brother was killed in a car accident."

"I'm very sorry for your losses. But what if I told you that you *could* tell her. Your stepfather too. Right now, as you sit there on your couch, during this meeting."

She frowned. "You mean using a Ouija board or something?"

"No. I mean that just because someone is dead or locked away in prison doesn't mean you can't tell them how you feel. Communication doesn't always necessitate a tacit response from the respondent. Preferable, yes, but not mandatory."

"Okaaaay…" she began. "So how do I do this?"

"Turn and speak to them as if they were sitting beside you. But before you do, know that if it's your stepfather, he has no ability to harm you. In fact, he won't have the ability to touch you or even speak. You're in control. Say your piece—anything you want, no matter how angry or vile or unforgiving it may be."

"Hmm." She bit her lip, then turned sharply on the couch, propping her knee onto the cushion, and folding her arms across her chest. "Hank, I've wanted to tell you this ever since I was little. You did those things to me knowing I'd never tell. That makes you a pedophile *and* a coward. Just know that I feel sorry for you. It must've been agonizing for you to wake every day and wonder if that'd be the day my mom would find out. She would've killed you. Horribly. Then *she* would've gone to prison. That's the real reason I never told. Because even though you stole my innocence, I refused to have it affect my mom, too."

Her breathing was coming shorter now, and her heart was pounding in her chest. But she felt better already. Empowered. She made a satisfied sound before turning back toward Harlon's image on her laptop screen. "Wow… "

He gave a knowing nod. "The best part of this exercise is that you get to do it whenever you need to."

"And every time, he can't speak or touch me?"

"That's how it works."

She did the same for her mother, telling her how happy she was her mother had lived her life free from the prison she surely would have experienced; and that despite that gratefulness, Abby wished she'd been somehow able to communicate to her what had happened. When she was done, she turned her gaze back out the same window and brushed aside a single tear. She'd expected more of them, but then again, she'd shed enough during her life to fill a river. Not wishing to dwell on the past, she concentrated on the bustling Uptown thoroughfare below. Early November in Minneapolis had brought with it the first frost of the season, as well as an explosion of reds and yellows from the maple trees lining the street.

During the second half-hour of the session, they spoke of varying topics. Included in them was talk of her most recent boyfriend, Anson, whom she'd broken up with two months ago. They'd dated for a year, their breakup due to them having grown apart. "Do you know where he is now?" Harlon asked.

"He lives right down the street," she said, her face a picture of resigned irony. "A mutual friend told me he's dating a girl I went to college with. I'm happy for him."

"Anyone since then?"

"No. I'm sure I will when I meet someone right for me."

At the end of the session, Harlon suggested, "How about we end with a pleasant childhood memory. Keep it brief."

Her brow wrinkled in thought. "My grandparents' farm. I spent a few weeks there every summer. One of my favorite things to do was walking through a large field of wildflowers. I'd walk with my hands at my sides, letting the flowers pass over my palms. I remember thinking that if I could only release all my pain and shame into them, I'd feel better. That it'd make what was happening to me easier to deal with. But the idea of giving those beautiful flowers something so ugly, so vile, disgusted me. I would've never forgiven myself. So I kept it from them. That always made me happy, knowing they'd stay pretty and innocent."

Abby uttered a contented sound as she turned her attention back onto the counselor. He seemed to be in his own thoughts while at the same time appearing to have listened closely to her.

She felt a sudden wave of gratefulness for having picked the man out of the dozens of potential counselors, even though her initial reasons had been selfish.

"That was a brave thing that little girl did, saving those flowers," Harlon said. He adjusted his position in the wheelchair, his smallish head stooped even lower than before.

Eying his hunched back and hump on his shoulder, Abby wished she could somehow reach through the screen and hug him. "I think I locked the memories away and only realized they were still there when I found out he was dying of cancer. I'm still going to visit him next week, but this really helped. Thank you."

"Good," he said. "Like I said, use this method whenever you feel the need. Think of it as your weaker self hypnotizing your stronger self. I do it all the time." He smiled. "Seems we've run out of time. Would you like to schedule another session?"

She nodded. "I'd like that." She reached for the box of tissues she'd placed beside her and used one to blot her eyes.

"Well, then..." She could see him reading something off his screen again. "How about next Wednesday, same time? That'll give you time to conduct your visit and let it settle."

"That works." She went to end the session when she paused. "Would it be improper if I asked you a personal question?"

The counselor shrugged. "Not unless you're going to ask me if I ate an entire pint of Ben and Jerry's last night." They both laughed.

"Do you ever wonder what it would be like, walking on your own?" As soon as the words left her mouth, she regretted them. They sounded horridly rude, even to her own ears. Clearly, she'd overstepped.

Instead of looking offended or becoming defensive, however, he smiled. "Every day. And no, that wasn't too personal. I'm glad to share it."

She sighed. The elephant, she realized for the first time, had risen off her chest. "See you next Wednesday," she said, and pressed "End Session."

After feeding Thomas Magnum and changing from her work scrubs into stylish jeans and a new sweater she'd bought at her favorite consignment store the week before, Abby grabbed the small gift off the counter she'd wrapped earlier that morning. Riding the elevator to her apartment building's lobby, she approached the doorman who was opening the door for her. "Evening, missy," he said, removing his billed cap to reveal a wisp of thinning white hair.

"Good evening yourself, Harold," Abby said, trying her best to mimic his formal air. She held out the package for him. "For Marna. Sorry to miss her birthday last week. I was swamped at work."

Harold's smile wrinkled the corners of his eyes. "Well now, you didn't have to do that."

"I sure did," she said, motioning for him to take the gift. "She remembered mine. Besides, I'm sure she's been a bit down after the surgery. How is she?"

He accepted the gift and slipped it into his doorman coat's inner pocket. "She's been better. The doctors say they got it all, but you never know." He grimaced. "Hard for a woman to lose her parts up there, even at her age."

Abby touched his arm. "I can imagine. Tell her I'll come visit this weekend when I'm off. We can watch Hallmark movies and bake cookies."

Harold laughed. "I may pass on the movies bit, but I'll take a few of those cookies." He winked. "Come over whenever."

She squeezed his arm then went to cross the threshold when he stuck his arm out to stop her. "You be careful out here, missy," he said in a low voice. He looked toward both directions of the street. "He's out here, plucking 'em right and left. Took that nurse from the hospital up the way. The rapper girl too, just last week. Finished her concert down at Club First Avenue, then poof—gone out of thin air!" He made an exploding hand gesture, his eyes widening as he did.

Abby smiled confidently. "I'm the last woman a kidnapper would be interested in. The most exciting part about me is coming home from work to watch *Wheel of Fortune* with my cat. But I promise I'll be careful." She stepped through the doorway and turned left down the sidewalk toward the bar that was her destination.

As she walked past familiar neighborhood shops and apartment buildings, she forced away thoughts of the serial kidnapper. Two dozen women since the previous spring, each one's profession represented by a different letter of the alphabet, and all abducted from their place of business. The police had witnesses and fingerprints, even surveillance video, but had yet to find the suspect. He'd had an accomplice on several occasions who had yet to be found either. Just like everyone else in the city and across the nation, Abby had initially been alarmed by the brazenness of the crimes. Since he'd preyed on local women in their 20's and 30's, Abby and other women in that demographic had had much more to worry about. But like many noteworthy crimes or traumatic news events, people tended to push the continual news flashes into the backs of their minds. As fantastic as those flashes were, people had lives to live. Abby was no different.

As she now walked down the busy Uptown street, the late-autumn sun just dipping below the horizon, she replaced thoughts of kidnappers and redundant news articles with those of the therapy session she'd just had. Now *that* was newsworthy to her. Long-dormant memories of her childhood had been disturbed, like a broom raising dust from a forgotten corner. She'd gone into the session hopeful she could come to grips with the possibility she may never get the chance to confront her step-father. She'd finished it feeling as confident as she could. But now, as she fought to push the dust cloud of memories back into its rightful corner, she decided she still needed that final bit of closure. Talking to the counselor had done what she'd intended —prepare her for Monday's visit at the prison (she'd preferred to go earlier, but the prison medical department had ruled it out due to her stepfather's recent procedure). It was a bitter irony that the man who had abused her for a large part of her childhood was now someone she hoped would survive through the weekend.

Ten minutes later, she walked through the front door of the Gimlet, the swanky Uptown bar. She'd only been here once, a brief visit about a year ago during a bar crawl with friends. Now, after exchanging polite smiles with the hostess, Abby stepped into the main sitting area and scanned the collections of heads. She didn't see Derek, her platonic male best friend. When she scanned the room again and still didn't see him, she checked her phone on the chance he'd canceled last-minute. No missed calls or messages from him. She took a lap around the bustling place, deftly dodging a woman in a cocktail dress and high heels carrying an extremely full martini. Still nothing. Derek must have gotten delayed at the shop, she figured. Turning back toward the front door to call him outside, she'd just taken two steps when she heard her name called out from her left. Looking in that direction, she saw the top of a bald, African American man's head and a waving arm from atop a row of potted plants. Weaving her way through crowded tables, she made her way to where he sat.

"Sorry I'm late—I got held up at the bank," she said, opting for a white lie instead of having to rehash her therapy session. She plopped onto the chair opposite him, took a sip from the glass of water already there, and gave a huge sigh.

"You were in a *bank robbery?*" Derek asked, eyes wide. He raised both hands with feigned melodrama and looked at an imaginary person beside him. "Excuse me, Mr. Robber, if you're looking for someone to strip naked and tie up, I volunteer."

Abby nearly spit out a mouthful of water. "You're terrible," she said, flagging down their waiter. She ordered them both a Cosmo, keeping with their hump day happy hour tradition. They made small talk for several minutes, during which she tried in vain to fully suppress thoughts of her therapy session. When their drinks came, she took a sip of hers and instantly felt warmth spread through her. The heaviness in her chest that had been present before and during the session had faded once the session ended; but now, as she smiled into her best friend's face, she felt guilty for telling him even a white lie.

He must have seen it in her eyes because he laid a hand on hers and asked, "Honey, you okay?"

"I'll be fine," she said, relieved he'd asked. "My bank visit was really the counseling session I mentioned."

Derek nodded knowingly. "How'd it go?"

She took a huge gulp of her drink, set the glass down, and stared at it.

"Say no more," Derek said, squeezing her hand. "Charles has been seeing a therapist ever since we've been together. I'm starting to believe that some skeletons are meant to stay buried."

"At least I didn't have to talk face-to-face. I found someone who does Zoom sessions."

"Ohh, I love Zoom. It's how Charles and I met. It's amazing how much of a connection you can have with someone through a computer screen. I've thought about developing a Zoom dating site called Leer the Queer."

Abby laughed. "I'm sure it'd be a hit, knowing your business skills. You may even give Grindr a run for their money."

Suddenly, Derek's expression turned serious. "Oh my God, you just reminded me, did you hear about the new Instagram post? They think it's *him* again."

"*Him* who?" Abby asked.

Derek gave her an exasperated look. "PK, who else? We were just talking about Nautinice yesterday. The cops got the post taken down right away, but everyone's saying it's him."

Abby nodded. "My doorman just reminded me about it. Everyone thought it was going to be a real estate agent or something exotic like a racecar driver."

"I don't know how much more exotic you can get than a rap star with a diamond-studded microphone," Derek said. "Her bodyguard went on the news saying he watched her walk into her dressing room alone after her concert ended. When he checked on her five minutes later, she was gone."

"I thought the cops said they got camera footage of the suspect," Abby said, indulging Derek's need to gossip, even if it now involved discussing the criminal the media had dubbed the "Profession Killer."

"They did, but it was inconclusive. Until we found out it was PK, everyone at the shop joked that maybe she got tired of all the fame and disappeared to the same island Biggie and Tupac went to." They both laughed. "But seriously, aren't you worried?"

Abby frowned. "Why would I be worried?"

"Because you're a D. Only that and V left."

She went to say something along the lines of him being ridiculous, that it was foolish to be worried about being one of dozens of potential professions and thousands of women whom the serial kidnapper could target, but even saying that seemed like wasted utility. "Derek, I appreciate your thoughts, but I have more to worry about than some weirdo who poses dead women in their work clothes. I'm a dietitian. We're boring. Mine is the last profession he'd target."

"True. Maybe he'll take a dancer."

Abby shook her head. "He already has the stripper. It's the same thing. At least he's equal opportunity." She felt warm all of a sudden. Digging into her purse, she removed a hair-tie, with the intention of putting her hair up. As she removed it, the clip from her work ID snagged on her thumb and the ID fell to the floor beside her. A man sitting by himself at a table near them paused from working on his laptop to bend over and pick it up. Handing it to her, he offered a brief smile.

"Thank you," Abby said, embarrassed at her clumsiness. Had the man's eyes lingered over her ID a second longer than necessary? She couldn't be sure and chalked it up to being paranoid over the discussion she and Derek were having.

"Remember the pool we have at the shop? No one's guessed right yet, so the pot keeps rolling over," Derek said, continuing in the same vein. "I put my money on him taking a dentist when he gets to D. If I'm right, I'm taking you to Cancun."

"I thought you liked your dentist," she said, taking another sip of her Cosmo. She set the half-full glass down and pushed it away from her. She hadn't eaten since lunch, and her head was already swimming.

"Duh, my dentist is a man. PK is clearly straight," he joked. "Good thing, because I've been waiting for my dentist to root inside my canal since I laid eyes on him."

She smacked him on the arm, looking around to make sure no one heard his comment. "I can't take you anywhere!"

"A girl's gotta dream," he said matter-of-factly.

"I suppose. But I hope it isn't a dentist. Mine is female, and I happen to love her."

"Let's make it a door-to-door salesman, then. Everyone hates them."

"Deal!" she said, reaching across the table to shake hands with him to seal it. "For once, I don't mind being in an obscure profession. But enough of that. How's the shop doing?"

That got them talking about work, mainly how his new position as head stylist at the hair salon was going. After talking about his oft-dramatic relationship with Charles, as well as Abby's recent breakup with her long-time boyfriend, Derek checked his watch. "Gotta run. My turn to cook tonight."

"What's for dinner?"

"Homemade carbonara. Trying it the true Italian way, without cream."

"Sounds delicious," Abby said, her eyes aglow. "No man with an apron cooking for me, so I'll settle for Marie Callender and a glass of wine."

After Derek paid the tab—since it was his turn—they made their way outside and stood on the darkened, relatively empty sidewalk. It was almost seven p.m. and already the early November chill made them both shiver. "Let me walk you home," he offered.

"I'll be fine. It's six blocks."

"I insist," Derek said, removing his jacket and draping it over her shoulders. He offered the crook of his arm, then stared straight ahead in the direction of Abby's apartment building. Knowing any further protest would be futile, Abby sighed and took his arm.

They walked mostly in silence, listening to the sounds of urbanity along the way. When they reached her building, Derek exchanged nods with the doorman, who stood ready to open the door for Abby.

"Thank you, Derek," she said, removing her hand from his arm. "For being such a good friend." For the first time since she'd left her apartment to meet him, the tightness in her chest was completely gone.

Taking his jacket back, he gripped her by the elbows and held them at arm's length. "Call me if you need anything. And I mean *anything*. I'm at the shop through Tuesday next week, but I'll push my appointments back if you need me before your prison visit. That weird old bag, Mrs. Wilcox will be first on the chopping block. She takes her hair home in a plastic bag because she thinks the CIA tracks people's DNA with it."

Abby stood on her tiptoes and kissed him on the cheek, then

turned to walk through the door. Harold exchanged a silent nod with Derek before watching him walk back the way he'd come.

Entering her eighth-floor apartment, Abby was immediately met by Thomas Magnum. He curled his body around her leg, his heavy black whiskers brushing her hand as she squatted to pet him. Fixing him dinner first, Abby popped a frozen pot pie in the oven then clicked on the TV. *Wheel of Fortune* had just started. Afterward, it wasn't long before she slipped into a luxurious hot bath while sipping an even more luxurious glass of merlot.

CHAPTER 2

The Next Day
4:45 p.m.

"Guard's here," Abby said, glancing through the Uptown Dietitian Center's front door. A tall, middle-aged Caucasian man in a baggy, familiar-looking black security company nylon jacket and matching cap stepped from a white van and walked confidently toward the front double doors. He made brief eye contact with both Abby and Belinda—the two dietitians on duty now—through the windowed doors and touched the brim of his cap. Handsome guy, Abby thought, at least from what she could tell from her brief glance at him. Dark blond hair peeking below the back of his cap, and a well-trimmed mustache. Before she could get a better look at him, he turned to face the parking lot. A radio sat clipped to one side of his belt, a holstered pistol on the other.

"Another new guy," said Belinda with a sigh. "I really liked the last one."

"Me too," Abby said. "But at least they finally sent someone who could actually protect us if he had to. The last guy was sweet, but he was two steps away from an assisted living facility." She glanced up at the clock on the waiting room wall before tapping Belinda on the shoulder. "Go ahead and get out of here. No reason to be late picking up Riley."

Belinda hesitated. "Are you sure? You know what Valerie said."

"I know, but it's a silly rule. Besides, the guard's here."

Belinda looked out the doors at him. He was a picture of protectiveness—solidly build, assured stance, hands on hips. "True. And Riley just texted me that practice is ending early today, so getting a head start would help. Still—are you sure?"

"Yep," Abby said, waving her away. "You'd better get to the field while all those hot soccer dads are still there." They both laughed.

"Okay, I'll run then," Belinda said, scooting her chair out and shouldering her purse strap. "There *is* a cute guy I've noticed lately. A lawyer, I think."

"Married?"

"Unfortunately," Belinda said, rolling her eyes. "All the good ones are. Oh well—see you tomorrow." She logged out of her computer, made her way through the waiting room, then pushed her way out the front door. After saying something to the guard, she climbed into her blue Corolla and pulled out of the parking lot before disappearing down the street. Alone in the clinic now but feeling an increased measure of safety, Abby began her closing procedures without worry. Due to the PK abductions over the past seven months, the clinic's owner had hired a part-time security guard to cover the openers and closers. She'd also insisted on those procedures going from the normal one employee to two, which was not to be diverted from under any circumstances. If she found out Abby had broken the rule and decided to close by herself, she'd be upset for sure. But Valerie was a fair woman, one who had clawed and scratched her way to owning her own business without her businessman husband's help. Abby figured she'd understand, especially since the rule had been broken on account of Belinda's difficult situation being a single parent. Valerie had been one herself. It didn't hurt that Abby was well-known to be Valerie's favorite and most experienced dietitian on staff.

At precisely five p.m., with the office still empty, Abby finished the last of her closing duties and logged out of her computer terminal. Turning out the lights, she grabbed her purse and armed the security system on the wall-mounted unit. Turning out the lights, she had just stepped outside to lock up when the guard's voice came from behind her. "Excuse me, ma'am, is there any way I can use your bathroom? I should have gone before I got here, and it'll be a bit 'til I get to my next assignment."

She turned to face the man, who stood several feet away, shifting from foot to foot. "Oh…sure, of course. I always need to go the minute I get in the car, so I'm familiar." She opened the door and held it open for him.

"You're an angel," the guard said. He smiled appreciatively, deep dimples appearing in both cheeks, then slipped into the clinic's unisex bathroom. Abby disarmed the alarm before the thirty-second timer ran out then waited patiently for him to finish, listening to the sound of him flushing the toilet. As she did so, she glanced through the front door and noticed a man in a baggy sweatshirt and ball cap pulled down over his face at the far end of the parking lot. He appeared homeless or working on it. This area of Uptown had its fair share of folks who were homeless, she knew, so she didn't sense any danger, even when he glanced toward the clinic's front door. But when he began walking in that direction, cutting directly through the parking lot and straight toward the clinic, Abby almost went to lock the door. But the sound of the running sink, followed by the familiar *whap* of paper towels being pulled from the dispenser, echoed through the empty waiting room. The guard would be out any second, she figured, and the man walking toward the clinic was still twenty yards away. Sure enough, a moment later the guard exited the restroom, a look of great relief on his face. "Whew, you saved me from finding a gas station," he said, re-fastening his gun belt. "The last one I used was a germaphobe's nightmare."

"No problem," Abby said with a laugh. "I'd probably rather go in the bushes than use most gas stations, so I get it." She glanced back out the front door and was glad to see that the strange man had disappeared. Probably to bed down in the alley behind the clinic, she thought, or rummage through the trash. As she turned to begin re-arming the security code, she detected sudden movement behind her. Not the guard beginning his path toward the front door as she'd assumed he'd do, but seeming to close the distance *toward* her. Animal instinct caused the hairs on the back of her neck to rise a split second before she began to spin to face him. But before she finished her rotation, the guard slipped his left arm around her neck, yanking her backward into his bulky torso.

At first, she believed he must be playing a joke on her. *Ha-ha, scared ya, didn't I?* But of course, that was ludicrous. He was the guard, for God's sake, the last person who would invade a woman's personal space in such a way. A half-second after that thought raced through her mind, realization kicked in and she bucked her body hard against his. But he was too strong, and with a squeeze of his arm around her neck, he cut off her air supply. Eyes bulging, Abby clawed and scratched in vain at the guard's arm. She twisted her body hard and scissor-kicked her legs in a desperate attempt to gain enough space to breathe, but his arm was tightening across her throat even more now. She'd been without air for about five seconds, but it felt like five minutes. Her lungs instantly began to burn, and tiny black dots pinpricked her vision.

Then, a sudden thought: If she could get to his eyes with her right hand, she might have a chance. She reached up and began to scratch at his face when she felt a moist cloth clamp down over her nose and mouth. As she struggled, a crazy thought struck her oxygen-deprived brain—that he felt bad for what he was doing to her and had decided to clean her makeup-smeared face. As Abby's eyelids fluttered and with her brain beginning to prepare for unconsciousness, the guard released enough pressure around her neck for her to breathe. Immediately, she heaved in a wheezing breath through the cloth. The black dots in her vision disappeared, if only for a moment, and for one amazing second her mind conjured an even better scenario—he was going to let her go. He'd realized his mistake and would even call the police on himself. *Sorry for choking you like that. I don't know what came over me…*

She inhaled again through the cloth, and just as her brain decided that thought too was ridiculous, she realized what he was doing. She tried to scream but couldn't; her throat was too damaged. She moved her lips uselessly, only the hoarse whispered words "help me" escaping them. And as the sweet chemical odor on the cloth finally registered to her senses, it all came together in a flash; she was about to become PK's twenty-fifth victim. This knowledge caused her to kick even more wildly. She gained a partial foothold on the wall and pushed off, spinning them both to the right. He corrected for it, though, and spun her back toward the wall, pinning her against it face-first. He pressed his shoulder into her back while keeping one arm tight around her neck, but giving her just enough room to breathe.

She wheezed again, fighting to keep her fluttering eyelids from snapping closed. She was fading fast. The black dots reappeared in her vision, even larger now. Her throat made a low guttural sound that reminded her of the gravely wounded deer she'd stumbled across in the woods near her grandparents' farm when she was twelve. It had been shot with an arrow and was too weak to run when she approached to try to help it. She was the deer now. Like a light switch inside her head flipping off, her eyelids fluttered once more before they slammed shut and her world went suddenly black.

CHAPTER 3

She came to sometime later—how much later, she couldn't be sure—and assumed at first that she was either dreaming or had awakened in some darkened room. A hard rubber ball the size of a golf ball sat wedged into her mouth. Similar rubber straps connected to it were wrapped tight around her head, making it impossible for her to dislodge the ball with her mouth. She tried to sit up but was instantly restricted by a heavy, plasticky bag of some kind covering the entire length of her body. A trio of tightened straps pinned the bag against her, her arms to her sides, and her legs together. Although her throat no longer hurt, it was hard to breathe normally due to the bag pressing against her face. A sudden panicked thought: she may be paralyzed, or even dead. This was what it would be like.

Closing her eyes amid the dark confines she was in, she forced herself to relax and concentrate on moving something small. A finger or a toe. No luck there. Nothing except the power to blink her eyes, her lashes brushing against the material over her face. She took a deep breath through her nose, realizing when she did that, she knew she couldn't be completely paralyzed. Okay, something else, then. Another deep breath as she concentrated solely on moving her right index finger. There! It moved, although just a flinch. Buoyed by that minute movement, next she tried to move her entire hand. Nothing at first, but then her other fingers twitched. Pinching her leg to ensure she wasn't dreaming, she exhaled gratefully through her nose when she felt the prick of her fingernails through her scrub bottoms. If only the goddamned ball in her mouth weren't there, she could take a proper breath.

With every passing moment, she regained increased sensation. First, the numbness in her hands lessened. Then her toes regained feeling, followed by her arms and legs. Finally, the leaden feeling in her limbs wore off with each passing second, until she was able to move her hands up to waist level. But the straps prevented her moving them up any further. Once she'd regained enough feeling in her neck to move her head slightly to the side, she saw through her peripheral vision a hand-sized circle perforation in the side of the bag. Faint light was coming through the holes, providing enough air for her to avoid suffocating. Moving her head in the other direction, she saw a similar set of holes on the opposite side as well. Had her nose brushed against a metallic seam running down the length of the bag when she'd done that? Yes, it had. A second later, her brain made the connection—a zipper.

Even more concerning was the fact she detected movement. Not near her. And not just the sound of it. The *sensation* of it. She was in a vehicle, she determined. She'd never ridden in this position before—flat on her back, strapped down, her head toward the back end of whatever she was begin driven in—so it had taken her longer than usual to orient herself. Another realization then—she was lying on a gurney, similar to the one she'd laid on six months ago when she'd had surgery to remove ovarian cysts. Just as her mind made that connection, she felt the gurney lift slightly in the air before slamming back down (a speed bump or pothole, most likely). Then a distant but nonetheless familiar sound—a car horn.

She finally managed to wiggle all her toes. Good, it was all coming back, albeit slowly. Thinking back to the last memory she'd had before blacking out, she remembered the guard approaching her. Now, she felt the vehicle turning, then accelerating as her weight shifted toward her head, followed by the metallic sound of gears changing beneath her. A second later it clicked—she was in was a body bag.

She recalled seeing the guard arrive in a white van and assumed it was the vehicle she was riding in. Valerie had several surveillance cameras in the clinic, with one covering the parking lot. Hopefully, they'd captured the man's description and the van's tag. As sensation continued to return to her body— spreading through her chest and up her legs, until finally she felt a cramp in her full bladder—Abby took note of whatever sounds she could hear through the perforations. Someone outside the van yelling. Other vehicles passing close by. Large tires beneath her moving over a concrete roadway. Minutes later, the tire sounds changed. They were no longer moving over well-paved roads. Still paved, but bumpy. Twice she felt herself being jolted, as if the van had run over more potholes. A minute later, the van paused, then progressed slowly up an incline before making a sharp right turn and cutting its engine. Two car doors opening then closing, the sound of a garage door lowering, and soon after a set of double doors opening behind her head.

The guard's voice: "Help me with her." Abby felt herself being rolled backward. A spring-loaded metallic mechanism opened beneath the gurney, followed by the sound of wheels striking concrete. "Take the feet. I'll unlock the door, then inside down the hallway," the guard said.

Abby wanted to cry out, but the ball gag prevented her. Although she couldn't form words, she could still groan. Loudly. She'd done so a few months ago during a bout with the flu, when Derek had come over to care for her. He'd commented about her midnight laments being loud enough to wake the dead. But a stronger sensibility overruled the urge to do so now, one that suggested she'd be best served not to appear more aware and able than these people obviously intended her to be. There was a reason people and animals often played dead, she thought.

She felt herself being rolled several feet before stopping long enough for one of them to unlock a door, then being raised over a threshold before being pushed another few seconds. She heard the loud click of a button being pushed, followed by the groan of what sounded like an aging elevator. "You're free to go now," said the guard. "The same way you came in." The sound of footsteps echoed, slow and languid, before they paused at what Abby presumed to be the doorway they'd just entered through.

"Thank you, I couldn't do any of this without you," the guard's voice called out, presumably toward the second person. The sound of the distant door opening then closing came to Abby through the perforations, leaving only the sound of the elevator door groaning closed, before they descended for what felt like an eternity. In reality, it couldn't have been more than a floor or two. On cue, the door groaned open, and she felt herself being pushed forward until the gurney finally stopped and the straps binding her legs and arms were removed, followed by the bag being unzipped.

Bright light and gloriously fresh air struck her senses like gold. She squinted hard against the overhead lights shining directly down into her eyes. As she blinked away the remaining fogginess that had plagued her since being drugged, the handsome face of a man staring down at her came into focus. White, early forties, with a healthy head of black hair touched by gray at the temples, and a strong jawline supporting a dimpled smile that, under any other circumstances, could have caused her heart to race. Despite the loss of the guard uniform, mustache, and blond hair, Abby was sure the man staring down at her was the same one who'd drugged her.

"Good morning, sleepyhead," the man said with what

seemed like genuine cheer. He looked the length of her body over, studying perhaps if she'd regained her ability of movement. After dabbing her sweaty face and neck with a handkerchief, he met her eyes again, his smile remaining as if painted there. "Nod, if you have feeling back. Don't lie to me if you do. I'll be able to tell."

Abby swallowed saliva that had accumulated in the back of her throat. She didn't want him to know she had feeling back, but something told her it would be best to be truthful to him. She nodded.

"I thought so," he said, clapping his hands together. He looked up toward something she couldn't see from her position. "I'll remove the gag and get you out of this thing on two conditions. One, you mustn't cry out. Not under any circumstances. It would ruin the mood. Not that anyone would hear you anyway, since the basement here is fully sound-insulated. And two, you must do everything I ask of you. Immediately, and without deviation. I'll have to put the gag back on you, among other punishments, if you don't. Trust me when I say you won't like what would be in store for you."

She looked away from him when he said that, and he said, "Look at me, Abby." She snapped her eyes back at him. *He knows who I am.* "Nod, if you understand." She nodded. "Excellent." He reached down and undid the bands holding the ball gag in place. A few strands of her hair that had been caught in the elastic were inadvertently ripped from her scalp, causing her to yelp. Still, it felt glorious to be able to breathe through her mouth again and stretch her jaw.

"Sorry about that," he said, giving the side of her head a stroke. "These implements can be troublesome. But now that you're here, I won't need to put it back on you, providing you keep your promise." He held up his pinky toward her, bent like a hook. She stared dumbly at it, unsure of what to do. The man raised his eyebrows, glanced down to her hand lying limply at her side, then looked back at her expectantly. "Well?"

Slowly, as if fearful that any sudden movement on her part would anger him, Abby slowly lifted her right hand and gave him the pinky swear he seemed to want.

"Now it's official!" he declared. He remained all smiles, his dimples deepening in his clean-shaven cheeks. "Now, let's get you out of this thing. I apologize for needing it. The thing with the cloth, too. Unfortunately, it was necessary to get you here. I've found that the last thing the police think of is unzipping a body bag in the back of a mortuary van. Even one with vents."

Abby stayed silent while he lifted her feet and legs free from the bottom of the bag before rolling her body toward him and doing the same with her upper body. The movement awakened a sudden urge to urinate, one she suspected had been masked by whatever he'd drugged her with. She couldn't recall the last time she'd wet herself—as a child, no doubt. Being kidnapped was one thing, she reasoned. Pissing herself in front of the man responsible seemed to her an even worse degradation, if that was possible. Feeling her bladder threaten to release, she squeezed her legs together as hard as she could in the desperate hope of holding it.

By now her eyes had recovered from the bright overhead lights and she saw that he'd wheeled her into a large room. The length of one wall was covered in wood paneling, with a cast-iron fireplace and ten-foot-long stack of wood in the middle. The opposite wall contained two doors, both closed, with a pastoral painting and several pieces of farm-related equipment hanging from nails. The opening to a doorless room hidden mostly in shadow could be seen along the third wall, along with what appeared to be a bathroom. An ascending wooden staircase stood opposite it. The man lifted her into a sitting position then stood directly in front of her, hands on hips. In place of his security guard uniform and gun belt, he now wore a gray jumpsuit with the words *Body Removal Specialist* sewn across the breast. He must have seen her pained expression and the way she clenched her legs together, because his expression changed from playful amusement to one of sudden apology. "How rude of me—you probably need to use the restroom. Let me help you. The drug takes some time to completely wear off."

He held out a hand to her. Tentatively she took it, sliding off the edge of the gurney and nearly collapsing in a heap due to the lingering wooziness in her head. He righted her and made a shushing sound like a patient parent attending to a sick child. Abby felt sudden nausea come over her, so much so she feared she'd throw up all over the both of them. But she shook the feeling away, determined to avoid any further act that could signify weakness. He tried to get her to sit back down but she shook her head. "No, I'm fine, thanks," she insisted, following on wobbly legs as he led her toward the small half-bathroom. He flipped on the light and motioned for her to enter. When she did, expecting him to allow her to close the door, he instead propped it open with his foot and leaned back against the jamb.

Realizing that he intended to stand watch while she went, Abby didn't hesitate. Turning toward the seat, she yanked her scrub bottoms and underwear down to just below her knees while keeping one hand covering her pubic region. She'd barely plopped onto the seat when a torrent of urine burst from her, splashing loudly into the bowl. Relief washed over her, making her eyes water and sending spasms through her abdomen. At least the man was decent enough to look straight ahead at the opposing door jamb. Finishing, she pulled her pants up then washed her hands. Glancing around, she noted no windows or other avenues of possible escape. Even the mirror was stainless steel instead of glass.

The man waited for her to dry her hands before turning to look at her. "I'll show you where your room is, so you can get your bearings. Then we'll take a trip upstairs. Remember your promise." She took his offered hand and followed him back into the main room. When they approached the fireplace, he bent to fidget with something in the stack of wood. While he did, Abby dared a quick glance back toward the darkened, doorless room at the end of the hall, but couldn't make out any obvious means of escape there either. Enough light was spilling into that room for Abby to make out what appeared to be some sort of steel table in the center of the floor, but not much else.

Manipulating a hidden latch in the wood pile, the man gripped a likewise hidden handle and pulled. Magically, one half of the wood pile, along with the wood-paneled wall, rolled on a concealed track to reveal a recessed wall behind it all. It featured two wooden doors side by side, as well as an industrial stainless-steel door akin to that of a walk-in cooler. As he went to unlock one of the wooden doors, he stopped, appearing to realize some obvious fault of his own.

"Where are my manners? I never introduced myself. I'm Frederik." He offered his hand. She looked at it as if it were something alien. "I promise it won't bite you."

She lifted her hand to his and shook it loosely.

"Glad to make your acquaintance," Frederik added matter-of-factly. "Normally I wait with new girls to show off my work. The first day tends to be a bit stressful, and some of them became hysterical when they saw my creations too early. But the way you fought me back there, something tells me you'll take it in stride." He winked, flashing that boyish, dimpled smile. "Aside from my brother, I don't have anyone else to show them off to in person."

For the first time, the specific thought of him killing her entered Abby's mind. The prospect of him raping her had also entered her mind on more than one occasion since she'd awakened. She recalled stories of kidnapped women kept in basements or homemade bunkers as sex slaves, some of them for years. But something in the man's manner, even the look in his eyes, told her that wasn't his endgame. *But if not rape, then what?*

Frederik, or whatever his name really was, opened the door long enough for her to see inside. Five by eight, and windowless, it was more of a closet than a bedroom. Just a mattress and box spring on the floor, with a plain bedspread. No other furnishings or decorations on the unfinished walls. Closing the door, he took her by the hand and led her toward the staircase. Abby was surprised when he allowed her to lead the way. With him still loosely holding her right hand, she climbed. An inner voice screamed at her to kick him and dash up the stairs, that if she hesitated for even a second, she'd never get the chance again. But a second voice, one that lived in an even deeper level of reason within her, told her doing so would not only be futile, but would cause him to make good on his promise of punishing her. Besides, it was doubtful that he'd have been foolish enough to leave an easy escape route for her. He'd mentioned no one being able to hear her down here if she cried out. Well-insulated and likely remote. A sickening feeling came over her as she mindlessly climbed the stairs. The image of a dusty file shelved in some police department's cabinet with her name, and the words "Cold Case" printed on it, came to her. Or worse, her bleached bones discovered by a group of kids playing in the woods.

When they reached the darkened upper landing, they faced a closed door. Frederik's voice came cold and direct from just behind her. "Open the door. I'm going to show you something you may find disturbing. I understand if it does. But please remember not to cry out or look away. It'll ruin it for me."

She reached out with a hand that suddenly felt not her own and opened the door. Immediately, cold air swooshed over her. It had to be forty degrees up here, a touch warmer than the outside air temperature. A shiver ran through her as her arm returned languidly to her side and she stepped out into a narrow hallway that looked like it belonged in a large residential home. "Left," he said. She turned that way and began counting her steps, perhaps to retain some part of the world she knew to be verifiable.

Abby had counted to eight when they reached a dimly lit formal living room. The home seemed to be of some bygone era —Victorian, perhaps—with ornately carved archways separating the rooms, peeling red wallpaper, and early twentieth-century furniture that could have been right out of the antique shop down the street from her apartment. All of it reminded her of one of her favorite black and white movies, *Gaslight*. Heavy red velvet curtains covered a pair of tall windows, their frames made of decorative wood. The curtains' natural splits had been sewn together, their edges nailed to the wall. She imagined the outside of the windows covered in burglar bars. He wouldn't want anyone peeking inside or breaking in through a window. As if reading her mind, he said, "The windows are barred and bolted to the studs. The upstairs ones, too. Even though we're a ways from the main road, someone could try to break in. That's how this place came up for sale. The old owners abandoned the place without removing a thing. Later, a group of kids broke in on a dare and, well…they got a shock, I'm sure."

Once they had fully entered the room, Abby was surprised to see three other women already present. The first—a curly-haired brunette of about thirty—sat staring in Abby's general direction from behind a desk and computer. Dressed in a knee-length black business skirt and white blouse, she appeared to be lost in thought or working through some difficult mental problem as she held the end of a pen between her teeth. She smiled brightly when Abby made eye contact with her. *Hello, so nice to meet you, D*, Abby imagined the woman saying to her. *I'll register you now. Is it "dietician" or "dietitian"?*

Something peculiar about the woman froze the thought in Abby's mind. She'd been holding the pen to her mouth for far longer than normal, given that two other people had obviously just entered the room. Looking closer, Abby realized the heavy makeup on the woman's neck wasn't enough to hide the top end of a row of stitches there. When Frederik touched a hand to Abby's back, guiding her a few feet to the left, she noticed a metallic brace fitted around the sitting woman's waist. It was connected to the chair she'd been propped up on, holding her rigid body in place. Something loosened in Abby's gut then, and despite her exposed skin having already gotten used to the cold temperature up here, gooseflesh spread out on her bare arms.

"Mina, my event planner," Frederik said cheerfully. He came up beside Abby and draped an arm across her shoulders. "I met her at a party she'd planned for an old colleague. There wasn't enough of a connection between us for me to be suspected. I waited a month to take her. Posed as a delivery driver. A close call; I was about five seconds from getting caught while I was stuffing her in a catering crate." He shook his head with the memory. "The biggest irony is that one of her co-workers helped me load it into the truck."

Abby was sure that had she not just gone to the bathroom, she would have wet herself right then.

"After I transitioned her, I had to keep her in the freezer downstairs until the others were ready. Needed to wait for cooler weather, too. I was worried she wouldn't thaw well, since I'd made a mistake with the embalming. Had to use the neck instead of the groin, but she still turned out just fine."

Abby closed her eyes. This wasn't happening. After a silent count to five, she slowly opened her eyes again, but the image before her remained. She shifted her gaze to the second woman, a young blond standing in the corner to her left, propped up by a similar bracket around her waist. It was connected to a heavy platform at her bare feet, itself barely visible through the heap of white sand on the floor. Dressed in a red one-piece bathing suit with a white cross on the front, she held a whistle to her pursed lips with one hand. Her other hand gripped a red life preserver ring. Her blue eyes stared ahead, the pupils fixed and dilated. Somehow, sadness seemed to communicate from them, perhaps due to the glue holding them open, some having dripped onto one cheek and drying there like a stream of frozen tears. Completing the beachy tableau was a hand-painted lake and sky scene on the section of wall behind her.

"Nicole—from Lake Harriet this past last summer," Frederik said. Abby heard his voice from beside her, but it seemed a million miles away. "Did you know that Minnesota has *more* than ten thousand lakes? 11,842, to be exact. They rounded it down to make it look better on the license plate." He paused. "And the butter package, too."

Abby stood speechless, unable to fully comprehend what she was seeing. Taking an instinctive step backward, she nearly tripped over her own feet. One hand went up to cover her mouth just as Frederik reached out to catch her from falling.

"Whoa there," he said, steadying her. He stood shoulder-to-shoulder with her, admiring the lifeguard. Even though she couldn't see his face, Abby knew he was smiling his dimpled smile. "I knew I had to have her the moment I saw her. I didn't visit too often after that first time, and waited for a windy day with few people at the beach. I stayed back until she got off duty at dusk and everyone else had left. I watched her go into a porta-potty, then made my move."

The third woman in the room—Asian and thirtyish, with black hair tied back in a ponytail—stood in a bent position opposite an aging settee and ornate Cheval mirror. Wearing red Converse All-Stars, rolled-up jeans, and a trendy, cropped-top t-shirt exposing her navel, she held an expensive-looking camera sideways to one eye, as if photographing someone on the settee. Her exposed eye and one side of her mouth had been glued and positioned in such a way to give her an expression of extreme concentration. Her body was supported by a similar-looking device as the other two women. The row of dark stitches on one side of her neck contrasted with her unnaturally pale skin.

Abby felt the flesh on the back of her neck and arms begin to crawl. She'd experienced many nightmares before, but never had she felt this innate sense of horror and disgust during any of them. Worse was the fact that she knew she wasn't dreaming. She'd made sure by pinching herself hard enough to nearly draw blood while inside the body bag.

"I'll introduce you to more of the girls later," Frederik said. "I only started bringing them up from the freezer last week. Such a shame to have kept them down there over the summer, but it's wakey-wakey time now. Finally cold enough outside. Speaking of, I apologize for having to keep the windows open up here and not heating the main floors, but we wouldn't want them to get sick, would we?" He slapped a hand on Abby's shoulder, as if they'd been lifelong friends. "But first, food. You've got to be famished."

As she followed his lead toward the nearby kitchen, Abby's mind spun in a hundred different directions. As unreal as all this seemed, she knew that it *was* real. She considered bolting and running, anywhere except right here beside him. She glanced through the adjoining foyer at the heavy-looking front door. Something seemed off with it. She quickly realized why—it pushed out farther than the surrounding walls. He'd apparently fashioned a vestibule of some sort behind it; she imagined there was another door leading to the outside, with only one being open at any given time, so to hide the interior from anyone standing at the house's open front door.

As they entered the kitchen, she swallowed hard. She realized that all the doors leading in and out of the house would have similar vestibules, and likely multiple locks. It would take an army to break in. And he'd likely have some intricate security system as well. He'd become an expert at being careful. After all, he'd done this two dozen times now without getting caught, all while being on the FBI's Most Wanted list. It said a lot that he felt comfortable enough to have her up here. Instinct told her she'd never escape this place completely on her own. She may as well be held captive on the moon.

It wasn't until he sat her down at a small Formica-topped table that Abby noticed the woman standing at the stove. She wore black pants, a chef coat and matching chef hat, and gripped the handle of a frying pan atop the stove. A few strands of black hair had fallen from the hat, and Frederik dutifully tucked them back in before retrieving some pans from the cabinet. Abby noted the same waist clamp and base platform supporting the chef as the other women. Other *corpses*, she corrected herself. Suddenly, a wave of nausea passed over her so strong that she was sure she'd throw up right there. Her skin still crawled, and when Frederik began rummaging through the fridge, she knew that somehow she was going to need to force herself to eat whatever he and the dead chef cooked up for her. He'd be angered if she didn't. Then, a woman's trembling voice came to Abby's ears. It took her a couple extra seconds to realize the voice was her own. "Are…are you going to kill me?"

Bent before the open fridge, Frederik paused for a moment before turning back to face her. His head tilted to the side and his voice came low and soothing. It might have comforted her in any other circumstance. Now it only chilled her to the bone.

"All in good time."

CHAPTER 4

The Minneapolis Police Department's Homicide Unit, part of the larger Violent Crimes Investigation Division, sat on the eighth floor of the city's Public Service Building in the heart of downtown. Detective Cal Randall, one of the unit's most long-standing members, pulled into the parking garage and rode the elevator to the same floor he'd worked on for the past twelve years. It was 8:45 a.m., Friday morning. He wasn't supposed to be on duty today; his three weeks of paid leave for what his superiors had referred to as a "psychological setback" wasn't due to end until the following Monday. But his ringing cellphone had awakened him from his early-morning stupor, Sergeant Fells' voice on the other end seeming like a dream.

"The chief reduced your leave," she'd said. *"He'd extended it longer than ordered just to be safe, but you passed your last exam. We need you, so get into the office ASAP. And by that, I mean immediately."*

Eyes slit against the bright overheads, Randall pressed his fob against the security reader. Waiting for the familiar buzz, he opened the tempered glass door into Homicide's reception area, then weaved his way through the labyrinth of cubicles until he came to his desk. Plopping down heavily in his chair, he dug a bottle of Advil from his top desk drawer and shook out four of the rounded tablets. Palming them into his mouth, he swallowed them dry. His head felt like a truck had ridden over it, and his stomach felt like it was tied in knots—both the result of the previous night's half-bottle of bourbon and two-day-old leftover Thai food. Having been awakened an hour ago, he'd showered in the dark to limit the light that seemed to pierce his brain like an ice pick.

He turned now to look out his slated office window and spied the familiar pitched, green roofs of the main City Hall building and attached clock tower. The five-story, rusticated granite seat of city government sat kitty-corner to the PSB, taking up a several-acre section of downtown. Since childhood, it had remained his favorite building in the entire city. Built over a century ago, the iconic edifice boasted turrets, arched entryways, and the striking roof he gazed at now. The roof, dozens of glittering skyscrapers, office buildings and hotels, and even U.S Bank Stadium where the hometown Vikings played just four blocks east, made for a great view. But ever since being assigned to Homicide, Randall had learned that along with those prime views came the knowledge that killers lurked among them.

Most notable was the serial kidnapper who had plagued the city for the past seven months. Randall liked to think that he'd stayed in VCID these past dozen years to catch bad guys and rid the city of its old "Murderapolis" moniker, something that for years had threatened to push it into the realm of its larger sister Chicago to the south. But he knew better. A small part of him had stayed because of the green roof itself and the comfort it brought him every time he turned in his chair—as he did now—and caught its image through the window. Even when engrossed in his work, the tolling bell in its monolithic clock tower often succeeded in soothing his soul. Strange, but true that for him it had become an oasis of sorts in a desert of murder and mayhem.

A female voice from behind him: "It wasn't always green,

you know." Startled from his fugue, Randall turned to see a familiar African American female's face standing above him. Sergeant Fells, with her short afro and angular face, smiled her usual thoughtful smile as she cast her own gaze out the window. "The original roof was terracotta, but they replaced it with a copper one in 1950, the year my mother was born. Turns out time gives Homicide sergeants wrinkles, just like it turns copper green. Just ask the Statue of Liberty."

Randall studied Fells' grim expression. "You're never philosophical. And the chief never reduces psych leave, even if the shrink signs off on it. One of those can be an accident, but both means there's trouble."

Fells looked away from the window and handed him a freshly printed bulletin she'd been holding. "Precinct Two just called it in. Dietitian center in Uptown. Looks like PK again, if that's trouble enough for you."

Randall took the bulletin and scanned it. The words seemed to dance across the page due to his doubling vision; it took him several tries to read it correctly. "Does it fit?"

"Only 'D' and 'V' left, so yeah. Plus, the responding officer watched the surveillance video. Suspect is wearing a mustache and probably a wig, but his other facial features and build is a match. Similar MO, too."

Randall massaged his temples. His headache was getting worse by the second. Nausea rippled through him, threatening to send him running to the restroom. He burped and gulped down a mouthful of something sour. "Di-e-ti-tian," he said, enunciating the word slowly. "Yep, last time I checked, that starts with 'D.' Any witnesses?"

"Sure, if you count the surveillance system."

"Forensics on it yet?"

"I told them to wait until you got there."

He eyed her. "So I'm officially back on duty?"

"I didn't wake you from…" She looked him up and down,

rolling her eyes. "From whatever you got yourself into last night to talk sports. Look, Cal, the chief pulled his own string. Which says a lot, considering he's the one who sent you up for the psych eval in the first place."

Randall couldn't argue there. "Whitlock and the FBI head the task force, so why bring me back so soon? The feds have ten times our resources."

"True, but the chief wants one of our own to assume lead from now on. Whitlock is on board. The FBI has been getting killed in the press, so I'm sure they have no problem having the heat taken off a bit. Besides, you're the most experienced detective in the department, and you've worked most of the kidnappings already, so…"

"But the chief said everyone works with a partner."

"That's already been taken care of. She won't be able to replace Pappy—God rest his soul—but then again, no one will."

"*She?*" Randall said, standing to his full six-foot-four-inch height.

"Yes," Fells said pointedly. "You know, the English pronoun to describe a female. Or the gender that makes up at least a third of the department, including half the command staff. Is that a problem?"

"I didn't mean it that way," he said, rubbing his temples again. "It's just that I'd rather not have *any* partner now that Pappy's gone. And I'd love to fly solo once during my time here."

Fells, five-nine herself, cast a motherly stare at him. "I know how much Pappy's death affected you, and maybe played a part in what happened. It affected all of us. But when a Black female Democrat working in the most liberal city this side of the Rockies can't convince the chief to break tradition in the unit, then there's your answer. Especially with this case."

Randall shrugged and said in a deadpanned voice, "If it means anything, you happen to be a very convincing Black female Democrat. But if it'll help convince him, I can loan you some of my privileged white male guilt." He knew better than anyone how the chief felt about VCID, and Homicide in particular. The well-respected lawman once joked to a reporter that if his house were on fire and the Homicide unit was visiting, he might rescue the unit members first before carrying out his wife and kids.

Fells' expression said she wasn't buying any of it. Still, her expression changed from serious to something almost reverent. "I know how you must be feeling, Cal. Ten years is an eternity to partner with someone. Especially someone as excellent as Pappy was. I won't try to guess if his heart attack had anything to do with your…issue, but either way, the chief won't budge on this."

Randall sighed. "Who am I getting?"

"Tan."

"Kelli Tan from Precinct Two? About yea tall and a hundred pounds dripping wet?" He held his palm five feet from the floor. He knew her from his days working street duty when she'd been a rookie officer. She'd immediately earned a solid reputation for being both competent and no-nonsense, but she was also the complete opposite in size to his former partner, Pappy, who at six-six and nearly three hundred pounds had resembled a bear more than a Homicide detective.

"She scored the highest on the detective test," Fells said. "She'll learn the most from you. Besides, the chief wants at least one female detective repping the task force, so there you go."

Randall should have guessed as much, since the other female Homicide detective was pregnant and on desk duty for the foreseeable future. "When do I meet her?"

Fells glanced over her shoulder. "In about five seconds." From behind Fells appeared a short Asian woman with hair slicked back into a tight bun. Laotian, if Randall guessed right, since he was familiar with the city's large population of that nationality. Squarish face, with a strong jawline and pert nose.

Attractive and plain at the same time. And the shrewdest eyes Randall had ever seen. He'd worked with her in passing several times before but had never seen her out of the normal black street uniform. Her tailored black business suit hugged her painfully thin frame. Besides her youthful features and perfectly smooth skin, she stood barely five feet tall. Randall spied the gold detective badge on her belt, and her exposed 9mm handgun. He thought back to the many female officers he'd worked with during his career, with each of them having come in at five-two and a buck fifty at least, big enough to hold their own in a fight. In comparison, the woman standing before him looked like an eighth grader dressed as a detective for Halloween.

"Detective Randall, this is Detective Tan," Sergeant Fells announced. Before Randall could fully extend his right hand, Tan shot hers out first and gripped his with surprising vigor.

"It's a pleasure to be working with you, sir," Tan said, her face brightening with a huge smile. She gave his hand a solid pump before releasing it. "I feel honored to be assigned to the PK unit with you. I've been following it closely since the beginning."

Randall nodded. "Yes…well, twenty-five women abducted in seven months is certainly newsworthy."

Tan's eyebrows raised high on her forehead. "There's been another one?"

Randall began to explain, but Sergeant Fells held up a hand to stop him, then motioned for Randall to hand Tan the bulletin. "Came in twenty minutes ago. Kidnapping MO fits. And the responding officer says the suspect description is a close match to the sketches and stills we have of him, despite the mustache and blond hair."

"He's worn disguises before," Tan said, removing her cellphone from her jacket pocket and opening her photo album. She compared the several pics she had of him with the well-known composite sketch every officer on the force had been given. She typed a note into her phone then slid it back into her pocket.

Sergeant Fells saw this and gave a tight nod of apparent approval. "We'll wait until we get more confirmation before we make a media statement. I want you two to head to the scene and give me a report as soon as you can."

"Yes, ma'am," Randall said, scooping his own cellphone off his desk.

Before he had a chance to say something to Tan, the keen-eyed sergeant stopped him. "I believe in you, Cal. There's a reason the chief got you back in action a few days early. Now that we're down to the last letter, he's realizing that we might not ever catch this guy. I agreed with the move, but I just need to know you're all right. You know..." She gave a quick glance down at his shoes before giving him a hopeful smile.

"I'll be fine, Sarge," he said. "Good as new. I'll let you know what we find."

Before they left, Fells asked Tan if she could borrow her for a second. Leading her into an empty office, she closed the door behind them. Despite the several chairs, both women chose to remain standing due to the decidedly formal air between them. The teacher and the student. Fells crossed her arms across her narrow chest and leveled a serious look at her young detective. "Forget for a second that you're new here. I don't have time to worry about tenure and experience. The women who've been abducted—whether they're dead or not—don't care about that. They don't need a good detective, they need a great one. Do you believe we picked the right person? Because Randall is the best detective in Homicide, and he also deserves the best partner."

Tan didn't hesitate. "This case has been in my soul ever since I got assigned to it last week. I've researched all the victims. I'm ready, Sarge. And Detective Randall is excellent at what he does. I've read his case files, and he has an impeccable reputation. He'll help me tremendously."

Fells nodded to herself. "You have an excellent reputation yourself. Even though you've already been picked by the powers that be, I needed to hear it from you. Which reminds me, I never had the chance to ask you about your extended background during your oral board. We usually go over that then, but the chief was in a hurry."

Tan took a deep breath. "Well, ma'am, I graduated from—"

"No, not your education or police background. We already know that. Your family, your struggles. And make it quick; you two need to get to the scene."

Tan seemed to understand why she'd been taken aside now. "My parents emigrated from Laos after the war. Weird how Minneapolis has such a large Hmong population, since the climates are so different, but they already had relatives living here so it was a bit easier. I'm the oldest of three. When my baby sister was five, she was killed by a stray bullet in a gang shooting. Went right through the wall of our home into her bedroom. I was twelve at the time. Even though it wasn't cool for people of my background to become police officers, I knew it was what I wanted to do."

Fells raised her eyebrows. "That isn't mentioned anywhere in your detective application or personnel file."

"I didn't want to come off as seeking sympathy. Everyone has their own story as to why they want to become a cop. That's mine. I wouldn't have shared it if you hadn't asked."

Fells glanced at her watch. "And what did you find once you got pinned?"

"That being a woman *and* Asian meant I had to work twice as hard as other officers."

"Hmm," Fells said, nodding thoughtfully.

"That's about it. I got married two years into my career, had my daughters, and focused on being the best mother, wife, and cop I could be. It's been hard. But if my parents could escape Laos by wading through rice paddies and dodging bullets, then I can make it here."

Fells stared at her for a second, then said, "Are you willing to put your life on the line to stop whoever's killing these women? I don't mean the normal pledge we give at graduation. I mean going above and beyond the normal above and beyond, even at risk of alienating family and friends. This isn't a movie. This is the biggest case any of us will likely ever work in our careers."

Tan didn't hesitate. "Absolutely."

"Okay. And I appreciate the insight. I never crawled through rice paddies, but as a fellow woman of color, I've definitely waged my own kind of wars."

CHAPTER 5

The detective pair stepped into Randall's black, unmarked SUV cruiser and made their way toward the Uptown Dietitian Center. On the way, Randall gave Tan the rundown of the most recent abduction cases. Other detective teams had worked the two cases that had occurred during his absence, but as the senior member of Homicide and being familiar with all the other cases, he was able to recite from memory nearly every detail of importance. News broadcasts showing both PK and his sometimes-accomplice's obscured photo, as well as hundreds of tips, had resulted in dead ends. Fingerprints taken from numerous crime scenes had all come back to the same unidentified adult male who'd posted mysterious Instagram photos of his victims, in addition to the fingerprint pad of his own forefinger. His calling card. The prints had come back clean. No criminal record, no prior military, and no linked professional certification.

Randall explained that in several of the cases, the suspect had been videoed spiriting his victims away in various containers and other inventive methods. Sometimes he'd been videoed simply carrying them out under cover of darkness. In about half the cases, no video or surveillance photos existed. License plates of no fewer than a half-dozen different vehicles known or suspected of having been driven by the suspect had come back as counterfeits. With plate readers in police cruisers having the ability to constantly scan for stolen plates or those connected to a reported crime, it had dawned on Randall and others in the task force that PK sidestepped this potential snare by somehow creating duplicate plates of known ones matching the make and model of his chosen vehicle. It had become frustratingly clear to Randall and the rest of the task force that they were dealing with much more than a psychopathic killer—they were dealing with one who was incredibly resourceful, and at times plain lucky.

They arrived at the clinic fifteen minutes later. As Randall lifted the crime scene tape to allow Tan to duck under it, he noted four other vehicles already present in the small lot—two marked, black department SUV cruisers, and two civilian vehicles. An unoccupied silver Hyundai Elantra sat by itself at the far-right end of the lot. A uniformed officer stood near the other civilian vehicle—a Mercedes Cabriolet—speaking with a fiftyish blond woman in a red pantsuit and matching heels. Another officer, a rotund African American man Randall had worked closely with during his time on street duty, stood guarding the clinic's front door. As Randall and Tan approached him, Randall extended his hand to him. "Hey, Enc, what's it been…a year?"

The name *Ennis* was printed on the officer's silver nameplate. He smiled to reveal teeth as bright as the shine on his bald head. "More like two, yeah? You been a busy boy lately, I hear." He glanced at Tan, who stood silently beside Randall. "New partner?"

"Yes. This is Detective Tan. It's her first day in the unit."

Ennis's caterpillar eyebrows rose toward his sizeable forehead as he offered his hand. "You're filling some pretty big shoes, young lady. Pappy was a legend. But glad to have you aboard!"

"Thank you," Tan said, pumping his hand. "I've heard a lot

about him. I'll do my best." She studied Ennis' face. "Didn't we work a detail together last year?"

Ennis thought about it. "Star Wars convention at the Radisson, right?"

"Yes. I remember breaking up a fight between C3PO and Han Solo." They both chuckled.

Wishing to get down to business, Randall asked Ennis if he'd run the Hyundai. He responded, "Comes back to our victim, Abby Carlson."

"Get a plate from the perp's vehicle?"

"Yep, got it on video. Registered to a guy living in St. Paul."

Randall planned to double-check it himself as soon as he watched the video, but decided to call it in to another detective team to check it out first. The serial kidnapper had used fake plates numerous times before, so odds were the plate seen in the video wouldn't help. He indicated the blond woman. "That the clinic owner?"

"Yep. Valerie Cowherd. A real mess. Franzese has been consoling her ever since he got here."

Randall and Tan made their way toward her and the officer. "Mrs. Cowherd?" he asked.

"Yes," the woman said, pausing in her conversation with the officer. She blotted her tear-streaked eyes with a tissue. "I'm the owner here."

Her cropped hairdo and husky voice reminded Randall of an older version of the actress Sharon Stone. He gave an obligatory nod to the patrol officer, signaling that they'd be taking over the questioning. The officer appeared relieved at the detectives' presence and hurried back to his cruiser to begin writing his report. After they introduced themselves, Randall nodded to Tan, indicating he wanted her to begin the questioning. They'd discussed it on the ride here.

Removing, then activating the digital recording device in her jacket pocket, Tan stated her own name, the woman's, then the date, time, and location before saying, "We understand you've already told everything to the responding officer, but we'll need to hear it too. Please start from the beginning."

"Belinda and Liz were supposed to open this morning. The rule is that two open and two close. Belinda got here first and saw Abby's car in the parking lot. She assumed she'd walked to one of the bars after work last night then Ubered home. A few of the girls have done that before. But when Liz got here and the guard never showed up when he was supposed to, they tried the door and found it open. They saw Abby's purse on the floor and got scared. When Abby didn't answer her phone, they called me."

"Abby is the employee who closed yesterday?" Tan asked.

"Yes and no. I mean, she was supposed to close with Belinda, but, well, you'll see on the video."

"So Abby did close by herself yesterday."

"Yes. Her full name is Abby Carlson, well I guess it's actually Abigail. I have all her vital information for you. With all the talk of that weirdo kidnapping women, I decided to have private security here fifteen minutes before and after opening. The same with closing, too, just to be safe. Everyone knew the rules—the guard had to be here before anyone got out of their cars in the morning, and before they locked up for the day at five o'clock."

"Did that always happen?"

"Yes, every day for the past month. Except for yesterday." She looked between both Randall and Tan, desperation in her eyes.

"How many total staff do you employ?"

"Four. They all work Monday through Friday, but like I said, only two open and close."

"Tell us about hiring the guard."

"Well, as you know, every time a woman's gone missing, it's gone viral. Once it got down to the last four letters and 'D' was one of them, I started getting nervous. The guard is only here an hour a day, but it was worth it to me. The girls and I talked about it every day. I even joked about PK being some fat guy who'd walk in some day and eat one of them." She shivered and hugged herself tightly. "I feel horrible having said that. It's like I talked it into existence."

Tan nodded regretfully. "What's the name of the security company?"

Mrs. Cowherd bit her lip. "Alliance something. No, wait— North Star Alliance."

Despite her digital recorder, Tan jotted down the information in a notepad, a habit from her patrol days. "I'm wondering why not just have all your employees arrive and leave together? I'd think that fifteen minutes either way wouldn't make that much of a difference."

"I'd considered that, but two of my girls have kids they need to drop off at school right at eight a.m., then pick up before five. Those are our hours of operation. I can sympathize because I raised two kids by myself. Besides, I felt better knowing an armed guard would be here. I never thought..." She placed a trembling hand to her mouth. "I never thought the person I hired was the one who would..." Tears welled in her eyes, and the pain in them told of a woman deeply troubled not only over her employee's disappearance, but her own perceived culpability in it.

"Where are Belinda and Liz now?" Randall asked, deciding to cut in temporarily so he wouldn't lose an important point he'd bookmarked in his head.

"At home. I just called them both and verified it. When Belinda called me about the front door being unlocked and seeing Abby's purse on the floor, I told them to go home until the police figured out what was going on."

"Makes sense," he said, jotting his own note for another detective team to swing by the women's homes to interview them.

Randall was about to ask a question about the guard when Tan beat him to it. "If this was the same suspect who abducted those other girls—and it isn't clear quite yet if that's the case—that's a pretty big coincidence for him to be an employee of the same security company you hired, no?"

Mrs. Cowherd nodded, her eyes afire. "That's exactly what I thought." Then, after thinking about it, she added, "But where's the guard who's supposed to be here? I called the security company, and they said the same man who's been here the past month checked in for the clinic job yesterday afternoon. But he didn't. I've got the video…" She dug into her purse and produced an iPad. Powering it on, she selected a pre-installed app then cued up the surveillance video in question.

"Can you start it a few minutes before Belinda leaves?" Tan asked.

"Of course," Mrs. Cowherd said, sliding her finger along the time counter until she got to the appropriate spot. She handed the iPad to Tan, who oriented it so that both she and Randall could watch.

"We have three interior cameras—one of the reception desk, one of the treatment room hallway, and one of the waiting room," Mrs. Cowherd explained. "The one exterior camera covers the door and the front half of the parking lot. I populated all four in split screens for you, so you can see what's going on in all of them at the same time."

"The date and time are accurate?" Randall asked, noting the video date as being yesterday, and the time being 4:27 p.m.

"Yes, you can see the clock on the wall. And I know it was yesterday because Belinda wore yellow scrubs for the first time since she's worked at the clinic. All of us teased her about how she looked like a walking banana." She uttered a humorless little laugh, but her eyes betrayed an even deeper sense of desperation than they'd contained before.

Tan pressed play, and the footage began to roll. Nothing of

much note in the interior, which encompassed a ponytailed woman in yellow scrubs sitting at the reception desk, identified as Belinda; a brunette in blue scrubs, identified as Abby Carlson; the empty hallway; and a sixtyish female seated in the waiting room. The lone exterior shot showed nothing of immediate note.

"Who's this?" Randall asked, pointing to the woman in the waiting room.

"Shirley Perkins, one of our long-time patients," Mrs. Cowherd said. "One of the sweetest ladies I know. I'd bet the clinic and everything I own that she had nothing to do with this."

Randall pointed to the exterior shot, showing three vehicles in the lot. "And the vehicles?"

"Mrs. Perkins' car, and the two girls who were supposed to close—Belinda and Abby," she said, pointing out each vehicle as she went.

They all watched in fast forward as the next several minutes on the video went by. Randall had seen plenty of dead bodies, some in such advanced states of decomposition they'd become virtual soup. But by far the worst part of his job, other than notifying victims' families, was watching video footage of an impending death or other serious crime. It had always given him chills watching as a person went about their life not realizing it was about to suddenly end or drastically change. Violently. Today was no different, save for the slim chance the Carlson woman might still be found alive.

"The guard arrives in the parking lot...now," Mrs. Cowherd said. On cue, a plain white van with dark tinted windows pulled into the lot and backed into a spot near the front door. Randall pressed the 1x option and the video slowed down to real time. A tall, middle-aged man dressed in a security guard uniform stepped from the driver's seat and approached the clinic's front door. Always attentive to detail, Randall noted the man's matching jacket and cap with the words "NORTH STAR ALLIANCE" written on them. Waving to both Abby and

Belinda through the front door, the man touched two fingers to the bill of his cap before pulling it down slightly, then turning to face the lot.

Randall and Tan watched as Mrs. Perkins and Belinda each left, at 4:49 p.m. and 4:51 p.m. respectively. "Belinda said that Abby told her to leave to pick her daughter up," said Mrs. Cowherd. "She's selfless like that. But I'm angry with her for putting herself in that position."

"What time does the abduction happen?" Randall asked.

"Just before the 5:03 mark," she said. "You'll see that Abby wipes the assessment rooms down and cleans the bathroom first —I ask the girls to do only a cursory job unless it's something bad, but Abby always makes them look spotless—then she'll turn off the lights before setting the alarm." She paused, then added, "I forgot to mention, there's someone else in the video."

Randall and Tan exchanged curious glances. "Who?" Randall said.

"After the guard knocks her out, he lets a man inside. I can't believe I forgot that part. My mind is a whirl. He came on foot. He helps…well, you'll see… "

They continued watching the next six minutes of video until Belinda left. For the next twelve minutes afterward, Abby was seen doing exactly what Mrs. Cowherd said happened. Randall knew better than to fast forward even a second of this footage, no matter how uneventful the action seemed. At the 5:02 mark, Abby could be seen shouldering her purse and turning out the lights. She pressed several keys on a wall-mounted panel then headed straight for the door. Opening it, she had just touched her key to the lock when the security guard approached her and said something that made her pause.

"He's asking to use the bathroom," Randall guessed aloud, noting the man pointing toward the waiting room and moving uncomfortably from foot to foot. A bit overdone, he thought, but effective, considering Abby could then be seen nodding and opening the door for him. After letting the man inside, she returned to the alarm panel and pressed more buttons before waiting for him to exit the restroom. "Tell us about the alarm."

"It's on a thirty-second delay and covers the front and back doors. Windows too." Mrs. Cowherd peeked at the running footage. When it got to the part where the guard exits the restroom and Abby turns to re-set the alarm, Mrs. Cowherd averted her eyes. "I can't watch it again," she said, her voice cracking.

Randall paused the video and suggested that she sit in her car to gather herself while he and Tan watched the rest of the video. He walked her there, closing her door for her, then watching as she buried her face in her hands. After giving her a moment, he bent and rested his elbows on her open window frame. "I'll share something with you, ma'am," he said, his headache subsiding for the first time since he'd woken up. "It never gets easier for me, and I've been doing this a long time. So don't feel bad for being emotional about this. What you saw is traumatizing. Just know that we'll do everything we can to find her." She nodded thankfully.

Randall returned to where Tan stood, and together they watched Abby's abduction. Once she fell unconscious in the guard's arms, they watched him lay her down gently on the floor, then open the door for a shabbily dressed, middle-aged Caucasian man in a black cap pulled low over his face. The accomplice removed a gurney from the back of the van and wheeled it inside. A black body bag lay atop it. The two fitted Abby's body into the bag and the guard affixed a ball gag into her mouth before strapping her down atop the gurney. After the guard changed out of his uniform and into a gray jumpsuit, they exited the clinic, loaded her into the back of the van, and drove away. To most people watching from outside, it would seem rather natural, if not alarming—someone from the clinic had died and had been taken to the morgue or a mortuary. The fact that

Randall and every other police officer knew that at minimum, an ambulance and police vehicles would be involved in such a case didn't matter. The general public was largely ignorant of realistic police work. Still, Randall found it curious that neither suspect had bothered to wipe away their fingerprints. Forensics was on the way, and Randall was certain they'd lift latent prints. He even made a private bet with himself that PK's would be among them. Success had either made him careless, or ruthlessly nonchalant.

Next came the actual inspection of the crime scene. Entering with Tan at his side, Randall noted black scuff marks on the white tiled floor in the same location the video had depicted the struggle taking place. A woman's purse lay on the floor with a car fob, wallet, and hairbrush lying haphazardly near the unzipped main compartment. Using his work cellphone, Randall took several photographs of the scuff marks, purse, and loose items while dictating his observations into his digital voice recorder. Squatting beside the purse, he removed a pen from his jacket pocket and used it to lift open one of the flaps. More of the expected women's particulars. Donning latex gloves, he opened the wallet and removed the driver's license from its clear holder. He immediately noted the photo of a brown-haired young woman matching the victim's computerized DVS photo. The name "ABIGAIL SOPHIA CARLSON" and date of birth were also a match.

"Victim's?" Tan asked from her position several feet away.

Randall nodded, then cast a curious glance toward the front door. "Assailants didn't bother to take it with them. Guard didn't wear gloves, either. All of this has PK's fingerprints all over it, no pun intended." He flipped through the wallet and removed a folded piece of paper with the words "Harlon Cromley," Wednesday's date, and "4:30pm" scrawled across it in neat hand-writing. Randall dictated what he'd read into his recorder and snapped a photo of it before re-folding it and stuffing it back into the wallet. Placing the wallet back where he'd found it, he asked

Tan to inspect and photograph the bathroom before forensics arrived.

The collective task force had agreed that PK's posting of the previous twenty-four bodies on Instagram, done anywhere from five to ten days after an initial abduction, would not constitute a true homicide investigation unless direct or overwhelming circumstantial evidence was gained. Photos could be faked, and already several copycats had posted similar photos of what had obviously been mannequins or likely jokesters posing as victims. For the families' and media sakes, the victims would be considered alive and breathing until proved otherwise. But Randall had been at this game too long to believe anything else than that each of them was dead. Or, in Abby Carlson's case, would be soon.

CHAPTER 6

Heading back outside, Randall and Tan watched the entire video several more times, focusing on the parts that included the guard. When the abduction was over and the two men loaded Abby's bagged body into the van and drove away, Randall pressed the pause button and found Mrs. Cowherd still in her car. She'd been crying again.

"Would you be willing to give us a copy of this?" he asked her. "If we have to go through the security company, it could take hours to get a warrant."

"Yes, of course," she said, looking up to him through her partially open window. She signed a consent form Tan retrieved from the cruiser, then emailed the video link to Randall's work address. Throughout the process, Randall paid special attention to Mrs. Cowherd's demeanor. She appeared completely genuine. His first impression had been that she'd known something she wasn't telling. She'd fit the cold, calculating businesswoman part at first, (if only because of her conservative clothing) with Randall's assessment of her initial tears suggesting she was more concerned with how the abduction could affect her image than the welfare of one of her employees. Now, he understood that she had real skin in this game. One of "her girls" had been kidnapped from her place of business, and by the one person she should have trusted to protect her. No, the Cowherd woman wasn't involved in this, Randall decided.

His mind went back to the thirty-nine-year-old quartz dealer who'd disappeared six weeks ago just after returning from a mine survey on Lake Superior's North Shore. Signs of a struggle in her suburban Minneapolis office had suggested the former college volleyball star had fought her attacker valiantly. But as Randall had driven to the location with his then-partner Pappy and one of the FBI agents assigned to the task force, he'd nearly driven off the road while glancing at his phone. Another Instagram post sent to him from one of the Intelligence members of the task force, assumedly authored by the kidnapper.

Hilda Demler, former University of Minnesota volleyball star turned precious-mineral expert, had been photographed seated at a desk and studying a glittering piece of quartz under a magnifying glass. A forensic pathologist had viewed the photograph and noted signs of apparent lividity on the woman's skin that makeup had not fully concealed. The final determination that had turned the case from one of kidnapping to also one of suspected murder had been the visible end of a stitched incision on the lower-right side of the woman's neck. Located in the same position where embalmers create incisions above the collarbone to access the jugular vein and carotid artery, it was perhaps the most damning clue that an embalming may have occurred. As normal procedure, the local FBI lab had conducted a forensic photo analysis and determined the photo to be unadulterated. Still, the family had not been notified due to the slim chance of her still being alive.

A sudden tightening in Randall's chest drove the thought away, and he winced as a familiar aura came over him. It was happening again. Looking down at his shoes, he tried to focus on something else to make it go away, but that only seemed to intensify the impulse to perform the task that at times seemed more needful than taking a breath. "Excuse me, I think I'm going to be sick," he mumbled to Tan. Holding the back of one hand to his mouth, he ran around the corner of the building and out of sight of anyone. If the impulse overcame him—the same one that had once caused him to suddenly drop to one knee in front of Sergeant Fells and a host of other high-ranking department heads —then let it happen where nobody could see it happen. But it wasn't working. No matter what he did, the same overwhelming compulsion that had resulted in his mandatory leave and subsequent treatment refused to go away. Feeling as though some hidden power were controlling him, he looked down at his shoes. The laces were still firmly tied. He looked up, trying to concentrate on some distracting object—a bird resting on a distant power line; the side of a graffiti-covered brick building. None of it worked. Biting onto his own fist, he groaned loudly. It was the only thing he could think of doing, as if the noise would somehow bury back into his subconscious the now impossible-to-ignore impulse to drop to one knee and do that thing that had very nearly forced him into early retirement.

And then he *was* doing it, dropping to one knee and cursing under his breath as he untied his left shoe with trembling fingers. He quickly re-tied it, stood, then paused for a moment before kneeling again. Cursing under his breath, he untied the same shoe, then immediately re-tied it again. He repeated the process several more times, this time with the other shoe, burning his gaze into his laces as he lipped the words his therapist had taught him to say if it ever happened again. *They're not going to become untied; you've already tied them. Now, stand up and walk away, and don't look down at them again...*

He managed to stand up when the compulsion beckoned once again. He spoke the reminder, but it wasn't any good because now he was dropping to a knee and repeating the same process. Mumbling to himself some complaint over why the therapist had cautioned him against wearing loafers, that he'd never get over his issue if he didn't confront the laces issue head-on, Randall was in the process of re-tying the laces again when a voice caused him to look up.

"Are you...okay?" Tan asked. She stood peering at him from around the corner, concern in her eyes. "I heard you making noises back here. I was worried."

"I'm fine," he lied, finishing his final tie job before forcing himself to a standing position. He was sweating now, despite the chill in the air. He swallowed the same sour something he'd burped up earlier back at Headquarters. It took everything in him not to puke it up right there in front of her. "It's...a thing I've been dealing with," he decided to say. "I might as well tell you about it now. When my partner Pappy died, I had what my therapist described as a 'temporary psychological episode.' Some past issues boiled to the surface. It's a long story, but basically it involved a compulsion to keep re-tying my shoes. I'm good, though." He made eye contact with her, and went to walk past her when she held a hand out to stop him.

"Look...I know I'm new. Hell, I don't even have my own car yet. But I've been a cop for ten years, and I know when someone's not well. You look..." She maintained eye contact with him. "You look like you're in pain."

He winced. "I'm fine. Thank you, though. It's something that will flare up from time to time. I appreciate your concern. Really." He managed a smile, and once they'd shared a nod of mutual acknowledgement they were walking back toward where Mrs. Cowherd stood in the parking lot.

"Sorry, something I ate," he said, snapping back into official mode. "You were saying?"

Mrs. Cowherd cast a worried glance to Detective Tan, shrugged, then said, "I was telling your partner that Abby never got a chance to re-set the alarm. I could tell from my phone app that it was off."

Just then, Randall turned to see a black SUV with the words

"FORENSICS DIVISION CRIME LAB" painted on both sides pull into the parking lot. A male and female tech, each dressed in khaki pants, boots, and black polos exited and retrieved several cases from the back of the vehicle. They approached the uniformed officer at the door and gave their names for the crime scene log. Randall sent Tan to coordinate with the techs, then began the line of questioning he was most interested in. Pointing to the frozen frame depicting the best view of the main abductor's face—a partially-obscured profile shot—he asked, "Have you ever seen this man before? Here as a guard, or anywhere else?"

Mrs. Cowherd shook her head. "No, it was the first thing I noticed when I watched the video from home. We've only had two guards. I had an agreement with the company that they notify me personally if they were sending a different one. The first guard was only here for one day. The second one has been here ever since, for the past month. A sweet old man—Willard. I've dealt with security companies before and know how their management can be with following instructions, so I didn't think anything of it when I saw this third guy show up on the video. That is, until I saw…" She placed a hand to her mouth and shook away what Randall guessed had to be a horrifying memory.

Randall stared hard at the main abductor's image, double-checking the other portions of video that included him. In every section, the man never allowed his face to become fully exposed to the camera. Frustrated, Randall looked around for Tan, who was just finishing her talk with the techs. She came over a moment later. "They've already lifted some latents to run through a mobile AFIS unit, so we should know pretty soon, unless the system is overloaded."

Leading her several feet away, Randall quietly asked her to contact the security company to verify Mrs. Cowherd's statement about the guards. That brought up another question in his mind.

He re-approached her and asked, "Has anyone else besides you and Officer Ennis seen this footage?"

Mrs. Cowherd hesitated, then seemed to be deciding on what to say. Finally, she said, "My husband's been gone on a business trip since last week. Europe. He goes with an associate of his several times a year. And by 'associate,' I mean the kind with a boob job and a habit of sleeping with other women's husbands. So, I guess you could say I decided to join him since I couldn't beat him." She folded her arms and set her lips in a firm line.

Randall and Tan, both accustomed to surprising revelations during routine questioning, showed no emotion. "So, not your husband," Tan said, jotting the note.

"I've known about Richard's philandering for years," Mrs. Cowherd said. "It's something I've gotten used to. I met Rory last year. We started as friends, but you know how that goes. We spent last night at a hotel, and he saw the video with me as soon as I got Belinda's phone call this morning."

Tan shot Randall a knowing glance. "And you called Abby immediately afterward?"

"Yes, but like I said, she didn't answer. Abby's only missed work once in two years, and that was when her grandmother died. She would never leave the door unlocked…and her purse on the floor. I knew right away that something terrible had happened."

"That's when you watched the video, then called police?"

"Yes."

"And the security company?"

"Yes. They said the guard—Willard—called in when he got to the clinic, just like normal."

Tan gave Randall an affirmative nod, then jotted the note. "Go on."

"But I told them that the guard in the video wasn't the guard they sent. They told me Willard was supposed to be here for closing. He was here in the morning—I'll show you." She scrolled the video back to the previous morning. The video showed an older man with white hair, shorter by several inches than the much younger-looking guard who'd abducted Abby, arrive at seven forty-five that morning, then leave at eight fifteen after the clinic had opened for business. "That's Willard."

Randall frowned. It didn't make sense for Willard to have called in his arrival in the afternoon when he hadn't been the one to actually show up. Mrs. Cowherd looked to Detective Tan and asked, "This may sound insensitive, but does any of this about Rory need to come out?"

"We're not in the business of getting involved in personal relationships if it can be helped," Tan explained. "But your boyfriend—this Rory—will be on the report as having seen the video footage of a crime, so we'll need to speak with him as well."

Mrs. Cowherd sighed. "It isn't fair that Richard gets away with what he's done for years without it being publicized, while I'm going to get outed because of this. Maybe it's for the best." Fishing in her purse, she produced a business card and extended it toward Detective Tan. She held onto it firmly for a moment when the detective went to take it. "He's married," Mrs. Cowherd said, cementing her eyes on Tan. "Not that I'm one to talk, but his wife is the type who'd take everything she could in a divorce. My husband cares more about what his friends would say than who I'm sleeping with. I'd appreciate as much discretion as possible." She glanced up to the clinic's parking lot marquee and sighed even deeper. "This place is my baby now that my youngest is away at college. It'd kill me to have its name dragged through the mud." She finally released her grip on the card. Tan took it and glanced it over before slipping it into her pocket.

"Our concern is with your missing employee, ma'am," Tan said without much sympathy. Randall offered a knowing nod. He'd danced this dance many times, both during his time on patrol and in Homicide. It never ceased to amaze him how selfish people could be, even when someone close to them was the victim of a crime.

As if reading Randall's mind, Mrs. Cowherd looked down at the ground and shook her head. "Look at me, worried about myself when Abby is the one in danger, or worse…"

"We'll do everything we can to find her," Randall said. As he said the words, it occurred to him that the task force that had been assembled to stop the city's serial kidnapper was no closer to having any answers now than they'd been when the first victim had been taken almost seven months before. He and Tan stepped out of earshot to converse. "Definition of cliché," Tan said, handing the card to Randall. He looked it over. The name "Rory McMichael" was typed across the top in a bold, masculine font. Below that, the title "Attending Surgeon," followed by the name of a major downtown medical center, cell and business phone numbers, and email address. Flipping the card over, Randall noted a scrawled smiley face. He imagined the doctor extracting a pen from his coat pocket and adding the personalization before handing it to Mrs. Cowherd during their initial interaction. Cliché indeed. People usually didn't keep secrets when said secrets didn't involve themselves, Randall knew. As if reading his mind, Tan asked, "You think the boyfriend's told anyone?"

Randall glanced to where Mrs. Cowherd stood on the other side of the parking lot, talking on her cellphone. She appeared to be crying again. "He's a doctor. He knows what he's getting involved in, so I doubt it. We can question him by phone just in case."

"Fair to clear her as a suspect?"

"Depends on what the security company said."

"They corroborated her story."

"Have a unit run by Willard's place, then. Something tells me he won't answer the door."

Ten minutes later, they received word from a patrol unit. The guard, Willard Knutson, hadn't answered knocks at his door. His truck wasn't parked in the driveway where it normally was, and neighbors hadn't reported seeing him since the day before. Also getting confirmation from another detective team that the plate seen in the video was indeed fake, Randall asked Tan to run through a likely scenario.

"Maybe PK stalks the guard and confronts him at gunpoint before he has a chance to get to work," she responded. "It would've had to happen somewhere else, since Willard never appears on the clinic camera in the afternoon."

"You think the guard's description matches PK enough for Willard's uniform to fit?" Randall asked.

"Willard's DL lists him at six-two, two-twenty, so…"

Randall nodded to himself. "PK forces the guard to call in his arrival, makes him disrobe, then assumes his identity." When he locked eyes with Tan, an extended beat grew between them as each of their minds appeared to simultaneously reach the same conclusion. Randall beat her to it. "Willard's dead. I'd bet my pension on it."

Five minutes later, forensics verified that several prints belonged to PK. No surprise there. Soon after, Randall's department cellphone rang. He spoke with the caller for several minutes before hanging up. "Precinct Two's got a Signal-Seven in a dumpster behind the coffee shop on Lyndale and Lake. White male, early sixties, dressed only in underwear and t-shirt. Blunt force trauma to the head. Willard's truck was found nearby."

Tan locked eyes with him. "Looks like your pension is safe," she said, straight-faced.

CHAPTER 7

With their jobs complete for now at the clinic, and forensics processing the crime scene, Randall and Tan left for the location where the body had been found in an alley two miles away. Located in a middle-class residential part of the city, the store served business commuters on their way downtown, as well as a mix of locals and students at the nearby community college. Randall had been here numerous times before, usually swinging through the drive-thru on his way to work. A small crowd had gathered at each end of the crime scene tape that had been stretched across both ends of the alley. Randall noted that responding officers had also erected sheets on either side of the dumpster. Grateful for their insight, he gave his and Tan's names to the officer in charge of the crime scene log, then lifted the tape for her. Ducking under it and approaching the dumpster, he asked her, "What's our order of operation?"

"First, assess the body and look for obvious evidence. Then question possible witnesses," she said confidently.

"Then?"

"Notify forensics and the ME if they haven't been notified. But they have already, so we update them when they get here."

"Good."

The man's body had been found a half-hour ago by a home-less man rooting through the trash. Randall slapped on two pairs of latex gloves and leaned to peer over the edge of the dumpster. Tan did the same. The body, matching the description they'd been given, was partially clothed and lying amid an assortment of bloated black trash bags. Someone (presumably one of the shop's workers) had thrown several bags of trash atop it. Easy to imagine someone not noticing the corpse if they'd simply lifted the lid and chucked a bag in without looking, Randall thought. It was darker back here, too. The man's head faced away from them. A large red gash along the rear of his head stood in stark contrast to the gray hair. The wound looked like a smiling mouth, the coagulated blood and shattered skull completing the morbid effect. Both arms jutted out at odd, stiffened angles, the fingers of each hand curled like a raptor's talon. He could have been a zombie in a horror movie. Despite the cool temperatures, a moving mask of flies had already taken residence on the face, with several crawling in and out of the half-opened mouth.

"Initial assessment?" Randall asked Tan.

"Blunt force trauma—open skull fracture. Probably fatal. Unclothed in a cold environment. Unnatural location of body. Obvious homicide."

"And?"

Tan looked the body over again. "Rigor and lividity suggest he's been dead at least twelve hours. Likely killed somewhere else and dumped here."

Nodding, Randall removed his cellphone and snapped a few pics of the body. Tan followed suit, with both of them adding more shots of the dumpster from a distance.

"How do we get him out?" she asked.

Randall considered. "Climb inside and lift him up under his arms. I'll pull him out."

She blinked. "Are you serious?"

He grinned. "Just kidding. We'll wait for the ME's direction. My guess is we'll need a city truck to dump him."

Randall had experienced this before. Murder victims had a habit of showing up unannounced in dumpsters from time to time. If a killer was lucky, a garbage truck would come by to empty the container, and the body would make its way to the incinerator without anybody noticing. If the body was discovered, all was not lost. Trash had a way of degrading evidence, and a dumpster's nature often increased the time that elapsed before the body's discovery. Insects and rodents feeding on the remains complicated things as well. Randall had once half-heartedly suggested that the city ban dumpsters all together, prompting another detective to quip that killers would then simply dismember their victims to fit them into smaller bins.

The twenty-two-year-old pimply-faced manager who'd called police stood just outside the tape, hands stuffed inside the pockets of his skinny jeans. His horn-rimmed glasses and '50s-style haircut made him resemble a modern-day Buddy Holly. Randall approached him then asked a series of standard questions while Tan paid close attention beside him.

"How long are you going to leave him in there?" the manager asked, eyeing the dumpster.

Randall removed his gloves and touched a hand to his temple —since arriving here, his headache had found its way back behind his eyes. He silently cursed himself for having left his pill bottle on his desk. "We're still waiting on forensics and the coroner. But I'd plan on around noon."

The manager threw his hands in the air. "That's three hours from now. What do I tell my customers?"

Tell them they're going to have to get their Caramel Macchiato somewhere else, because there's a dead guy in the trash with his skull caved in. Randall settled for something more diplomatic. "Blame the police. We'll let you know when you can re-open." The manager shot a resigned look toward the hanging

sheets, then walked to the side parking lot where a few of the
store's employees had congregated.

The African American homeless man who'd discovered the
body stood outside the line of tape, shuffling from foot to foot
and mumbling to himself. Sporting a shaggy salt-and-pepper
beard, beanie that looked like it had gone through World War
Three, and several layers of foul-smelling clothing, he looked up
in recognition when he saw Randall approaching.

"Hiya, Cap'n!" he shouted, despite the three-foot distance
between them. He snapped his heels together and executed a stiff
salute. Randall returned it, knowing from experience that the
man would hold it indefinitely if he didn't. He knew him, as he
did many of the local homeless men populating this section of
the city. A Vietnam veteran, the man had once told him in a
moment of clarity that his hearing had been severely damaged
during the war. Randall had lost count of how many of the man's
salutes he'd returned over the years.

"Long time, no see, Vern," Randall said, turning toward Tan.
"This is my new partner, Detective Tan. She's going to ask you a
few questions if that's okay."

"Suh thang, Cap'n!" Vern shouted back. He grinned to reveal
several rotten teeth that jutted from the otherwise empty space of
his mouth.

Randall stood by while Tan questioned him. Twice he felt
tempted to interject, but remembering that one of the tenets of
good field training was that minor mistakes should be over-
looked in the moment, he bit his tongue. It didn't matter that she
used street cop verbiage instead of detective-speak, or the order
in which she asked certain questions. He'd go over those unim-
portant things with her later. Besides, he knew that the witness in
question ate out of garbage cans and held regular arguments with
himself—the perfect sort of witness for her to continue getting
her feet wet with.

When it was over and they'd sent Vern on his way (Randall

had him scratch out his illegible signature on his witness statement card first), Randall had Tan read back her notes aloud. It
was a trick he'd learned early on in his time with Homicide to
help understand if he'd missed an important detail.

"He's up at six a.m. before anyone else can get to last
night's trash," she began. "He works his way down the alley
until he opens the lid here. He begins to climb in when he sees
an arm. Thinks it's one of the dummies from the consignment
store down the street, but when he leans in closer, he sees the
blood."

"Did he report touching the body?"

"Says he never touched it. Notified the store manager who'd
just arrived to work."

Randall nodded. "What else?"

She rolled her eyes. "He asked if I was from Vietnam. Said I
reminded him of a few women who'd kept him company during
the war."

"Try not to be offended," Randall said, noticing Vern
muttering to himself outside the tape.

"I'm not," Tan said. "I got my share working patrol. And
growing up, my mom taught me to grow thick skin. She said that
if half the things that happened here had happened back in Laos,
you'd be lucky to still be alive."

Randall nodded thoughtfully, remembering the stories his
own grandfather had told him about his time in Vietnam. Just
then, an early-model white BMW pulled into the side parking
lot. A tall, attractive woman of about forty, wearing green
hospital scrubs and dark tennis shoes, stepped out. She showed
her ID to the cop with the crime scene log, then ducked below
the tape and made her way toward them. With her dark blond
hair put up in a clip, and turquoise browline glasses perched on
her face, her clinical appearance clashed with the alley's rundown urban setting. Alicia Lampley, one of Hennepin County's
eight current medical examiners, and the only one officially

attached to the PK task force. They'd dated several years ago, hot and heavy for six months, then off and on for another year.

As she approached and offered him a warm smile, Randall couldn't help noticing the yellow honeybee ring on her right ring finger. He'd bought it for her birthday—her thirty-fifth—during their hot and heavy days, after learning that she'd helped her grandparents raise honeybees as a kid. Randall had surprised her with it during the birthday dinner and movie date he'd orchestrated. A lover of the local music legend Prince, she'd once lamented that she'd never watched *Purple Rain*. Randall hadn't forgotten the comment. He'd picked her up from her inner-city lakeside home and driven to a working-class section of the city near a set of railroad tracks. Parking on a tree-lined residential curb, they'd eaten take-out Chinese food and watched *Purple Rain* on his laptop, right there in the car. When she'd asked him why he'd driven to such a random spot to watch the movie, he pointed to a plain clapboard house nearby and explained that it had been Prince's character's house in the movie. Then he'd driven downtown and parked along First Avenue, near the still-functioning club where Prince had filmed much of the movie's concert scenes. The two of them had had their first kiss then.

Randall snapped out of the memory. Alicia had said something he hadn't heard. "Sorry?"

"I asked if you were going to introduce me to your new partner," she said, raising her eyebrows toward Detective Tan.

"Oh...yes," he said, maintaining extended eye contact with Alicia, a glimmer of fondness in his gaze. A second later, Alicia gave an impatient sigh and looked at Detective Tan, who'd stood silently while watching their interaction.

"Hello. I'm Dr. Lampley, ME's office." She extended her hand.

Detective Tan shook it and introduced herself. "Nice to meet you. I hear you're a part of the task force?"

"On an auxiliary basis, yes. The powers that be think it

makes sense to have one of our examiners work closely on the PK cases, even though we don't have physical bodies yet." Her face went circumspect, and she said to Randall, "Speaking of bodies…"

He indicated the open dumpster. "May be connected to an abduction we just worked down the street. Wanted to wait to get your opinion on getting him out. I suggested my new partner do it herself, but she respectfully declined."

The doctor donned a pair of blue latex gloves and approached the dumpster. Rising onto her tiptoes, she gripped the edge, studying the body and the dumpster's contents for a full minute before turning back toward them. "Smart girl, not listening to smartass detectives," she said to Detective Tan. "It'll be a lot easier if we dump him. Any way we can get a truck from the city?"

Tan looked to Randall for help. "Absolutely," he said, instructing Tan on which city department to notify to request a garbage truck capable of handling the job. While they waited, they erected more sheets to block the entire alley from both sides. Half an hour later, a truck arrived and, under the ME and detectives' guidance, carefully dumped the container's contents onto the ground. An unceremonious way for a body to be extracted, Randall thought as he and Tan carefully removed bags of trash and a few loose pieces of rubbish from atop it. The forensics team had since arrived and, along with the ME, began the process of examining and photographing the body. Randall talked Tan through the entire procedure. She'd witnessed the process numerous times during her time in patrol, she said, but never in such an investigative capacity. At one point she asked the ME if she could crouch beside her while she inspected the body.

"Even better—you can help me roll him."

Eyes aglow with curiosity, Tan assisted with rolling the near-naked body, noting the lividity that had settled along the entire back portion. "He was probably killed somewhere else, then dumped here shortly after death," the ME declared. Forensics took his prints and were awaiting word from AFIS, the national fingerprint database. Randall already had the missing guard's driver's license photo from the wallet found in the truck, a close match. Still, he wanted to be sure. They didn't have to wait long to discover what Randall already suspected—the dead man was indeed the missing security guard. Randall crouched beside the body, studying the deep fracture in the man's skull.

"You should've called in sick yesterday, Willard," Randall said, his voice thoughtful. He instructed Tan to take a series of close-up photos of his face on her department cellphone. "You get his next-of-kin info from the security company?"

"Yep."

"Ever done a notification?"

"Twice," Tan said, her voice reverent. She stared into the man's half-open eyes. "But it's been a while."

"May as well start getting used to it," Randall said. He disliked training new detectives, mainly because he already knew the proper procedures inside and out. He also knew that wasting even a few minutes explaining necessary procedures and details could set them back hours, or even days, as an investigation rolled along. Still, he knew that those methodical explanations were necessary; he'd gone through them himself after he'd made detective. But as fresh as she was, Tan appeared to be inquisitive, and had already proved to be a quick learner. Despite that, it didn't help ease Randall's apprehension, since her first case was shaping up to be one associated with the city's notorious serial kidnapper and likely murderer.

"What do we do after the notification?" Randall asked her.

She looked up and scanned the building's back wall, which was devoid of any security cameras. "Neighborhood canvas and CCTV search. No cameras back here, though. That's why the killer dumped him here."

"Good."

"It was well-planned," she continued. "This is a busy part of the city. People drive through this alley all the time. I've done it myself about a hundred times when I was assigned to this district. We'll pull intersection video and try from surrounding businesses and homes, too. Six blocks in every direction. We can expand if we need to."

Randall nodded his approval. While Tan got with the department specialist responsible for street cameras, he went back over his own notes. His headache was finally gone. It was time to get to work. He took an extended moment to scan both ends of the alley. The crowd had grown in number, a mix of locals on their way to work, a few homeless men and women, and several employees from area businesses. Some were taking cellphone photos and videos from their positions behind the tape.

Maybe one of you could do us a favor for once and videotape our guy without a disguise, he thought. It was ten-thirty, Friday morning, with a noticeable chill in the air. Winter was coming. And if Randall was right, PK wouldn't wait for snow to finish his collection.

With the dead man's next of kin—a cousin living in Montana —notified, Randall and Tan coordinated with other elements within the task force to inspect surrounding intersection and business CCTV cameras, as well as private home Ring cameras. Videos showed a white van with the same plate as the one from the clinic abduction entering and leaving the alley at 4:32 p.m. the previous afternoon. Also, forensics had confirmed identity of PK's clinic accomplice—Ernie Potts, a local vagrant and low-level criminal whom Randall had arrested several times for petty misdemeanors during his time on regular patrol, and whose prints had been found exactly where the accomplice was seen touching. No violent crime arrests per Randall's NCIC query. His address was listed as "transient." Curious why Ernie had gotten wrapped up in a crime of such magnitude, Randall wasted no time in forwarding the information as a nationwide BOLO. Within seconds every local, state, and federal cop had access to the information, along with a request to immediately place the man in custody once found. In addition, an entire undercover unit had been mobilized to canvass Uptown and the surrounding neighborhoods.

In the meantime, Randall called the office line of Dr. McMichael, Mrs. Cowherd's illicit boyfriend. He listened to several rings before it went to voicemail. Trying the listed personal cell number, he was mildly surprised when someone answered. "If you're selling something, take me off your list," said a gruff-sounding voice.

Randall introduced himself, then dove right into the doctor allegedly having watched the video of Abby Carlson's abduction. "How do I know this is really the police?" the doctor responded, suspicion lacing his voice. "People impersonate you guys all the time."

"You're free to call the department's main line. They can transfer you back to me."

Another pause. Randall imagined the man looking at his caller ID and seeing *City of Minneapolis*. "No, you're the police; you all talk the same." He heard the sound of footsteps on tile, followed by a door opening then closing, and a heavy *click* of a latch. "You've got two minutes, Detective. I'm just about to prep for surgery."

Randall gave him the full rundown as quickly as he could, asking the doctor if he had any more involvement with the case than being a witness to the video. "None at all," he replied pointedly. "Look, I didn't even want to watch the damn thing, but Valerie got hysterical when she saw it and begged me to. I've never seen the guy before. Hell, I've never even met the girl who…well… "

Randall considered the doctor's words for a moment, then made a judgment that he was telling the truth. What he said made sense, and there wasn't any obvious connection between him and the victim. He thanked him and gave him his number in case he knew of any information he later thought could help them. Hanging up, he checked with Tan, who'd been busy coordinating with Detective Haag's secondary detective team. "They got a call from a man named Derek Kinney. Claims to be Abby's best friend," she said.

"And?"

"He said he hung out with Abby Wednesday night at a bar down the street. Sounded distraught. He's meeting Haag and Pedersen at Precinct Two in thirty minutes."

Randall checked his watch. It was nearly eleven a.m. "Call Haag and tell him to wait until we get there," he said. Dr. Lampley had finished her preliminary examination of the body and held up a questioning thumbs-up to Randall. When he nodded to indicate he and Tan were done with the body, two ME workers in white jumpsuits and latex gloves rolled it into a black body bag before lifting it onto a collapsed gurney. Randall watched the process, an eerie sense of déjà vu coming over him as he watched them load the body into a newly arrived van. Eighteen hours ago, a young woman had experienced that same process, albeit alive and with a ball gag in her mouth. It was his job to find her, just as it had been his job to find the other two dozen abducted women. Even if he'd been batting .200—the Mendoza line that no self-respecting big leaguer wanted to dip below—he would've solved three or four of the cases. As it was, he and the rest of the task force were batting triple zeros—not even good enough to make a beer league softball team.

After he and Tan completed the final procedures to clear the scene, he said goodbye to Alicia and asked her to notify him as soon as she conducted her autopsy. Due to the association to another confirmed PK abduction, she'd already pushed back her other cases for later, keeping to the ME office's pledge to give any PK case priority. Every other case deserved answers too, she'd explained to Randall more than once. But unlike this case, those others didn't involve a young woman's life dangling precariously in the balance.

CHAPTER 8

Chatham, MN
(130 miles northwest of the Twin Cities)
September 1982

"I'm sorry, Mrs. Derring, but perhaps a different school would be a better fit for your family," said Mr. Phillips, principal of the Harding K-12 School, the only school serving the town of just under two thousand. He sat with hands folded atop his desk, his bug-like eyes shifting uneasily between the middle-aged woman sitting across from him and her five-year-old twin boys beside her.

"But this is the only school in the county," Mrs. Derring reminded him. "The next closest one is thirty miles away."

"I'm aware of that, ma'am. The problem is...how shall I put it...the boys may become too much a distraction to the other children if they were to attend school here. Although I feel Frederik would do quite well on his own, Victor here..." He smiled uneasily at the quieter boy of the two. Victor slouched forward and absently ran a toy car back and forth over the arm of the chair. He gripped his brother's hand tightly with his free hand. In contrast, Frederik sat up straight, a polite smile on his face. He had either resigned to accept his brother's grip, or welcomed it willingly, Mr. Phillips couldn't tell which. "I'm sorry, Mrs. Derring, but there's no delicate way to put it. Victor here just wouldn't fit in."

"I see," said Mrs. Derring. She glanced at her hands in her lap. "Maybe you could place Victor in a special class at first? Frederik wouldn't mind attending with him for the first year, maybe two, if his brother is slow to adapt. Your school has a special education class available. I know because our neighbor's son down the road took one last year."

Mr. Phillips's smile faltered as he looked into the desperate face opposite him. "That's correct, we do offer a special ed class —two of them, in fact. But I'm afraid the upcoming year's classes are full already." He gave the sort of smile that suggested he expected the matter to be dropped.

"You're the top administrator here, no?"

"I am," he said, blinking with frustration.

"You would have the power to offer accommodation. My boys scored well on—"

"Mrs. Derring," Mr. Phillips interrupted, his voice considerably firmer than before. "I don't think you understand the full circumstances here. I'm sure your sons are fine children. And I'm aware of their test scores. They're above average in every category, tops in two of them, even. And I can see that they are very close to one another. That's the problem."

Mrs. Derring scoffed. "Close? They're inseparable. What does that have to do with schooling them?"

"That's my entire point, ma'am. Due to their...unusual togetherness, I'm not sure a formal school setting would be appropriate for them. You must consider the other children, and their teacher, of course. Whomever taught them would no doubt need to dedicate undue attention to them. It wouldn't be fair." Mr. Phillips shifted his gaze from Frederik's stoic expression to Victor's languid one, then finally down to their tightly intertwined fingers. They'd been holding hands since they'd arrived with their mother ten minutes ago. Despite the boys' mother already having described their inseparability during a prior phone call, Mr. Phillips had insisted he see firsthand how they interacted with one another. He had not been prepared for what he was seeing.

He'd been told that the boys' closeness was "unusual," creepy even. But sitting across from them had been the true test. He was now convinced that the twins would be teased mercilessly. Playground fights would break out over hurt feelings, and ribbing over the brothers' inseparability would no doubt morph into bullying, regardless of his or a teacher's warnings. Mr. Phillips' own children attended the school, although in different grades than the Derring boys. He'd told his wife about this scheduled meeting and the particulars behind it. She'd warned him to not allow the Derring boys to attend, stating she'd be ostracized from her church group if he did. The only thing Mr. Phillips loved more than his wife was God Himself. He intended to stay in good graces with them both.

Mrs. Derring nodded her head deferentially. "I understand your concerns, Mr. Phillips. But my boys are well-behaved. Ever since they were born, they've depended upon each other for everything. We live at the edge of town, with few children around. I do think that if you gave them a chance, they would thrive in a real school. They crave normalcy. Frederik is the athlete, and Victor is more studious. Keeping them away from other children would be detrimental to their development. Over time, I promise you'll see that they require less attention than most other children."

Mr. Phillips forced a polite smile. It was the well-worn expression of a school administrator who was accustomed to such delicate issues with parents. "I'm sure your sons are delightful children, Mrs. Derring. And you could very well be correct. Many students without your sons' special attachment have proved to be lesser students, and even disciplinary problems. Just last week I had to suspend a first-grader for placing a piece of bubble gum in a classmate's hair. The poor girl had to have half her hair cut off." He gave a good-natured laugh.

"I can assure you neither of my boys would ever do something like that," said Mrs. Derring. Her breathing had begun to shorten since they'd arrived, and beads of perspiration now stood out on her furrowed brow.

"Indeed, they may not," the principal said, a bit more pointed than was necessary. "Still, the attention they would assuredly attract would become a detriment to their learning, and to that of the other children. I've already mentioned the unfairness of it."

Mrs. Derring's hand went out to touch Frederik's arm. She sat up straight in her chair and looked the principal in the eye. "Sir, I didn't come here to beg you. In fact, I haven't even considered speaking with the county—"

"The commission will see things my way, trust me," Mr. Philips said, now uncaring how sharp his voice was. "As you know, this is a small town. Farmers and factory workers, mostly. Church-going people…" He raised his eyebrows at his mention of "church."

"If this is about my family's absence in church, I can assure you it isn't—"

"That has nothing to do with it," Mr. Phillips said, interrupting her again. He leaned forward in his chair. "I'm afraid my answer is no."

Mrs. Derring lifted her chin proudly. "There is nothing unusual about brothers loving one another, Mr. Phillips. Especially twins. My sons may not act alike, but their minds are linked to one another. Since they were babies, I knew what one felt, the other did too. Sharing a womb and a crib only helps that."

Mr. Phillips placed his hands flat atop his desk. "I do appreciate everything you're saying, Mrs. Derring. I have children of my own. If it makes you feel any better, part of the issue is your husband's work."

Mrs. Derring frowned. "So this is about my husband's *profession*?"

"Not entirely," he said, holding his palms up defensively. "I just meant—"

"That *is* it, isn't it?" she said, her voice rising. From beside her, Victor raised his head in alarm, concern flooding his eyes. Frederik, ever the stoic twin, increased the grip on his brother's hand and made a shushing sound. "My husband provides a *service* to this community. To numerous communities, in fact. People from all over the Midwest do business with him."

"I know," Phillips said. "That's part of the problem as well, to be perfectly honest. Personally, I have no horse in this race. But the grapevine grows quickly in a small town."

Mrs. Derring shook her head in disgust. "Do you think we don't know how people call us freaks behind our backs then pretend to be our friends the next day? But to shun two innocent boys—intelligent boys who by your own admission scored higher on the entrance tests than most of the other children here —is unacceptable." She reached out and grasped Frederik around the shoulder, hugging him tight. Victor, still grasping his brother's hand tight, was pulled over with him.

"Mrs. Derring, please don't—"

"Don't what?" she snapped.

Mr. Phillips shot a nervous glance toward his closed office door. "Please don't raise your voice. I'm trying to be diplomatic."

"No, you aren't," she said, rising to her feet and yanking Frederik's hand. Eyes widening as if they were unaccustomed to hearing their mother raise her voice, both boys wrapped protective arms around her legs. "You're just like the rest of them, judging my sons because they're different. They may be, but they're still human beings."

"I know that," he said, lowering his eyes to his folded hands.

"Then look at them," she said. "Look at them as if they aren't what you think they are. Sons of the town freaks."

Mr. Phillips raised his gaze at the boys, but without Mrs. Derring's requested humanity. His eyes blazed anger. "Mrs. Derring, it's time for you to leave. I'll arrange for my secretary to refer you to a more appropriate school. Now, I have work to do…"

Mrs. Derring opened the door and took one step into the hallway with Frederik and Victor in tow, before turning around to face him again. Nearby, the plump, bespeckled secretary sat staring from a nearby desk, her fingers frozen on her typewriter keys. "I can see it in your eyes. You think my husband makes zombies out of people. But that's not true. He gives people *comfort*. We had to move all the way out here because no one would sell to us, knowing what he intended on doing, and now that we're here, we're being treated as outcasts." Tears pooled in her eyes, but a fierce look of pride on her upturned face prevented them from spilling. "I'm going to make it easy on you, Mr. Phillips. Not for your sake, but for ours. My children will never again set foot inside this school, no matter what you or the next principal decides. I'll arrange it with the school board to teach them at home myself."

Chin lifted, she gathered herself and walked out, pulling Frederik behind her, with Victor being pulled along with him as he clutched onto his brother for dear life.

After they'd left, Mr. Phillips sat back in his office chair and expelled a breath of relief. Yes, the meeting had been uncomfortable, albeit necessary. His staff knew a decision had to be made about whether the children of the local undertaker known for his unusual practices would be allowed to attend the town school. It was true that the boys weren't normal. One look at them together was all a person needed. Fawning over one another, communicating without words, it seemed. And the almost constant holding of hands, their fingers intertwined as if some invisible force threatened to arrive at any moment and break them apart. They'd only separated their grip once during the meeting, and that had been for mere seconds.

Mr. Phillips would have to deal with whatever came from this, he knew. The children's father would be upset. He'd perhaps curse him, or even barge into his office and accost him. The man did have a reputation for drink, after all. And there was the possibility of a discrimination lawsuit. He'd done his research. There was no real reason the boys could not attend school here. But he'd done his job. The teachers' comfort level was what was important, and in the end, it was his job to appease the masses. Let the boys attend a different school in a neighboring county, one more fit to handle their unique situation. Or, as the mother had suggested, let her teach them herself. As for her husband's profession—namely, the ghoulish way he practiced it—avoiding *that* topic in the teacher's lounge, classrooms, and even his own office may prove to be the biggest benefit of all.

CHAPTER 9

They stopped for ice cream on the way home, the three of them ordering from the to-go window at the local creamery. The boys—Frederik, chocolate; Victor, strawberry—licked their cones with youthful exuberance the entire ride home. Pulling off the main rural road bordering their combined business/home, Mrs. Derring guided the aging pickup into the garage, careful as always to avoid the gleaming black Cadillac hearse parked in its usual position along the far-right side of the spacious interior. She cut the ignition and waited for several moments, closing her eyes and breathing deeply. The meeting had been a disappointment, which wasn't to say she hadn't expected as much. Indeed, since early in the boys' development, she'd envisioned an eventual meeting going exactly the way this one had. Her sons *were* smart, and there should have been no reason they couldn't attend regular school. Politics had won in the end, as it usually did, and although she understood the powers at work, it by no means made it any easier to take.

Under normal circumstances, people who first met the boys often regarded them with a polite smile and a genuine "hello," followed most times with curious stares as the boys innately found each other's hands, their fingers intertwining in wakefulness and sleep just the same. It was as if their hands had minds of their own. To most, what was at first regarded as a sweet and tender display of brotherly affection quickly became a perceived obsession. You'd interact normally with Frederik while Victor occupied himself with a toy or some other distraction and seemingly oblivious to his brother's conversation. Eventually, you pretended Victor wasn't there at all, if for no other reason than to avoid added awkwardness to an already awkward situation.

The boys had no close family other than their parents, the only blood relative being a sickly uncle in North Dakota. Their few family friends had slowly drifted away as the boys aged, finally realizing that their own children no longer enjoyed interacting with them due to their incessant togetherness. Like most instances, such as what Sarah Derring did today with the ice cream, the boys' social interactions had been reduced to short ventures into town, insisting on taking them places to escape the boredom of farm life. The family home being five miles from town notwithstanding, she considered the possibility that the boys may only encounter other people during bi-weekly trips to the grocery store, and occasional visits to one of the town parks when other children were not there yet.

She opened her eyes and gave a deep sigh before getting out to unbuckle the boys. They each happily popped the final bit of their cones into their mouths. As usual, she took Frederik's hand as she hobbled up the stone walkway to the raised front porch. Also as usual, Frederik grasped Victor's hand as the latter drooped his head languidly toward the ground, the toy truck still firmly gripped in his other hand. The final days of an Indian summer had waned, giving way to crisp mornings and cool evenings, with intermittent rains that in little as a month would become snow flurries.

Once inside, Sarah sent the boys to their room then found her husband at work in the small chapel, preparing for a viewing later that day. She stood silently in the open entryway, arms folded across her ample chest, and watched as he put the finishing touches on the deceased, a seventy-six-year-old man from a Minneapolis suburb. He'd died of cancer—a common cause, Sarah had learned in the ten years she'd now been married to her funeral director husband. The man's death had been attended by a physician, the release of his body swift. No autopsy was necessary. Several signatures at the hospital morgue, a few pleasantries with the staff, then the loading of the refrigerated, wrapped body into the hearse.

Sarah and the boys had accompanied Mr. Derring on account that she had wanted to take the boys to one of the city malls and let them ride the merry-go-round. When they arrived, Frederik had been game, his eyes widening with excitement. But Victor had responded with worry about the rotation and speed, frightened of the smiling wooden horses that seemed somehow alive. Their mother had solved the dilemma by reminding the boys they would need to agree, for or against. Victor had won out, and so neither of them had gone. No reminders had been needed of the family's long-standing rule: the boys would have to agree on everything. They may not require holding hands for their entire lives, but even doctors and psychiatrists had agreed that during their childhood, allowing them to remain so close would be best. They would have differences in opinion, but in the end, what one did, so did the other. Happiness would come from cooperation and compromise.

"The family will love him," Sarah said, her voice echoing in the near-silent chapel.

Yves, her husband, lowered his hands from the deceased man's collar and turned to fully face her. "How did the meeting go?" he asked, ignoring his work for now.

She sighed. "As expected."

"Hmm." He nodded. "What will we do about it?"

"I told him I'll teach them myself. And I will."

"They need to be around other children. You and I can handle being isolated out here. It'll affect them."

"It's too late for them to not be affected," she said. "Yesterday, Frederik wanted to ride the merry-go-round. Victor said no."

"It's not the first time they've disagreed. I'll take them another time when Victor feels more up to it."

"No, you won't," Sarah said, moving down the chapel's aisle and past the neatly arranged rows of chairs to stand near her husband. "I know you mean well, but Victor...he's changing. Becoming more withdrawn."

"Frederik has always been more outgoing. I think if he talks to his brother, he can make him become less timid. Less afraid."

She hugged herself, something she did often when speaking of her sons' difficulties. Shifting her attention to the dead man standing three feet away, she asked, "Was it difficult—getting him that way?"

The deceased man had been an avid golfer in life. So loving of the sport, he'd arranged his own funeral in the months before his impending death, down to the smallest detail. The Derring Living Funeral Home, two hours' drive away, would be the location of his final golf outing. Family and friends—fifty in all—would come to see him posed in full links attire: his favorite cap, knickers cuffed just below the knee, red socks ending with his spiked golf shoes. Posed in a standing position, his body was braced with a hidden metal support which was in turn connected to a heavy platform base to hold his emaciated yet still substantial one hundred and twenty pounds. He'd wavered on several poses, first electing a simple putting scenario complete with indoor-outdoor carpeting, flag, and hole spaced ten feet away. But he'd decided it to be too tame, too predictable. No, if he were to do this thing right, to truly send himself off into the ether in a style and manner fitting how he'd lived his entire life, it would need to be something much grander—a tee shot, with his favorite wood driver. The action evoked power and health.

Cancer had robbed him of his body, but it had not been his entire existence. He'd met with Yves at the same home he himself would soon occupy in death. In his last precious weeks where he could breathe and think for himself, he'd made the decision that would cause a smile to remain on his face for the entire drive home.

Yves, answering his wife, focused his attention on the man's straightened arms extended in post-swing, the driver gripped in his bony fingers. A painted temporary wall in front of him depicted a fairway, complete with trees, a sand hazard, and a cloud-filled sky. A real golf ball hung suspended from a string two feet from the driver's head, its path seemingly toward the fairway. "The fluid sets the muscles quick, so I only had one chance to get it right. Thank goodness for the pulleys."

Sarah placed a hand on her husband's shoulder. "Some call you a monster. I call you a saint."

He sighed. "If not me, someone else would do it."

"No," she said, her voice assured. "Only two in the entire country, and no one else in the Midwest. Others have tried, but no one else can do...*that*." She indicated the dead man, his facial features so life-like that he could have been alive. The eyes glued open, their pupils dilated and fixed but otherwise glowing with what could have been pride at the perfect swing. Plastic forms placed between the teeth to open the mouth just so, and hidden stitches along the corners of the mouth, to pull the lips upward in an expression of exultation at completing his final instruction for Yves: to depict him achieving in death what he had never achieved in life, written out on a banner above him—*Hole in One!*

"I try," he said. But his shoulders slumped as he remembered how their conversation had begun. "I worry about Victor. Frederik too. We won't be around forever to care for them."

"We live as long as God chooses," Sarah said, coming to him and kissing him softly on the cheek.

"You're an angel," he said. "I couldn't do any of this without you. Especially the boys…" He hugged her tight, then held her at arm's length so that he could look into her eyes. "Now, I've got to finish this up before the guests arrive. Service is at noon."

Three years later, while doing laundry one morning, Sarah Derring collapsed from a major heart attack. Her husband was in town at the time conducting business, and her only children, the twin sons she'd doted on since their birth, had been sleeping in their shared bedroom. Two hours later, Victor awoke first then woke his brother, as was their custom. They dressed then went downstairs expecting to find their mother in the kitchen cooking breakfast as she did every morning. But the kitchen was empty, no food prepared or dishes set out. Concerned, since they'd seen their parents' bedroom and both of the home's bathrooms unoccupied, they searched the rest of the house until they found her body sprawled in front of the washing machine. She was cold to the touch, her eyes frozen open.

Frederik screamed and fell to his knees. While his brother begged and pleaded for their mother to wake up, Victor averted his eyes from his mother's lifeless body, his hands coming up to cover his ears so that he could block out Frederik's wails. They sounded like those of a gravely wounded animal. Victor's lips formed soundless words as he attempted to make the image before him go away—this impossible thing that in one moment had changed his life forever, his brother's too, because their mother had been the rock of the family—but now she lay stiffened and cold, not warm and cuddly as she'd been every night while tucking them in to bed, something she'd done since the day they'd been born. Just like the old man their father had brought to the home the day before to prepare for a living wake. The boys had even helped their father move the man's tattered recliner from the truck into the chapel. It had been the man's favorite place to sit in life, and his will had declared that his funeral viewing would include him being seated in the chair, right leg crossed over left, one hand holding a folded newspaper and the other a cup of coffee. But that wouldn't happen now. The man's family wouldn't come, because a different death had occurred, one much closer to home, and one that would shape the boys' lives from that moment on.

Frederik wept over his mother's corpse for the next hour; Victor pressed his face against her chest and mumbled incoherently to himself. When their father came home, whistling a country tune he'd just heard on the radio, he found the kitchen and family rooms empty. He checked the boys' bedroom and found it empty as well. Alarmed, he checked the rest of the house before he finally found them—Frederik having cried himself to sleep atop their dead mother's chest, Victor gripping both his brother's hand and that of his mother while humming a nursery rhyme to himself. When their father pried Victor's fingers from those of his dead wife, he pulled so hard he snapped two of her stiffened fingers like twigs.

CHAPTER 10

A bby's first night as a hostage wasn't anything like she imagined it would be. Images of women kept in virtual dungeons or chained to beds to become sex slaves filled her head. She slept on and off, her brain still affected by whatever drug he'd used to knock her out with. That, and the pure trauma of what had happened. After introducing Abby to several of the other "houseguests," Frederik had taken her back downstairs and locked her in one of the hidden bedrooms. Barely large enough to fit the double bed, the windowless room was lit by a low-powered, battery-operated night light. No electrical outlets, from what she could tell. At least he'd left her a makeshift toilet comprised of a five-gallon home improvement store bucket half-filled with water, covered with a sheet of plywood with a large hole in the middle. A stick glued to one side acted as a holder for the half-roll of toilet paper hanging from it. Soon after Frederik had left, Abby remembered listening to the sound of two heavy bolts sliding home, then of something heavy being rolled across the door. She'd blacked out then. When she came to, she wasn't sure if it had been for ten minutes or ten hours. Her entire world had just become unraveled. In one moment, she'd been ready to close the clinic for the day, planning on going home to lie on the couch and watch her favorite Netflix show with Thomas Magnum, then the next moment...

She bolted upright in bed, propping herself up on one elbow. A new panic swept through her, one that had nothing to do with her own safety. Her cat was locked inside her apartment. The usual routine was to feed him twice a day—once at seven a.m. and once again at seven p.m., regardless of if it was a workday or not. Several times she'd forgotten to feed him for one reason or another. But that had been over a two-year period, and on those occasions she'd remembered several hours later and either left work or darted home from an outing to feed him before going back out. He'd never gone twenty-four hours without food since she'd had him, however. He was her constant companion, the mixed-breed tabby she'd rescued from...what was the place called? She searched her mind, desperate to hold onto one of her favorite memories of the brindle feline that had more so chosen her than she'd chosen him.

As she blinked in the room's near-total darkness to clear her fuzzy vision, she focused on that scene she usually remembered so well, the one she loved to re-tell people when they asked about the only pet she'd had during her adult life. If she were to die here, then at least let her recall entering the Uptown cat-adoption café with the four-foot-tall cat statue beside the front door. The Café Meow, that was it. Fitting name for a coffee shop that, from all advertisements, combined a fully functioning café and no-kill cat shelter. Located on Hennepin Avenue, one of the busier streets in this part of town, she'd either driven by or walked by the place a thousand times without ever visiting. The day she'd actually gone inside should have been no different. Before heading to happy hour with Derek, she'd changed out of her scrubs and into a new outfit she'd been waiting to wear for months, then decided to walk the one-mile route from work instead of driving. A beautiful spring afternoon in the city. The last of the winter snow had melted several weeks ago, and the

mild temperature combined with clear skies seemed a harbinger
of good things, despite the fact she was still mourning the end of
a year-long relationship. She didn't remember why she'd
suddenly stopped at the cat statue and decided to go inside. A
lark. Pushing her way inside, she'd seen an interior nicer than
what she'd always imagined. Recalling it here in the semi-darkness, the pleasant memory helped comfort her.

"Welcome to the Café Meow," said the twentysomething girl
behind the counter. Abby noted the girl's lip ring, arm sleeve
tattoo, and pink mohawk. Appropriate. "Will you be using the
cat lounge today?"

Abby scanned one of the printed menus. 'Oh, I don't know,
maybe just a tea to go. I've been by this place a million times
and just wanted to check it out."

"If you change your mind, the cover charge to sit in the cat
lounge is five dollars for fifteen minutes, ten for a half-hour."

"Just the tea is fine," Abby said, looking around the place.
The normal café was well-appointed with wooden bistro tables,
black wire-backed chairs, and the expected cat-themed art. The
checkered tile floor and variety of live plants gave the place an
especially homey vibe. When her hot green tea was ready, she
thanked the girl and headed for the front door when she paused.
Turning around, she walked back to the counter. "Oh, why the
hell not. I'm already here."

"If you're interested in adoption, let me know when you're
done, and I can fill you in on the paperwork. Standard background check takes about a day to process."

Abby waved her off. "I can barely keep a plant alive. I'll just
sit and visit with them."

After paying for a fifteen-minute session and receiving the
low-down (visitors should allow the cats to sit or lie where they
were unless it was obvious that they wanted to be picked up;
petting was fine, but no feeding them), she entered a small
vestibule and waited for the door behind her to fully close before

opening the cat lounge door. Immediately, she understood why the place was so popular with locals. Even more homey than the people café, the cat portion was also complete with several bistro tables and chairs, with the addition of several carpeted cat towers and wall-mounted lounge platforms. Fake trees, a pair of well-worn couches, and cat-themed paintings completed the space. But the main objects of interest were the residents themselves— about a dozen cats of various breeds occupied the space. Several lay curled on or in the towers. A gray Chartreux sat perched atop the back of one of the couches, and a sleek black shorthair sat along the large picture window's sill to gaze lazily at passersby. Others lay napping on the checkered tile floor. Abby smiled as she looked around, wondering why on earth she'd never stopped here before.

When she sat at one of the tables, the black shorthair on the windowsill jumped from its perch and approached her. Before she could reach down to pet it, the animal jumped onto her table. Not to be outdone, a calico-tabby in one of the towers jumped down and leapt onto her lap. For the next ten minutes, she took dozens of photos of the two, as well as of the others. But she felt an instant connection with the one on her lap, loving how it turned to look up at her appreciatively with its green eyes and heavy set of black whiskers as she stroked its sleek coat. Others came to investigate her, brushing against her leg or sitting several feet away to stare inquiringly up at her. Wishing to allow others time to sit with her, she nudged the Tabico several times to get it to jump down, but it sat stubbornly in her lap until her fifteen minutes was up. Finally, she had no choice but to pick it up and set it down. She finished the last of her tea, said goodbye to the group of cats, then let herself back into the people café.

"How was your experience?" asked the girl behind the counter.

Abby smiled from ear to ear. "I loved it. I've got to come back with my friend Derek. He's a huge cat lover." She thanked the girl then exited onto the sidewalk, preparing to continue down the street to the bar she was meeting Derek at. She took two steps then stopped and glanced back at the cat lounge's picture window. Instead of the black shorthair, the same Tabico that had sat on her lap now occupied the sill, staring at her. After an extended moment, she said, "You aren't going to take no for an answer, are you?" and went back inside.

The following day after work, and once her background check came back, she bought a cat carrier then stopped by the café to pick up the Tabico she'd adopted. She went straight to Derek's place. "What's *that*?" he asked as soon as he opened the door.

"Uh, it's called a cat," Abby said sarcastically, entering then placing the carrier on the floor. She opened the carrier's door and removed the creature. "They're common domesticated pets. Cleopatra even owned them. And unlike any of the men I've dated lately, he appreciates public displays of affection."

When she and Derek sat together on the couch, the feline curled in her lap and began to purr luxuriously. His own two cats regarded it suspiciously from their towers. "Snarky today, eh?" Derek said half-jokingly. When Abby extended the feline for him to hold, he accepted it with enthusiasm. "Black whiskers, and thick!" he said, holding the cat up to inspect at arm's length. "They remind me of that actor from *Magnum P.I.*..."

"Tom Selleck."

"That's it." He placed the cat in his lap and began stroking its back. "Hey—if he doesn't have a name yet, maybe you should name him that."

Abby wrinkled her nose. "He was a stray, and I don't like the temporary name they gave him. But I don't think that fits him either. Shame, since the whiskers do."

"How about Thomas Magnum?" he offered. "That was the character's name on the show."

Abby's face lit up. "Simple and mysterious, just like his personality. I love it."

Derek gave the cat back to her then brushed his own collar with dramatic flair. "Once again, I've proven my brilliance."

Abby snapped out of the memory when a sound came from outside her door. Lying back onto the bed, she pulled the covers up to her chin and closed her eyes. If she couldn't play dead, she'd fake sleep. But then again, if Frederik had meant her immediate harm, he would have already done it. What had he said in response to her questioning if he was going to kill her? *All in good time…*

She heard the sound of the bolts sliding free, followed by the heavy rolling of the wood pile, then the squeak of hinges as the door pushed inward. She did her best to keep her breathing consistent with a sleeping person's, slow and even. Devoid of sight, her other senses intensified. Heavy footsteps made the wood floor creak before they paused, then approached the bed beside her. She smelled the odor of aftershave and a bitter chemical scent she couldn't place. Her heart pounded so hard, she worried he'd hear it. Was he standing there with an ax gripped in both hands, ready to bring it crashing down on her head the moment she opened her eyes? Was he pointing a gun at her, or was he doing something more subtle like wrapping a length of cord around each hand? As she pondered her fate, her mind went back to her original thought, Thomas Magnum. She tried to remember if she'd left the toilet cover up—a water source she knew he'd have until someone eventually checked her apartment —but she couldn't recall.

A man's voice then, from where the footsteps had paused beside her. *Him*. Frederik, if that was his real name. "You can open your eyes now. I know you aren't sleeping."

Her heart stopped for a beat, and the hairs on the back of her neck stood on end. Then a moment later, her heart began pounding again, only harder this time. She wanted very badly to open her eyes, to at least confront whatever fate surely awaited her, but her lids felt glued shut.

"I have a camera installed in here. Not to spy, but to make sure you don't do something both of us might regret. I don't check it all the time, but I did peek in at you just now, so…"

With the rest of her body remaining perfectly still, she opened her eyes and confirmed that it was indeed Frederik standing beside her. The rectangle of light created by the open doorway illuminated half of his face, the other half remaining in darkness. She wasn't sure if a person could smile and scowl at the same time, but she imagined if it was possible, he'd be doing it now. At least he wasn't holding anything. "You slept all night. The first day can be sort of stressful, so I'm not surprised. Hungry yet?"

No, but my cat will be. She scrunched the covers tighter around her neck. For the first time since she'd awakened, she realized she was still fully clothed. Had he raped her? She forced her mind to recall every waking memory from the time she'd been kidnapped until now. Even the unconscious memories too, because since a child she'd become ultra-sensitive to them. Finally sure that he hadn't violated her, she said, "My cat is home alone. I need to let someone know he needs food and water."

He moved a bit to his right, exposing his full grinning face. "The police just left the clinic, so I imagine they'll search your apartment soon. And then Mr. Kitty will be…" He performed a chef's kiss. "…eating his little heart out." He extended a hand toward her. "I assume you have to tinkle. You can use the upstairs bathroom to freshen up. These old homes weren't built with showers, and I never added one so a bath will have to do. I took the liberty of setting out some fresh clothes for you as well. Hopefully I got your size right."

So, she had been here overnight, after all. Unsure what to do, Abby opted to push the covers down and tentatively take his hand. Rising to her feet, she instantly felt the same heaviness in her bladder that usually followed her usual eight-hour sleep sessions.

"Same rules as before. I'll trust that you won't break them." His eyebrows raised. She shook her head. "Excellent. I've got a sweatshirt for you to wear, to handle the cold upstairs. Now, shall we?" He led her out the room and handed her a hoodie with a familiar M-shaped emblem in maroon and gold. Obliging him, she slipped it on then allowed him to lead her through the same open room she remembered from the day before and back up the stairs. A blast of cold air met them as soon as they breached the doorway. Abby had lived in Minnesota her entire life and knew the temperature to the degree just from skin sensation alone. It had to be in the upper thirties up here, cold enough to see her own breath. She wondered how he'd gotten it so cold but then remembered the open windows behind the nailed curtains.

He led her into the same kitchen as yesterday. It was semi-dark in here, and until he flipped the wall switch all she saw was the small Formica table and chairs she remembered sitting at. As the overhead fluorescent lights flickered on, Abby saw a woman standing at the stove. Confused at first over who might be cooking for him, reality hit her like a punch to the gut a second later. It was the same woman from yesterday. Abby remembered the women in the other room at the same moment her brain registered the metal brace holding the chef's body upright.

"This is Petra," Frederik said, resting a hand on the woman's shoulder. "She's a local celebrity chef I discovered on YouTube. I would have formally introduced you two yesterday, but when you didn't eat her cooking, she got offended. Chefs are funny like that." He slipped a hand around Abby's waist and squeezed that soft part she hated people to touch. "Breakfast is her special-ty," he continued, leading Abby to her seat at the table. "So hopefully you'll eat something now." He stood behind Petra and whispered something in her ear. While he had his back turned,

Abby dared a glance around the small galley kitchen. Nothing of any use to her, from what she could tell. None of the drawers had knobs; she guessed they were empty anyway. No knife rack for her to pull a blade and sink between his shoulder blades. In fact, every surface of the dated yellow Formica counter was bare. Stealing a quick glance toward the way they'd come, she calculated that she'd get about a ten-foot head start if she decided to bolt through the parlor for the front door. But as quickly as she considered the possibility, she remembered the vestibule door system and the nailed curtains. He'd mentioned the camera in her room, and it only made sense that he'd installed other security measures she hadn't seen yet.

With mechanical lethargy, she looked back toward the stove in time to see him place both hands on the dead woman's hips and kiss her cheek. "Good morning to you too, love. What, an omelet? I'd *love* one!" He turned to face Abby. "Care for one after your bath? She makes them super cheesy." Again, that dimpled grin.

Abby shook her head, or some unseen force shook it for her. "I'm not hungry, thank you."

Frederik shrugged, his smile faltering a bit. "Well, then, bath time." He led her upstairs then indicated an open door at the end of the hallway. "Towels and a change of clothes are beside the sink. Toiletries too. You'll forgive me for insisting the door remain open." He did his eyebrow thing then extended his hand in the direction of the open bathroom door. She looked at it dumbly for a moment before forcing her feet to move in that direction. Propping the door open with an unworn boot, he walked down the hall out of view. The sound of his weight settling onto a chair, and his low whistling reached her. He was giving her a bit of privacy, but obviously didn't trust her. Abby immediately scanned the interior for a camera, or a possible way out. He'd either hidden a camera well, or decided not to place one here. The porcelain pedestal sink was bare of anything except a single bar of soap still in its cardboard container, a new-looking toothbrush, and a fresh tube of toothpaste. A pair of black sweatpants, a t-shirt, bra, and a pair of underwear all with tags still attached were neatly folded atop a wicker bin. Noting the mirror on the medicine cabinet, a thought crossed her mind: she could break it if she got desperate enough. She could use a shard on him, or herself if need be. Running the tap, she dared to open the cabinet door to inspect it. Not only was it empty, but she discovered that this mirror was made of stainless steel too. Closing it, she noticed her fingerprints clearly standing out on the mirror. Grateful she'd noticed, she breathed on it then wiped her prints clean with the hand towel.

Similar to the windows downstairs, the bathroom's only window was covered by a heavy curtain and nailed around the edges. She didn't even try prying it free to look outside. Realizing she had little choice, she opted to placate him for now. She dropped the plunger and cranked the tub's squeaky knobs. Steaming water poured from the old-fashioned spigot to a point where she felt it wouldn't overflow with her added weight. Undressing to her bra and underwear, she glanced around at the walls and ceiling once more to check for a camera. As sure as she could be that there weren't any, she stepped into the bath. Clothes he'd given her to wear were one thing, but she drew the line at placing anything over her most private parts that he'd shopped for, that grin of his likely on his face while he did so.

After she bathed and dressed, (her bra and panties still damp) he led her back downstairs. Apparently he'd cooked since two omelets sat on separate plates, and were still warm. Frederik had changed too, from the pajamas, slippers, and loose robe he'd had on before her bath into jeans and a long overcoat. An odd choice for breakfast at home, Abby thought, but dismissed it just as quickly as it passed through her mind. Nothing about this situation was normal.

"Eat," he said flatly after five minutes had gone by and she'd only poked at it. He said it while pausing with his fork halfway to his mouth and staring at her plate. His calm demeanor and subtle tone of insistence told her if she didn't do as he said, he might pick the food up with his fingers and jam it down her throat. She cut away a small portion of omelet and scooped it with the plastic spork he'd given her to use. Raising it toward her mouth, she touched it to her trembling lips before lowering it back onto her plate. Despite her grumbling stomach, she couldn't do it. She'd vomit if she ate it. He'd become angry, no doubt, but something inside her demanded she not show him any amount of weakness, even if that was just throwing up.

"I...I can't. I'll be sick. Please..." She fought with every fiber to keep it together. She had allowed herself to cry quietly while in the bathtub but doing it in front of him would strip her of the minute shred of dignity she had left. It was bad enough that he'd sat her to face the dead woman. Worse still was the fact he'd turned Petra's body in such a way to partially expose her frozen smile and glued-open eyes. Averting her gaze from the standing corpse the best she could, Abby focused on the omelet that was growing colder by the moment. It felt even colder up here than yesterday. She fantasized that when she looked back up, the dead woman's head would miraculously be facing the sink again, her limbs re-animated somehow and in the process of cooking. It would've been part of this sick joke. The women from the other room, plus the others he'd suggested that may already be in different rooms or were waiting in the downstairs freezer would all be in on it. *Surprise. Haha. Gotcha real good, didn't we?*

Frederik pushed his chair out and stood suddenly, hands on hips. Abby looked up at him. The hairs on the back of her neck stood out, and despite the warm sweatshirt covering her arms, she could feel the flesh beneath it turn to gooseflesh.

"Petra, our guest still isn't hungry," he said flatly. "Are you okay with that?" It was as if part of him knew she was dead, and another part of him thought that her stillness was caused by some perceived insult. He didn't speak or change expressions for several agonizing moments. Just the pounding of Abby's own pulse in her ears. Then, as if a switch had been thrown inside him, his angry expression softened to one of regret and contrition, and he came to embrace Abby's upper body and head in a giant hug.

"Aww, I scared you," he said soothingly, rocking her back and forth. "You won't make me take a nap because of it, will you? Tell me you won't. I promise to be a good boy…"

Abby sat frozen in his tight embrace. Her heart was yammering so hard in her chest, she swore it would burst through her ribcage. And despite her arms remaining pinned at her sides, her fingers still managed to clench into fists, the nails gouging her palms. Then an absurd thought: she had a nail appointment today at five-thirty, at her favorite place down the street from her apartment. She'd never no-called, no-showed in the three years she'd been going there. She imagined somehow having the opportunity to call them now to cancel. *Hello, it's Abby Carlson. I'm trapped in some lunatic's house with a bunch of dead women dressed like they're going to a job fair, and I really doubt I'll be making it today, so sorry.*

CHAPTER 11

After speaking with Dr. McMichael, Randall and Tan grabbed a quick to-go lunch at the PSB's lobby café. While waiting for his order, Randall remembered to query the name Harlon Cromley. Only two such names came up in the state—an eighty-seven-year-old man living in Bemidji, and a forty-five-year-old licensed mental health counselor operating a local online practice. Eliminating the elderly Cromley, Randall decided to begin with the counselor then go from there. He called the number on file and left a voicemail asking the man to call him back as soon as possible. When they got back to the Homicide office, Sergeant Fells was waiting for them near the elevator. She held an enlarged driver's license photo and a familiar-looking stat sheet in one hand. "Letter twenty-five headed to the board," she said, grim-faced. She led Randall and Tan through aisles of cubicles occupied by both civilians and sworn members, to the elongated PK bulletin board that had dominated one wall of the department's main Homicide office for the past six months. Of the twenty-four women's photos already tacked along its length (inverted three-by-five index cards had been tacked above them, with successive letters of the alphabet written out in black marker to indicate each profession), only two missing letters remained, D and V. As Randall watched Sergeant Fells tack Abby Carlson's photo and stat sheet below the index card marked "D," he thought to himself how much the index cards resembled tombstones.

"D..." he muttered under his breath. He stared intently at Abby's photo—her expressive brown eyes, Roman nose, and bright smile exposing well-maintained teeth—and wondered where she currently was. She'd been gone for nearly twenty hours, day one in PK's playbook. If he kept to his schedule of killing and posing her, Abby had anywhere from four to nine days to live. PK had gone off schedule before, though, so that time frame wasn't guaranteed. Assuming he did kill her, her corpse would make a short Instagram appearance before the IT folks in the task force ultimately took it down. But Randall and the rest of the task force would be left as they had after the previous twenty-four cases: scratching their collective heads.

During his three-week hiatus following his mandated psychological evaluation, Randall had poured over his own notes from the other abductions and apparent killings. He'd surprised himself by losing ten pounds, something he concluded was the combined result of getting more than two hours' sleep a night and eating food that didn't come from a drive-thru or was wrapped in cellophane. No one had been more surprised than himself when Fells had called yesterday morning. His paid leave had been cut short by three days, the result of politics, he'd concluded. The PD and FBI—and of course, the task force itself —were under immense pressure. Minnesota was making national news again and, similar to the riots several years ago, it wasn't in a good way. A shame, since the state had largely enjoyed positive press for Randall's entire career prior to those events. He may have been relatively low on the PD's totem pole, but he was savvy enough to know his re-instatement wasn't just an attempt to save the lives of twenty-four women (twenty-five now), but also a last-ditch effort to avoid an indelible black mark for them all, professionally and personally.

"Crew's here," Fells said, waving Randall and Tan toward the nearby conference room for their daily briefing. The "crew" meant the other core task force members, beginning with a secondary PD Homicide team comprised of Detectives Haag and Pederson. Both detective teams and all others serving as axillary units were commanded by Fells. Agent James Teague, the force's IT and flight liaison from the state's Bureau of Criminal Apprehension, was also present. Topping off the core members were two contingents from the FBI's St. Paul office across the river— Dr. Irene Hoffman, the Midwest's foremost forensic psychologist and criminal profiler, and Senior Special Agent Dean Whitlock. The latter had assumed formal leadership of the task force when it had become obvious the department was dealing with a serial killer. A team of agents had been assigned to the force, their main missions focusing on cybercrime and intelligence. Although Agent Whitlock was in charge on paper, he had quickly determined that the city's PD detectives (and Randall specifically) held the greatest expertise in local, on-the-street investigative skills. This was their turf. As such, Whitlock had smartly asked Sergeant Fells and her teams to assume de facto leadership roles. In his view, egos didn't win wars, but only prolonged them. Seeing Randall enter the room, the barrel-chested, mustached Whitlock stood and extended his hand. "Welcome back, Cal. We've missed you."

Randall pumped his hand. "Good to be back," he said, meaning it. He turned and indicated Tan, who stood beside him with a polite smile on her face. "This is my new partner, Kelli Tan. It took me a week to get my feet wet. She's gotten neck deep before lunch."

Agent Whitlock shook Tan's hand and offered her a

welcoming smile. "Nice to meet you, Detective. From what Sergeant Fells says about you, they picked the best person for the job. I hope you like swimming, because the pool you're jumping into is pretty deep."

Tan gave him an appreciative smile. "Thank you, sir. I'm honored to be on the team. I'll do my best."

Whitlock pulled out the empty chair next to him and motioned for Tan to take it. "No 'sirs' around here. Call me Whit."

Tan sat despite appearing surprised that she was being offered the seat nearest to Whitlock at the table's head. Randall took the empty seat beside Fells and removed a notepad and pen, his old-school method of note taking. Tan followed suit. The other members had their laptops open and at the ready. After Whitlock called the meeting to order, Agent Teague, the bookish-looking BCA liaison, was the first to get Tan up to speed. "BCA serves two main purposes here, Detective. We coordinate with programmers at Instagram to detect and remove PK's posts as soon as possible. We also provide airborne surveillance units that MPD doesn't have, should they become necessary."

Agent Whitlock pointed at him. "You guys have been on top of those posts, James. Our techs don't hold a candle to you state guys."

"We try," Teague said, shrugging. He turned to Detective Tan and added, "When we started the task force, BCA's goal was to keep a full-time IT tech on the lookout for his posts the minute we had a confirmed abduction. In all but three of them, he posted photos of what we suspect are his victims' corpses in that five- to ten-day window. One was posted four days after the abduction, and two after eleven days."

"Does his posting their pictures suggest psychosis or narcissistic personality disorder?" Tan asked.

All heads in the room turned toward Dr. Hoffman. She nodded in Tan's direction, seemingly impressed with her question. "Both, actually. He's clearly psychotic, and his self-aggran-dizing behavior does suggest extreme narcissism. He adds photos of his own fingerprint with the posts to differentiate himself from the many copycats who've surfaced. It also speaks to his level of commitment that he's willing to risk unnecessary capture by abducting women on the job."

Randall nodded his agreement. "You've heard of his MO, but you probably didn't get a real sense of how it unfolds until the clinic video."

"For sure," Tan said. "He must increase his odds of getting caught a hundred times by doing that."

"Even more when you consider that people's awareness increases with every letter he takes," the doctor explained. "The methodology of the letter sequences was the most diffi-cult aspect of his profile. We didn't realize until he was about halfway through the alphabet that the letters themselves weren't his goal. Yes, the pattern provided him with notoriety. It's easy to keep track of, and every working woman in the city between twenty and forty works a profession beginning with one of them. But digging deeper into his psyche, I found it much more likely that some childhood trauma—perhaps an absentee parent due to different jobs creating opportunity for abuse or neglect—led him to focus on the alphabet specifically."

Tan frowned. "But it hasn't helped us predict his next victims."

"I've never been good at math," Whitlock said, "but I know that twenty-six letters multiplied by thousands of different professions equals one hell of a clusterfuck for our undercovers to pull surveillance on. It's not a needle in a haystack, it's a needle in a field of haystacks."

By far, the biggest clue to PK's profile were the posts' subjects themselves. Tan brought up what they'd all discussed ad nauseum. "He obviously has mortuary science experience. What have we found with former funeral directors, or funeral homes themselves?"

"Not much," Randall said, answering for them all. "We started in Minnesota, then branched out to the entire Midwest. The FBI here was a big help, but it still took weeks to visit hundreds of operating funeral homes and interview directors. All of them checked out. We also queried every certified school in the country, although you'd be surprised how many people have, and are taking formal mortuary classes. We did a cross-comparison of the white men in them with PK's general description. That narrowed it down, but we still came up empty."

Everyone went silent for a moment, until Agent Whitlock changed the mood of the room by fishing into his briefcase and removing a copy of Abby Carlson's enlarged photo. He stood up abruptly and held it up for them all to see. "This young lady is out there, people. Twenty-four hours ago, she was minding her business at work until someone decided to kidnap her. We all know who that individual was. We've *all* failed finding the other victims. Don't think it doesn't disrupt the little sleep I do get. I don't intend on ever seeing Ms. Carlson's Instagram post, is that understood?" A chorus of assents came from around the table. He sat down and slapped the photo hard atop the table.

Sergeant Fells had been relatively silent for the first part of the meeting. Her narrowed eyes had focused on each individual speaking. Now it was her turn. She pulled up a file on her department cellphone, which included a since-deleted Instagram post of bright-eyed nineteen-year-old Edina resident Frieda Gustafson, PK's first confirmed abductee. Fells slid the phone across the table to Detective Tan. "The post you're looking at was from this past April—letter one, 'I.' It stayed up the longest because we didn't know about it yet."

Like most members of the department, Tan knew the story well enough. But this was the first time she'd had an official examination of the post she and thousands of others had briefly seen before it and all re-posts of it had been forcibly taken down. Tan went through the three photos, beginning with the now infamous shot of the unfortunate college student who'd been abducted from her job at a local ice cream shop. Her smiling corpse (she, like all the others, hadn't been officially declared dead by police, despite a forensic examination of the photograph having verified it as being unaltered) had been posed behind a small display case of various fake ice cream containers, extending a likewise fake ice cream cone in one hand. The second photo depicted the interior of the shop she'd been abducted from. The last photo had been the most puzzling to police at first—a focused shot of a human fingertip, proved by the FBI to be authentic. Only until police had viewed surveillance footage from the shop had they understood the significance. The suspect's fingerprints had been traced to a disguised, middle-aged white male, per the footage showing him abducting her after the manager on duty ran a quick errand. Tan read the post's caption: "Letter One, but far from done." Her frown deepened. "But what about locating his photos or pinging the posts themselves?"

"No-go," Agent Teague said from his spot at the far end of the table. "He's posting from crowded public areas. Pretty simple technique to defeat the technology the FBI and we have, which is some powerful shit."

"I get us not being able to shut down the Mall of America, or legally search everyone leaving Valley Fair. But I'm talking about discovering the location he actually took the photos from."

Teague shot a look toward Randall that said the issue had already been addressed. He explained it to Tan in as simple terms as his nerdiness allowed. "He's taking a digital picture of a physical Polaroid from the same place he posts from."

"Aha," Tan said, full understanding flooding her eyes. "He keeps us running around in circles while making sure we spread our resources thin. It's not cat and mouse; it's a cat and a thousand mice."

"Pretty much," Teague said. He brought up a file on his laptop and had those beside him hand it her way. "Whomever this is, they're the biggest PK copycat out there right now."

"A hundred thousand followers. Not bad," Tan said, scrolling through the series of faked corpse poses which became more extravagant as they went along.

"He doesn't try to pretend he's PK, he's just spoofing him," Randall added from experience. "In fact, he gives a lot of credit to the suspect for being so creative. If you scroll through the comments, you'll see how pages like that generate a hundred times more bad tips than we already get."

Tan read the first dozen or so comments before looking up with another question in her eyes. "I'd think PK would be upset that someone else is receiving all the attention."

"It isn't all ego for him," Dr. Hoffman said. "PK enjoys a practical benefit from social media pages like this. He probably knew going in that authenticating his work created the likelihood his own posts would be removed. That isn't his main goal." The doctor paused with raised eyebrows. It was a clear sign that she expected Tan to come up with her own conclusion.

Tan squinted at the screen in deep thought. "I just read a dozen hypotheses in under a minute. There has to be a hundred more just on this one post. PK would see for himself that a page like this is allowed to remain because it's obviously a fake. I'm a cop, and it's only taken a minute for me to think of a few theories of who he is. I can see how the task force has been flooded with BS tips." She went through a few more of PK's authenticated posts that Agent Teague had saved, most of which she'd never seen for herself. Twenty-four women, each dressed in the clothing they'd worn at the time of their abduction from their places of business. An African American artist wearing a tank top and overalls sitting before an easel, her paintbrush poised to touch the canvas. A short-haired, Latina hairdresser standing behind a fully-dressed, seated mannequin, a pair of open scissors held to a length of the dummy's hair. And a figure skater captured in the perfect Biellmann pose—one leg stretched up behind and above her head, one hand reaching back to grip the blade and the other grasping the forearm for support. Her killer had even taken the time to manipulate the frills of her sequined performance dress to make her appear in forward motion. Twenty other posts the task force IT folks had saved for investigative purposes, all of which Tan scanned with increasing amazement. When she finished, she handed the laptop back down the line to Agent Teague, who regarded her with a somber expression.

"It's obvious he's keeping the victims as trophies," Whitlock told Tan. "Part of these meetings is trying to discover what makes him tick, outside of the obvious. If the women he's abducted are truly dead—and Dr. Lampley at the ME's office seems to believe they are—then our next question is how long he can realistically keep doing this before they all fall apart. We've verified with local funeral directors that embalming only keeps a body fully preserved for a week, maybe two, until a funeral is held."

"Could he be refrigerating or freezing them?" Tan asked.

"Maybe at first," said the doctor. "But his profile suggests he wants to keep them displayed for as long as possible. I've dealt with serial killers like this before. A common denominator is their need for instant access to their trophies. Keeping them on display together would require a warehouse or somewhere large enough to refrigerate twenty-six staged bodies at once."

Randall added, "It's counter-productive for him to take all these risks just to store them inside a fridge or freezer long-term. Wherever he is, it's a large space where he can work in private. Some of the scenes he produces take up an entire ten-foot wall."

Agent Whitlock folded his hands atop the table and leaned

forward, his expression grave. "We sent the photos to D.C and had them examined. You'd be amazed at how paint and wall patterns can be forensically stripped away or compared, much like rifling marks on a bullet. At first, we considered that he might be posing each body in the same place and re-decorating the backdrop, but we ruled that out. We did the math and agreed on an area no smaller than three thousand square feet. Fells's teams queried sales on every model of commercial cooler and freezer that size as far back as we found records for. There were hundreds in Minnesota and western Wisconsin, the furthest he's operating. All of them checked out."

"How about slaughterhouses?" Tan asked.

"We checked those too," Whitlock said. "Nothing, except me never wanting to eat hot dogs again. At least he's letting us view the bodies."

The room went quiet, with each member pausing to presumably take in what most of them already knew but had rehashed for the sake of the newest member of the team. For his part, Detective Randall leaned back in his chair, a distant and troubling memory surfacing in his mind that had remained tucked away for months—one of a sixteen-year-old girl lying in a casket. In his mind, he pictured himself standing over her lifeless form, crying. Immediately, as if turned on by a switch, he felt a familiar sensation wash over him whenever he'd conjured the memory. His skin grew cold, and his mouth went dry. It was coming, he knew. Looking around at the faces surrounding him, he tried to think of a plausible reason to excuse himself before it happened again. His mind was so confounded that he didn't even think to say he needed to use the bathroom. He licked his lips. The others' voices turned into a jumble of distorted sounds. He felt trapped, like a man surrounded by captors speaking in foreign tongues. At any moment it would happen. When it did, like earlier outside the clinic, he would feel helpless to prevent it. And if he allowed it to happen in front of everyone, he'd be left to mumble an explanation as to why it had occurred, or more specifically, why even after weeks of department-ordered therapy it was *still* occurring. He'd be removed from duty again—maybe this time for good.

"Excuse me," he said to the group, then hurried to the men's room. The compulsion to kneel and re-tie his shoelaces was overpowering. But he resisted it. Running the faucet, he splashed cold water on his face as a detective from the surveillance unit came in to use the bathroom. As the detective stood washing his hands at the sink next to him, Randall breathed deeply for a moment as he detected the man's concerned look in the mirror. "You okay?" the detective asked.

"Cafeteria's fish sandwich strikes again," Randall lied, glancing at him in the mirror.

"Probably catch them in the river," the detective said with a laugh. When he left, Randall leaned onto the counter and stared hard into the mirror.

"Hold it together, Cal," he spoke aloud. After he collected himself, he walked back to the group. He could tell he'd been discussed. His assumption was confirmed when Fells took him by the arm. "Excuse us," she said to the others, then escorted him into a nearby empty office. Closing the door, she turned to face him with arms crossed. "Did it happen again?"

"No, I swear. I just needed a second to let it pass."

She burned a look into him that said she was wavering on a decision. Finally, it came. "I'm recommending you go back on leave," she said matter-of-factly.

"But, Sarge—"

"But nothing. I can't have you in the field if it happens again. Your triggers are between you and the counselor, but even I can tell when it's about to happen. And that was in a controlled setting."

"I know what it looks like. I'll be fine."

"I'm not convinced you are, Cal. It pains me to say that, but it's true. You need more time."

"We don't *have* more time," he said, pointing toward the door. "There's another victim out there who'll be dead soon if I don't help find her. No one else knows the case like I do. It's why you brought me back."

She shook her head. "Correction—it's why the *chief* brought you back. I agreed with him, but that was before I saw you run out of there just now."

"Koenig puked during a shootout last year and didn't even have to get screened," Randall said.

"That may be the case, but it still doesn't take away the fact you aren't well," she said, her tone softening. "Look—I know how much this means to you. Lord knows I've lost just as much sleep over these past six months as everyone else. But I can't in good conscience let you go back into the field with you still affected the way you are. Whatever's going on with you, you've got to get your own head straightened out before you can help anyone else."

He planted his hands on his hips. "I was fine while I was on leave."

"That's exactly my point."

"I'll make a deal with you—if it happens again, the actual shoe thing, I'll come straight to you and hand over my gun and badge. I'll re-submit my FMLA and stay away until my other six weeks are up. Next time, not even the chief can make me come back. And that's not counting the fact he could put me on psychological fitness for duty leave afterward."

She began to protest but stopped herself, appearing to ponder a thought for several moments before finally looking toward the ceiling with raised hands. "Why, Lord...why?" she pleaded, then bored an intense look into him with an extended finger. "You have one more chance. One. If you touch those shoes when you don't need to, even if you're alone and no one is around to see it, you self-report. Understood?"

"Yes, ma'am."

"I mean it. I'm sticking my neck out for you by allowing you back in the field. More important than that is your well-being. Don't make me regret doing this."

"I won't, Sarge, I promise." He stepped toward her and extended his hand. She stared at it for a moment before shaking it, albeit cautiously. "I'd never risk your reputation or position here if I didn't mean it," he said. "I can beat this thing. Abby needs me. The other victims do too, even if they're dead. They deserve justice, and their families deserve answers."

She nodded. "Okay. I'm inclined to regret my decision, so I suggest you leave right now before I change my mind."

"Yes ma'am," he said, moving toward the door.

"Cal, wait," she said. He stopped and turned to face her. "While you were out, the chief called me into his office. He told me not to tell anyone. I haven't yet, but you have just as much right to know as I do. The city commissioners are considering disbanding the Homicide unit. Half of the commission is up for re-election, and they're getting hammered in the press."

"What are they going to replace us with, mall cops?" he asked, his voice indignant.

"Worse. Civilian leadership and hand-picked investigators from outside the department."

He shook his head. "Just like they were threatening to do with the entire department after the riots."

"Which they would have if half the department hadn't threatened to get blue flu."

"For what it's worth, I'd trade going back to patrol tomorrow if it meant getting Abby back alive," Randall said. "I'm not in this for glory."

Fells' previous hardened expression softened. "I know that, Cal. And so does the chief. It's why he did what he did."

"Ten-four. And thank you for believing in me. I won't disappoint you." He shook her hand again then walked back into the conference room from where Agent Whitlock was just exiting. "UC unit just picked up your clinic accomplice in Uptown. They're bringing him in now."

Randall smiled. Finally, a break. "Can we give Abby's friend Derek to Team Two?" he asked Fells. "I want the accomplice."

"You read my mind," Fells said, shooting him a relieved smile. At least it was something.

CHAPTER 12

She's cold.

That's because the thermostat is set to fifty-five. To save money, her mother says. The cold, dark shape of the radiator crouches beneath her frosted-over window like a forgotten promise. Her bedroom window is the only one on the second floor absent the insulating plastic film Hank used to cover them with before winter set in. He'd only had one of the expensive sheets left for either Abby or her younger brother. Hank had asked her to choose, explaining whoever's room didn't get it would get much colder than the others during winter. He'd even gone so far as to tell her that he was sure Bobby's asthma would be fine if he didn't get the plastic, that despite him being five years old, he was still a boy, and boys were stronger than girls. Abby had of course offered to go without it, telling Hank that since she was three years older than Bobby, he should get the plastic. Hank had patted her on the head and told her she was a good sister. Then he'd checked over his shoulder before whispering to her that he'd make it up to her later that night, that he'd do that thing to her he'd shown her last week, when her mother had stayed the night in the hospital due to her kidney stones.

That had been a month ago, before the first real snowfall and *before the red line on the thermostat hanging outside the kitchen window dipped below thirty degrees for the first time that season. It hadn't risen above it since, and probably wouldn't until after Valentine's Day three months from now. The comforter would have to do. Abby huddles under it now, clutching her favorite dolly and stuffed bear against her nightgown-clad body. Her dolly and teddy are also eight years old, or so she's declared since she's had them as long as she can remember. Gifts from her mother and father, God rest his soul. It's just her mother and Bobby now, if you don't count Hank. He prefers plain old "Hank" versus "stepfather." He doesn't like that word, says it makes him seem less than what he is, which is the man of the house. But Abby uses "stepfather" when referring to him to her friends at school, because "father" doesn't sound right coming from her own mouth. And "Hank" sounds too informal, friendly almost.*

Once, she slipped and referred to him as "stepfather" to a family friend in Hank's presence. His face growing red, he'd taken Abby forcefully by the hand and led her to his truck. When her mother had asked where he was taking her, Hank had told her to shut up and mind her business, that he was going to teach the girl a lesson. With Abby seated beside him, he'd made the truck tires kick up rocks from the gravel driveway as he'd torn out onto the main road. He'd driven to the local cemetery and stopped the truck on a road familiar to them both, then taken Abby by the hand and led her to a gravestone with her father's name written on it.

"If your daddy wanted to be with you, he wouldn't have got himself killed," Hank had said, plumes of his breath rising in the frigid air. Then Hank had knelt on the frost-covered grass and taken her by the shoulders. "I'm your daddy now, and you'll do as I say, hear?" Abby had nodded, thankful for the bitter cold because it froze the tears in her eyes.

Then Hank drove her home and sent her to her room where

she'd played with her dolly and teddy. She'd heard her mother and Hank's raised voices from downstairs, followed by the sound of someone being slapped and a chair being overturned. Then silence. Abby remembers this as she huddles beneath her covers, trying to force the memory away, and that of others like it because they're numerous and unpleasant. But she can't help it. Thinking about them has a strange way of preventing them from taking root in her mind, like weeds in her mother's garden.

It's ten thirty, an hour past bedtime. Her room is dark, the sort of dark where shadows don't exist, not even when her little brother wakes up like he's done just now to shuffle in his onesie pajamas to the half-bathroom, turning the light on in the hallway on the way there. She can hear the plastic bottoms of his pajama feet scratching along the hallway's wooden floor. Then the flick of the light switch, and now a rectangle of light appearing beneath her door. She moves the covers past her eyes and makes out the faint globe of her doorknob. The keyhole that is normally empty no longer is, because she's fashioned a makeshift skeleton key from one of her mother's bobby pins and half a roll of tape, since Hank threw away the only key for the door. It took her several tries before her skeleton key would turn the lock. She'd let out a cry of self-accomplishment when it had clicked home, despite her knowledge that locking the door was a hollow victory, that to Hank it would be like pushing your finger through wet toilet paper. Thinking of Hank, she pulls the comforter even closer around her body. Sleep will be difficult tonight, if possible at all. Hank had been in a foul mood today. Something about a job his boss said hadn't been done right and Hank not being paid what he said he deserved.

Abby hears the splashing sound of urine forcefully striking the water in the bowl, followed by the metallic clank of the tank lever being pushed down, and finally the familiar chug of water. Hearing the squeak of the sink knobs, she imagines Bobby standing on his tiptoes to turn them, that look of determination

on his face. *That look always reminds Abby of their father whenever he'd whittled a stick or worked on his truck. Now the rattle
of the bathroom towel ring, then the flick of the light switch, and
just like that, the rectangle of light beneath her door turns to
black.*

*Immediately, her heart begins to pound as she listens to
Bobby shuffle down the hall past their mother and Hank's
bedroom to his own room. She hears the faint squeak of his door
hinges, the click of the latch, and now she's truly alone because
her mother is drunk again. Abby knows because she helped her
to bed after supper. The third time already this week. The first
two times had been without much apprehension on Abby's part,
because Hank had been away on business selling farm supplies.
But he's home tonight, having returned unexpectedly a day early
because something had happened to his truck. Earlier, as Abby
had fixed dinner—macaroni and cheese, hot dogs, and canned
corn—she'd stood at the stove while her mother lay half-dozing
on the couch and Hank sat behind her reading the newspaper at
the table. He'd rustled the pages every so often as if he was reading, but she'd felt his eyes on her the entire time. She always felt
his eyes when she knew he planned on visiting her that night. It
was like an electric current in the air. Later, as the four of them
had eaten in relative silence, Abby had kept her eyes focused on
her plate until she'd finished. She'd been glad that Hank had
retired to the living room while she washed the dishes.*

*Blinking now in the darkness, she thinks she hears her moth-
er's snoring, but that would be unlikely through two closed
doors. It's probably her own quick breathing. Abby wishes she
could hear it, though. She needs to. To give her a semblance of
comfort for what she knows is about to occur, even though her
mother will surely wake tomorrow morning, bleary-eyed and
mumbling, "Good morning, honeybun," or "Have you seen my
cigarettes?" She'll sit across from Abby at the breakfast table, a
cigarette hanging from the corner of her mouth. Abby will make*

sure to avert her eyes, lest her mother read them and know what had happened the night before. And believing her little girl is just tired or bored as she often believes her to be, her mother will smile that crooked smile of hers and reach across the table to ruffle Abby's hair. "Dontcha know I love you?" she'll say, her voice thick and hoarse.

"I know," Abby will say as Hank walks into the kitchen, out of her mother's view. He'll lean against the archway, inspecting his fingernails then grinning at Abby. It says a lot, that grin. Mostly, it says he's proud of what he's done. It also says he knows without a shadow of a doubt that Abby will never dare breathe a word about it to anyone, let alone her mother. Hell will freeze over and angels will descend from heaven first.

But her mind is getting ahead of itself. That will be tomorrow. This is now. To arrive at that place of relative safety, where daylight streams through her windows and her brother and mother are awake and aware of Hank's whereabouts in the house, Abby will first need to endure the night. Endure him. Her heart skips a beat when she hears a sudden noise. Just the house settling from the cold. For a moment, she allows herself to believe he isn't coming tonight. That he's fallen asleep or has been satisfied with her mother, as he sometimes is. Abby knows this because she's heard his grunting and the knocking of the headboard against the bedroom wall, followed shortly by his heavy snoring. Several times he'd come anyway, smelling of beer and cigarettes and, worst of all, her mother's perfume. But mostly, he'd come to her room well past midnight after watching TV downstairs. She'd hear his heavy footfalls on the staircase, counting them as they reached the landing—three to her brother's room, seven to the master, and eleven to the hallway bathroom. Abby's bedroom is always fourteen. She hates that number.

Now she hears his footfalls up the stairs, then a pause. He's on the landing. Abby imagines Hank peering down the hall *toward that dark rectangle that is her bedroom door. His eyes are like an owl's, large and accustomed to the dark. She imagines his tongue moving out to lick his lips, a hunting snake. One of his hands moves down to massage his crotch, something he's done before when it's just him and her in the room together and he knows she can see it. One step down the hall, then two. Three. And four. Abby's heart pounds faster in her chest. She clutches her dolly and teddy to her chest. She burns her eyes into the door as she tries to stop the footsteps with her mind. It'll work if she concentrates, she tells herself, because unlike her body, her mind is strong enough to defend herself against him. His body is three times her size and ten times stronger. But not his mind. She knows this. It is weak and subject to periods of laziness, where hers is sharp and resourceful. She's the one who thought of the key, after all.*

If she can ward him away, then she will prove her theory of mind control. She's seen it in a movie before. But if her mind cannot stop him, her body surely won't. She's only fought him once, in the beginning when he pinned her to the bed and shoved his hand up her nightgown. He'd yanked down her underwear while fumbling with his belt, yelling out when she'd bitten him. She'd done it out of desperation, not aggression. Then his hand had clamped over her mouth, cutting off her breathing, his stinking breath in her face as he promised to make it hurt bad if she dared fight him again. Or tell. That would be worse. They'd never believe her anyway. And in the small chance someone did believe her, he'd run for the hills and live out his days a hermit. Plenty of folks did that.

Eleven footsteps, a pause, then another. Abby's heart sinks. He'll be angry about the lock. He may even be rougher with her because of it. But it's all to plan. He'll know why she'd done it. A purpose of righteousness, an exclamation of disobedience. He'll get what he claims is his right, but if it takes him one second longer than usual, that'll be her victory.

The fourteenth step, then a pause. The knob rattles but does not turn. Harder now, but still it holds fast. "Open the door," he says, his voice slurred. But Abby does not move. She's made him wait one moment longer than he's used to, but now she presses for more. She accepts the damage that will come, that she'll have to avoid her mother's curious eyes for a day, maybe two, but in the end it'll be worth it. When she grows up, she'll never let a man control her like this, and perhaps someday she'll hear footsteps that won't make her skin crawl.

Two quick knocks and a single word, "Now..."

Drawing her covers aside, she gathers her dolly and teddy in her arms, then climbs out of bed. She kisses them both, then places them atop her dresser facing the wall.

Then, she unlocks her door.

CHAPTER 13

Like most homicide detectives, Randall preferred to conduct suspect interviews at headquarters prior to them being booked into jail. Despite the custodial aspect an interrogation room held, it paled in comparison to the finality of the bars and gates of jail. A suspect's home turf was preferable in many instances, but PK had yet to send Homicide his return address. Randall had long decided that if forced to choose between making a suspect uneasy or completely freaked during an interview, the uneasy route was always preferable. Once the heavy gate of a jail cell clanged behind a person, their perception of reality changed. Another bonus of conducting suspect interviews before booking them in jail was simple—they often still wore their own clothes. It was even more reason they chose to talk versus lawyering up.

After verifying that the interrogation room's audio/visual recording devices were operational, Randall researched the suspect—Ernie Potts, a small-time criminal and oft-homeless man whom Randall had arrested a half-dozen times during his time in patrol. As grateful as Randall was to have the alleged accomplice in custody, it didn't make sense for the man to have gotten caught up in such an elaborate abduction. Likewise, it didn't make sense that PK would use someone so undependable. The man had left his fingerprints on the clinic's inner door handle. Video had shown him removing his gloves and wiping his nose, forgetting to replace them before pushing his way out the door. Then again, PK himself held no regard for concealing his own involvement. Either way, Randall was chomping at the bit to interview Ernie, their first solid suspect any of the investigators had had during the case. Randall wanted Tan in the room with him, but told her, "I'd like you to read him Miranda, then explain that we've got some questions for him if he'd like to speak with us. He knows and trusts me, but I've locked him up before. I'll join you, but it's best if you start him off by yourself."

"Got it," Tan said, appearing excited. "I'm learning more than I thought I would."

"Like Whit said, you're swimming now. I know this stuff is coming at you fast. Your job is to keep your head above water. The rest is instinct."

Five minutes later, with Randall, Fells, and Agent Whitlock watching on a monitor, uniformed officers escorted their handcuffed suspect into the interrogation room. He was dressed similarly to PK's accomplice as seen on the clinic video footage. Uncuffing him, they asked him if he'd like something to drink. "Coke," he said, scratching his beard. The officers returned moments later with a can of Coke. Ernie guzzled it in ten seconds flat.

"Looks like the same jacket," Randall noted, bringing up a side-by-side image of the clinic surveillance footage and the live interrogation room feed. They'd asked Ernie to remove his hat, which matched the one seen from the clinic. Randall froze the images then enlarged them. The olive drab army jacket was distinctive enough, with its subdued shoulder patch depicting the screaming eagle of the 101st Airborne Division, and Ranger tab arching above it. Several other pins adorned his filthy-looking jacket, all of which matched those seen on the clinic video. The dirty jeans and boots he wore today appeared to match too.

The group watched as Tan entered the room and took a seat opposite Ernie. She read him his Miranda warning from a card then explained he'd been brought to the PSB to "help clear up some issues." Randall had told her to keep it vague for now, assuming the man didn't lawyer up. To Randall's surprise, he didn't, not only agreeing to speak with Tan but appearing completely relaxed in doing so.

"He looks sober," Fells observed.

"He didn't look under the influence on the clinic video, either," Randall said, shooting Fells and Whitlock a curious look. "If he'd been drunk, I could see him taking cash to help someone remove a body from the clinic, but not even Ernie would have done something like that sober."

As planned, Randall entered the interrogation room after Tan had asked several introductory questions to gain rapport with him. He re-introduced himself to the suspect. After answering a few basic questions surrounding his whereabouts over the past two days, Ernie's demeanor changed from good-natured to confused. "Whatchu pick me up on this time?" he asked, scratching his head. "I ain't been in none of them stores that trespassed me."

"Well, Ernie, this isn't about any of those stores," Randall said, deciding to turn the questioning into a straightforward accusation. "It seems you're on video helping a man abduct a woman from the Uptown Dietary Clinic yesterday. Can you explain why you'd do something like that?" He maintained eye contact with Ernie, making sure to keep his voice level and as empathetic as possible.

After it sunk in, Ernie frowned and cocked his head confusedly. "Abduct. Ain't that another word for kidnap?"

"That's right."

"That can't be right, boss. I ain't never messed with no woman like that. That was someone else, for sure."

Randall paused to allow the tension in the air to settle over Ernie. Tan did the same. Silence was a highly effective interrogation technique, he believed. Best to let a suspect stew in it. But after several excruciating moments, he elected to let a bit of steam off by saying, "We have your fingerprints on the inside door handle, Ernie. From the same place the suspect can be seen touching it on the video. He wore the same jacket you have on now, too. I can show you the video if you'd like."

Ernie's frown deepened. "I tell you, boss, I ain't touched no lady like that. It ain't me on no camera, promise!" He nodded once to emphasize his point, holding up the palm of his right hand. Randall noted the man's open body language and his own direct eye contact. Even more telling was his immediate rejection of the accusation thrown at him. This caused Randall to frown as well, but for different reasons. In his experience, a guilty person rarely made an outright denial seconds after being accused of a crime. Initially, they tended to act confused or offered a host of excuses as to why they couldn't have done it, their mind's way of biding time to concoct a story. And he could never recall someone who'd turned out to be guilty having done what Ernie had just done: immediately raise his right hand. It was a small gesture, one that adhered to the tenet of truth pouncing quick, while a lie slithers slowly through the grass.

Despite having the man's fingerprints and the video—enough for an arrest, and probably a conviction—Randall brought up the clinic surveillance video on his laptop. Like always, his goal was a confession. "Ernie, I want you to look at that jacket. Can you see the patches on the left sleeve?"

Ernie leaned forward on his elbows and squinted at the screen. Soon, recognition set in as he grinned and pointed at it. "Yup, they're just like mine!"

Randall shot a glance toward Detective Tan beside him. Her

raised eyebrows echoed Randall's own curiosity. "Ernie…it's not just the patches that look like yours, it's the whole jacket. Look at the pins. And while we're at it, that man sure looks a lot like you."

Ernie squinted at the screen again. He came away shaking his head. "You ain't wrong, Mr. Randall. But that can't be me in that picture. I woulda remembered."

"I've watched every second of this video, from the time these two individuals abducted that woman until police arrived on the scene the next morning. The front door remained unlocked all night, and no one else entered until the police arrived the next morning." Randall levied a patient look at Ernie. The man was shaking his head confusedly. "Ernie, I've known you a long time. I've run you, but that was small-time stuff. This is big-time, big enough to put you away for a very long time. I don't want to see that happen. But I can't help you if you don't help me explain why you were there helping that man." Randall let the rest of the video play out, including the footage of PK and the entire abduction sequence. He watched Ernie's reaction closely. What he saw disturbed him. Randall had memorized the sequence after having watched it several dozen times, so he knew exactly what happened and when. Ernie's facial expressions, even down to the micro-expressions that Randall had learned people couldn't control, appeared consistent with someone genuinely surprised at what they were seeing.

When the footage of the two men loading then driving Abby away ended, Randall paused the video. For the first time, Ernie seemed aware of the implication at hand. He sat back in his chair and folded his arms across his chest. "That wasn't me, Mr. Randall. Maybe someone stole my jacket."

"Your fingerprints, remember."

"They ain't mine!" Ernie shouted, leaning forward as he spoke the words. His dirty face tightened, and his blue eyes glared out from the filthy folds of skin that weren't covered in gangly beard. "I ain't talkin' no more. I want a lawyer."

Randall leaned back in his chair and expelled a breath of frustration. He gathered his laptop and briefcase and stood, along with Tan. "If you change your mind and want to talk to us, just let them know at the jail."

～

After a pair of patrol officers handcuffed Ernie and took him away, Randall and Tan met up with Detectives Haag and Pederson. The two had just finished their interview of Abby's friend Derek. "Anything?" Randall asked them.

"He said that she had a Zoom counseling session with someone the afternoon before her abduction. Said something about him being disabled and it seeming to help her get through it."

Randall had hoped for more but jotted the info anyway. Likely a reference to the note he'd found in Abby's purse. After walking down the line of victim photographs on the bulletin board, re-reading each information sheet for what seemed the hundredth time, he returned to his cubicle and stared out at the green roof. The first snow flurries of the season swirled in the slate-gray sky, falling toward the columns of half-bare maples lining the street below. Winter was approaching, but seeing those flurries sent a different chill through him. PK was almost finished, and it made sense for him to do so before the elements made it much more difficult for him to move about easily. Letting his mind wander to more abstract aspects of the case and allowing the seemingly thousands of bits of information to coalesce into several more easily consumed ideas, Randall slipped into one of his working daydreams he so often experienced when consumed with multiple aspects of the case. To him, that sort of meditation was necessary for not just him individually, but practically everyone on the task force. They'd each spoken of it during formal meetings and private chats, sometimes over a beer on a rare day off or cup of coffee, as their eyes invariably drifted off to some place that only they could see.

Several minutes later, his ringing department cellphone snapped him out of his meditative trance. His caller ID read *Cromley Mental Health*. "Detective Randall, Homicide," he said, sitting up straight in his chair.

"Yes, this is Harlon Cromley," came the refined male voice. "I had a voicemail from you asking to call this number regarding a possible patient of mine?"

Randall grabbed a pen and notepad. "Yes, sir. We're investigating a young woman's abduction yesterday, Abby Carlson. Is she a patient of yours?"

"Oh dear…I did see a young lady by that name two days ago. Via Zoom session. Age thirty-one, brown hair and eyes?"

"Yes, sir. Do you have a birthdate to compare with our victim?" Randall listened to the sound of clacking computer keys.

"My Abby Carlson is September 16, 1991," the counselor said.

"That's her," Randall replied with regret.

"How terrible!" the counselor said, his voice relaying deep shock. "Kidnapped! By whom?"

"We have an idea, but what we'd like to speak with you about has more to do with your session with her. Nothing too involved, but there could be information that could help us if you're willing to waive your client-provider privilege. We have consent forms for that."

"Of course. I'd be happy to help any way I can, Detective. A young woman's life is in danger. Is it…that man who's been kidnapping all the women and posing them?"

Randall shook his head. He hadn't wanted to discuss that, but he supposed he shouldn't be surprised that the man had asked. If most fifth graders knew about PK, then it made sense for a business professional to know, too. "We aren't at liberty to discuss details of the case, sir, but I won't hide the fact that there's a serial kidnapper at large who could possibly be a suspect in this case. Do you know where the downtown Public Service Building is located?"

"I do, but my disability usually prevents me from venturing into downtown. Is it possible to meet me here at my office, say in forty-five minutes? I rent one for my Zoom sessions."

Randall said that was fine and wrote down the man's office address. It would be a twenty-minute drive for them, enough time to further search the man's background. Typing his name into the DVS database, Randall re-read his driver's license information (surprising that he had one, based on the severe physical deformity he apparently suffered from) and verified that his disability had been confirmed by the state. Then, a more in-depth criminal history and warrant check, both standard procedure prior to contact with any witness or victim. He wasn't surprised when the man came back clean. As a licensed mental health counselor, he'd been required to have his fingerprints taken and forwarded to the national database. No suspensions or revocations. Still, Randall had learned early on to never assume anything.

"Let's take a field trip," he said after swinging over to Tan's desk. She'd been busy researching Abby Carlson's extended background to give to the FBI profiler.

"Museum or cultural center?" she asked sarcastically.

"Maybe next time. We're meeting Abby's counselor at his office. I'll drive this time. Headache is finally 10-6."

CHAPTER 14

They made it to the counselor's office five minutes early. Emerging from the cruiser, Randall decided to don his gray suit jacket, something he personally disliked wearing in the field, but felt added formality to an interview with a business professional. Walking through the mostly empty parking lot, he noted a black, late-model Chevy cargo van parked in the small lot's lone handicap spot. Randall shielded his eyes and pressed up against the van to peer through the driver window. Both front seats had been removed to assumedly accommodate an electric wheelchair behind the wheel. Fitted with special steering wheel controls and an inner-loaded ramp that appeared to extend out the side double-doors when needed, it appeared similar to a vehicle Randall had once seen driven by a disabled relative.

He opened the front door of the nondescript single-story office building, allowing Tan to go first before following her inside. For a Friday, the place was surprisingly empty. Comprised of a single corridor with about a dozen offices on each side, only two of the ten-by-ten doored spaces appeared occupied. The first was near the entrance, where a middle-aged woman could be seen through the open door typing on her laptop. She glanced up when the detectives passed. Her eyes moved toward their exposed badges and pistols, then quickly returned to her work. The other occupied office sat at the far end of the corridor on the left, where a rectangle of light showed from beneath the closed door. The plaque on the door read *Cromley Mental Health Services*. Randall knocked.

"Please, come in," a man's voice called from inside. Opening the door, Randall observed a wheelchair-bound, bespeckled man one-third the size as a normal-sized adult man sitting behind a desk. He bore a close similarity to the DL photo Randall had queried earlier. Most of his lower body was obscured by the desk, but the top half—what there was of if—stood out plainly for them to see. "Hello, Detectives, please have a seat," he said, indicating the two chairs positioned against the wall opposite his desk. His malformed arms and hands resembled those of a small boy. He craned his smallish head upward and twisted his severely bent torso to look at them, as a biologically normal person might do when peering through a door's keyhole. The motion appeared uncomfortable, if not painful, in part due to his grossly enlarged upper back and the massive hump on his right shoulder. Randall immediately understood why the man conducted his counseling appointments via Zoom. Not only would his condition likely be more off-putting in person, but conducting his sessions via Zoom in a rented space like this would no doubt allow him the occasional freedom a home office wouldn't.

The detectives sat in the chairs he'd indicated. Randall, who'd once arrested an armless, one-legged man for driving on a suspended license, neither felt nor showed any shock about the counselor's condition. "Thank you for meeting with us, sir," Randall said. "Hopefully we won't take up too much of your time."

"Not at all. I was just finishing up some notes from an earlier session," he said, pushing his wire-rimmed glasses up on his nose. A thinning wisp of hair swept over his balding pate, and the long shawl covering much of his dress shirt-sweater combo completed his clinical, if not abnormal, appearance. "You mentioned that Ms. Carlson is in danger. How can I help?"

"It's a formality, but we should begin with the waiver we discussed," Randall said, producing the two-page document they'd brought with them. He rose slightly and placed it atop the desk where the man could reach it.

"Yes, of course," the counselor said without more consideration. He removed a pen from the desk drawer and despite the obvious difficulty he had writing, scratched out a surprisingly legible signature. "There," he said, leaning forward to push the paper back toward the detectives' side of the desk. "I don't always discuss my sessions with police. But this certainly qualifies as an exception. You were saying about Ms. Carlson?"

"Thank you," Tan said, collecting the waiver. "We'd like to audio-record the interview, and will be as general as possible." She produced a digital recording device, switched it on, and set it atop the desk. "If there's anything you wish not to discuss, we understand."

Mr. Cromley folded his hands atop the desk. "Go on, Detective. I'll answer whatever you ask."

"Did Abby mention anything about romantic partners, past or present, who may have done her harm before?"

"None. There's an ex-boyfriend she mentioned, but they broke up several months ago. It was amicable, and there'd been no abuse, from what she said."

"How about any suspicious men she'd noticed lately, at work or otherwise?"

"Nothing she mentioned."

"Any threats she'd received in the past six months, written or spoken?"

"No."

Tan referenced her notes. "Male family members she had any negative issues with?"

The counselor went to speak, then stopped. The corner of his mouth twitched. It happened so quickly, Tan missed it. But Randall didn't. One of the many micro-expressions he'd become acutely aware of when interviewing people. They lasted only milliseconds, and were well-known to be the body's uncontrolled, physiological response to certain emotional stimuli. In his judgment, the man was deciding on whether to divulge sensitive information about a young woman already in the most vulnerable position she could possibly be in.

"Her stepfather," the counselor said, having obviously decided to honor his earlier promise. "She stated that he sexually abused her as a child. I won't go into the specifics since it doesn't matter, but I will say that he's currently incarcerated at Stillwater State Penitentiary for other crimes. I verified that he's been there for the past ten years, but of course you can, also. Unfortunately or not, he isn't expected to live much longer."

Randall nodded, glancing over toward Tan who jotted down the note. "No issues at work?" she asked.

"No issues; she seemed very comfortable there. Uptown Dietary Clinic if I remember correctly."

"That's right. And you're sure she didn't mention any strange interactions recently, no matter how minor?"

"Nothing of that sort, I'm sorry."

While Tan jotted those notes, Randall took the opportunity to ask a few follow-up questions of his own, namely if Abby had talked about anything embarrassing or that she was unlikely to reveal to friends or family. "It was fairly straightforward, Detective," replied the counselor. "I took the time to go over my notes from our session—we only had one, by the way—and couldn't formulate any issues of importance." He shook his head. "Such a shame, what the world has come to. Do you really think it could be…him?" He raised his eyebrows at them.

Randall shrugged. "It's still an open investigation, as we discussed."

"Well, if there's anything else I can do to help, don't hesitate to ask."

"We appreciate it," Randall said. They wrapped things up and stood to leave, thanking the man for his time. On their way out, Randall took note of a bookcase in the corner, specifically a sizeable tome on the top shelf.

"*The Hunchback of Notre Dame*," said Mr. Cromley, seemingly pleased that Randall had noticed it. "I was telling Ms. Carlson that I have much in common with the book's hero. Hugo wrote him well. Have you read it?"

"In high school," Randall said, recalling the AP literature course he'd once taken.

"The story holds many lessons," Mr. Cromley continued. "Like Frankenstein's monster, our ugly friend in the tower dealt with a society that valued vanity over character. The first time I read it, I believed him to be a victim of his times, Medieval Europe. On later readings, I realized I was wrong. People similar to him—and me for that matter—will always be looked at differently, no matter the era they live in. I've learned to not take it personally."

"Wise words," Randall said. He didn't remember the character's name, but per his assertion that Google amounted to cheating his mind from its deduction powers, he refused to look it up or ask the man to remind him. "Please call us if you can think of anything else pertinent about the victim."

Mr. Cromley sighed. "'Victim.' It rings with such finality. I do hope you find her in time." He gathered the shawl closer to his body and shivered. "They keep this place so cold. Sometimes I wonder if they even bother to heat it at all."

Randall thanked him and handed him his business card. Once they returned to his cruiser, he smiled to himself. "I just remembered his name."

"Whose name?" Tan asked, sliding into the passenger seat.

"The hunchback in the book. It's Quasimodo." He started the

engine and pulled out into mid-day traffic. "That would have bugged me all day."

On their drive back to the PSB, Randall turned to Tan at one point with a thoughtful expression. Something had been bothering him since they'd left the therapist's office. "His comment about it being so cold in there, that it seemed like the office owners didn't heat the place. What if PK is operating somewhere more common, in a place we've never thought to look?"

"Like what?" Tan asked.

"I feel like it's coming to me. A large enough space he can cool easily, but has access to funerary equipment. His criminal profile says he's embalming the bodies himself, but it stops short of suggesting actual locations."

"But we've already cleared all the funeral homes where he'd be operating, current and not. Plus all structures that can realistically be cooled to the temps he needs. That doesn't leave many options."

"I know. I just can't help feeling that we're missing the obvious." His gaze drifted momentarily toward a row of Uptown businesses still shuttered from the riots. One of them attracted his particular attention, namely the faded storefront sign that read *FROM OUR HOME TO YOURS*. Doing a double-take, he nodded to himself. "I think I know where to look. And it gives me another idea, too. I want Fells in on this."

CHAPTER 15

Once they made it back to the PSB, Randall led Tan into Sergeant Fells' office where he immediately planted his hands atop her desk. "What if he's hiding in plain sight?" he said.

"As in?" Fells asked, looking at his hands then meeting his eye.

Randall removed his hands and smiled apologetically. "He's building a corpse museum. For something like that, he needs to refrigerate enough square footage *and* have access to the necessary equipment. But more importantly, he needs it to be somewhere we'd never look. He's smart. Abducting twenty-five women from their places of business proves that."

"Where's he building it, City Hall?"

"That'd be convenient. No—a residential home, one big enough and properly equipped. It's where I'd do it."

Fells nodded slowly to herself before shifting her inquiring gaze at Tan. "What say you, rookie? And don't tell me what you think I want to hear. Or him, for that matter. I voted for you mostly because of your outstanding arrest stats. But part of it was because we're embarrassingly short of female intuition in this unit. No offense," she added, glancing toward Randall.

Tan considered for a moment. "It's only my second day, but I'm already jibing with Detective Randall. That said, when he first mentioned it, I was skeptical."

"And now?"

"The more I think about it, the more sense it makes."

"I'd be glad to petition the chief for a hundred thousand more detectives to search all the homes in the metro area, but I doubt the budget will allow it. Or the Constitution."

"We don't need to search them all, Sarge," Randall said. "Just the ones capable of handling the embalming process."

"But we've already done that."

"We investigated *modern* funeral homes, both operational ones and those that went out of business. We never checked non-traditional ones that have been shut down or changed business practices. It never occurred to anyone to check those since they're technically residential homes now."

Fells thought about it. "Like the ones where families lived upstairs and did viewings on the main level?"

"And did the dirty work in the basement. Probably what puts the 'home' in 'funeral home.' But none of those old-school places are still in operation around here, or even the country. With the task force scrambling to investigate two dozen abductions, we never thought to look for every old business large enough for an operation like that."

"But you're forgetting his profile," Fells said. "It says he isn't storing them away. And the whole Madame Tussauds concept means he'd have to display them all at once. The ME says he'd need to keep the bodies at around freezing, even if they're embalmed. They'd fall apart, otherwise."

Detective Tan took the opportunity to interject. "I think the house concept works if he simply doesn't heat the floors he displays them on. He may have needed to store them in a cooler or freezer after posing them at first, but winter's coming. Just keep the windows open and obscured, and if the house is big enough, he's got a five-thousand square foot cooler to keep them together until spring."

Fells thought about it briefly, then gave a nod of assent. "Do what you feel is best, but get Whit up to speed."

Randall checked his watch. It was just after one p.m. "I still have the physical file of all current and former funeral homes over the past hundred years in my garage. The task force only investigated the ones with business designations since we never thought to check houses. I think there's a couple dozen of those old homes not in operation anymore, if memory serves me correct."

"How much time are we thinking?"

"A few days, but I got another idea on the ride here that might make it quicker. Let me do some research on it first."

"I can have another team cover some of them," Fells offered. "Not sure we can lift any more off what they're already doing."

"Don't bother, I'd rather us check them personally," Randall said. "And it'll keep everyone else on task. Besides, I have trust issues."

Fells agreed and sent them on their way, with Randall asking Tan to coordinate with several surveillance teams while he darted home to grab the physical files. When he opened his front door, his Golden Retriever Daisy met him with a round of licks.

"Hey, beautiful," he said, bending to return her kisses. Since being assigned to the task force, Randall had understood that his responsibilities as a single dog father couldn't be properly kept. Not to his standards, or what Daisy deserved, anyway. For the first six months, he'd broken down and asked his kindly, widowed neighbor, Lena, if she'd come by twice a day to feed and let Daisy out to run around the backyard. She'd done so, adding in walks, too, but refused to take the money he'd insisted she take. But his three-week mandatory hiatus had allowed him to spend every day of that time with her. That alone had helped tremendously in his recovery. Now, that would change again, at least until this PK business was over. He popped by next door and asked Lena if she'd resume watching Daisy for the foreseeable future. It killed him with all the back-and-forth he was placing on both Daisy and Lena, but he didn't feel right leaving his furry best friend alone for such long periods.

"Of course I will, I love watching her," Lena said, the spryest eighty-year-old Randall had ever known. "I'll just plan on keeping her here at the house if it's all the same to you. I know how it is, not having family around. Just pop on over whenever you want to visit. She misses you, but there seem to be other young ladies who need you more." She gave him a brief yet knowing smile. After giving Daisy a kiss and pat on the head, Randall reminded himself to pay Lena for her services as soon as this business was over, no matter what she said. Then he ran next door and immediately dug through a box of files he'd labeled "PK 1-22." He'd been on leave for two of the abductions, but he had computerized notes from the detective team who'd worked them. Re-familiarizing himself with his own handwritten notes in the typed margins, he moved on to entries centering on defunct, family-style funeral homes that had since been deemed "residential." It was Dr. Hoffman's belief (and Randall's too) that PK didn't personally know any of his victims. And in Randall's experience with Homicide, he'd learned that kidnappers of adults unknown to them shared a common denominator—an overriding fear of discovery during transport of their victims. Every block traveled or intersection crossed increased the risk that someone would plow into them, or a cop would notice a license plate hanging askew and pull them over. Disaster lurked at every turn.

The biggest clue that PK lived within the agreed-upon twenty-five-mile radius of downtown lay in the location of his Instagram posts. All two dozen of them had been traced to heavily populated public places in the metro area. Not a definitive clue itself, until the kidnapper had slipped. In one of his posts' photos, he'd inadvertently captured the very edge of a cellphone screen in the background. Specifically, the blurred image of the current temperature—seventy degrees. An easy thing to overlook when busy abducting women and mounting them like wild game trophies, Randall reasoned. FBI technicians had focused the blurry background through painstaking forensic analysis. Had it not been for an unusual weather front in the area —the westernmost and easternmost edges being ninety degrees, with a thirty-mile strip of land through the state that included the bulk of the Minneapolis metro area being twenty degrees colder — Randall may not have ever made the connection. But he had, with help from from a local weather expert he'd interviewed. If the task force believed the photo had been a mistake on PK's part and not an intentional ruse, then he was most certainly storing his victims in the greater Twin Cities metro area. By Randall's official count, that put the number of defunct, family-style funeral homes-turned residential properties in their target area at thirty-five. More than he'd remembered. Choosing to take Fells' approval to proceed as wholesale, he forged ahead, eliminating twenty-one of them due to them being under two thousand square feet, per Zillow records—much too small for such an operation that PK was conducting. That left fourteen. If no leads were gained with the homes on his 'good' list, he reserved the right to check the others later. Cross-referencing his initial find- ings with owner information from the Public Appraiser's Office, he felt confident that if anything were to be found up this tree, he'd find it. He also did more research on his other idea that may help them, a grand type of advertisement they'd tried before, but without a certain specific element he hadn't thought of until their drive back from the business office.

After he communicated his results to Tan, he met her back at the office to review his notes. Venturing out together, they struck out with the first five homes. Waiting until tomorrow to check the remaining homes was a gamble, since there was no guarantee PK would stick to his previous average of a week between abduction and Instagram post. But part of good police work was knowing when to take things as they came, he knew. Not like playing conservative during the first two dozen abductions had worked for them. Besides, November dusk came early this far north. As the sun touched the western horizon, Randall swore he felt an electric current pulsing through the air. Through the entire city, even. He knew that a host of events had been planned over the weekend, despite another victim being taken twenty-four hours ago. Life had to be lived, and in a pulsing metropolis full of vibrant people of all ages and backgrounds, enjoying oneself wasn't just a luxury, it was often necessary to fight a thousand other issues besides a killer hiding in their midst. But for most of the PK task force members—many of whom had toiled for weeks without a day off—enjoyment would come in the form of dinner eaten from to-go bags at their desks, a hot cup of coffee inside a freezing cold surveillance vehicle, or even a stolen moment to speak to loved ones on the phone. If the killer refused to rest, so would they.

CHAPTER 16

Orchestra Hall, a Modernist 1970s venue built along the locally famous Nicollet Mall area of downtown Minneapolis, buzzed with excitement. It was Friday evening, just before eight p.m., and still day two of Abby Carlson's abduction at the hands of the notorious 'Profession Killer.' Despite the unseasonably chilly early-November temperatures outside, a gratifying warmth filled the hall's enclosed mezzanine. Men in smart formal wear, and women in an array of glittering evening gowns and trendy faux fur coats, stood in groups chatting and drinking pre-performance cocktails. They'd all come for the same reason—a special rendition of Beethoven's Symphony Number Three. Since the hall's summer and fall schedules had ended (among them, the wildly popular "Music and Movies" series that treated guests to real-time orchestral soundtracks of famous movies), more traditional works had been offered. Tonight was no different. Comprised of woodwinds, brass, and strings, the chamber orchestra planned to deliver a rousing rendition of one of the German composer's most famous works, an ode to Napoleon before he'd crowned himself Emperor of France.

Frederik stood tall and refined in a black-tie tuxedo as he

sipped a glass of champagne at the edge of the crowded mezzanine. His eyes, relaxed and happy, surveyed the eclectic mix of folks from behind the thick-framed eyeglasses he'd chosen as part of his disguise. He didn't need them; his vision was perfect. But he knew how glasses changed a person's recollection of a stranger's description and thwarted facial recognition cameras. For good measure, his scholarly salt-and-pepper wig lent him added refinement, as well as ten years to his features.

Known mainly for its Scandinavian roots, Minneapolis also held a large influx of Asian and African immigrants. All were represented in the crowd. Despite the occasional Somali *shaash* and East Indian *pagri*, as well as groups speaking languages he didn't understand, Frederik was pleased to see everyone had followed custom by adhering to the event's formalwear doctrine. It had been months since he'd done anything truly social, having spent much of that time preparing for what he hoped would be his favorite winter ever. The past several women he'd abducted had proved especially difficult—indeed, he'd nearly encountered disaster on more than one occasion. He'd considered the folly of rushing things, that to do so would invite unnecessary risk. But with just one letter remaining to complete his list, and winter expected to be especially cold this year, he understood the possible reward for finishing his masterwork earlier than later. He had every intention of finishing before November's end; all the better if it happened before Thanksgiving, so that he could enjoy the holidays with them all. But work was work, and play was play. With "D" safely locked away in the house, he'd decided to take the night off and treat himself to an old pleasure —live classical music created by actual humans, with real instruments. Adding to the symphonic experience was the irony that such complex compositions created over two centuries ago were rarely duplicated in today's vastly more technological world.

When the doors opened to signal that seating would now begin, guests hurried for a final cocktail before filing into their seats. Frederik drained the last of his champagne then took the elevator to the third-level, side-oriented balcony, his favorite location. Orchestra Hall had been designed with acoustics in mind. One hundred and fourteen large sound-reflecting cubes had been built into the ceiling and wall behind the stage to amplify each note. The striking visual effect kept with the city's diverse, artistic flair. Taking his seat at the end of the last row and closest to the stage, Frederik was pleased to see that the other three seats to his left were empty. Good, no need to have the usher kick people out who'd moved seats. Per usual, he'd bought up the entire row to ensure he sat alone in the one balcony area that lay in near-total darkness. Once, and despite his plan, a couple had been moved into his row after one of their seats in another section had experienced a technical issue. He'd smiled politely as the couple had taken the row's two far seats, but even with a seat between them and himself, he'd been prevented from undoing his bow tie and several top buttons of his shirt. He enjoyed wearing formal attire, but it quickly over-heated him. All the more reason the added expense was worthwhile.

When the audience was settled, the conductor, done up in white tie and tails, stepped onto his raised podium and intro-duced the program. The thirty-plus musicians took their seats and thumbed their music sheets. Moving his eyes among them, Frederik paused when he spotted a fiery redheaded female violinist in the front row, closest to the conductor. Like the other female musicians, she wore a long black formal dress. But with the humdrum black dresses and tuxedos, and the sea of black-, blond-, and gray-haired heads, she stood out like a beacon in the night. Enthralled, Frederik leaned forward in his seat, his eyes widening. About thirty, the woman held a dignified air about her as she sat expressionless in her chair, her feet planted modestly together, her instrument and bow resting in her lap. High cheek-bones and strong jawline, with smooth alabaster skin and a figure that suggested both good genetics and regular exercise, she was everything he coveted in a woman. Intriguing him almost as much as her hair was the top of what looked to be a large back tattoo peeking above her dress's neckline.

The conductor tapped his baton. A rush of excitement surged through Frederik as the redhead was first to ready her instrument by raising it to her shoulder and resting her bow on the strings. In unison, the other musicians followed suit with their respective instruments. Her short-nailed fingertips arching onto the finger-board, she moved her bow in a measured upward thrust—an E flat chord. Frederik, who had taught himself to play several instruments in the past, recognized it from memory. In unison, the other musicians followed suit, a few of them adjusting their tuning when they'd finished. After several more adjustments from the other musicians and the overture was over, the redhead nodded to the conductor, who in turn raised his baton to signal the start of the performance.

In a frenzied burst, the beginning notes of the sonata rose and reflected from the dozens of sound-improving cubes. Frederik felt a familiar excitement beating against his chest. His tongue flicked out to wet his lips, and his fingers gripped the side railing. On reflex, he untied his bowtie knot, then unbuttoned his top three shirt studs. A familiar longing came over him as he focused again on the redhead. She appeared perfect in every way, from her silky, shoulder-length hair to her exquisite figure. Frederik dropped his gaze to her feet, modestly covered in the same type of closed-toed heels as the other female performers wore. He imagined what color her toenails were painted. French tips, possibly, or red to match her hair. Yes, that would be it, he decided. The thought alone caused his cock to stir with excitement.

He flipped through his program until he got to the musicians' biographies and photos. Finding the only redhead, he read her name—Nicolette Dunn, the First Chair violinist. Even her name was perfect. An asterisk beside her name noted that she was a native of the Twin Cities area, and not only was she a first-time performer here, but that it would be her only concert at the venue before embarking soon on a year-long residency in Austria. If that news wasn't disappointing enough, Frederik's excitement was further dashed with the recollection that he'd already taken an "M," a young female mascot from a local college football game last month. A shame he couldn't take the enthralling musician. But as quickly as he'd become disappointed to miss out on her, a sudden realization struck him so forcefully he sat up straight and gripped the arms of his seat. The redheaded beauty who so deftly moved her bow across the strings was more than just a musician. She was a violinist. "V." His last remaining letter.

Taking her here inside the building would be difficult, he knew. Perhaps the most difficult one of them all. Being so unprepared presented many dangers, chief amongst them being the fact that he wouldn't be the only one to notice her like a beacon in the night. Him coveting her did not make her invisible to others, he knew. And him taking his "D" just yesterday had no doubt thrown the police into full alert mode. They would be in their usual pattern of initial response, something that tended to relax a bit after the first several days when they failed to make an immediate arrest. If he wasn't careful with the redhead, if he didn't use every fiber of skill and exercise every ounce of precaution he possessed, he'd be captured before he took one step outside the concert hall. Then what would all of this have been for?

As the music continued, Frederik's mind worked. He considered using a ruse of some kind to lure her outside. But he quickly discounted that, due to the unlikely chance a woman of normal intelligence would follow a man unfamiliar to her that far from where they'd first met. He *had* done it that way with several of the other women he'd taken, but those situations had been unique. And in those occurrences, a week or more had passed since he'd last struck. With so many gang shootings and other crimes in the daily news, people had tended to forget about his newest abduction after several days in the news cycle. A shame, really. The mere fact that the police had teamed with Instagram's developers, as well as both state and federal agencies, to remove his posts seconds after they appeared, had been unfortunate if not expected. Fortunately, Twitter feeds, Facebook discussion groups, and even the more antiquated *Star/Tribune* had picked up where his deleted posts had left off.

He considered the possibility that he would have to kill her here. There must be two thousand people packing the auditorium, and that wasn't counting the musicians and venue workers. The violinist's fellow musicians would present the greatest risk, of course. Getting the chance to speak with her wouldn't be difficult; he'd done so with other musicians in orchestras before. But separating her from the others *would* be. Even if he was lucky enough to get two minutes of alone time with her, perhaps posing as a reporter and requesting an impromptu interview in the lobby or quiet area of the mezzanine, he could expect others to see their interaction and remember it. He hadn't brought enough supplies because he hadn't expected to take another victim tonight. His face (although disguised) had already been seen by dozens of people, and the many cameras that undoubtedly blanketed the place would surely be recording his every move. He estimated his chance of subduing her without being noticed at less than ten percent. He'd become very good at his job, but getting her body—either alive or dead—to his car without anyone noticing would further reduce his chances to about one in a hundred, he figured.

Still, he had to try. She was too perfect. The poetry of it all was something that had been largely absent from any of the others. Here he'd come to enjoy a classical performance, and like a gift from Beethoven beyond the grave, he'd been presented with a priceless opportunity. To waste it would be a travesty of art itself. Above all else, Frederik had to find a plausible way to get her out.

Intermission came. He'd use the restroom, then figure out a way once he cleared his mind. Before the house lights came on, he re-buttoned his shirt and re-tied his bowtie. As he rose to his feet and began to move down the empty aisle, he paused when something near the back of the stage caught his eye. Some*one*, more specifically—the double bass player. The distinguished-looking man of about fifty bore a striking resemblance to himself (albeit with a full head of gray hair, an age-marker Frederik had eluded so far). The man appeared a few inches shorter than Frederik, and about thirty pounds heavier. Good enough. But it was the bass's hardshell case the man now bent to open that attracted his real attention. Unlike most of the other musicians who propped their instruments onto stands to prepare for their break, the bass player had chosen to set his instrument—at least six feet in length, from end pin to scroll—into the case. Likely to prevent it from falling or being knocked over, Frederik assumed. Whatever the reason for the man putting it away, it gave him an idea. If he could somehow assume the bass player's identity and gain access to his case...

Making his way onto the crowded mezzanine, Frederik passed a crowd of mingling people sipping cocktails and commenting on the performance. He needed advice about his plan, from someone he trusted explicitly. Although he knew that the hall's security cameras didn't record audio, he knew full well how people's ears listened to, and their minds remembered unusual conversations. After using the restroom, he exited and found an unoccupied area near it to talk, preferring not to step outside into the freezing temperatures. Removing a cellphone from his coat pocket, he pressed an icon beside a familiar contact's info then held the phone to his ear. "I have an idea," he blurted excitedly several moments later.

A pause, then Victor's reply: "An...idea?"

"Yes. A violinist. I want her."

"You can't be serious. Tonight?"

"Yes, tonight. I think I found a way."

Victor sighed. "Tell me."

He did. "What do you think?" he asked after finishing. When a group of concertgoers passed by, he smiled and offered them a friendly wave.

"You can't chance it," Victor said.

Frederik shook his head in frustration. "If it works, it'll be done, and much quicker than I'd planned. I could have all of them ready by Thanksgiving."

"You could also be in jail or dead by then. The police murdered a man not far from here for doing basically nothing. What do you think they'd do to you if they discovered what you've done?"

Frederik huffed. "That's different. Besides, I'm not worried about going to jail." A glimmer came to his eye, and a grin touched his lips. "I'm asking what you think of the plan itself."

Victor hesitated. "I can't deny your past successes. And you'll have to finish it, either now or later."

"So you're telling me to do it."

"I'm saying no such thing. Just that it's doable."

"Anything is doable. I just need an answer, yes or no."

"You'll be able to subdue her quietly?"

"I've got that covered. I keep a bottle of the chemical in the car for contingencies."

"Remember the mascot..." Victor said. How could Frederik forget; he'd just thought of her. Just a month ago, he'd attended a college football game and had taken a stroll behind the bleachers during halftime. To his surprise, he'd found a young woman sitting on one of the bleacher supports, nursing what she described as a sprained ankle. An oversized, fur-covered moose mascot costume in separate head and body portions had lain on the ground beside her. Frederik had offered his assistance, pretending to be a physician whose nephew played for the opposing team. After listening to the doe-eyed brunette lament how a backup would have to take her place if she reported her injury, Frederik had told her to remain there, ostensibly for him to retrieve an ice pack and ACE bandage from his car.

Luckily, the sympathetic gate guard had allowed him back in on account of his medical supplies. Frederik had kept the bill of his ballcap low, and his mirrored sunglasses firmly on his face. After icing then wrapping the thankful woman's ankle, he'd stood behind her while she gathered her costume. He'd dabbed a cloth with chloroform without her noticing. It had taken the spirited young woman twice as long as usual to be subdued, and he'd been forced to drag her writhing body behind some tall bushes when someone had approached. Thankfully, the screams of fifty thousand fans had blocked out all sounds of the struggle. After she'd finally gone limp, he'd climbed into the comically oversized body portion of her costume before squeezing her inside with him. It had been incredibly tight, but they'd both fit. One advantage of the cramped space was him keeping her upright more easily. While loading her into his car, he'd been forced to use more of the chemical on her after she'd woken up and began resisting again. He'd nearly been discovered because of it. After getting her home, he'd sworn to use ketamine injections or some other method of sedation in the future. The chloroform was just too unpredictable. While the mascot had kicked and scratched at him for several minutes, the lifeguard and several others (the dietitian included) had succumbed in mere seconds.

"I do remember," Frederik said. "But I don't have the ketamine or any hypos with me."

"You'll have to run home. I'd help, but we can't risk them seeing us both."

Frederik checked his watch. He'd be late for the second part of the performance, but he judged he'd have just enough time if he left now. "I knew there was a reason I decided to speak with you first."

A pleased murmur in response.

"So, it's decided then?" Frederik said, his pulse pounding.

"I suppose."

Again, that dimpled smile.

CHAPTER 17

He hurried home and filled a hypodermic with an amount of the sedative ketamine he felt would render a woman the violinist's size unconscious, adding a few more milligrams just to be safe. He'd obtained the powerful tranquilizer through one of his pharmaceutical contacts as a high-priced "recreational drug." It had proved its usefulness on his first try when he'd taken the artist inside her studio, knocking her out with little fight. Now, after returning to the hall's parking garage, and thankful that no one had taken his previous spot since he judged no garage cameras focused on it, he went to close the car door when he remembered something. Reaching into the glove box, he removed the expandable baton he kept there for both personal security and as an emergency means of incapacitation. Only eight inches long when retracted, the easily concealed weapon expanded to a full twenty-one inches with a forceful downward arc of the hand. Better than a gun or knife at times, as it could produce little if any blood in the right circumstance.

He re-did his shirt buttons and tie, then rushed back inside just as the house lights dimmed to signal the start of the second half of the performance. So, he hadn't missed any part at all. Re-taking his seat, he undid his tie and top three buttons once more.

All this activity had begun to overheat him again. He forced himself to relax and cool down, taking in slow, measured breaths. If he were to succeed (and even more important, avoid capture), he'd need to summon every bit of calm he possessed. He went over his plan frontwards and backward. He'd have to leave before the end, a shame since it truly was a thrilling rendition. As his mind worked over the details, accounting for every possible hazard and delay he could imagine, his eyes moved over the violinist's form. How elegant she moved the bow across the strings. The angle of her arm, her head bent toward the instrument's body, trapping it between her chin and bare collarbone. Two quick upstrokes to mark dramatic G and F majors, followed by a long downstroke to evoke a saddened E flat minor. It was almost a shame she'd never play again, Frederik thought. But knowing how he'd have her forever dispelled any regret. Besides, he already planned for how her music would live on. The surround sound system he'd recently installed in the house would ensure symphonies of all kinds would be enjoyed, including a recording of this very performance he could attain. Just the thought of the other girls listening to it excited him, although he suspected several of them may become jealous over the house's talented newcomer.

He checked his watch—nine-thirty. The main performance would end in about twenty minutes. As long as he left his seat during the expected encore, he figured he'd have enough time to slip away under relative darkness and into a mostly empty mezzanine. From his past visits to Orchestra Hall he'd learned that the service entrances led almost directly to the parking garage. There was a connected, second-level skyway leading to it, too. If he could dispose of the bass player and hope the violinist didn't know him well, he figured he'd have an outside chance of getting her away from the others. The program mentioned that she'd been tonight's guest First Chair, and as such had never performed with this particular orchestra. Still, they would have had rehearsals. He'd have no room for error. If someone heard her cry out and found him struggling with her, he'd be finished. All his past work would be for nothing. Despite the possession of an ace up his sleeve—one he was certain would allow him to evade prison if he were caught—discovery of any kind would mean an instant end to his dream of completing his collection. His girls would be taken away, an abomination. He shuddered at the thought, refusing to consider the possibility. Best to concentrate on the positives. The same police detectives who had so far failed to solve even one of his abductions were not here. Only Victor knew of his plan, and he was so trusted that God Himself would be able to verify the fact, if necessary.

As the end of the main performance neared, Frederik made his move. Slipping into the empty hallway, he kept his face averted from the cameras as he made his way toward a service door he remembered seeing past performers go through. He tried it but found it locked. Moving on, he discovered another service door and found this one unlocked. It led to a staircase, which he descended one level before coming to an empty kitchen area. Thankfully, he didn't pass anyone as he went through it then out another door until he found himself at a second staircase. He flew down another level, hopeful it led to the restricted back-stage area. It did. Hearing approaching voices, he eased the door closed behind him then ducked behind some floor-to-ceiling curtains. A woman and a man, talking about the performance and how best to break down the set. When they passed, Frederik made his way toward the faint music. He could tell he was behind the theater's back wall now. While the embedded cubes reflected sound outward, they provided insulated soundproofing back here. Turning his ear, he listened for the bittersweet notes of her violin. Nothing for one measure, then two, until finally they came lifting in the air. He smiled. There were several other violins, he knew, but as First Chair, the redhead led. Besides, her

talent far surpassed that of her cohorts. He swore he could tell
them apart, note by note.

Without warning, a stagehand appeared seemingly out of
nowhere, not giving Frederik time to hide or obscure his face.
But the young man hurried past him and barely paid him any
attention. As he was dressed similarly to the formal-attired musicians, Frederik figured he'd been mistaken for one of them,
perhaps having ended his part in the performance or experiencing some instrument issue he had to fix. Decorum said that all
musicians remained in their chairs until the end of a performance. But even Frederik knew that no two shows were the
same. And with myriad factors that went into putting on such a
grand production, calamities were expected.

With the end of the main performance's final crashing notes,
the audience erupted in applause. From his hidden spot behind
the wall, Frederik imagined them rising to their feet, smiling as
they brought their hands together and shouted to one another at
how excellent the show had been. The applause lasted a full
thirty seconds, after which the conductor could be heard tapping
his baton on his music stand. The encore came, a reprise of the
performance's theme, followed by another round of thunderous
applause once it ended. Frederik waited as the murmuring crowd
became a smattering of words, until after ten minutes he could
tell most of them had filed out of the auditorium. As musicians
began to appear from the stage door, he kept his head low, trying
his best to appear as though he belonged there. He hoped that as
First Chair, the redhead would be one of the last musicians to
exit the stage. So far, he hadn't seen her. He also hoped that the
double bass player would enter backstage alone and not be
engaged in conversation with anyone. If the man chose to talk to
another member for any length of time, Frederik doubted he'd
have a realistic chance at him.

Seconds later, he got his answer. The man walked through
the door on the heels of a cello player. Each pulled their instru-

ments in their respective hardshell cases, rolling them like over-sized, wheeled suitcases. "Excuse me," Frederik said, stepping forward to stop the bassist.

The man paused a second to look at him. "Yes?"

"One of the flutists has had an attack. Asthma, I think. Can you help me with her?"

The man looked Frederik up and down, then cast a concerned look toward the sea of musicians congregating in an open area backstage. "Is it Lydia? She didn't look well earlier."

Grasping onto this detail, Frederik nodded. "Yes. She's in there." He pointed to a nearby closed door marked *Electrical Room—Caution*. From where they both stood, the door was plainly visible, but he estimated that by walking just a few feet toward the musician's lounge area, it would likely be cut from people's view due to the floor-to-ceiling curtain.

"Why is she in there?" the bassist asked, frowning.

"She needed somewhere dark and quiet to recover—it's too noisy out here. Can you help me carry her out to the auditorium? I think she'll be fine once we get her there." The man looked back toward the milling musicians, who now numbered a dozen. One by one, more of them appeared from the stage door. Fearful that at any minute the flutist he'd referred to would materialize through the door unscathed, Frederik reached out to grasp the man's arm. "Hurry, please. She doesn't look good."

The man looked at him skeptically, as if about to question who he was, but the concern on his face as he glanced at the electrical room door appeared to override it. Nodding, he set his instrument case down and followed Frederik to the door in question. When Frederik reached to open it and found it locked, panic seized him. Putting on a nervous smile, he said, "It must lock automatically," and drove his shoulder into it as hard as he dared. Thankfully, the deadbolt wasn't secured, and the latch splintered past the wooden jamb as the door opened to a large, darkened space.

"Are you sure she's in here?" the man asked, dubious. He took a step backward as he once again searched the milling musicians at the other end of the room. Feeling that he only had seconds to act, Frederik stepped behind the man and shoved him into the room. Stumbling forward, he crashed to the floor face-first.

"What the hell..." he began, gaining his feet much more quickly than Frederik had expected and turning to face him. But he never finished his sentence. In one fluid motion, Frederik removed the retractable baton from his coat pocket, expanded it with a sideways chopping motion, then aimed a strike at the side of the man's neck.

He'd only meant to incapacitate him, targeting the cluster of nerves between the collarbone and base of the ear. But seeing the strike coming, the man turned away at the last second. Instead of the targeted muscle area, the segmented steel club struck the back of the man's skull. A sickening cracking sound was accompanied by a warm spatter of blood striking Frederik on the face. The man grunted once then collapsed to the floor, his legs exposed through the doorway. Ensuring none of the other musicians had appeared from around the curtain, Frederik grabbed the man by his hands and dragged his unconscious body all the way inside. He closed the door behind him and flipped on the light before removing both his coat and the man's. Although Frederik's was also formal black, it lacked tails. He shrugged into the man's coat, feeling it to be a bit short in the arms but plenty big enough in the shoulders and chest. Seeing that their bowties were different styles but at least the same color, he judged them to be close enough to do the trick. He didn't have time to re-tie it anyway.

He knelt to check the man's pulse—a heartbeat, albeit faint. Dark-red blood oozed from a huge gash at the back of his head. He may live, assuming someone found him before he lost too much blood. Thinking of this, Frederik touched a hand to his own face. His fingertips came away bloody. Using his discarded coat, he wiped his face and hands clean. Double-checking, he removed his cellphone and used the selfie feature on his camera to view his face. He'd missed two spots of blood on his cheek. Grateful he'd thought of this, he wiped them clean, imagining the redhead's reaction if he hadn't. *Oh, this? I just smashed the bassist's skull in with a baton. But you were saying...?*

Frederik drove the striking end of the baton straight down into the concrete floor to collapse it. Pocketing it, he switched off the light. The room was instantly cast in a wash of green and red blinking lights from an exposed electrical panel. He cracked the door and made sure no one was watching before he stepped from the room and shut the door behind him. With a familiar excited pounding against his chest, he walked as naturally as possible around the curtain and scanned the group of musicians. No blazing head of red hair in the mingling sea of black- , blond-haired, and bald-headed folks. Checking again that no one was watching him, he picked up the bassist's case and wheeled it back into the electrical room where he laid it on the floor. Shutting the door behind him, Frederik noted that the bleeding man's breaths had grown labored and shallow. His body had begun twitching involuntarily. A brain hemorrhage, Frederik figured. Major skull fractures to the back of the head—an area he knew controlled basic life functions—often turned fatal if left untreated. If the man should die, then so be it. Fitting that he'd become something similar to what he'd just used himself—an instrument.

Flipping open the case's latches, Frederik lifted the heavy bass from its felt lining. As he propped it against the wall, he heard approaching voices. He froze. If someone saw the broken door latch and investigated, he'd never be able to explain his presence here with the bleeding man. Even if he abandoned his plan and ran, he wouldn't make it ten steps before the alarm was raised and someone called the police. Perhaps he *had* over-reached. In his blind lust for the prize he considered greater than any other he'd taken so far, he'd missed the obvious signs of danger he'd once listened to. For the first time during his collection process, he felt a pang of regret. Standing there in the semi-darkened room, those blinking electrical lights seeming to taunt his arrogance, Frederik wished to be magically transported back to the safety of his home. He'd tell the girls he loved them as he caressed the contours of their faces. How foolish he'd been to risk them all for this one wild chance. The mere possibility of never seeing them again, not even having the chance to say goodbye, horrified him. Only now did he understand the folly of acting with such reckless impulse. He felt himself a fool, like a man playing Russian Roulette with all the chambers full and pinning his hopes on a misfire.

But just as the voices neared, they passed. All became quiet again. Daring to slip back through the door, he peered around the curtain just in time to see the redheaded violinist pass through the backstage door from the auditorium. She came around to stand nearest him at the rear of the group of mingling musicians, her case's handle gripped in one hand as she listened to the conductor speak. An inner clock in Frederik's mind told him he must act now, or never. Stepping fully around the curtain, he made his move.

"You were magnificent," he said from beside her as the group applauded something the conductor said.

She turned toward him, a warm smile on her lips despite a momentary confused look in her eyes. Frederik was taken aback by her beauty from up close. Intelligent green eyes, perfectly proportioned nose, high cheekbones denoting strong Nordic roots. He'd chosen all his women carefully—even the dietitian, after his chance encounter with her. Beauty *and* brains were his standards. But the violinist had exceeded those lofty ideals by a mile. From her silken red hair to her spray of freckles across her nose and cheeks, down to the hint of cleavage peeking out above the top of her dress, she was the model of perfection in his eyes. Even her assured yet demure stance thrilled him. The fact that he'd happened upon her in such an unexpected manner only intensified the excitement that coursed through him now.

"Thank you," she said after looking him up and down. "You're bass, right?"

Frederik made a snap decision that the truth, or a portion of it, would serve him best here. "I wish. I played a bit of sax and guitar in high school, but I gave it up. It was my cousin who performed. I watched the performance and asked him who you were. He got me backstage so that I could speak with you about the violin."

She nodded, seemingly impressed. "Let me guess—you wanted to up the ante by wearing his coat and tails too?"

Frederik gave a self-effacing shrug. "Desperation isn't my greatest trait."

She laughed. "So, true honesty from a man. I didn't know it was possible."

"Barely. I think they're doing a Netflix special about it. It comes out after the one about it snowing in hell."

She laughed again, then extended her right hand. "Nicolette Dunn. And seriously, it's nice to get a bit of truth from a man, even if it's from a fellow musician's cousin stalking me backstage." She eyed him with playful suspicion. "But my Spidey sense tells me you're not a stalker."

He shook her hand, conjuring a name out of thin air. "Alex Hill. And I always preferred Batman. To me, 'Caped Crusader' has a better ring to it than 'Webbed Wonder.'"

She nodded. "I like a man who can analyze fictional characters swinging between buildings in skintight outfits."

"You should hear me analyze violinists," he said with a wink.

She sized him up. "So, what's your story, Alex Hill?"

When he extended his arm toward the unoccupied curtained area near the electrical room and suggested they speak where they wouldn't have to compete with the raised voices around them, she checked to see that the conductor had ended his speech. He had and was talking with a smaller group of musicians now. "I'm meeting some of the others at the bar soon, but I suppose I have a minute," she said.

Frederik led her to behind the curtained area, suspecting she'd never agree to speak with a stranger in a secluded backstage area had said stranger not been as handsome as himself, and wearing formal dress. It never ceased to amaze him, the power of human assumption. The stories of Little Red Riding Hood and the Wolf in Sheep's Clothing came to him. "I'm curious how you were introduced to the violin," he said, choosing to get her discussing herself right away.

She sighed. "My mother played professionally. During my senior year in high school, she was diagnosed with Parkinson's. She'd always wanted to teach me, but I was too busy hanging out with friends and working to pay my car insurance. By the time I decided to take home lessons, her disease had progressed to the point where she couldn't play or even instruct anymore. It made me feel like total shit. One day, I picked up her violin and started teaching myself."

"That's a powerful story. Proof there's no motivation like self-motivation," Frederik said, his eyes glowing with excitement. He was already imagining how and where to position her in the house when a man poked his head around the curtain, startling them both.

"I thought I saw you sneaking away over here," the man said to Nicolette. "We're heading to the bar. Coming?" Frederik recognized him as an oboe player from the orchestra. Not wishing for the man to get a close look at him, he lowered his head and placed a hand to his temple, feigning a headache.

Nicolette held a finger up to the man. "I'll meet you there." Then, before the man ducked away, "Oh, hey, can you grab me a glass of chardonnay? Those bar lines remind me of Disney World."

"You got it," the man said. He offered a thumbs-up then disappeared around the curtain as quickly as he'd appeared.

Smiling, Nicolette began to turn back toward Frederik and said, "If you'd like to grab a drink with us, we could talk long—"

Before she could finish, Frederik reached up and grabbed a handful of her hair and forcefully tilted her head back. With the creamy white skin of her neck now exposed to the backstage lights, he stepped forward so that their faces were just inches apart. He pulled the hypo from his pocket, removed the cap with his teeth, and jabbed the needle into her jugular vein a split second before depressing the plunger with his thumb. At first, Nicolette's eyes widened with surprise, perhaps thinking maybe he'd leaned in to kiss her neck unexpectedly, his teeth scraping her skin. Or he'd seen an insect biting her and had thrown her head back to look for the culprit. But with the immediate shock of the moment wearing off, her eyes widened even more with the apparent knowledge that both of those scenarios were ridiculous. Trying in vain to twist from his steely grasp, she reached up to grab the needle with the one hand that wasn't blocked by his pressing body. But he detected the movement and released his grip on her hair in time to catch her slender wrist.

She began to cry out, but his free hand clamped hard over her mouth at the same time he slid the needle free from her neck. "Shhh, don't fight it," he whispered into her ear. Even as she began writhing against him, struggling to free herself from his strong grip, he could feel her body growing limper by the second. But then, just as he felt her body begin to go fully limp, he felt her suddenly stiffen. She cried out into his hand, a gurgling sound coming from somewhere deep in her throat. Frederik twisted her around so that the back of her head was now buried in his chest. She writhed and kicked, her legs fruitlessly striking air as he lifted her body upward. Looking toward the curtain and praying no one would peek around it or come walking by, he began walking her backward, twisting left and right to counter her wildly shifting weight. Despite the lack of voices coming from beyond the curtain, he couldn't risk a noisy fight on the ground. He'd just carried her to the electrical room doorway when her eyes rolled back in her head, and she went under. Holding her limp body up with one arm, he opened the door and dragged her inside. Since the lock was broken, he'd have to work with the hope that no one would come back here looking for her. If that happened, he still had the baton.

Measuring the instrument case's interior visually, Frederik determined she'd never fit inside of it right side up. He'd have to reverse her, placing her head at the bottom then folding her legs atop one another in the much-narrower neck portion. It worked, although he realized doing so would mean wheeling her in an inverted position. That could be problematic due to the drug he'd injected into her bloodstream pooling in her head. He'd have to risk it. Closing the top, he found it wouldn't close without him having to kneel atop it first. Doing so, he succeeded in fastening the four metal clasps. The case bulged more than would have been normal, but she was in, nonetheless.

Standing to wipe sweat from his forehead, he looked beside him at the bassist's pitiful form. The man was having a full-blown seizure now. His entire body shook violently, his glazed eyes stared vacantly, and whitish foam bubbled from his lips and down his cheek. He'd become incontinent at some point, a dark blotch of wetness growing from his crotch and down his pant legs. Careful to avoid the ever-growing pool of blood seeping from the man's head, Frederik grasped the case's upper handle and lifted the neck portion of the case. When he did, he felt the violinist's body shift slightly downward. He knew there was nothing he could do but hope the drug didn't affect her more, or her airway didn't get cut off. Collecting himself, he opened the door and wheeled her out, switching off the light as he went. The room was cast into its previous blinking green and red low light. The bassist had stopped seizing, his body rigid now, the rise and fall of his chest nearly imperceptible. Frederik closed the door, not caring to wipe away his fingerprints from the knob. A calling card. Besides, none of that would matter anyway if he didn't make it out undetected.

As he made his way beyond the curtain, he spied the redhead's instrument case on a table near where they'd first talked. Opening it, he found the violin and bow tucked inside the red-felt interior. Frederik's eyes widened, and a grin rose to his lips. Unable to resist the temptation, he closed it and decided to take it also. Guessing as to where the musicians may exit the building from back here, he balanced the larger case's neck portion on one shoulder as he pulled it behind him down an empty corridor. Should one of the real performers spot and question him as to why he carried two cases that didn't belong to him, he'd have to decide on the spot to talk his way out of it or try to escape. He could only pin his hopes on no one seeing him emerge from the hall into the bitter early-winter night, the downtown skyscrapers blinking above him as he spirited away a living human being inside the bassist's case.

As it was, no one did.

CHAPTER 18

Thanking himself for leaving the performance early, and even more grateful that most of the audience members had already exited the hall and driven away, Frederik nonetheless used the case's prominent neck to hide his face during the hundred-yard walk back to the parking garage. Feeling like a soldier crossing no-man's land by himself, he'd expected at any moment for a police officer or venue worker to yell out for him to stop, that he was stealing the performers' instruments. But as he struggled under the larger case's weight, its wheels grinding loudly into the concrete walkway as the frigid night wind whipped into him, he finally came to the garage entrance. For the first time he allowed thoughts to enter his mind that he might succeed. The garage was mostly empty; the performance had ended thirty minutes ago, but per usual with orchestral performances on a weekend night, several attendees had wished to soak in the atmosphere by enjoying a post-performance drink in the lobby's bar area. But soon they'd begin filtering out to their Volvos and BMWs to drive toward home or places unknown, their exhaust fumes billowing into the icy November night.

He'd driven here in the Bronco for no special reason other than it was the most comfortable of the several vehicles he owned, and the seat warmers worked especially well. He'd just painted it three weeks ago (having done it himself in the garage), and for the third time in the six months he'd owned it. Gun metal gray this time. Now, after pressing a button on his key fob and hearing a familiar "pop," he lifted the back window up then swung the side gate open. He thanked himself for having brought it instead of the Miata. He never could have dreamed of pulling something like this off had he driven the tiny sportster. Although possible to have switched cars when he'd gone home, there'd been no guarantee changing one element wouldn't have created a new disaster. The mere thought of possibly missing out on her over a blown tire, getting pulled over, or an ill-timed act of God made him shudder.

He checked left and right. The only people he saw in the garage were a middle-aged couple walking up toward the second level of the ramp. Frederik wasted no time. He propped the neck end of the case onto the edge of the Bronco's cargo hold, then came around to the bottom end and lifted it to waist-level. He shoved it into the hold, the heavy plastic case scraping along the carpet until it struck the back of the front seats. The last foot of it remained outside of the hold, though. He opened the front passenger door and climbed in, lifting the neck portion and pulling with all his might. He didn't have much leverage this way, and the woman's dead weight combined with the bulkiness of the case itself made pulling it in far enough difficult.

He finally succeeded in wedging it atop the console and firmly between the front bucket seats. Should a cop stop him on the way home, or God forbid he got into an accident, it was plausible enough keeping to his planned story that he'd just returned from a gig at some random downtown venue. The only wild card was the bassist himself. It was vital that his body remain undiscovered until Frederik made it home. If it were discovered before that, and if some unseen person had happened to spot him lugging the case into the Bronco, every cop south of the Canadian border would have a BOLO matching him and his car. Street and exterior business cameras were commonplace these days, he knew, with any one of them having the potential to cause him ruin. He decided right then that if he were pulled over, he would voluntarily exit the vehicle and then do his best to incapacitate the cop. In that event, he may only have time to race home and say goodbye to the girls before deciding to either run or end things for himself.

He was being paranoid, of course. No one would have found the bassist yet because they had all left the backstage area for the bar. They'd be on their second drink by now. Conversation would flow more freely, laughter would be louder. Someone might initially ask where their missing colleagues were, but soon enough they'd become distracted and forget about them. It was entirely possible the bassist's body wouldn't be found until the next day or later, provided someone didn't need to reset a breaker or his decomposing body hadn't begun to stink.

He'd just closed the door and slammed the window down when a set of headlights swung around the corner from the second deck. Frederik ducked behind the far side of the Bronco, desperate not to be attributed to the vehicle. The car's driver stopped at the automated security bar and slipped a ticket into the machine. After the driver paid, a red light beside the security arm turned green, and the bar rose. The car crept forward then turned right out of the garage before disappearing into the night.

Frederik climbed into the driver's seat and tried his best to relax. His heart raced in his chest. He undid his tie and tossed it onto the floorboard, then unbuttoned all but three of his shirt buttons. Falling back against the seat, he closed his eyes and caught his breath. The hardest part was over. He'd gotten her out unseen, or assumedly so. Knowing he wouldn't truly be able to relax until he got her home, he pushed aside a hundred doomsday scenarios that played in his head. Now was not the time to get scared. A certain amount of risk came with this project he'd embarked on seven months ago, he knew. Close calls were to be expected. Discovery could occur at any moment. He'd reckoned with the possibility that his entire dream could come crashing down upon him like a house of cards, without notice. He would sit here to gather his wits and relax before making another move. Better a lost minute or two than a lifetime of regret in some dungeon.

Once the heat coming from his chest abated and his breathing returned to normal, he opened his eyes and spoke aloud to the quiet stillness of the Bronco's interior. "Fifteen minutes and it will be done. Now drive from this place and everything will be that much closer to perfect." He decided to check on her first. Cracking open the case, he was met by a wafting mix of women's perfume and years-old felt. Her upper body had indeed shifted downward during their walk, but only slightly. Her legs remained firmly wedged in the narrower neck portion, and her head lay facing him. She could have been sleeping. Or dead. Thinking of that, Frederik smiled.

"Soon enough, my love," he whispered, smoothing out a stray lock of her fiery red hair that lay matted against her wet cheek. She'd begun to sweat heavily, no doubt due to her inhaling more carbon dioxide than normal. The cramped confines of the case itself would have insulated her against the cold as well. The drug he'd given her had had the benefit of reducing her respiration rate by half. As a result, he'd leave it closed during the ride home since he wouldn't have time to properly close it if he were pulled over. He only needed her alive for the trip, and afterward when he planned to purify her. But the dietitian would be first, of course. He'd had them all in order so far, and that's how it would remain if he could help it.

When he guessed that she'd gotten enough fresh air to last the short ride home, he closed the lid and re-fastened the latches. He started the engine and was careful pulling out of the space, wary of the car beside him. Before he approached the lowered security bar, he donned a ballcap he'd never worn during his abductions and pulled it low over his face. He inserted his ticket in the machine. As always, he paid with cash. For one agonizing moment, the arm didn't rise. A malfunction. Or an alarm had been raised in the hall, freezing vehicular movement to and from the garage. That thought caused him to scan for more security cameras. He saw one to his right, grateful that it wouldn't capture his full face from straight on. It would record his plate on the way out, no doubt, but the plate was fake. If he were stopped by a cop, he knew the Bronco would come back to a similar make and model vehicle as his, registered to a man whose driver's license photo closely matched his own. In that event, he'd have "forgotten" his wallet at home, as well as insurance and registration cards. His gig tonight had distracted him. Part of his many painstaking precautions. When another moment passed and the security arm still didn't rise, Frederik considered ramming through it. But a second later the light on the arm turned green and it raised, and Frederik eased the Bronco beneath it before turning east into the freezing Minnesota night. Even to him, the darkness seemed like a mouth stretched wide to swallow him whole.

He made it home in fifteen minutes, taking as many back roads as possible. Once, during a short ride on Interstate 35, he passed a cop who'd pulled a vehicle over. He offered himself extra thanks for taking such extreme cautions with his vehicles. Knowing he sometimes would take a victim with little to no notice, it had behooved him to not only keep professionally made fake IDs and plates, but to religiously obey all traffic laws. Every time he drove one of his vehicles, he meticulously inspected it for maintenance issues that may attract scrutiny, whether he planned to hunt or not. He'd considered carrying a loaded gun in the console as a last-case option but had decided against it. Even though he had several of them (both legally obtained and illegally), he'd figured it best to avoid the issue of firearms altogether. A cop's nervousness always increased in their presence, even if carried by another cop who was off-duty. And a cop he certainly was not.

As he turned off at his exit and traveled the three miles through residential neighborhoods toward the house's main road, he fought the urge to relax even a bit. He felt like a man who'd won the lottery and had to wait until morning to collect his winnings, paranoid that some freak accident would either ruin his ticket or kill him during the night. He drove past the familiar abandoned warehouse and the crumbing Dutch Revival home that fire had ravaged last year, then turned onto his road. Fifty yards of relative darkness, since the city hadn't bothered to install streetlights to illuminate a lonely, wooded road with a single home at its end, shuttered for two decades before he'd moved in. When he came to his driveway, he pressed a button on the opener and waited for the wrought-iron gate to open before pulling up the sloped drive. Parking beneath the awning, he got out and opened a security app on his phone to manually turn off the delayed floodlight. He hadn't had a trespasser in over a year —a vagrant who'd managed to scale the spiked fence had been the last—but he couldn't risk discovery now. He recalled buying the dilapidated property two years ago, after the bank had finally gotten serious about selling the place just to rid themselves of it. Slow fixes at first, with his decision to mostly keep the house as-is to preserve its century-old elan. He'd added the false wall, basement soundproofing, and secret rooms himself once his idea had become reality.

Opening the oversized garage door now, he pulled in between his vans (each of them the third different make and model he'd bought since beginning his collection) and the Miata, then lugged the case inside. It hadn't been long since he'd given her fresh air, but for one heart-stopping moment after he unlatched the case and opened it, he thought she'd suffocated or that he'd given her too much of the drug.

"No!" he yelled, falling to his knees and lowering his ear to her nose and mouth. Nothing. Eyes wide, he straightened and stared down at her chest, willing it to rise. No movement for a full ten seconds. Panicked, he pressed the pads of his first two fingers against her carotid artery and felt for her pulse. Nothing there, either. "Breathe!" he yelled, his voice higher in pitch than normal. Lifting her from the case, he laid her flat and had just interlaced the fingers of both hands atop her breastbone when she took an involuntary gasp of air.

"Yes!" he rejoiced. Relief poured through him as her blue-tinged face turned pinker with each breath she took. He fanned it, looking her up and down. Her head rocked from side to side, and her lips formed soundless words. Bending over her semiconscious form, Frederik placed his hands on her cheeks and kissed her forehead. "Thank you," he whispered. "Thank you." One more minute inside the case and she would have been lost for good, he thought with horror. And him, like the lottery winner who slipped on the front stairs and broke his neck, the ticket clutched in his dead hand.

~

THIRTY-FOUR YEARS EARLIER

The boys' father stood at the embalming table, scalpel in hand, and looked down at the elderly woman's strangely positioned corpse. Several straps and pulleys connected to the walls and ceiling held the legs at a ninety-degree angle, while others held the hands in a resting position over the lap. Rubber bands twisting the curled fingers, and hidden foam inserts in her partially closed hands gave them the appearance of performing some sort of manual task. She'd died yesterday, finally succumbing from Alzheimer's. Her family had called on the boys' father to prepare her for a viewing tomorrow. Not just any viewing, but a special one she'd planned herself just days after her diagnosis three years ago. A lifelong knitter, she'd especially loved creating afghans for family and friends. Knowing she would soon lose her cognitive power, she'd contacted the controversial undertaker and requested he eventually position her not in a casket like normal but sitting upright in her favorite rocking chair with a pair of knitting needles in her hands. A spool of yarn and the afghan she herself had completed the day after signing her contract were to complete the tableau. The family had given the undertaker the completed work—depicting a tree with the names of her closest family members representing the branches —to drape over the dead woman's lap during the wake.

After inspecting the various parts of the body he planned to soon work on, the undertaker looked into the curious faces of his twin ten-year-old sons. "Tell me, Victor, where do we make the incision?"

Victor went to speak, then paused. His father had taught him this before, he recalled, but he'd forgotten which side of the neck, or if it was the femoral in the groin. Another moment of indecision passed before he shook his head in frustration. "I don't know."

"Frederik?" the father said, shifting his eyes onto his other son.

The boy frowned, in thought, then answered with a question of his own. "Will she wear a dress that exposes her neck, or will it be covered?"

The father, who up until now had kept his lips pressed tight under the growing frustration of this latest teaching lesson, smiled. "The family requests a high collared dress."

"The jugular and carotid, on the right side of the neck then," Frederik said, his voice soft yet confident. "The femoral is more common with women, but it would be difficult with her legs this way. And the neck stitches will be hidden by the dress."

The father's smile widened. "Very good. Do you want to make the cut?" He extended the scalpel toward where the boys were positioned in the doorway.

Frederik's eyes widened. "Me?"

"Yes. I won't be around forever. Someday one of you can take over the business."

Excited, Frederik nodded but then paused after looking at his downtrodden brother. "It's okay, Vic can do it this time."

"I don't know..." Victor said, shrinking down within himself. "I don't want to make a mistake."

"If so, I can fix it," their father said patiently. "Come. Victor can help today, then Frederik next time."

When they approached, Frederik's eyes moved over the dead woman's body. Or what remained of it after age and disease had done their ghastly work. Soon, he knew the embalming would begin. What Frederik had once considered taboo, something unspoken that his father performed in the basement of their rural home, had become routine to him as he aged. Watching the process dozens of times along with his brother had helped dispel those thoughts. Death was a natural part of life, Frederik had learned, something that every living organism experienced. His father had taught both boys that only in our modern culture was the preparation of the dead considered morbid. Pharaohs had been mummified then entombed with living people, doomed themselves as they'd been chosen to accompany their masters into the afterlife. Ancient Greeks, the Vikings, and even American Indian tribes had all regarded death as merely a gate through which the eternal soul passed from this life to another. As Frederik and Victor had sat and watched their father work on bodies, they'd listened to him lecture and describe what he did and why. But never had he invited them to actively help. Until now. They moved a step closer to the embalming table, Victor's eyes downcast as normal, Frederik's alert and curious.

"Victor, take it and begin the cut…here." Their father held the scalpel out for him to take and placed the tip of his finger just above the corpse's right collarbone, near the shoulder. "And end…here." He placed his finger at a spot several inches up toward the ear. Victor took the razor-sharp instrument and did as he'd been instructed. "Skin is thicker than you'd think, and the tissue tough. Even hers. Use the point and press downward, firmly, as you go." Victor's hand began to tremble. "It's okay, son, you can do it."

"I can't!" Victor said, releasing the scalpel where it clattered noisily against the table's stainless steel surface. Throwing his hands up to cover his face, he shook his head and said, "I'm sorry, Father, I've failed you."

The father smiled a well-practiced, fatherly smile. "You didn't fail me. I misjudged. Perhaps when you're both older." As their father reached down to pick up the scalpel, Frederik snatched it up first and, with a fierce look of determination burning in his eyes, pressed the point into the first spot their father had pointed out. It slid in to about a half-inch depth, after which he drew it upward several inches to the second spot. When he removed it, a red, bloodless incision stood out in stark contrast to the corpse's pale white flesh.

An astonished gasp escaped the father's throat, but he quickly regained his composure. Straightening, he peered curiously into his son's fierce eyes before shifting his attention to the incision. Inspecting it closely with a pair of tongs, he nodded. "Good job, Frederik. I couldn't have made a better cut myself."

The embalming process had begun. Victor uncovered his eyes and watched in silence, his arms hanging limply at his sides. As he'd done before, their father spoke first of the precision required for such specialty viewings. Unlike normal casket viewings, with the body lying supine with arms folded at the waist, those that included the body standing, sitting, or in an action pose required innovative embalming techniques. Last month, the boys had observed with fascination as their father had masterfully embalmed the corpse of a twentysomething man bent over a pool table in shooting stance. The family had wept with happiness at seeing their beloved son and brother with a cigarette in his mouth, positioned to sink the eight ball in a corner pocket.

"The fluid sets the muscles quickly," their father reminded the boys. "We need these to keep her in position." He touched the pulleys and straps, reminding the boys that an embalmed body was so stiff it was nearly impossible to move the body parts afterward. He'd installed the strap system himself several years before, after adding his specialty viewing option to his existing traditional wakes. Supervising Frederik as he finished the required cut through the corpse's skin and flesh, he placed a hooked instrument in one of the boy's hands. "We raise the vein with this, then slide it beneath it so that it does not slide back inside the body." It took him several tries, but finally Frederik succeeded. "Very good." Their father cast an impressed look at his eager-looking son. "Now, the artery."

Frederik repeated the process, this time with the shallower carotid artery. As their father walked him through the next steps, he re-told the story of one of his first specialty wakes, where he'd made the mistake of waiting too long to position the body. He'd massaged the wrongly stiffened limbs for hours afterward, his hands aching inexorably, but had still been unable to set them correctly. He'd regretted having to tell the grieving family that their plan to pose their loved one on his favorite motorcycle would be impossible. He'd given them a traditional wake instead, free of charge. Never would he make the same mistake.

When the work was complete and the body had been dressed (the clothes had been cut lengthwise, wrapped around the body, then carefully sewn back together again due to the body's new position), the boys helped carry the corpse to the elevator. The chapel sat on the house's main floor, and it was here where the three of them placed the body in the rocking chair. Her knitting needles, yarn, and afghan sat on a nearby table, ready to be positioned in her hands and lap just before the wake.

"Won't she stink if she's not in the cooler?" Victor asked, wrinkling his nose.

"Did you forget?" asked their father. "Embalmed bodies can last several days without refrigeration. Months if so, years if frozen. Us three have business tomorrow morning in town before the service, so now is a better time to position her."

Suddenly, a woman's voice came from behind them. "You expect me to be alone with *her* sitting in there like that?" The boys turned to see their stepmother, Naomi, leaning against the room's open double door jamb. A glass half-filled with wine hung from one hand.

"I'll shut the door, of course," their father said.

"I don't care," said Naomi, her voice gaining its familiar rancor. "I'll know she's there. Sometimes I feel their eyes following me through the walls when I pass by the chapel. It's creepy."

"But we've already placed her."

"Then place her again before the wake. Take her back downstairs, Yves. I insist." She burned her eyes into him.

Frederik and Victor looked from her to their father, silent. After their beloved mother had died two years ago, they'd watched their father mourn her for a full year. Then he'd met Naomi—slightly older than him, and childless—from a neighboring town while buying home supplies. They'd married a month later. Grudgingly tolerant of her husband's business and its connection to the home she shared with him and his sons, their stepmother had quickly settled in as master of the home.

While their father was mild-natured and soft-spoken, she'd proved to be bossy and loud-mouthed, especially when she drank. She wasn't at her height of inebriation yet, Frederik assessed, but she was getting there.

Their father dropped his head and sighed. It was always like that with her. He motioned for the boys to take one side of the corpse, and together they moved her back downstairs.

It wasn't until the next day after the viewing, when their father was away on more business, that Naomi appeared to them again, this time after they'd eaten dinner and were in their bedroom. "Come downstairs," she said drunkenly from their open doorway. A few strands of graying hair had fallen across her face. As usual, a glass of wine hung from one hand.

Frederik, who'd been playing with an action figure, looked up and froze. Victor, half-asleep already, woke with a start.

"Did I stutter? I said come downstairs. Now."

They followed her down the staircase into the kitchen where she stood with fists planted on her ample hips. "The dishes are to be done *before* you go to your room. How many times must I repeat myself?" The boys looked dumbly to one another. "I asked you both a question," she said, her voice turning venomous.

"Sorry, ma'am," Frederik said, and started toward the sink.

"No, Victor can wash them. You did them last night."

Frederik stopped in his tracks. "It's okay, I don't mind. Victor's not feeling—"

Before he could get the sentence out, she stepped forward and grabbed him by the ear, twisting it upward so hard he was forced onto his tiptoes. The movement was so sudden, her wine sloshed over the lip of her glass and splashed onto the floor. Bending down so that her mouth was mere inches from Frederik's face, she said, "I didn't ask you how he was feeling. I told *him* to do them."

Frederik screwed up his face in pain but didn't cry out. "Yes, ma'am."

"If I wanted you to do them, I would have said so. Why do you insist on disobeying me, boy?"

Victor looked up into his brother's contorted face. When he began to protest, their stepmother saw this and swung the back of her hand toward him, smacking him on the side of the face. "Shut up!" she yelled, slurring her words. Victor, stunned by the sudden strike, touched a hand to his cheek then lowered his head.

Their stepmother dragged Frederik by the ear to the sink. Victor, clutching desperately onto his brother's hand, followed. "Maybe this time you'll mind what I say," she said, turning on the hot water. She maintained her upward hold onto Frederik's ear as she grabbed his left wrist and forced his hand under the stream. Even as the water turned from cold, to warm, to scalding hot, Frederik grimaced but didn't make a peep.

"You're hurting him!" Victor cried. He reached out to try pulling her arm backward, but due to her work on the farm, she was much too strong. As she looked down at Victor's desperate face, his hands pawing uselessly at her arm, she uttered a drunken laugh that reverberated through the entire main level of the house.

After steam began rising from Frederik's reddening skin, she turned the water off and released her hold on his wrist. For the first time, Frederik made a sound—a whimper—as he held his hand close to his body and turned protectively away from her. Laughing, she retreated to the other end of the kitchen to retrieve her bottle of wine. While Frederik turned on the cold water and thrust his already blistering hand beneath the stream, she pulled the cork out with her teeth and re-filled her glass. She stumbled toward the living room, pausing to look over her shoulder and point a wavering finger in the boys' direction.

"A year I've lived here. An entire year and I never go into town because of you two. I'm like..." She hiccupped once before finishing. "I'm like a prisoner in my own home." She cast a resentful glare at them before staggering into the darkened living room. The sound of her clicking on the television, and then nothing except the running cold water, and Victor consoling his weeping brother.

CHAPTER 19

Abby startled awake, sitting upright in bed so fast the comforter flew onto the floor. It took her a few moments to differentiate between the dream she'd experienced and reality. She'd had a nightmare about being chased by a faceless monster when a noise had awakened her—voices, or a door slamming shut, she wasn't sure which. As she lowered herself to one elbow, she tried to remember how she'd gotten here. She remembered preparing to close the clinic, and the security guard asking to use the bathroom...

Full realization hit her then. Collapsing onto her back, she expelled a breath of frustration. Frederik. She was inside his home, of course, or wherever he'd taken her. Abby didn't remember much after her bizarre breakfast and house tour, except being locked back in here for several hours until she'd somehow forced herself to fall asleep. With no real sense of time, she'd begun to slip into a vacuum. Her brain had begun to play tricks on her. Old, well-maintained memories she'd always held as inviolable she now questioned. She wasn't even sure whether some recent memories were real, such as if she'd really gone to work on Thursday, or if the happy hour with Derek hadn't been her mind conjuring some pleasant scene to interrupt the terror she was experiencing. Because like what she'd just dreamed, this was exactly what nightmares were made of. Every scary movie or book or story she'd heard over a campfire in her youth had coalesced into this waking abortion of reality.

As if to solidify her thoughts, she heard the rolling of the woodpile from in front of her door, and then something unexpected—the notes of a familiar '80s pop/rock song coming from the crack below the door. The song reminded her of her high school prom, when she and her date had joined a group of their friends in a raucous dance line that had snaked around the entire dance floor. It struck her as funny that she could remember such a tactile memory like that while being locked away in someone's basement.

She heard the sound of a different door opening, one apparently just beside hers, followed by Frederik's muffled voice either through the wall or the ventilation system. Abby couldn't make them out, but his words seemed soothing. Her heart began to pound as she imagined who he could be speaking with. Surely, if it was a man or someone he was in cahoots with, he wouldn't be speaking to them in such a manner. He'd spoken to her that same way, she remembered. The other girls upstairs, too. Then, a woman's ear-piercing scream emitted from the same nearby room. Abby bolted fully upright. By now, her eyes had fully adjusted to the semi-darkness, and she was finally able to verify she was in fact in the same room as before. The instinct to try escaping came over her. But as quickly as it had come, she dismissed it. He'd mentioned having a camera set up in here. And her own door, as well as every other one leading upstairs or outside for that matter, would certainly be locked as well.

Another scream, followed by Frederik's raised voice: "Quiet, you'll wake her!" A final scream, this one more muffled, as if the woman had uttered it into her hands. Or his. Then nothing but the music (conga line!), and Abby's heart pounding in her ears. Her concern for her own safety turned into curiosity moments later when she heard the door close, a heavy-sounding lock turn, and Frederik's voice arise over the music. "Which one should I take first?"

A second voice, a man's, so low or far enough away that she almost couldn't hear it above the music, responded, "You've taken them in order so far. Why change now?"

"You're right. The dietitian is spunky, and she's curvier. But the redhead is exquisite. She'd be the perfect way to end the collection." Abby pictured him standing out there staring at each of their bedroom doors, considering.

"So…the dietitian, then. Will you need help transitioning her?"

"I should be okay. I'm thinking of teaming her with the X-ray technician; she doesn't really have a scene of her own. Maybe the dietitian holding a tape measure around her waist or taking her body fat reading, since the X-ray woman is the biggest of them all."

"Yes, that would work."

Abby turned her ear to the doorway to better gauge the voices. Now she wasn't sure if she was hearing someone else who was physically in the room, or if Frederik was speaking with him on speakerphone or FaceTime. She forgot herself by swinging her legs out of bed and standing up, when she froze. Surely, he'd be angry if he looked at the camera or decided to open the door and saw her like this. Prepared. What for, she couldn't guess, but her pose was anything but what a submissive captive was expected to look like. She started to lay back down on the bed when a voice inside of her started shouting, so forceful it was almost as if someone was in the room with her.

If you're going to get out of here alive, you can't lie back down! Not yet. That's what he wants, for you to give up. You need to look at what he's doing. The crack under the door is big enough to see under. You used to look under your door as a little girl, and that was smaller than this one. Do it before you lose your nerve.

Abby squatted and placed her palms on the floor, easing herself down first to one knee and then the other. She remembered how the floorboards had creaked when Frederik had entered her room the day before. The music still played; he'd even raised the volume. Her heart hammering in her chest, she closed one eye and placed the side of her face against the cold floorboards to peer through the crack. Due to her limited field of vision, she could only see three feet off the floor, and the portion of the room directly opposite her door. Soon, there was movement into her field of vision—a pair of feet dressed in men's dress shoes, and the lower half of a pair of slacks-covered legs.

"It's getting cold down here. I'd like to throw another log on the fire," the second voice said.

"I'll do it," Frederik said. Immediately, the slack-covered legs walked out of Abby's view. There was the sound of the fireplace door opening, followed by that of a log being inserted. *Someone else* is *here, then.* She didn't know if that was a good or bad thing. Him acting alone would have meant a relative bit of safety in that no one would be able to implicate him. She'd taken a criminology class in college and learned that criminals exponentially increased their chances of being caught with each added accomplice. She'd learned this lesson the hard way herself (albeit in a non-criminal way), recalling the time she'd told a close high school friend a deep secret and sworn her to secrecy, but soon after everyone found out. On the flip side, him having an accomplice also meant double the risk of something bad happening to her. Two minds, four hands, and, well, two dicks...

Abby forced that thought away and focused on the pair of legs. She needed to see more of what was happening; only seeing half of it was worse than confronting the entirety of it. When she adjusted her positioning, the floorboard beneath her left knee creaked. She froze. Those feet turned in her direction. The music stopped a second later, and the room turned deathly silent. Knelt there with her face pressed to the floor and her butt in the air, she felt more helpless than ever. She cursed her decision to peek under the door. Such a stupid thing to do. And needless. What did it matter, anyway? If anything would help her escape this situation, this wasn't it. But she felt stuck. She couldn't risk rising to her feet and getting back into bed. He'd know she'd been peeking, or at least doing something she wasn't supposed to do. That would anger him. Perhaps more so than her breaking her promise not to run or cry out, since it involved subterfuge on her part. Whatever his mental state, either result would unlikely cause him to pat her gently on the head, telling her he understood her needing to see what was happening. Then he'd sigh and apologize for what he was about to do to her.

Heart in her throat, Abby felt a sudden loosening in her bladder. She may have wet herself right there if the music hadn't started back up just then, and Frederik hadn't turned back to face the other direction. As the other person in the room coughed—a loose, chesty sound—Frederik's final words became lost under the combined noise and music. Straining her ears more than she had before, due to her knowledge that he was referring directly to her, she thought he'd said *purifying her*.

She hoped he'd repeat what he'd said, but the distraction apparently caused him to forget. Instead, he said, "You're getting sick again."

"It's nothing," spoke the voice, now just a hoarse whisper above the music.

Frederik walked out of Abby's view. Panicked, she decided to take her chances with him hearing her move about in here than to throw the door open to find her this way. Easing first to one foot, then the other, she kept as much pressure against the floor as she could as she raised one hand at a time. Her back and knees hurt from kneeling that way. It had only been a few minutes but already she felt her head begin to swim. *Might not be the best time to faint, girlfriend. Get it together long enough to see if he and his buddy intend on taking turns with you. Unless both at once is their thing...*

She'd just eased back into bed and pulled the covers up to her chin when a key rattled in the door's lock. A second later, as if he'd wanted to surprise her, he pushed the door open quickly. Abby's eyes snapped closed at the same time. Remaining as still as possible, she counted in her head to ten then stirred. She could feel him watching her from the doorway, and smelled that same sickly-sweet odor she'd recalled from the day before, a mix of aftershave and chemicals. Unable to place it, she concentrated on her breathing, wishing to appear as naturally asleep as possible. When at last she felt it appropriate to do so, she opened her eyes in mock sleepiness and propped herself up on one elbow.

"What...where am I..." she said, feigning confusion as she settled her gaze on Frederik's form. He was leaning against the door jamb with one of the same dress shoes she'd seen propped against it. A slender, wooden object hung from one hand. Light reflected on it, and for a second she was sure he was holding an ax. But when he dropped his foot to the floor and turned to fully face her, Abby saw the object for what it really was—a violin.

"You're right where you belong," Frederik said. Despite him standing with his back to the light, Abby could tell he was grinning. "I've got a surprise for you," he said, drawing out the word *surprise*. "Do you like music?"

She clutched the blanket up tighter around her neck. "I... um...I suppose so..."

"She *supposes* so?" he said, presumably to the other person who was still out of sight of her. After placing the violin atop the table, he pointed a remote control at a black box beside it. Soon after, the music changed to Sade's "Smooth Operator."

"I'm going to purify you now," he said, turning back to face her. He began unbuttoning his dress shirt as he entered the room. "You mustn't cry out or resist me. It'll ruin the moment. I understand if you're afraid, but as long as you don't resist, I'll be gentle."

Abby felt her chest tighten. The elephant was back. As if the stress of the past two days hadn't been enough, she was now being confronted by the only thing she feared more than death itself. With his shirt only half unbuttoned, he went to remove his belt, that dimpled grin visible on his face despite the room's semi-darkness. He was one of those guys who liked to do it partially clothed, she thought. Her ex had been that way too, preferring both of them to wear shirts so that their combined sweat didn't make them too slippery. He'd even said it turned most men on to see a woman partially clothed versus nude anyway. Watching Frederik toss his belt to the floor and advance on her, Abby made the decision that not only wouldn't she submit to what he intended to do to her, she promised herself that she'd survive this entire ordeal. Not so much to live out her days into old age, surrounded by friends and family in some nursing home, but for a larger purpose altogether. One that involved her driving an hour away and sitting tall on a prison visitation room stool to confront the one person on Earth responsible for every sleepless night and failed relationship she'd ever had since her childhood. The madman in front of her wasn't going to stop her from doing that, no matter the perceived impossibility of her ever actually achieving it.

He must have seen the decision transmit across her face because he paused while unzipping his slacks. "Now, this is going to go one of two ways. Both result in me getting what I want. Do you understand?"

Nodding, she scooted back toward the head of the bed as far as she could go. Almost unconsciously, she reached down and tied the drawstring on her bottoms as tight as they would go, double knotting them.

"Now be a good girl." He moved much faster than she'd expected. She shrieked the moment she felt his weight atop her.

He pawed at the covers, ripping them from her grasp and casting them to the floor beside the bed. With seemingly superhuman strength, he flipped her face-down with one hand while yanking his slacks and underwear down to his knees. Abby managed to turn onto her side and claw at his face with one hand, her survival instinct at full alert. She couldn't allow him to pin her face-down again; she'd have no leverage. For the first time since college, when an upper-classman she'd met at a party had tried to force himself on her, she was transported back to her childhood bedroom, when her stepfather had visited her during all those nights her mother had been passed out drunk and unaware of the things her husband was doing. Nasty things he'd made her promise to never repeat to anyone. Because if she did, her mother would kill him, he'd said, and Abby had not just believed him, she had conjured up the image herself. Her mother was a drunk, yes, but she loved Abby and would have certainly killed for her. It all came rushing back to Abby's mind like one of the Viewfinders she'd used as a kid, only instead of pressing the lever down to progress the pictures one at a time, the one in her mind went so quickly that the photos became like an animated flipbook.

"Stop…fighting me!" he demanded. "You're ruining it!"

"No!" she yelled, her voice desperate in her own ears. Despite her struggle to prevent it, he succeeded in flipping her back onto her stomach. She grunted as she fought with all her might to keep her legs pressed together. He drove a knee between her thighs, his weight pressing on a cluster of nerves she had there. A lightning bolt of pain shot through her legs and involuntarily drove them apart. At least her bottoms remained tight around her waist. He'd have to yank them down over her spread legs now. A crazed thought crossed her mind just then. For the first time in her adult life, she felt grateful for having wide hips. A maddened laugh escaped her, and even though none of it was funny at all, it rose from somewhere deep inside her anyway. Fuck rules at this point. The guy hadn't just kidnapped her, now he was trying to steal that part of her she'd spent almost twenty years trying every day to recover. That was the most bull-shit thing about it. She'd prefer for him to simply put a bullet into the back of her head. If the guy wanted to be fair about it, he'd pose her just as she was now, clawing and scratching and fighting him, a wild animal bent on the survival of her spirit as much as of her life, instead of some stupid pose of her taking someone's body measurements.

When he reached around to grab her face, apparently with the intent to force her head around for her to face him, she lowered her head and bit into the fleshy part of his thumb. He hollered and pulled it free of her teeth. Then nothing except the sound of his heavy panting and the love song pouring from the speakers in the other room.

"You bit me," he said simply. He climbed off the bed, leaving her face-down and twisted like a human pretzel.

"You were trying to rape me," she said hoarsely, surprised at the frankness of her words.

"I didn't expect you to fight me. I'm sorry."

She turned onto her side and wiped the taste of his hand from her mouth. Looking at his silhouette standing there in the door-way, she wondered how much more quickly he was going to kill her now that she hadn't given him what he wanted. If he had an idea, he didn't say, because without a word, he stepped from the room and shut the door to leave her in darkness again.

CHAPTER 20

The FBI's St. Paul office sits downtown between the state capitol and the Mississippi. Being nine o'clock on a Friday night, the Federal Building was mostly a ghost town, save for several security guards, a few staffers making up for lost time due to the recent presidential visit to the city, and several agents working on special assignments. Among them was Special Agent Whitlock. With only a small desk lamp illuminating his office, he stood at the large window staring down at the nearby river. Downtown lights cast its darkened surface into a shimmering, multi-colored snake that wound its way between the Twin Cities, south through St. Louis and Memphis, before spilling into the Gulf of Mexico at New Orleans. Whitlock had driven here an hour ago from his home in nearby Apple Valley after his wife had tired of watching him pace the living room while flipping through stacks of PK files. She'd risen from the couch and placed her hands on his shoulders, telling him that she knew he felt guilty about taking a night off.

After sleeping in his office every night for three straight weeks, he'd finally relented and assigned another senior agent, as well as several MPD detective teams to take that night's workload. Like himself, Randall and Tan would still be on call.

Despite today being Detective Randall's first official day back in weeks, Whitlock was not of the opinion that mental health leave was vacation. Arguably, the man had been through as much, or more, as the rest of them during that time. Tan, although it being her first day in the unit as well, had been given the choice to remain in the office or be on call. Partners to the end. Despite Whitlock's wife articulating her appreciation that her husband had taken a night for the family, she'd looked him in the eye and told him that once he read bedtime stories to their two young daughters, he should go back to the office. She could tell that's where he felt he needed to be, in that quiet space where he concentrated best. She'd missed him these past six months, she'd explained, and so did the girls. But women throughout the city were dead or close to being so, and even she reasoned that the case would soon end one way or another. Unselfish to her core, she'd waited until the girls were tucked in, then led her husband into the bedroom for twenty minutes of alone time before sending him on his way.

As Whitlock stood watching the river, going over in his mind the thousands of details of the case, he couldn't help but liken his position to that of a military commander in the midst of a difficult battle. Guessing where the enemy was entrenched and when he would strike was a start, but at some point soldiers had to fix bayonets and climb from their trench to fight them. He'd joined the Marine Corps during those confounding years after high school, when his then-fiancée had abruptly ended their engagement and he'd become disillusioned with life. Having spent two tours dodging insurgents' bullets and seeing more than a few of his buddies stuffed into body bags, he'd left the Marines for the FBI. Considering himself lucky to be assigned to his home state, he'd dedicated himself to the preservation of law and order, an ideal he felt he could control much easier than the deadly and fruitless missions his military commanders had once given him and his men.

That the joint task force he led had only managed to arrest a blubbering homeless man who'd been an accomplice to one (and possibly more) of the kidnappings did little to instill pride in him. Women were still being stolen and likely murdered on his watch, and he felt helpless to stop it. Part of the reason he'd relented and chosen to come back to his office tonight had been the innocent looks on his daughters' faces during story time. All the female victims had been someone's daughter too, and no doubt they'd once lain in bed and been read stories in a similar fashion. It disgusted him to even imagine a world where the task force never caught the maniac responsible for snuffing out the lives of so many promising, happy young women.

Just one letter remained, V, and if PK achieved it before the task force could catch him, Whitlock knew it would be game over. Although everyone attached to the case longed to see the man responsible captured, an almost perverse apprehension had fallen over them in recent weeks. In a bitter paradox, many members, Whitlock included, had privately hoped for PK to continue his work if he should complete the alphabet. Even if he didn't and got spooked beforehand, or simply moved out of the area never to return, there was a real possibility he would never be caught. Twenty-five women snatched seemingly out of thin air, their families left devastated. Never had Whitlock felt more anxious about a crime that hadn't been committed as Abby Carlson's impending murder. And whomever "V" wound up being, she likely now walked the city streets unaware that she too would become an addition to the suspect's maniacal museum.

Against his better judgment but needing an understanding ear to talk things over with, Whitlock called Detective Randall. His counterpart picked up on the second ring. "Hey, Cal, sorry to bother you at home. You busy?"

"I'm in the office, actually. Took Daisy for a long walk then tried to watch some TV, but my brain wouldn't stop spinning, so I came in."

"Same. I'm looking out of my office window as we speak."

"Rachel didn't throw a plate at you on your way out?"

Whitlock huffed. "She's the one who sent me here. I guess she got tired of watching me wear out a strip of carpet."

Randall sighed. "I felt like a box of assholes sitting at home on my first day back. Especially with the news tonight. Folks at the city are openly calling for the chief to resign."

"If anyone were to resign over this, it'd be me," Whitlock said. He moved his gaze along the river's shimmering surface, then onto the brightly lit downtown skyscrapers that bordered it. "I was thinking that if we had a thousand more plainclothes covering the city, it still wouldn't mean a thing. Do you know how many jobs start with 'V'?"

"Tell me about it. My dog's veterinarian closed her office yesterday. *Closed*, Whit, until PK takes the last victim. She's afraid one of her pet owners is going to kidnap and pose her giving a dog a check-up. That's real fear."

There was a longer pause from the other end of the line, then Whitlock's voice came back with a tinge of irony in it. "Two grown men alone in their offices on a Friday night off. I remember a time when I'd call us pathetic for that."

"Well, technically *I'm* not alone. Tan was already here when I walked in."

Remembering something, Whitlock selected a personnel file labeled "Tan, Kelli" from a stack of files on his desk. Opening it to the first page, he read a line in a section marked "Demograph-ics," then smiled. "Hey, you two want to meet up for a bite to eat? We can unofficially discuss official business."

He heard the sound of Randall covering the phone and his muffled voice calling out to Tan, then, "It's a date. Where are we meeting?"

Whitlock thought about it. "Rachel's been begging me to take her to that place in the Foshay, toward the top. I forget the name."

"Prohibition?"

"That's it. It's close enough to walk for you two, and I can do some date night recon. Meet you in thirty."

"Perfect," Randall said. "I've been doing more research on a billboard idea I have. I'll explain more when we see you."

A half hour later, Whitlock entered the Foshay Tower, a white stone monolithic office building turned W Hotel that, from 1929 (when it had been completed) until forty-four years later, had been the tallest building in Minnesota. Built by Wilbur Foshay, an eccentric utilities magnet, as an homage to the Washington Monument, it had remained one of downtown Minneapolis's most iconic landmarks despite later skyscrapers surpassing its nearly 450-foot height. Whitlock had been here only once before, for a co-worker's going-away party at the hotel's ritzy first-floor bar. The group had later visited the building's museum and observation deck. Surprising that he hadn't been here more, since he prided himself on his Minnesota roots and took every opportunity to explore the state's many historical landmarks.

He read an incoming text from Randall that he and Tan were already here and had indeed walked. Passing through the lobby to a set of gilded elevators, Whitlock pressed the button marked "Prohibition Bar," then entered and rose to the twenty-seventh floor. When the doors opened, it seemed as if he'd been transported back a hundred years to one of the city's luxurious speakeasies. An ornate wood bar fronted the red-carpeted space, with velvet couches and plush wingbacks bookending a host of candle-topped tables. The place was packed with smartly dressed folks chatting and laughing. Whitlock searched the crowd and finally saw Randall's waving hand above the collection of heads. He wove his way through the sea of people until finally reaching where the detective pair stood near a set of floor-to-ceiling windows. "Glad you made it," he said. Each of them were dressed business casual, and were armed. The FBI and PD both had a policy forbidding a member or agent from being armed while visiting an alcohol establishment off-duty, but their on-call statuses overrode that. A technicality, but Whitlock knew they wouldn't be drinking anyway.

"Have you been here before?" Tan asked Randall.

"Once," Randall said, surveying the place. "It's changed over the years. Crowd seems younger than I remember, or maybe it's me who's getting older."

"You in the over-forty club yet?" Whitlock asked him.

"Yep, three years ago." He turned and raised his eyebrows at Tan.

"I thought it was rude to ask a woman her age," she said half-jokingly.

"When you're a homicide detective, you cease being sensitive to age, since your victims will never get any older," Randall deadpanned. "Perspective."

Tan considered what he'd said, then said, "In that case, I'll join the over-forty club exactly one year from today."

Randall stared at her, wide-eyed. "Today's your birthday?"

"Yes. It's no big deal, though. Like you said, most of our victims will never have another birthday. Besides, it's only my first day. No reason I can't pull a twenty-four."

"Still," Randall said, knowing she may not get another free evening for weeks. "It wouldn't take you long to respond if you get called in."

She waved him off. "Don't worry about it. My husband and daughters promised to make me breakfast in bed next chance we get. That'll be the best birthday present I could have."

While Randall ordered them several shareable small plates, and waters to go around, Whitlock excused himself to the restroom. When he returned, their talk turned to Randall's idea of using a billboard advertisement. They'd used various advertisements and social media posts with this case before, but never a billboard. "Shoot," Whitlock said, interested to hear his plan.

"During our interview with Abby's counselor, he talked about how cold it was in the office building. He said he wouldn't be surprised if the owners didn't keep the heat off altogether. It was pretty cold in there. That got me thinking that maybe PK is using an actual house to stage the bodies. Maybe a former home-style funeral home, since he'd have all the equipment he needed and could live in it. Tan made a good point about him simply not heating the floors he displays them on during cold months. And what better place to hide than in plain sight surrounded by a quarter million other homes in the city?"

"Good point, but where does the billboard come in?"

"We've done Crime Stopper billboards before, but most of those messages were too broad, like our Facebook and news-paper ads have been. And instead of scrolling past a post, or people channel surfing past one of our TV news conferences, we'd force half of everyone driving into downtown to see it."

"What's the new message?"

"We'd target local real estate professionals who may have shown or sold that style of house to someone matching PK's description in the past five years. His profile states that he started his kidnappings soon after choosing his location to store them. Even if someone with direct knowledge doesn't see the billboard themselves, they all have friends, family, and colleagues who might spread the word."

Whitlock nodded slowly. He liked the idea. "I'd rather have a few hundred folks with specific knowledge of that issue seeing the message, than a million people who don't and are burned out from the same old broad messages we've been jamming down their throats. Maybe add a QR code. Folks already text and TikTok while driving, so why not let them take an extra second to scan a code and read it when they're not driving."

"Folks visiting the Spoonbridge and Cherry could probably

see it, too," Tan added, her voice hopeful. The iconic statue garden across the freeway from downtown attracted both tourists and locals by the thousands most days.

"You can—I already checked the location. There's an open board for rent right there," Randall said.

Whitlock jotted a note about it in his phone. "Why not. It could even spook him if he sees it himself. Maybe gift us an extra day or two."

After their food came, they ate in relative silence. It was the last real meal any of them may have for the foreseeable future that wasn't from the PSB cafeteria or a drive-thru. When they finished eating and their plates were cleared, the waitress returned shortly afterward with a single cupcake on a saucer. A burning candle was stuck in the middle. "Make a wish," Whitlock said to Tan, placing a hand on her shoulder. It took a second, but Tan's previous expression of tight and focused thought turned into one of surprise and deep appreciation. When she looked to Randall, he shrugged and said he'd had no idea. Both he and Tan looked to Whitlock, who simply grinned as a response. "Thank you, that was sweet," she said, smiling. But it quickly disappeared as she shook her head with apparent guilt. "It feels wrong to be celebrating when Abby's the one out there needing help."

"One of my captains in Iraq once organized a birthday party for one of our guys while we were in the Green Zone," Whitlock said. "He'd had his legs blown off by an IED. The captain rounded up everyone in the company who wasn't on alert and had them sing him happy birthday bedside on his birthday. Even made him a homemade cake out of MRE desserts since they'd run out of cakes. My point is, don't ever stop celebrating the small things in life, if you can manage. We're not on this rock for very long. Some of us may only have days or hours." Tan and Randall went quiet with that. A moment later, Whitlock's cellphone rang. Answering it, he held up one finger to them, then went to go talk in a quieter area.

Randall signaled for the check, telling Tan, "He's right, you shouldn't feel bad. None of us can go at it twenty-four hours a day without catching a breath. One thing to remember is that in this line of work, you've got to *be* human to *help* humans."

Tan nodded appreciatively, then took a small bite of her cupcake. When the waitress dropped off the bill folder, Randall slipped three twenties into it and told her to keep the change. Seconds later, Whitlock came hurrying back to their high-top with a sober look on his face. "OIC just notified me," he said, pocketing his phone. "A male Signal-Five over at Orchestra Hall. And a missing female musician." He paused. "A violinist. I already told them we're on the way."

CHAPTER 21

The three of them burst through the street-level front doors and raced to Whitlock's issued vehicle parked down the block. The agent didn't wait for his passengers to buckle themselves in, activating his emergency lights and siren and popping the gear selector into drive. Pulling out of his curbside parking space, he executed a tire-squealing U-turn against oncoming traffic, cutting off a rideshare driver who screeched his car to a halt several inches from them. Lowering his window, the Somali man shook his fist and unleashed a line of curses in his native tongue as Whitlock straightened the SUV and roared up the street. He made it to Orchestra Hall in one minute flat, having been forced to wait for cross traffic to slow at several red lights. When they reached the hall's fountain-fronted plaza, he hopped the curb and screeched the cruiser to a halt. A dozen other cruisers (both marked and unmarked), a fire truck, and an ambulance sat parked at odd angles around the plaza and along the curb.

"Nicolette Dunn is our missing person," Tan said, having just communicated with dispatch. "Caucasian, thirty-two years old. Five-eight, one forty. Redhead. Last seen wearing a black formal dress. Confirmed as tonight's lead violinist." A couple walking along the sidewalk stopped and shot curious looks their way as

the three bounded from the unmarked SUV, the siren de-acti-
vated but the emergency lights still flashing. Entering the hall's
front lobby, it didn't take them long to meet up with a group of
uniformed patrol officers and the female sergeant who'd first
responded to the call. The on-call FBI OIC who'd notified Whitlock was further away and would be here soon, although Whitlock insisted on assuming command anyway. The female
sergeant who'd taken over the scene approached Randall. He
recognized her from his days on the street.

"Hey, Cal, if this was a normal 10-89, I wouldn't have notified the task force," she said. "But when I found out a female
violinist was missing too, I figured you'd want to respond."

"Start from the top," Randall said as the sergeant led the trio
through a door marked *RESTRICTED ACCESS*. From here, they
wound their way through back corridors until they arrived at an
area behind the main auditorium's stage where officers were
keeping EMS personnel and several hall employees at a distance.

"After the performance, one of the musicians saw our
missing violinist talking with an unidentified man over there."
She pointed toward a curtain separating a lounge area and an
open mechanical room guarded by a uniformed officer. A line of
crime scene tape extended around the room's exterior, tied to
stanchions hastily borrowed from somewhere nearby. Just inside
the tape lay a woman's dress purse, denoted by a yellow crime
scene marker. A middle-aged Caucasian man's body lay just
within view on the mechanical room's floor. Positioned on his
back with his feet toward the door, the man's clothing appeared
consistent with that of an orchestra musician: black slacks,
matching dress shoes, and white formal button-down, complete
with black bow tie. A black tuxedo jacket lay beside the body.
The entire left side of his shirt was stained with blood, more of
which pooled out from the back of his head, extending to a point
just past the door's threshold.

Avoiding the blood, Randall stepped into the room and bent

over the body to look for a wound. Due to the head lolling to one side, he observed the tell-tale jagged whiteness of an open skull fracture there. It reminded him of the wound found on the security guard. Unlike with the guard, this death appeared recent—within thirty minutes or so, due to the lack of coagulation to the blood. One of the body's legs was straight, while the other lay bent at a forty-five-degree angle. His right arm extended straight to the side and the other lay across his chest. He could have been dancing with an invisible partner. Stepping further into the room, Randall was surprised to see a stand-up bass resting against one wall. Donning a pair of blue latex gloves, he gently lifted it away from the wall, checking the back side of it and the wall it rested against for any obvious evidence. Nothing. Inspecting the rest of the room, he noted a blood spatter pattern consistent with the blow from a blunt instrument on the door of a circuit breaker panel. No signs of a murder weapon, and no other points of entry into the room.

"Who found him?" Randall asked the sergeant.

"One of the oboe players," she said. "He came backstage to say goodnight to the violinist before he went home. Said he figured she'd lost track of time talking to the man he'd seen her with. When he saw blood coming from under the door, he opened it and saw his friend lying there bloody."

"Where is he?"

"We've got him standing by in one of the offices."

"He try CPR?"

"No. Said he got scared when he didn't find a pulse or him breathing, then called 9-1-1."

"Well, tell him if he's got a date tonight, he'd better cancel."

After learning that a doctor had spoken with responding paramedics by phone and authorized them to officially declare death just twenty minutes ago, Randall stepped back outside the room to check the purse. "Our missing violinist's?" he asked the sergeant.

"No one else reports missing one. I ordered my folks not to touch it until you guys got here."

He knelt beside the purse and carefully opened it, déjà vu coming over him. The usual woman's articles, most notably a wallet, cellphone encased in a glittery case, and car fob attached to a ring of keys. He opened the wallet and removed a driver's license with Nicolette Dunn's name on it. The photo matched the one from the DVS query Tan had obtained on the ride here. Placing the license back where he'd found it, Randall eyed the surrounding walls and ceiling. No visible cameras. He verified with the on-duty security supervisor that there weren't any back here at all. "How many cameras does the building have?" he asked the man.

The supervisor, a tall, dour-looking man of about fifty who reminded Randall of the character Lurch from the TV show *The Addams Family*, made his way forward through the crowd of assembled officers. "Twenty-six. Five each for the building's points of entry—interior and exterior—and panoramas of the auditorium and lobby. Six on the mezzanine level, and another four on the balcony level. Plus one in the gift shop." He nodded assuredly to himself, then quickly corrected himself. "No, wait— twenty-seven. I forgot about the loading dock."

"Where's your video control center?" Whitlock asked him, stepping forward.

"In our office behind the ticket counter," the supervisor said, looking between the agent, Tan, and a still-crouching Randall. Either by some pre-determined agreement or natural ability, Randall appeared to be in charge. Settling his gaze back on the dead man, the security supervisor asked, "Who do you think killed him?"

Hearing the man's question but choosing to ignore it, Randall felt a curious sensation creep up the base of his spine, one he immediately recognized as his mind's way of telling him he'd missed something important. But yet another sensation lay behind it, one he knew could threaten to compel him to repeat that same action that had almost derailed his entire police career. Looking down at his shoes, he took a deep breath, counted to ten in his head, then stood.

"You okay?" Tan asked.

"Yeah," he said. Looking back through the open doorway into the room, he frowned. Why a professional orchestra musician would bring his instrument into such a place, without its case no less, he couldn't fathom. Pointing to the bass, he said to Tan, "Have the uniforms search for the case...Wait, there should be two of them. No one's recovered the missing woman's violin, right?"

"Correct," the sergeant offered. Tan conferred with her and quickly arranged for a search of the general area. She volunteered to aid a group of uniformed officers and the newly-arrived agents who'd originally been assigned lead tonight, all of them combining to complete a full search backstage, of all the building's offices, as well as publicly-accessible areas. Whitlock and Randall remained behind, speaking on their cellphones as they coordinated with other elements of the task force to assemble at the hall to await further instruction. Several minutes later, Tan, the group of agents, and the uniformed officers returned empty-handed. "Nothing," she said, her face grim.

Randall stood looking between the dead man and his instrument. That feeling crept further up his spine, causing his frown to deepen. As he'd done countless times before, he slipped into the killer's shoes. "I'm attending the performance, with or without the intention of taking a victim," he said, his voice introspective. "Either way, I spot her in the orchestra. She's a 'V,' the perfect end to my collection. It fits my MO to take her from her place of work, and even though I took a victim yesterday, I act on my impulse tonight. But I wouldn't have time to find a way to get her out..."

As soon as the words left his mouth, he understood. "The

case," he said, motioning to the security supervisor to take the three of them to the control center right away.

To save time, they took the witness with them and interviewed him there. He gave a voice recorded statement, which included as detailed a suspect description as he could. Almost two thousand people attended the performance. Isolating every middle-aged white male between the ages of thirty-five and fifty and in formal wear would take hours, considering how many camera shots they had to search, something they didn't have time for. Randall suggested they begin by concentrating on the movements of the various musicians as they left the building. He'd reviewed enough security footage to know the next best thing to isolating a suspect from the beginning of the crime was finding them by the end.

Inside the security room, a series of large monitors sat atop a table, each with real-time, split-screen camera images of various parts of the hall's exterior and interior. The security supervisor entered a password into a computer, brought up the camera program, then turned to face the trio. "Which cameras would you like me to pull up?"

Whitlock began to answer when the door opened, revealing a harried-looking Sergeant Fells. "Starting the party without me?" she said, her manner official. "Sorry it took me so long, I forgot my wings at home."

"Perfect timing. We're just starting the show," Randall said. He raised his eyebrows toward Whitlock, then to the bank of cameras. Keeping true to his preference for Randall and the task force's senior PD detectives to handle most of the meat and potato investigative aspects, he nodded his head deferentially toward Randall. *I'm letting you handle this*, that nod meant, so Randall turned his attention back to the security specialist. "Let's start with the main exits, lobby, and the auditorium's backstage doorway. Throw in as much of the outside walkway as you can get."

"Want me to add the loading dock?" the man offered. "We only use it for deliveries and trash pickups, but technically someone could exit there. Not trying to tell you guys how to do your jobs…"

"Yes, please," Randall said, asking the man to begin playing the footage fifteen minutes before the end of the performance, and to fast-forward until Randall asked him to stop. The four task force members stood silently watching the screens while the supervisor inputted the time—9:45 p.m.—then clicked the "play" icon, followed by the 8X selection. A second later, the previously frozen images on the screen began to play out like a 1920s-era silent movie. After the performance and most the concertgoers had left, scattered couples could be seen moving through the main mezzanine toward the lobby, along with a few lone persons, none of which even remotely resembled their suspect. Select musicians could also be seen leaving, but none of them with cases or a container large enough to fit a person inside in any fashion. But then at 10:27 p.m., less than a half-hour after the performance had ended, the image of a man fitting the suspect's description was seen walking out one of the employee exits pulling a large, wheeled instrument case nearly as long as himself.

"Go back to when he exits, then stop and zoom in," Randall said. The others leaned in closer with him as the supervisor rewound the video to a point just as the suspect exited the building. Pausing the video, he zoomed in on the man's face, captured in profile and heavily shadowed due to the back lighting. But it was definitive enough for Randall, despite this man wearing glasses and having graying hair.

"Ballsy for him to attend the symphony, even with a disguise," Randall said, removing his cellphone and pulling up a saved photo from a previous PK case. He recalled a similar-looking man—from the glasses and hair down to his height and build—from a confirmed PK case three months ago. A stripper working at a downtown gentleman's club had been kidnapped near the end of her shift. A fellow dancer reported seeing her friend and a graying man with glasses slip into one of the club's VIP rooms but couldn't remember seeing them leave. She'd done a private dance of her own and had gotten distracted by the DJ afterward. Security footage had shown the same man carrying the victim's scantily-clad body—her nipple tassels swinging as he went—out the club's back-alley door. How he'd gotten past the hulking security guard with an unconscious, mostly naked woman in his arms, the club's manager couldn't guess. The guard couldn't, either. But Randall could, knowing the frequency of shady characters slipping twenties or even hundred-dollar bills to doormen when indiscretion or even a bit of illegality was at hand. In the end, they'd gotten a palm print from the door matching that of several prior abductions attributed to PK, and a shadowy still-shot of his face. It had been dark, the alley's street-light partially obscured by a tree branch. To date, it was the best photo of the elusive kidnapper and suspected killer they had that was devoid of any sort of mask or head covering.

"Guess all the kidnapping he's been doing stoked his musical ear," Fells said from behind them. "Speaking of, have we confirmed there was only one bassist tonight?"

Tan nodded. "Yes, ma'am, it was the first thing I verified. The only other instruments tonight that were even remotely that large were cellos—three of them, a man and two women. The man is Asian and five feet nothing. We confirmed they have their instruments and cases."

"Are there any views from inside that door that can re-trace his movements?" Randall asked the supervisor.

"I'll check, but I'm pretty certain there isn't. I've watched these cameras every day for the past three years. If he started from backstage and went through the employee hallways to that exit, we wouldn't see it."

Everyone in the room grew quiet as the man selected every camera that could possibly show the suspect from a point just prior to him exiting the building. He got what he'd said he might —nothing. They'd already searched the parking garage, but sent another officer to confirm that a camera indeed covered the only exit, albeit partially. The city owned and operated the garage. Several phone calls later Randall discovered the entity responsible. Although no one answered, a recording stated that an on-call technician could be made available to law enforcement during off hours, if needed. Frustrated this had occurred on a weekend evening, Randall took the opportunity to speak with Sergeant Fells away from the others. "Any way we can get that billboard up and running by dawn, Sarge? We don't have time to waste now."

"I already notified the chief on the way here and asked him to put a rush job on it. He said he would."

Randall should have been satisfied with that, but he wasn't. That old sensation was back again, drawing up his spine like a cold finger. He was fairly certain it wasn't something he'd forgotten. It was more the possibility that he'd unknowingly seen a ghost when he and Tan had walked to the Foshay, one in the form of a passing vehicle that very well could have been spiriting away the final piece of PK's ghoulish collection.

CHAPTER 22

Sergeant Fells and the secondary detective team worked with task force agents in handling the hall's murder/kidnapping crime scenes. Randall and Tan tackled the parking garage issue. Since the hall video cut off at the far curb of the property line and only showed the suspect wheeling the case across the street toward the parking garage, it wasn't certain if he'd parked there. But conventional wisdom went that a kidnapper wheeling a woman's body inside a giant instrument case wouldn't wish to traipse across the city that way. Randall bet that the garage was by far their best option, especially since the city operated the camera system there versus private companies for other nearby garages. The prospect of discovering exactly who owned those garages and who on a Friday night was in charge of their video system was an avenue he preferred not to have to travel.

Still, dealing with the city parking authority during working hours was cumbersome; at eleven p.m. on a weekend night it was like molasses in January. As he paced the hall's security control center, listening to elevator music drone on in his phone's earpiece, Randall fought the urge to scream. He'd called the authority's main line for the purpose of paging the on-call tech responsible for all city-owned parking garages over the weekend.

He'd been waiting to talk to a human for the past five minutes, his inner clock seeming to tick at double time. Forced to wait while their killer was likely miles away depositing his next victim into his hideout was beyond frustrating. Just when he was ready to hang up and request a unit drive to the local answering service office to physically get the tech's name and phone number, someone came on the line. "Minneapolis Parking Authority," said the bored-sounding young woman. "What is the nature of—"

"This is a police emergency," Randall blurted, giving his police credentials and why he needed the tech. He had to stop himself from adding, *You'd think it was an emergency too if it was you getting ready to pose dead with a phone in your hand.*

"Oh snap, for real?" the woman said. "Hold on a sec." Maddeningly, she put him on hold, this time for only a few seconds before coming back on the line to say the tech had been notified and would notify Randall on his department cell when he arrived. In the meantime, Randall met up with Sergeant Fells, Agent Whitlock, and Detective Tan back at the murder scene. Forensics had just arrived and were busy snapping photos and gathering evidence. The ME was there too—Alicia again.

"Come here often?" he said over her shoulder and out of earshot of anyone else. She was crouched beside the dead man's body, inspecting the gash in the back of his head.

"As a matter of fact, I was here last month," she said without turning to look up at him. "Orchestra played the soundtrack to *The Godfather* while the movie played."

He crouched beside her, careful to avoid the thickened blood. "Don't you see enough death not to watch a bunch of mafia hoods gun each other down?"

"It makes me appreciate death more. It's strangely therapeutic to dig into a dead body one minute, then watch a depiction of those same insides get splattered over an elevator wall the next. Call me strange."

He canted his head as he watched her lift the corpse's closed eyelids. "Is that your way of inviting me to watch a movie with you sometime?"

She huffed. "It isn't, but I do enjoy your movie ideas. But not tomorrow; I'll have a date with Mr. Electrical Room here. And tack on an extra week or two, even after this whole business is finished—I need to make you wait since you stood me up for rollerblading at the lake."

Not wishing to argue with her here, and definitely not while she prodded in a dead man's skull, he said, "Okay. But technically I didn't stand you up. I had to notify the hairdresser's family after her Instagram pic was posted. They thought I was their Uber Eats delivery."

She turned to look at him, her blue eyes softer and more sympathetic than they'd been the last time he'd seen her. "Oh, Cal, I'm sorry. You've got to be at your wits end with this PK shit."

"I think my wits ended a long time ago," he said. He looked away and sighed resignedly. "That's it, all twenty-six of them. He did it. We don't have long before he posts on the Carlson woman, and maybe a week on this one unless he gets froggy and decides to finish it while he can. I don't know what I'll do if we don't find him in time."

She removed her gloves then placed a hand on his knee. "If it were me out there, I'd want you looking for me. Just saying." He managed a brief smile and patted her hand.

Thirty minutes later, the bassist's body was bagged and loaded into an awaiting ME van. Alicia said that after the autopsy tomorrow, it would take a few days for toxicology to come back and a definitive cause and manner of death to be made. The electrical room and hallway where Nicolette's purse was found were fully processed by forensics. To those involved with the investigation, it was no surprise when PK's fingerprints were found on the electrical room's doorknob. Still, the assembled employees and musicians who had not already left before police arrived were questioned by additional detectives and agents. One musician—a flutist—said she'd seen the bassist walk behind the curtained area with a man matching the suspect's description. She'd left with everyone else for the bar area and didn't remember seeing either man again.

"Tech's here," Randall said to Fells, having just received a phone call from the man. Giving Whitlock a heads-up (he'd been busy assembling a group of agents from D.C called in for an emergency assignment), he and Tan met the tech at the garage and immediately asked to view the footage he had available on his iPad. No shots existed showing the suspect or anyone else wheeling the case into the garage. But one did exist of a dark gray Ford Bronco exiting the garage twenty minutes after the main rush of concertgoers had already left, and just several minutes after the man had been seen wheeling the case toward the garage. The male driver's face had been obscured by a hat, with only the lower half exposed. At the point the man leaned out of the driver's seat to first insert his ticket into the machine, then several bills, Randall asked the tech to zoom the image. The man hadn't been wearing gloves. Also, the curve of his mouth appeared the same as that in other confirmed PK sightings. The jawline also. The Bronco's tag came back to someone who looked vaguely like PK, but Randall suspected he'd done as he'd seemingly done before and manufactured a fake tag that would take police time to trace. A convoluted trick, but once again, potentially effective. If PK were ever stopped by an officer who had no reasonable suspicion that he'd committed a crime, the cop wouldn't have a valid reason to detain him longer than was necessary to either issue a warning or a ticket. A VIN check would of course trip PK up, but most traffic stops didn't include that unless the vehicle was suspected of being stolen.

After examining the video several more times and having the link emailed to his department account, Randall informed both

Fells and Whitlock of his suspicions. The tingly feeling along his spine had been replaced by a confident one that said although the suspect had gotten away, at least they had a partial ID on the vehicle he'd likely used.

"We'll need those tickets," he told the tech, indicating the ticket machine. With Tan playing traffic cop for the straggler vehicles she'd cleared and that needed to exit via the entrance lane, Randall supervised as the tech opened the ticket machine and began sorting through the last several days' deposited tickets. He preferred to double-check each of the tickets' timestamps and compare them to the video footage of when the Bronco exited the garage—10:34 p.m.—here beside the machine instead of inside the hall. Despite the freezing temperatures, he felt too anxious to wait even another minute. Since the video indicated that no other vehicle had exited the garage three minutes before and four minutes after the Bronco left, all he needed was the ticket corresponding to the time it left. He just prayed that once they found it, a clear print could be lifted.

Randall donned a pair of latex gloves and began searching the first bunch of tickets. The process went fairly quickly—glance at the timestamp and discard until he found the ticket in question. He finally found it, albeit in the next batch of hundred or so tickets, since the machine was programmed to cycle them for some strange reason. Placing it into a plastic evidence bag, he tucked it into his pocket then proceeded to check all the others to verify none of them had been stamped incorrectly with the same time. They hadn't. Satisfied he had the suspect's ticket, he and Tan raced back to the building where forensics was waiting for him, according to instructions. Handing them the ticket, he exchanged hopeful glances with Fells and Tan. It wasn't long before they got their answer—the prints on it belonged to PK.

CHAPTER 23

Twelve-year-old Cal Randall runs his hand over the car's hood and grins. *"You're sure you gonna let me drive?"*

His cousin, Winnie—four years older than him—looks at him sideways. "You getting chicken on me?"

"Naw, I'll do it. I was just checkin'," Cal says, eyeing the two-door '77 Ford Pinto—white on red, with its trademark slanted rear hatch window. He's never driven before, if you didn't count his grandfather's tractor.

"You cannot tell my mom," Winnie says, pointing at him. "She'd kill me if she found out."

"I won't. And don't worry, my mom would kill me first." He starts toward the open driver's door but steps onto one of his untied shoelaces, falling onto his backside on the rural highway road top. From her position standing over him, Winnie doubles over in laughter.

"You won't have to worry about your mom killing you... you're going to kill yourself first tripping over those laces!" She wipes away tears of laughter and shakes her head pitifully as Cal picks himself off the ground.

"You're a real comedian," he says, brushing himself off.

"Why don't you ever tie your laces, anyway?"

"Because it's cool. Don't they do that up here?"

"No, silly. We actually have sense up here."

He eyes her widening grin, feeling something else is coming.

"Why did clumsy Cal get married?" she asks.

"I don't know," he says, rolling his eyes because he knows what's coming is one of her usual jokes at his expense.

"Because he fell in love!" she says and howls more laughter. Recovering, she puts on a serious face and stands akimbo. "I'm in high school now, so I won't be around during summers much anymore when you visit. Take these lessons serious. No one else up here will teach you at your age, so pay attention. Got it?"

He looks her in the eye. She jokes a lot, too often sometimes. But he knows she's serious now. "Got it."

"Got it, what?"

"Got it, cuz...becuz...I wuz...a little buzzed...on Granny's guzz..."

They both laugh. She places the ignition key into his palm. "Tell me how you'll do it."

He takes a deep breath. "Start the car...two hands on the wheel—ten o'clock, two o'clock—look over my left shoulder to make sure no one's coming behind me, 'cause you can't always trust your mirrors...press the clutch...put the gear in first, then accelerate slow as I ease off the clutch."

She smiles. "Good, just like we practiced in the driveway. Try to get through all four gears. Just make sure to pull over at the mile marker so we can switch seats."

"Okay." He begins to say something else but she's already skipping around the front of the car, her tanned legs scissoring below her short shorts. She slides in the passenger seat, but he's still standing there beside the open driver's door, awed by what's about to happen. Both their mothers are waiting for them a mile down the road, at their grandparents' farmhouse. Winnie has ostensibly driven back to her house to change clothes, Cal asking to tag along so that the two can "talk sports."

He gets in and slams the heavy door shut. He's warm all of a sudden, so he cranks the window all the way down. His heart pounds in his chest as he sits up tall behind the wheel. Their granny is even shorter than him, and if she can do it, so can he. In goes the clutch, then the key—a quarter-turn clockwise and the engine sputters to life. The gauge needles jump, and an old country song croons through the speakers.

A long look over his left shoulder—all clear. No on-coming cars, either. When he begins as instructed, the car lurches forward and stalls. He tries again. This time he gets ten feet before it stalls a second time. Frustrated, he tries yet again, but this time he lifts off the clutch more slowly and the engine smooths out. Getting the hang of it, he shifts smoothly into second and gets the Pinto up to fifteen, still on the shoulder.

"Pull onto the road," Winnie tells him, her voice excited. She turns to face him, one leg propped sideways. He does as she instructed him, and now he's doing it, he's driving. Still in second, Cal is afraid to shift into third because he doesn't want to ruin his progress, but she's encouraging him by shouting, "Third, third, put it in third!" and so he does, a nervous laugh escaping him as he completes the gear change. He gives it more gas, and now they're flying down the road, or at least it feels that way because the fastest he's ever gone himself was twenty, and that was downhill on his bicycle.

"Woo-hoo!" he hollers, gripping the wheel like she'd told him to. His teeth are bared, and when he leans forward in the seat, his eyes widen as the broken yellow lane markers blip by faster and faster. He checks his mirrors then faces ahead—still no vehicles behind him or on-coming. Their grandparents' farmhouse is only a white speck between the trees up ahead, so he knows he has another half-mile to go before he must pull off and switch with her.

"You're driving, Cal!" she yells above the radio and the wind. She's hopping up and down in her seat, her hair whipping

in her face, and in that moment he loves her more than ever, because she believes in him, and it's nice to be believed in. He enjoys seeing her, but only gets the chance two or three times a year since her parents stayed in the small town when his moved to the Cities before he was born. He's smiling from ear to ear as he bobs his head to the music. He's watching her smile too, but then her smile disappears and her eyes go wide as she suddenly points a finger at the windshield.

It happens quicker than he remembers it years later, on sleepless nights or long walks around the lakes, or even while working a case and he learns someone's name is the same as hers. Winifred, but he knows it's really Winnie. Memories can be cruel, he'll discover. Cruel like a knife twisted in your guts. Afterward, the sight of a deer will induce crippling anxiety. A girl's high-pitched voice will make him shiver. Even the sound of crunching metal and the smell of pulverized glass, things he won't experience often, will make it feel like it's happening all over again.

Worse than the sight of her blood and brains all over him is the memory of sitting dazed on the shoulder, his mother and auntie and grandparents running down the road toward the wrecked car, yelling. And him looking down at his untied shoes, knowing he could have braked in time had the laces not become tangled in the accelerator.

CHAPTER 24

A bby dreamed of zombies chasing her. After she woke, Frederik allowed her to dress in a fresh change of clothes he'd either bought or already had stored away. Contrary to the day before when he'd been first gracious, then aggressive as he'd tried to force himself on her, his demeanor now was markedly reserved, distant even.

"You can use the real bathroom," he said, leading her out of the room once she'd dressed in the blue jeans, long-sleeved undershirt, and sweater he'd thrown on the bed beside her. At least grateful she didn't have to use the bucket, Abby walked tentatively toward the bathroom, thinking she heard a woman's soft whimper from behind the door of the room beside hers. Entering the bathroom, she dutifully left the door open and had just dropped her jeans and underwear and sat down when she emptied her full bladder. She washed up, not bothering to look for any avenues of escape, or a weapon to use against him. The room was just as barren as it had been the day before—only a plastic garbage can, toilet paper and hand towel, and a travel pack of pink tissues in the cabinet. When she exited, she half-expected him to be leaning against the wall and watching her, that sick grin on his face. He wasn't. Instead, he was sitting on the same chair he'd sat her in the day she'd arrived—*when was that, two days ago, three?*—when she'd had that fucking ball-gag in her mouth. As she walked across the cold floor in her stockinged feet, she watched in amazement as Frederik stretched his head so far back and to his right that it seemed to touch his shoulder blade. When he noticed her looking at him, he turned on the chair to face her. The violin and bow lay in his lap. "Eighteen hours sleep, impressive. You'll probably be up all night now."

She searched his expression for anything that would tell her if he was mad or not, but his face was a blank canvas. He must have read her mind because he said, "I'll forgive your rejection, for now. But your transition process can't happen until you're purified. I've taken all the others in order, but..." He shrugged, a little pout appearing on his face. It disappeared a fraction of a second later. "Have you ever been to the symphony?" He plucked one of the violin's strings.

Abby wanted to break his eye contact but couldn't bring herself to. Hell, she wanted to fly away. "I've never been, but I've always wanted to play the violin," she said, surprising herself with her candidness. *What do you have to lose? He's going to turn you into a goddamned doll soon enough.*

He shot to his feet so quickly she flinched. Initially, she thought she'd said something to upset him. But as soon as that thought passed through her brain, she realized she'd done the opposite when she saw his expression brighten. "How wonderful!" He set the violin and bow on the chair then came to her. In the span of ten seconds he'd turned from a pouting middle-aged man into an exuberant little boy. "I know the perfect after-dinner treat for later. A concert for you and me—with her on the violin." He turned to look in the direction of the closed door where Abby had heard the muffled cry, before meeting her eyes again. Smiling, he took her by her limp hands and leaned toward her. At first, she thought he was going to kiss her. Instead, he moved his mouth to beside her ear and whispered, "But for now, I've got a different surprise for you."

Before Abby could utter a word, Frederik spun her around and began leading her forcibly by the arm toward the darkened, doorless room at the end of the open space. When they crossed beneath the room's archway, he flipped on the bright fluorescent overheads, temporarily blinding her. "Stay here," he told her, rummaging through a nearby drawer. When her eyes adjusted to the light, she noticed a stainless steel table large enough to hold a person's body, in the middle of the tile floor. A black, rubber block with a head-sized indentation rested at one end of the table. Affixed to the ceiling above it was an industrial sprayer, the flexible steel hose enabling its user to easily wash whatever lay beneath. It reminded Abby of a hospital surgical room. A black machine containing a five-gallon tank sat on the floor beside the table. Two plastic hoses were attached to opposite sides of the tank's base and lay coiled on the counter above it. Several jugs of pinkish solution and a couple more of clear solution sat beside the hoses, while a full makeup kit and an assortment of hairstyling equipment occupied the counter's far end.

Suddenly, everything clicked in Abby's mind. His comments about having to first keep the women in the cooler...one of the upstairs rooms that had reminded her of a small wedding chapel...the service elevator...it all made sense now. She was in an old funeral home, one that families used to both live in and operate the business. Her mind spinning, she realized something else that should have been obvious right away—this room is where he "transitioned" the women.

As the thought connected in Abby's brain, Frederik positioned himself behind her and placed both hands on her slumped shoulders. She flinched, sure he was going to place her atop the table and begin to do ungodly things to her body, either alive or dead. He'd mentioned a surprise for her. But instead, he led her to a high-backed wooden chair positioned several feet beside the table. "Sit, please," he said. When she did, he brought her arms behind her back and began handcuffing her to a metal ring attached to the chair. She badly wanted to struggle. In a host of horrible things she'd seen and experienced already, some inner sense told her what was about to happen would be much worse. But she knew better than to resist him, remembering his earlier warning that if she did, she wouldn't like the punishment.

"I'll leave your legs alone if you promise to sit still," he said, coming around to squat in front of her. He fed a padlock through a hook attached to one of the chair's legs, then again through a hook bolted to the floor before securing it. When he looked up at her, his smile was gone. In its place sat a curious expression that suggested he was both sorry for what she was about to endure, and excited. "I'm going into the other bedroom now. When I come back, you'll see something that may upset you. But it's important for you to watch. I wouldn't want to cheat you out of what the others all got to see." His smile returned then, if only for a flash, and then he stood and walked out of view. She heard the sound of a key into a lock, then an opening door.

"Hello, sweetie," Abby heard him say before the door closed. For a moment, no response came, but soon she heard Frederik's muffled voice through the door. Abby caught about every second or third word, piecing together the conversation through context. He was telling someone how beautiful they were, and something else about him being honored if she would have him voluntarily, because having to force her wouldn't be the same thing. A woman's sudden sobbing then, her words sounding like, "Please don't kill me...I'll do whatever you want..." but Abby couldn't be sure, because now the woman was sobbing uncontrollably. Frederik's voice, low and soothing, telling her to stand and undress, then to kneel on all fours on the edge of the bed because that's the way it had to start. Strangely, the woman's sobbing stopped when he said that. It was as if the act of sex—or more aptly, rape—had ignited some distant hope inside of her, that pleasing him with her body might preserve the tiniest chance of salvation she had left. Her own heart thudding inside her chest, Abby adjusted the position of her arms behind her. He'd placed the cuffs tight. But whatever his reason for doing so, he'd wanted to ensure she would hear what was happening. That smile of his when he'd told her he was going next door...

Soon, the sound of creaking bedsprings came through the door. As Abby adjusted her position, she bent her head back to stretch her neck and noticed an air vent in the ceiling. Staring at it, she realized the sounds she heard weren't coming through the distant door like she'd figured, but likely through a shared vent. Closing her eyes, Abby tried her best to block out Frederik's grunts and the coinciding creaking bedsprings—the combination forming a grotesque harmony—but she couldn't. Beneath those noises she heard the woman's cries, muffled as if through a blanket or pillow. It went on for what could have been minutes or hours, it seemed. Throughout, Abby felt her flesh grow cold with her own distant memories of her past, ones she'd tried to drink or eat or cry away over the years but had been unable. But chained up here, she knew that if she was going to properly confront those demons, in particular to ever get the chance to finally stand up to the man who for years had made her feel subhuman, she'd have to do it by using every bit of mental strength she possessed. Opening her eyes, she lowered her head and stared dumbly at the table, imagining what had occurred there while processing the familiar sounds of custodial rape that were coming through the vent. She decided right then that if she somehow made it out of here, she'd crawl on her hands and knees all the way to the prison if she had to.

Frederik's voice came again through the vent, thick with lust. "I want you...Turn around...Tell...that you love me... "

Something told Abby that if she didn't try something now, she'd never have the chance again. She pulled and twisted against the cuffs with all her might, but the metal strands dug painfully into her wrists and wouldn't budge. She'd never get the cuffs off without the key, and he likely had it on his person. She looked around the room for anything she could use as an aid. A rubber-matted tray lined with surgical tools sat on the far counter. But the embalming table was in the way. Spotting the nearest drawer and estimating it might be close enough for her to reach with her foot, she managed to remove one sock by stepping on it and pulling. Twisting her upper body to allow her hip more movement, she stretched her leg toward the drawer. But even with her pointed foot, her toes were still several inches from the handle. Lowering her leg, she paused a moment before lifting it again, this time rotating her hip the way she did sometimes to kick higher during her body combat class at the gym. This time her toes got to within an inch. On her third try, they barely brushed the handle, not quite close enough to get them wrapped around it.

Taking a deep breath, she'd just tried again when the woman in the other room let out a bloodcurdling scream. Abby's leg froze in mid-air, as did her own heart in her chest for several beats. Lowering her leg and bending as far forward as the cuffs would allow her, she tried to see the doorway where the scream had come from, but the angle was too great. Then, the woman's voice cried out in a pitch higher than her speaking voice: "No! Oh God, no!" Frederik said something in response, but his voice was too low to distinguish his words. Then the woman's voice again, this time with increased desperation. "Please...I can't do that...I'll do anything else..."

Abby wasn't sure, but it sounded like Frederik was trying to soothe her. He could easily overpower the woman and get what he wanted, but Abby sensed that he preferred to be pleased by a willing partner—if you could call anything done under these conditions "willing." She herself had resisted him without being sexually violated, but she knew he'd try again. As for the violinist, she'd apparently already submitted to him. But whatever he wanted her to do now sounded far worse than what he'd already done, judging from the woman's pleas. A pause, then something happening that Abby fantasized was him telling the woman that he'd let her go when he was finished with her, the dietitian too, because he finally realized what he was doing and how wrong it was. He was making her hook her pinky finger with his and promise that she'd never tell. The woman would be nodding furiously, her tears streaking her makeup. But her face would be a mixture of gratefulness and relief, because although he was readying to violate her in some awful new way, she would survive.

Whatever did happen ended several minutes later, followed by a momentary pause, then the woman's voice, each word clear to Abby because she was shouting them, their tone haunting and animalistic as if she sensed they may be the last she ever spoke. "No! Don't kill me! I did what you wanted! I'll move out of state if you let me go! Wherever you want! I won't tell anyone! I won't even come back to visit family! Pleeeeease!"

A shushing sound from him, followed by the sound of a violent struggle. It seemed to go on forever. Abby hummed to herself, trying to block out the noises, but it was no use. The thrashing and banging of bodies and limbs on the bed and walls was too much to block out. Finally, a period of eerie silence as the struggle died down to what sounded like someone pressing a weighted object down hard into the bed several times, until even that stopped. Abby strained her ears to hear any clue about what else may be happening. Nothing for several agonizing minutes, until the sound of an opening door, then approaching footsteps, and finally Frederik appearing in the room's entranceway with the woman's limp, naked body draped in his arms. Her face was turned toward Abby, the wide-open eyes resembling a horror movie poster girl. Mouth hanging open, her tongue lolled from her parted, bluish lips. The unnatural paleness of her skin contrasted with the flaming red hair hanging from her head. A matching triangle of hair sat above her pubic region.

Abby glanced away guiltily. Having heard what had happened to the woman was bad enough. Seeing her in such a vulnerable state seemed so much dirtier with her being dead. An affront worse than anything that she could have endured in life, if that was possible. Although barefoot, Frederik was fully dressed, his baggy dress shirt untucked and the top several buttons undone. His hair was mussed, and a fresh, bleeding scratch ran down one cheek. Abby stared first into the woman's dead eyes, then down to the bright, finger-sized marks around her throat.

"It was beautiful," Frederik said simply, his eyes dreamy. He stood there holding her like that for what seemed an eternity. Then focusing his next words directly to Abby, he spoke as a teacher would to a student before an especially important lecture. "When I begin, you mustn't look away or cry out. It'll ruin the experience for both of us. Plus, it's imperative I get her right the first time. Understand?"

Abby nodded once.

"Excellent," he said, smiling for the first time since he'd been standing there. He laid the woman's body gently atop the table, taking extra care in placing the base of her head in the block's crook. The result was the woman now lying perfectly supine, with her chin slightly raised and the back of her head lifted a few inches off the table's surface. A sink and long-armed faucet sat at the table's head. The table itself was tilted slightly toward the foot end; a welled depression that ran the entire inner edge of the table ended with a drain hole, spout, and high-lipped floor drain. She'd somehow missed seeing a set of ceiling-mounted pulleys and cinching straps bolted to all four walls, each appearing capable of supporting a significant amount of weight held in adjustable positions. Unhooking one of the straps at the head of the table, Frederik looped one end through a ceiling pulley then fastened it around the corpse's left thigh. He pulled the other end of the strap until the leg bent at a forty-five-degree angle, then locked it into place. After repeating the same process with the right leg, he tilted the corpse's head to the left so that the ear was several inches from the left shoulder. Leaving the room momentarily, he returned with the violin and bow. Careful to tuck the instrument's chin rest between the corpse's cheek and the left shoulder, he adjusted the positioning of the head several times before appearing satisfied with the fit. Using another strap, he positioned the left arm, hand, and fingers to grip the violin's neck. He did the same with the right arm and hand, manipulating the fingers to grip the bow. Taking a step back, he assessed his handiwork. In spite of the corpse being naked and on its back, it was easy to imagine her later seated in a chair while playing her cherished instrument. "What do you think?" Frederik said aloud without looking away from the corpse.

From her seat five feet from the dead woman, Abby blinked. "Are you asking me?"

He turned to her and frowned. "Well, I'm certainly not asking *her* how she thinks of herself, am I? She isn't vain like that."

"I...I think her knees should be higher," Abby suggested. "If she's going to be playing, she wouldn't be sitting straight up. She'd be leaning a bit forward with the emotion of the music, like this..." Despite the handcuffs biting into her wrists, she demonstrated the best she could, adding the effect of tilting her head to the side to mimic someone holding an invisible violin to their shoulder.

Frederik looked between Abby and the strapped corpse several times before nodding. "You're right. And it'll be easier to get her legs higher than tilting her body forward. You're such a good helper." He adjusted the leg straps and locked them in place before looking over his shoulder at her. "Like this?"

She nodded, knowing he was pleased with her. Still, she dropped her head submissively, remembering where she was and what was occurring, but mostly to not appear any more complicit to his actions than she'd already been.

Frederik retrieved a scalpel, a thin metal instrument with a blunt hook at the end, and pair of elongated clamps from the tray. "Since you won't get to see your own transitioning, make sure you pay attention," he said, turning a studious eye toward Abby. "I'd rather do this in her groin to keep her neck pretty, but her legs are bent." He stood on the opposite side of the table so that she could see what he was doing. Angling the woman's head toward him and exposing the right side of her neck, Frederik picked up the scalpel and made a four-inch-long incision beginning just above her collarbone and ending below her ear. A thin line of blood dripped down her neck as the skin and underlying tissue separated, but nothing came from the wound after he wiped it clean with gauze. "Afterward, maybe you and I can go upstairs and visit some of the others you haven't met yet. I'm sure they could use the company." When he said that, his smile broadened, and a sparkle came to his eyes. Bending over the body with the confidence of an experienced technician, he inserted the hooked end of the thin instrument into the incision and raised the deeply-set jugular vein above the skin's surface, sliding the instrument beneath it so that it wouldn't slip back in. It resembled a worm being pulled from a white patch of earth. Tying the vein off at a point closest to the ear, he pricked a small hole in it with a pair of tweezers. Retrieving a thin, L-shaped metal tubular device containing a plastic cannula, he inserted the end of the metal tube into the vein in the direction of the feet. He then fed the cannula through the metal tube and several inches into the vein, leaving the exposed end to lie in the table's welled depression. Next, Frederik raised the carotid artery, tied it off, and inserted a second cannula into it, all in a similar fashion. The other end of this tube was connected to the machine on the floor.

Stepping back behind the table, he poured the contents of all the jugs into the machine before returning to the table and tilting the corpse's head toward him so that Abby could see what he was doing. When he reached behind him and flipped a switch on the machine, the sudden buzzing sound it made caused her to jump in her seat. He must have noticed because he turned to her with a look of deep regret.

"Yeah, I should have warned you about that. It's an older system and can be cranky sometimes, but it works better than the new one I bought last month. Too bad I couldn't return it used." He patted the machine's top like a proud father. Ensuring that the embalming fluid was properly flowing through the artery tube, thus forcing the blood through the body's veins, he made a satisfied sound when blood soon began pouring from the exposed jugular tube into the table's edge depression. He turned the sink faucet on, and water mixing with expelled blood turned the table's ringed depression into a flowing pink river. When the expelled fluid turned clear several minutes later, he tied off the punctured area of the vessels with suturing string, then sewed the wound closed with a baseball-type stitch. As he worked, the last of the fluid in the depression dribbled through the tube and gurgled down the drain.

"Unfortunate that she won't get to watch a transitioning too," Frederik said as he unhooked the ceiling-mounted sprayer. "But life isn't always fair." He shampooed and rinsed the corpse's hair, then scrubbed the body using a soapy-smelling solution. Working quickly over the perky breasts and pubic region, he rinsed the body then finished by cleaning out the mouth, ears, and nose with chemical-soaked Q-tips. Into her cheeks went a handful of cotton balls, followed by him inserting a wire suture into her upper mandible and lower gums with a gun-like device, then twisting the wires to close the mouth. He placed a plastic hook into each corner of her mouth, tied strings to the eyelets, then pulled upward. When her smile was just right, he tied the strings around her ears. He finished by dabbing a spot of glue onto each of her eyelids, then lifted them and held them in place for a full minute. When he released them, the eyes remained open.

As Abby watched Frederik apply a floral-smelling lotion onto the body and begin massaging first the limbs, then the face and torso with loving strokes, she understood that he wasn't just preserving the woman's body, he was preserving the moment for himself. The kidnapping itself wasn't his thing. It wasn't even killing them. This was the ritual he performed in front of each victim. Whatever he did to them sexually in the next room was just a preamble to his ultimate ecstasy. His true orgasm had nothing to do with his dick or mouth or fingers. It wasn't until this moment that Abby understood his terms of "purifying" and "transitioning" meant much more than rape or a physical conversion from life to life-like; he successively became a part of them one at a time. The other women in the house—many with hopes and dreams and perhaps painful pasts like hers—hadn't stood a chance with him. Even scarier than the thought of death itself was the thought of being forever frozen in form, with no one she had left in the world—Derek and her best girlfriends from the center, mostly—ever getting the chance to see her again.

Abby began to feel light-headed. The combination of Frederik's playful attitude, the sound of the machine, and the room's overpowering antiseptic smell finally hit her full-force. It reminded her of her high school science lab when she'd dissected a frog, except instead of a stone-faced instructor droning on about preserved amphibians, it was a serial killer turning female corpses into dolls. She continued watching like someone forced to witness a slow execution. Each time she glanced away she quickly looked back when she detected Frederik glancing over to check if she was still watching.

"Now, the fun part." He cast her a wicked grin and made his eyebrows do a quick *here we go* motion. Picking up the scalpel again, Frederik made a small, bloodless incision near the corpse's belly button then retrieved a foot-long, pen-shaped steel instrument from the surgical tray. Its solid triangular head was razor-sharp, with an elongated hole an inch down its length to collect fluid through an inner metallic sleeve. The device— similar to those used in arthroscopic surgical procedures—had a grip at its opposite end, enabling its user to easily probe into a body. A long plastic tube was connected to the sleeve and the grip's base, which Frederik in turn connected to a different section of the machine. After selecting the "suction" option, he returned to the body and placed the instrument's point into the belly button incision. Leaning over like a billiard player about to take a shot, he planted one hand on the corpse's stomach and pushed the skin above the incision taut toward the head. He angled the instrument toward a specific part of the abdomen and was about to push it in when he paused to look back at Abby. "This part may be the worst for you, but it's vital to the process. We wouldn't want the girls to get sick, now would we?"

Moments after he drove the instrument deep into the body, an audible chugging sound came from the machine as fluid and gases began to suck first through the instrument, through the length of clear tubing, then into it. When that happened, the abdomen depressed slightly, as if the corpse had just expelled a deep breath. As Abby watched, she became even more light-headed. Her stomach knotted and her mouth began to water, all familiar indicators that she was going to throw up. Desperate to avoid doing so, lest he become angry with her, she pretended the body had not once been human. A doll, or mannequin built for practicing such things, like the dummy she'd once worked on during a high school CPR class. But she knew the body *had* once been alive; she'd heard the woman's pleas and screams, even her involuntary groans when Frederik had raped her. And the music-themed tattoo with floaty music staffs and notes visible on her sides and upper back only confirmed that. The more she watched, the harder Abby fought to keep herself from being sick. But when the hose jerked as more material passed through it, Abby's stomach lurched. Turning her head to the side, she vomited onto the floor, some of the sour-tasting fluid dripping down her chin. It felt warm against her skin. For some reason, perhaps because it reminded her that for now, she was still alive, the warmth comforted her.

He alternated withdrawing and inserting the instrument at different angles within the chest cavity, careful to avoid withdrawing it back through the skin during the fluid suction. When that was done, he did the same to the abdomen. Like before, the machine made its wet chugging sound and the hose did its jumping thing. Abby flinched every time, despite knowing what was coming. He could do it a thousand times and she'd never get used to it. When he was finally finished, several lines of reddish-clear fluid extended from the incision down the corpse's sides.

"This last part doesn't take nearly as long," he said, affixing the stabbing instrument's hose to a large bottle of clear solution marked "Cavity Fluid." He held the bottle above his head with one hand then fitted the instrument's tip into the belly incision with the other. "When I'm done, you can help me dress her and do her hair. I always appreciate a woman's touch."

CHAPTER 25

When he finished and enough time had passed for him to be satisfied that the corpse would remain in its manipulated position, Frederik went to uncuff Abby. She became aware of the time, date, and day of the week—2:10 a.m.; November 9; Sunday—when he reached across her to undo the lock securing the chair to the floor, exposing his digital wristwatch. He caught her looking at it but didn't seem to mind. When he uncuffed her, she brought her arms from behind her and groaned with relief. Her shoulders ached inexorably; they'd been in that position for hours already. She shook them out, as well as rubbing her wrists and kneading the blood back into her hands and fingers, not bothering to ask his permission to do so. He stood patiently by while she did so, humming to himself. Rotating her arms to stretch her shoulders, Abby averted her eyes from the weirdly positioned corpse. He noticed and tsked. "Now, now, no looking away. Remember our deal."

She forced her eyes back onto the body, rolling them in the process and not caring if he noticed. Fuck him. He did seem to notice and lowered his head as if to try drawing her gaze onto him. She refused to make eye contact with him, though. If he was going to make her watch what he was doing, fine. But he hadn't yet insisted on her looking at *him*. She would if he promised to hurt or force himself on her. But he didn't. Instead, he seemed content with having her help him comb and do the corpse's hair, at times running his fingers through the strawberry-hued locks while he gazed into the glued-open eyes. He undid the strap holding the left leg in place and tried to press it down flat. It didn't budge. Doing the same with the other limbs achieved the same result. Grabbing the body around its shoulders with the apparent intention of turning it on its side, he paused and shot Abby a hopeful expression. "Mind giving me a hand? She's more awkward than heavy."

Like a robot, Abby went to stand beside him. Her shoulders slumped; her arms hung limp at her sides. "What should I do?"

"Be a sweetie and take her feet. I'll hold the heavy end." Abby looked dumbly at the corpse's bent legs before grasping the cold, hard-as-concrete ankles. She shuddered, but did her best not to show it. "There you go," he said, gathering the makeup kit. "We'll dress her upstairs. On three…" When it was time, they lifted together and carried the naked corpse into the main room. As Abby shuffled behind him, she tried to block out the thought of what she was doing. She was an actor carrying a prop, nothing more. Still, some inner purpose drove its way into her consciousness as she reminded herself that she had to do something to try to save herself. As ridiculous as it seemed, she understood that she was literally carrying a giant piece of evidence.

When they reached the elevator, he keyed it then led the way inside. Due to the cramped space, he couldn't fully turn to face her. He pressed a button, and the elevator began to slowly rise. Soon they'd be on the main floor. Desperate to do anything constructive, she tried to think of how to possibly inform someone on the outside of what was happening. Perhaps to somehow put a mark on the body in case it was discovered after Abby herself was dead. Anything to let the authorities know she'd been here and at least tried to notify them. But that seemed just as impossible as escaping, she decided. She almost laughed with the ridiculous notion that in carrying a dead woman, she'd even have one chance in a million of letting the authorities know she was doing so. But before she could think of anything, the elevator stopped and the door creaked open, then he led them into the frigid hallway. *It must be forty degrees up here*, she thought. "Right through here," he said, leading her through the living room and into an office. Panicked, Abby realized that this would be the only time she'd have access to the woman's body —and probably any of the others—outside of his direct view. After she placed the corpse's feet on the floor and straightened, he knelt facing away from her and began to adjust the feet. Standing behind the corpse, a sudden thought struck her. Instead of *leaving* a trace on the woman, she would *take* some. Reaching out, she plucked a wild hair from the corpse's head and quickly wrapped it around her finger. A second later, Frederik snapped his head around, his eyes narrowing with what seemed like suspicion. "Nope..." he began.

Abby's heart stopped in her chest. She balled her fingers into a tight fist, fearful that he'd uncurl them one at a time and discover what she'd done. When he did, he'd unwrap the hair and shake his head. *I told you what would happen if you tried anything. Now instead of making it last hours, I'll make it last days...*

But instead of grabbing her hand and forcing her fingers to uncurl, he straightened and pointed past her at the open doorway across the hall. "The study. I should have thought of that." Abby almost cried out in relief when he instructed her to pick up the corpse's feet again. They carried the body to where he'd indicated, this time Frederik directing Abby to help him set the body on its back. The result was the violinist appearing like some mannequin discarded on a department store floor. Bringing Abby with him to another room, he picked up a chair, a music stand,

and a plastic bag and carried them back into the study, setting them down in the room's lone empty corner. Abby had kept her head low, but now she looked up to see a short Latina woman in jockey gear against a long wall, crouched atop a galloping carousel horse. Her riding boots set into the metal stirrups, she held her whip victoriously aloft. Wallpaper depicting a cheering crowd scene took up the entire ten-foot wall behind her. At one of the shorter walls, a mid-thirties, olive-complexioned woman dressed in blue jeans, a cream-colored blouse, and a hijab stood at a blackboard. She touched a piece of chalk to the board; behind her a row of life-sized plastic children's dolls sat at toy school desks. A third woman—a smiling brunette in tight blue jeans and a low-cut t-shirt—stood behind a mini bar with a Boston shaker held over one shoulder in the classic double-handed grip. A pair of martini glasses filled with clear liquid and an olive garnish sat on the bar top in front of her.

"Would you like a drink?" Frederik asked Abby, making her jump. He'd approached beside her silently, like a cat.

"No, thank you," she said, rubbing the goosebumps that had risen on her covered arms.

"Well, let me know if you'd like one in the morning. Brittany here makes a mean Bloody Mary." Motioning back toward the violinist on the floor, Frederik dug into the bag and handed Abby a pair of items. "I'll let you put these on her. I'd imagine she'd be a bit shy if I did it." Abby dutifully accepted the pair of lacy black panties and matching bra he offered. "Let me know when you're done." He cleared his throat and turned to the side.

For an insane moment, Abby considered stepping behind him and wrapping the bra around his throat and trying to strangle him. But that wouldn't work, of course. He'd spin around and overpower her in seconds. Two hours from now she too would be sitting like concrete beside the redhead. Of all the things she'd seen or experienced in the past two days, the prospect of what she was now forced to do filled her with the most revulsion yet.

But it had to be done. Dreading her task, she knelt and fitted the panties first over one hardened foot, then the other. Sliding them up the likewise hardened legs and bent knees, she adjusted them over the corpse's slender hips, glad at least she no longer had to look at the exposed tuft of red hair between her legs. Once that was done, she did the bra, doing her best to slide it up and over the perky, hardened breasts without touching the clammy skin. "Okay, I'm done," she said, stepping backward and wiping her hands on her pants legs.

He turned and glanced the body over. "Thanks for doing that. It saved her and me some embarrassment. Almost done now." Digging into the bag and removing the same black evening gown the woman had worn the night of the performance, Frederik bent and slipped it first through her left arm, over her head, then through her more awkwardly bent right arm. After zipping her up, he extracted the same black low-heeled shoes she'd worn and placed them onto her feet. To Abby, that last part reminded her of the prince in Cinderella, kneeling to slip the lost glass slipper on every maiden in the land.

"Over there," he said, nodding toward the chair and music stand he'd arranged.

When the violinist was properly seated in her chair, Frederik secured her to it with a support bracket around her waist. He did the same to each of her legs, securing them below the knees against the chair's front legs with Velcro straps, then draping the dress over them. After positioning the violin and bow to his satisfaction, he adjusted the music stand in front of her. Last came her makeup, a task he seemed intent on doing himself, applying foundation, eyeliner, lipstick, and a bit of blush from the case he'd brought from downstairs. "There!" he exclaimed, clapping his hands together. A huge smile spread across his face, the dimples in his cheeks deeper than ever. He stood there a moment to take in his finished work, a sculptor appreciating his own masterpiece. His eyes gleamed with pride. His chest heaved in excitement. Removing a Polaroid camera from a desk drawer, he snapped a series of instant photos, each taken from different angles. After choosing the photo he liked the best, he cut each of the others into a dozen pieces with a pair of scissors then set them atop the desk. "We'll burn those later. As for her...what do you think?" he asked, indicating the violinist.

Abby forced a smile and used a word she knew he'd appreciate. "She's...beautiful."

"I'm so glad you aren't the jealous type," he said, beaming. He pulled a book from the bookcase and plopped down onto an oversized chair. Propping his feet on the ottoman, he opened the book as if to gauge the reading experience with his newest addition. "Yes, having her in here is perfect. I always love reading to music."

CHAPTER 26

At nine-thirty Sunday morning, all fifty-five members of the PK task force assembled in the PSB Homicide office. Not that it hadn't been all together before during the abduction spree. But for the first time since a twenty-year-old professional figure skater from White Bear Lake had been abducted early on in the spree and her apparently embalmed body photographed and posted on Instagram, all members of the force were present at the same time.

"I hope everyone got a few minutes of sleep last night, because it may be the last you get for a while," Whitlock said from the front of the room, diving straight in. He looked around at the various faces staring back at him, the bags beneath each of their eyes evidence that they'd indeed gotten little sleep. After the Dunn woman had been abducted Friday night, they'd all been ordered to remain on standard duty until further notice. Since then they'd worked through the first half of the defunct funeral homes on Randall's list. No leads yet, per the UC's assigned to watch them.

"As you know, we've confirmed victim twenty-six," Whitlock went on to say. "Sergeant Fells just briefed the chief and city manager, and I've spoken with the FBI director. If we need an airplane to buy a pencil in Seattle, make it happen. We've got the keys to Ft. Knox from here on out." He flipped off the lights and powered up the overhead projector. "Case in point, we implemented Detective Randall's billboard idea yesterday afternoon. For those unfamiliar, it's located on the I-94 downtown approach, near the Spoonbridge and Cherry. Not a new idea, as you all know, but the message is. We're deploying surveillance teams for a series of out-of-date funeral homes, but it could take a few days to eliminate them all. The billboard may be a long shot, but even one solid tip could save resources."

A photograph image of an electronic billboard appeared on the screen. It depicted a giant magnifying glass with the words *HELP CATCH PK!* emblazoned across the top. A grainy black-and-white surveillance photo of their suspect's face sat along the board's lefthand side, with the message *TO ALL AREA REALTORS—SEEKING INFO ON PAST HOME-STYLE FUNERAL HOME SHOWINGS/SALES TO PERSONS MATCHING THIS DESCRIPTION.* Along the bottom was the taskforce hotline number, along with the logos for the MPD, and both local offices for the FBI and BCA. A large QR code sat at the board's bottom right.

"I want our hotline phones manned twenty-four seven," Whitlock explained, turning the lights back on. "I don't care if those folks need to piss in a milk jug, no one leaves those desks unattended."

After the meeting broke an hour later and with surveillance teams already in place on the next batches of homes, Randall and Tan rode down to the building's café to grab a quick to-go breakfast. While still in line, Randall got a call from a detective who'd been assigned to triage incoming hotline tips. "We've got three possibles since daybreak, he said.

Randall stepped out of line and found an empty space on the

counter. He pulled a napkin from a nearby dispenser and removed a pen from his jacket pocket. "Go ahead."

The detective described three tips deemed "hot" from the billboard ad. The first two were too far off the mark to expend immediate resources on, Randall judged, but the third piqued his interest. A caller said he'd sold a defunct, family-style funeral home nearly two years ago to a single man intending it for residential use. White, mid-fifties, six foot, and maybe two hundred pounds, from what he remembered. Not exact, but eyewitness testimony was often sketchy, and the suspect could have had the foresight to disguise himself then, too, Randall judged. "Thank you," he told the detective, jotting the listed owner's name and address down. It corresponded with one of the homes he'd planned on personally checking today. He met Tan at the café's exit and gratefully accepted the egg bagel she'd gotten him, then described the tip during their elevator ride back up to the office. He gave her the task of further researching the home's ownership record and the man's background, while he coordinated with an undercover team. They'd move this home to the top of the list. Assuming the owner was home, Randall would pose as a salesmen or some other unofficial citizen when knocking. If the home was deemed suspicious, or if anyone matched the suspect's description, they'd request a probable cause search warrant and enact full surveillance. If no one answered, they'd place a team on it until someone showed. An iffy proposition, for sure. But they'd endured a thousand disappointments with the case already. It was all a reminder that the killer was always one step ahead, while they were left chasing their own tails.

A half hour later, he and Tan prepared to head to the property with an undercover unit serving as backup. Selecting a stack of homemade religious pamphlets he kept in his desk for such occasions, Randall shrugged on a plainclothes jacket over his ballistic vest, and switched to an ankle holster. He stuffed his badge into his pocket. It was important that whoever answered the door or anyone in the immediate area see no connection to the police.

They parked a block away. The house, a century-old, two-story Victorian, sat in a non-descript, middle-class residential neighborhood fifteen minutes' drive from downtown. Using binoculars, Randall checked for movement to or from the home, or obvious indicators of criminal activity. Nothing suspicious. "Keep watch, and don't transmit or call for backup unless you see me shooting," Randall said, handing Tan the binos. "UC unit is half a block back if you need them."

"You sure you don't want me coming with?" she asked.

"Yep. Too many chefs spoil the soup," he answered, hopping out with the bag of pamphlets. As he approached the home, Randall noted its wrought-iron fence as well as burglar bars on the first- and second-floor windows. A long driveway led up to a side entrance then an attached garage. The burglar bars weren't unusual for this type of neighborhood, but were still something to consider since the suspect's criminal profile indicated he'd take extreme caution with his hideout. Randall tried the spiked pedestrian gate and was surprised to find it unlocked. Walking up the staircase to the covered wood porch, he peeked inside the barred bay window but found it covered by a heavy curtain. He knocked on the front door and waited patiently until a fiftyish white male with graying hair and glasses opened the door. The man stepped halfway out, his body blocking Randall's view past him. "Can I help you?" he asked, eyeing Randall suspiciously.

Randall went into his rehearsed spiel declaring himself a member of a local spiritual organization, and offered the man a pamphlet. When the man respectfully declined, Randall shifted his attention to the home itself. "Beautiful place. Looks big enough for a B&B."

The man shrugged resignedly. "I thought about doing that when I first bought the place. A good way to make money while living in your business. Unfortunately, the girls had something else to say about it."

Adrenalin surged through Randall's veins. He forced a congenial smile. "Aha. Would the ladies of the house like some of this literature? I don't like being pushy with our group's message, but Jesus didn't save humankind by taking no for an answer."

As the man paused and seemed to consider something, Randall committed every aspect of his physical description to memory. Six-foot-one, early fifties (or maybe younger, if the gray in his hair was the result of a wig), and although the build wasn't the same, the man's clothes were baggy. His facial features seemed a bit off, too, but the composite sketch they'd created for PK wasn't from a full-frontal shot of his face. And he'd always worn a disguise. They'd need a close-up shot, including both of his eyes without glasses, to even consider facial recognition comparison at some point. Randall considered pulling out his phone and snapping a picture of the man, maybe by faking an internet search or asking to photograph the home out of his own expressed interest in it, but decided not to risk it. A law-abiding civilian might not detect the trickery, but PK would be ultra-aware of any such move. The last thing Randall wanted in the event they ever encountered him was to spook him unnecessarily.

"Hmm...the girls tend to be a bit shy with strangers," the man finally answered. "But thank you anyway." He stood there, seemingly waiting for the usual "no problem, but here's my information in case you change your mind" speech. When Randall didn't budge, the man's polite smile faltered. "If you'll excuse me, sir, I've got things to do."

"I understand," Randall said, keeping his feet planted where they were. He wasn't sure what his next play would be. Aside from his own hunch that the man may be hiding something, he knew they had little if anything to even hint at reasonable suspicion, let alone probable cause. And judging from the man's attitude, it was unlikely he'd consent to a cursory search of his home if they returned in official capacity. Randall had seen his type a thousand times—not necessarily anti-police, but not helpful either. Likely a result of the riots, when local law enforcement had become mostly pariahs. But he figured that despite him only getting a brief look at the place close-up, they may have zeroed in on a potential suspect. Definitely worth continued surveillance. Just as he thanked the man for his time and walked halfway down the staircase, the man called out and told him to wait. Randall turned around in time to see him open the door fully while looking back at someone approaching the doorway from within the house. From his position on the stairs, Randall now had a clear view into the home's interior, which appeared surprisingly modern comparted to the antiquated exterior. Two women soon appeared at the doorway. One, easily in her seventies, clutched a bathrobe around her frail body. The other appeared no older than forty and regarded Randall with an apologetic expression.

"I'm sorry…my uncle can be a bit over-protective sometimes, especially with all the kidnappings," the younger of the women said. She glanced at the stack of pamphlets Randall was holding. "Are you a preacher?"

Randall opted for a half-truth. "No. But I am part of an organization seeking answers to crime in our city, so it's ironic you mention that. I thought that maybe spreading the Lord's word might help us."

The two women, standing on either side of the man who'd answered the door, smiled appreciatively. The older woman took a half-step forward and said, "My Raymond passed last year. I heard you now from inside, and it made me think it might be him sending me a message. It would have been our fiftieth next month." She went misty-eyed, her smile suggestive of a long life lived with the man she'd spoken of.

"My deepest condolences," Randall said. "The road to salvation is wet with tears of the living."

The woman smiled at that. "I'd like to see what you have there."

Surprised, Randall said "of course," then climbed the stairs again. The three occupants conferred briefly amongst themselves, after which they invited him to step into a small foyer directly inside the front door and out of the cold. Randall accepted, immediately noting the home's modern furniture and artwork. Politely declining their invitation to sit, he handed them each a brochure, which they all briefly scanned before the younger of the women said, "After Dad died, Uncle Gerald here helped Mom and me out quite a bit. He even bought this place for us all to live in."

"Well, you know…" Gerald said, with a self-effacing shrug.

The older of the women placed an appreciative hand on his shoulder, her eyes shifting to Randall. "You were saying about our city's crime problem?"

He glanced around at the updated interior complete with new-looking carpet, then looked back at the woman who'd spoken. She smiled warmly. He returned it, his previous excitement dissipating. Nothing about the three people or the home remotely matched PK's criminal profile.

Ten minutes later, after bullshitting his way through a quasi-religious opinion on the decline of the city's moral and lawful fabric, he thanked them for their time and was on his way. Once he'd gotten back to the waiting unmarked cruiser and slipped into the driver's seat, Tan asked him how it went. "True story— the first time I ever played the lottery I hit four out of six numbers," he said dejectedly. "Only eighty bucks. I would've rather got none of them."

"At least you'll get to try again soon," Tan replied. "Another tip got flagged while you were inside. A local realtor was on his way downtown for today's game and saw the billboard. Said he remembers showing an old-style funeral home a few years ago to a man fitting the suspect's general description."

"Guy's name wasn't PK, was it?" he joked.

"No. But he does remember the guy saying something about his father having been an undertaker and being raised in a house just like it."

CHAPTER 27

Frederik secured the deadbolt and slid home the two steel bolts located at the top and bottom of Abby's bedroom door, then pocketed the key. The reinforced door and surrounding walls were rated strong enough to withstand a sledgehammer, and the steel-framed false firewood wall was yet another barrier that would make it virtually impossible for someone to escape or gain entry to the bedrooms and freezer without cutting through with heavy machinery. The hidden handle in the firewood had been his idea; he knew that police would likely never guess that other rooms existed behind it since two other bedrooms existed down here in plain view. As an added precaution against his captives escaping from the basement, he'd reinforced the stairway door, too, and removed the aging elevator's fuse whenever he left the house.

After climbing the staircase to the main floor and securing the heavy wooden door behind him, he made his way toward the garage when he paused at a closed hallway door. Reaching out to turn the doorknob, he stopped himself. "I'm leaving for a bit," he said, loud enough for his voice to be heard through the door. "I'll have time to visit with you later." Remembering something, he went to the hallway credenza and removed two tubes of face paint—one purple and one yellow—from a drawer. By aid of a hanging wall mirror, he applied paint to his face in a checkered pattern, then opened another drawer and removed two charged burner phones he had stored there. Slipping the phones and the violinist's Polaroid into his pocket, he added a pair of white-framed sunglasses for good measure. He hadn't worn them since his abductions began, and knew better than to wear any of the others he'd worn recently. Besides, the white frames were snazzy, and along with the face paint they made him look ten years younger.

Donning a baggy purple Vikings jacket and matching ball cap hanging from a wall hook, he made his way through the vestibule doors leading to the attached five-car garage. It was large enough to fit the several vehicles he kept at any given time, and many of the necessary supplies he'd used to pose the girls. The lone pedestrian door leading to the expansive backyard had not originally been secure enough in his eyes, even after he'd added extra slide bolts and barred window. Out of an abundance of caution, he'd added a vestibule here as well, in the off chance an enterprising policeman with binoculars or a helicopter's camera watched from afar. Several acres of woods stood between his home and the neighboring properties. Frederik had arranged for the vacant land around the home to be bought up during the property sale, wishing to guarantee it wouldn't be built on while residing there. These measures, including barring off every window in the home, had led him to the conclusion that if someone ever entered the home against his wishes, they'd need a battering ram to do it. As he prepared to climb into his Miata (he'd just bought it last month, and loved how zippy it was), he glanced at a covered vehicle parked along the far wall of the garage. He'd more or less forgotten about the Camry since stealing it last June. But now as he glimpsed a bit of red fender below the slightly upturned cover, he suddenly remembered something. Checking his watch, he considered if he'd have time now. Traffic would grow worse by the minute. Cursing himself for forgetting about the vehicle (and the special attachment to it), he was reminded of one of his late father's favorite sayings—*out of sight, out of mind.* Finally, he decided. Yes, he'd do it now before he forgot again.

Letting himself back through the vestibule and stairway door, he raced downstairs and slid the false firewood wall aside. Lifting the freezer's heavy-duty combination lock, he aligned the numbers 4-9-2-2—the month, day, and year of his first abduction —and yanked it open. Pulling the door open and flipping on the light, he stepped into the thirty-one-degree interior and saw what he'd come for—a lone figure wrapped in plastic leaning against a metal supply rack. The letter "U" written in marker on the plastic was barely visible from where he stood, but he knew it was her. It had to be, since she was the only one he hadn't placed yet, besides the dietitian in the bedroom.

Donning a pair of yard gloves from the rack, he carried the wrapped figure into the main room. Locking the freezer and sliding the firewood wall home, he carried the figure upstairs and into the garage. He tore the cover off the vehicle, a red Toyota Camry (he'd covered it in case someone had happened to find their way into the garage or saw inside, a decision he now felt had been made out of paranoia), and opened the driver's door. After removing the double layer of plastic and chucking it into the corner, he took a moment to inspect her. Just a bit of freezer burn on her ears and nose, but other than that she appeared fine. More importantly, she was still positioned in the same seated driving position he'd embalmed her in.

Once he positioned her in the driver's seat—her curled fingers fitting nicely around the wheel as he'd been careful to measure—he reached across to fasten her seat belt. Coming around to stand outside the open passenger window, he removed one of the cellphones and mimicked checking his Uber app. "Tonya, right?" he asked her. She stared stonily ahead in her frozen position. He'd asked her the same thing when she'd picked him up for real that moonless summer night, confirming the ride on a dummy Uber account with fake bank info he'd created in anticipation for a rideshare abduction. Frederik recalled how she'd leaned forward to smile at him through the open passenger window and cheerily responded, 'Yep! Charles, right?' Frederik had said it was him, then climbed into the back seat. He'd given the address to an abandoned house on an isolated street absent any streetlights. When she'd stopped and peered curiously at the darkened home, he'd reached up with a length of cord wrapped around both fists and strangled her. Killing her on the spot had been a snap decision, one he'd made due to the fact she was behind the wheel of a running car and could have temporarily sped off causing an accident if he'd chosen to subdue her. After she was dead, he'd torn the lit rideshare device from the dash and thrown it into a nearby trash bin before going home along a route he knew was absent of intersection cameras. Most of the lower-income businesses and homes along the route didn't have exterior cameras, either. He'd done his homework. Still, it had been risky stealing the car, something he'd never done before nor since. The thought of posing her inside of it had been too delicious to resist once he'd seen her smiling, girl-next-door face come up on his app. Thank goodness he'd remembered her in the freezer; she'd be a great compliment for what he planned tonight.

"Downtown, please—the stadium," he said to her in a formal yet friendly tone. He eyed her silver nose ring, particularly the condensation that had begun to form on its surface due to the higher temperature here inside the car. He recalled how it had torn through the cartilage during the struggle after one of his fingers accidentally snagged it as she'd thrashed. Afterward, Frederik had carefully sewn the jagged wound, insisting on keeping the ring in place where it had been. It would've thrown the whole thing off if he hadn't. He hadn't fixed the crack in the windshield, though, for obvious reasons. After she'd created it with her desperate kicking, he'd almost decided against stealing the car and just abandoning her body inside the trunk. It was risky driving with a cracked windshield, as he knew police often stopped vehicles for minor violations on pretext. He'd agonized over the decision. But he'd already killed her, and to his knowledge no one had been the wiser. Finding another "U" wouldn't be too difficult, but the allure of having an Uber driver—especially one with her pretty freckles and bubbly personality—had been too great to resist. Only after he'd verified that no GPS device was present (he'd quickly scanned for one with a detector he'd bought) and parked in his home's garage, had he breathed a sigh of relief. He'd lamented that she wouldn't be properly purified, and that she'd been cheated out of witnessing a transition. But he'd made up for it by allowing the glassblower he already had in one of the bedrooms to help with the particularly difficult transitioning process.

The temperature in the garage was ten degrees higher than outside, but it was still cold enough for Frederik to see his breath. Perfect. She'd last out here until March, April maybe if the groundhog didn't see his shadow. Then, back in the freezer she'd go with the others until the following autumn. It saddened him knowing he'd go six months each year without their constant company. Although he believed that absence made the heart grow fonder, he feared that such a lengthy break could make them feel unwanted. He'd visit them weekly, at a minimum. On their birthdays, and every holiday during those warm months, too. When he leaned over and planted a kiss on the Uber driver's frozen cheek, the difference in its warmth left perfect lip marks. "Any way you could swing by White Castle on the way, hon? I'm famished."

CHAPTER 28

Downtown, the purple serpents snaked their way along the crowded streets, through bars and eateries and beneath tents erected by horn-wearing, animal-fur-clad warrior-wannabes of all ages, creeds, and genders. From time to time, *gjallarhorns* sounded, their trademark blasts rising in the air as a call to arms, or in this modern case a call for local football fans to descend upon their menacing Viking ship of a stadium and root against the invading team. Frederik, dressed similarly in purple to blend in, walked among the masses of *skol* chanters along a packed Washington Avenue. Thousands of them marched to rock music blasting from one bar to the homegrown Prince songs from another; the familiar one-two beat of the drums people on the street used to simulate the giant one overlooking the stadium's field provided a pulse-pounding base note.

Stepping into the camera-less, sunken doorway of a closed business he'd visited before, Frederik removed the Polaroid photo of the violinist and one of the burner phones from his pocket. Turning its camera flash on, he pointed the lens at the Polaroid and snapped a clear picture, then saved it to the phone's library. Connecting to the business's free Wi-Fi network and entering the required password he'd memorized, he downloaded the Instagram app. He opened it and created a basic dummy account complete with false demographics and a dummy Gmail account he created on the spot. He disliked the quality of Polaroids, but it was the simplest method to ensure no digital marker could be traced back to the house. Navigating the phone's photo editing function, he turned its location metadata off before attaching it to the post. Not wholly necessary, since he didn't plan on keeping the phone, but the added step had the potential of delaying the police's response a bit longer. Ensuring no identifying street or business markers existed in the shot, he held the pad of his right forefinger in front of the lens. When his fingertip came fully into focus, including the unique arches, whorls, and loops that no other human on earth possessed, he snapped a photo of it. He turned its location metadata off as well before attaching it to the post. He'd rightly expected copycats to emerge as the media continued to report his exploits. It had become all the rage to impersonate him on social media, with viral TikTok challenges of teen girls posing as his victims in increasingly ridiculous ways. Imitation was the best form of flattery, of course, but Frederik also believed the work he performed, and the risks entailed, demanded proper credit.

In the post's caption, he wrote, "Letter 25—V. Enjoy the late Halloween treat." His handle, as always, was some form of "Yours truly," with a rare, specialized character that he hadn't previously used. As usual, he added the singular hashtag #pktaskforce since he knew the police would see it; they publicly called on citizens to use it when sending social media tips. As he saved the draft, drunken fans continued to pass by him, oblivious to what had just occurred in the darkened doorway. Good. He'd accomplished his previous posts in similar fashions, and always in crowds so that the police could not isolate him with the blankets of surveillance and cameras they had throughout the city. Better still that he'd likely catch them by surprise today by doing something new—posting a victim's photo less than forty-eight hours after her abduction.

Stepping from the doorway, he walked for three blocks amid hundreds of yelling fans ready to watch their team take the field. As he passed the green-roofed City Hall and its similarly-roofed clock tower, he couldn't resist the temptation of stopping to look at the Public Service Building across the street. He trained his eye on a row of slated eighth-floor windows. Somewhere behind them, he knew, sat the contingent that for the better part of seven months had been confounded in their pursuit of the man responsible for gripping the city in fear and anguish. It caused pride to swell through him, knowing that after all he'd been through, he was free to stand here among this winding purple serpent and look upon that very place where plans were being made to stop him. God Himself must be looking down from heaven with admiration in His eyes.

As Frederik stared at those windows that resembled so many eyes peering out at the city, his mind did that thing it often did when he reflected deeply. It visited that time in his past when light had begun to fade into darkness, when one door had closed and another opened.

～

Their father isn't expected back until midday tomorrow. Business in the Cities two hours away, twice as far as St. Cloud. It's dinnertime, and Naomi is in a foul mood. She's drunk again. Both boys can tell because she's crossing her arms atop the table and leaning forward, a glazed look in her eyes. And her glass of red wine has been perpetually half-full for the past two hours.

"Don't pick at your food," she tells Victor, her speech slurred.

"I'm not hungry," Victor says. He takes a nervous glance

toward his brother Frederik, who gives an almost imperceptible shake of his head. Don't make her angry, *the shake says.*

"I didn't ask if you were hungry," Naomi snaps. She leans so low across the table that her shirt dips into her gravy-topped mashed potatoes. "I said not to pick at your food. There are starving kids in China, for Christ's sake." She burns a look of disgust toward Victor, but he avoids her glare by focusing on his still half-full plate of food.

"Yes, ma'am," Victor says and stabs at a piece of fried Spam. He lifts it toward his open mouth, but he cannot eat. He drops his fork, where it clangs noisily on his plate. Both boys look to see Naomi's reaction, but for now she hangs her head and pokes at her own plate of food. When she does look up, she stares at Victor's fork so hard, her eyes look like they'll fall out of her head. "You'll pick that fork up and eat the food I cooked you, understand?"

Instinct kicks in and Victor reaches for his brother's hand. As soon as the boys' fingers interlace, an electric current passes through each of them. It's happened thousands of times before, but it feels different this time. Naomi isn't just drunk and angry; she has a look in her eyes that promises a lengthy time for one of them beneath the hot water if she gets her blood up.

And just like that, she's up out of her chair in a flash, her hand slicing through the air in a backhanded swat against the boys' joined hands. Immediately, their hands separate, but a second later they re-join, the fingers once again interlacing, only tighter this time. Naomi's jaw drops. Her eyes bulge. Then a look of snide understanding crosses her face. "I get it now—you really are inseparable. Your father warned me when we first met. But I didn't think it would be a problem. Even though I didn't have children of my own, I'm a woman. I should know. But now I see. You're both born of the devil. It's why we aren't allowed at church."

Frederik looks at her in shock. "That's not true. We don't go to church because Father says—"

A split second later her hand flies out and slaps Frederik hard across the face. The resulting whack *reverberates in the otherwise quiet dining room. Other than a few spankings for minor offenses, Frederik has never actually been struck by her before. Not like this. In response, Victor sucks in air through his teeth in an expression of shock. Not even their father has ever struck the boys in the face. And never in any way by their mother while she'd been alive.*

"Don't you backtalk me, boy!" Naomi says, wagging a finger at Frederik. She's breathing hard now, her large bosom heaving in and out as she leans even closer to him. "Not ever. I'm the woman of the house, and don't you forget it." She pauses to look around; her lip curls. "If you call this place a house. More like a house of horrors, with what your father does." Her eyes widen when she sees Frederik staring up at her, a prideful resistance in his eye. "Does that upset you, me saying that this house is a freakshow? Because it is, with those...things he creates. My mother warned me. 'Never marry a widower,' she said. 'You'll live in his dead wife's shadow,' she said. Well, she was right. I was a fool then, but I refuse to be a fool to a child. Now, apologize for your mouth and I won't take you to the sink."

Frederik and Victor lock eyes. It's been several months since Naomi has brought them to the sink. The last time she'd done it to Frederik (for forgetting to pick his dirty clothes off the bedroom floor), their father had returned from a business trip and questioned him at length about his burn. He'd narrowed his eyes and made a sound that made Frederik think he hadn't believed his lie. Then he'd told the boys to stay in their shared bedroom and went downstairs to talk to Naomi. Their slightly raised voices had floated up the staircase before exploding into a heated argument. During it, the boys had interlaced their fingers and sang songs to soothe one another—Michael Jackson's "Billy

Jean" from Frederik, The Beastie Boys' "Fight for Your Right"
from Victor.

Stronger emotionally now than he'd been that day, Frederik
shoots a defiant look up at the giant-like Naomi. "I won't let you
take me to the sink anymore," he says. He's surprised that he's
said it, but despite his fear for having backtalked her, it feels
right on the inside. "I won't let you take Victor either."

Naomi flinches, then her lips twist into a cruel smile. "Oh, I
see...all grown up now, eh? Little Frederik has become a man.
Well, how do you propose to stop me from disciplining a child
living in MY HOUSE!" She screams the last two words as she
bends lower. Warm spittle strikes Frederik's face, but he makes
no move to wipe it away.

"If you do, I'll tell Father," Frederik says, his chin raised.

She straightens and cocks her head as if she doesn't believe
what she's hearing. Then she throws her head back and roars
laughter. "You'll tell your father? He's less of a man than either
of you. And I should know; I've seen you both take a bath."
When both boys gape at her, she laughs even harder, doubling
over with tears spilling from her pudgy face. "You'd be surprised
to know he barely compares to a pair of ten-year-olds!" she says,
holding two fingers an inch apart.

She barely has time to wipe her tears of laughter away when
Frederik's hand shoots out from seemingly nowhere and slaps
her hard across the face. She stumbles backward more out of
surprise than from any real force behind the strike. Frederik is
sitting down, after all, and she'd been bent forward with her feet
wide apart. As she straightens, her face reddens with sudden
realization. Not only has the boy talked back to her, he's dared to
put his hands on her.

"You...you little shitbird!" she stammers. She points a trem-
bling finger at him. "I should whip you to within an inch of your
pathetic little life. Look at you both, holding hands like a couple
of pansies. I should be glad we're not welcome in church."

Victor looks at Frederik with panic in his eyes. "Freddie, don't make her mad."

Naomi laughs at him. "Mad? I'll show you mad..." In a flash, she lunges forward and snatches them both by their clutching hands, pulling them off their chair so hard that their free arms knock their plates off the table. Hunks of Spam, peas, and mashed potatoes spill onto the rug.

Frederik struggles to free himself from her grasp, but she's too strong. "Father will believe me!" he yells, wriggling and writhing against her, but he is still unable to break free. She drags them both from the dining room into the kitchen, toward the sink, and Frederik screams, "He questioned you last time, I heard it!"

She stops so fast that the boys bang into the back of her legs. Naomi, strengthened from a lifetime of farm life, looks down at Frederik with a quizzical look. "You...eavesdropped on me?"

"No, you were both yelling. We couldn't help—"

Instead of dragging them the rest of the way to the sink, she reverses course, dragging them instead back into the dining room and through the living room until she stops at the chapel's closed double doors. She releases the boys' hands, and they crumple to the floor. But Frederik still maintains his grip on Victor's hand, then goes to hug him tight. Naomi digs into her pocket and removes a set of keys. Inserting one of them into the lock, she throws the doors open. It's dark in here. And cold. The boys' father doesn't heat the room until a half hour before a viewing, for reasons he's explained to them a dozen times.

"Maybe your pencil-dicked father would believe you. But that gives me an even better idea," she says, flipping a switch on the wall. A set of track lights at the front of the small chapel illuminates a bier, atop of which rests a closed white casket. Fresh flowers stand on either side of it, along with an enlarged photo of an elderly woman on an easel. Naomi reaches down and

grasps the boys' hands. She makes it two steps when Frederik realizes what's about to happen.

"Noooooooo!" he screams, kicking wildly and clawing uselessly at her hand. But she's been beaten by grown men before, her daddy too, she's said so during many of her drunken stupors. Frederik tries to pry her fingers loose, but her grip is like a vise. Victor, weaker and less assertive than his brother, curls into himself and begins to bawl.

Naomi reaches the casket, undoes the locking mechanisms on both lids, then throws them open. The dead woman lies on a white satin pillow and matching liner. She's been done up in a green dress, her favorite color. Her wrinkled, age-spotted hands are folded at her waist, and her lips press firmly together, sewn closed the day before by their father while Frederik assisted.

"It's a good thing she wanted the box, and not one of those morbid poses," Naomi says, reaching down to lift the boys up. Victor freezes in terror; Frederik kicks and screams bloody murder. It takes her three tries to fit the boys inside, but she finally succeeds by pushing Frederik's flailing arms inside as she shuts the lids. Holding her weight atop them as Frederik desperately pushes up from beneath, she reaches down to secure both locking mechanisms, their purpose to prevent the lids from accidentally opening during a service or transport. Panting, she straightens and smooths out her mussed hair. She returns to the doorway and listens to the banging and muffled screams coming from inside the casket. Grinning, she turns out the light and leaves, closing the doors behind her.

Frederik knows they'll both suffocate if they don't calm down. He grips Victor's hand, doing his best to push the corpse's cold, withered body away from them. But it's too cramped, so he stops trying.

"Victor...Victor...you need to calm down," Frederik whispers in the darkness. He's turned his brother away from the corpse, using himself as a buffer. He can feel the corpse's rigid *body, and its face pressing against the back of his neck; it feels like one of his old baseball gloves. The body gives off a strange chemical odor, like their father's embalming room but stronger.*

Victor stops his crying as Frederik lies behind him, smoothing out his hair and shushing him. "It's going to be okay," he whispers. "She won't leave us here for long." He tries to remember how long it's been, but time feels warped. Once, during a lesson when Victor had asked what would happen if a dead person woke up inside a casket, their father had laughed and said he doubted that had ever happened, but added that in Victorian days, not only did families pose for photos with recently deceased loved ones, but they sometimes buried them with strings attached to bells above the grave in case they woke up buried alive. Thus had been born the phrase, 'Saved by the bell,' he'd said. But they had no bell to ring. Even if they did, there wasn't anyone to help them. Frederik tells Victor to take shallower breaths. They'll save a few minutes that way. Then a new fear grips him, that Naomi has maybe passed out drunk. She's done so countless times before, not waking until the next morning, or perhaps in the middle of the night, stumbling half-asleep to the bathroom before going back to bed. Frederik had seen this himself on several occasions after waking to pee. But even if she woke in an hour or two and remembered, both he and Victor would be long dead.

Reality sinks in as Frederik takes in a shallow breath and realizes almost all the oxygen is gone. He listens in the darkness as Victor's own breaths shorten considerably. They're raspy, like the ones he takes when he catches a cold, or when he speaks too fast and his tongue becomes tied. And in moments like that, when Victor had begun wheezing and Frederik had looked on help-lessly, both brothers had done as they'd done countless times before—they'd grasped hands and communicated in either spoken or unspoken ways, and always in the end they'd known they'd come away just fine.

Frederik's breaths become even shorter now. White dots appear in his black field of vision, and he becomes light-headed. He'll pass out any second, and when that happens he knows he'll never wake up again. He senses that Victor is also moments from unconsciousness. But by some grace, the sound of the locks sliding open comes to his ears, and the casket lids lift. Frederik and Victor bolt upright as they inflate their nearly collapsed lungs with huge sucking breaths. It's the sweetest air Frederik has ever breathed. The corpse beside them lies oblivious, one of its hands still in its lap, the other having been pushed onto its side. A few strands of the previously well-done hair fall over the wrinkled face, while others stick up at odd angles. The head tilts slightly to one side. She could be sleeping if she weren't dead.

And now, Naomi's hands reach in and lift both boys out, then set them down on the floor at her feet. The brothers collapse upon each other, gasping, murmuring, praying. While Naomi fixes the corpse good as new and closes the lids, the boys lie at her feet, crying softly. Frederik is the first to stop. He cups Victor's face and tells him that it's over now, that everything will be okay. Then Naomi says something that chills the blood in Frederik's veins, something even more frightening than what just happened.

"If you tell your father, I'll kill him in his sleep, then I'll kill myself," she says, then shuffles off to bed.

After that first time, Frederik coached Victor on how to handle things if Naomi put them into an occupied casket again. Do not resist. Do not cry or complain. It wouldn't make it any better if they did any of those things, and it would communicate to her that what she was doing worked. The second time came a month later, when their father went away again on business. Twice more in the six months after that, one of them occurring when their father had been home. That had been the most disturbing occasion for Frederik. Their father had been on the tractor in the field when Naomi quietly rose from her knitting and motioned for the boys to follow her into the chapel. A young man from a neighboring town had drowned in a lake and been picked at by fish...

Two years later, the boys' world tilted on its axis as they sat in that same chapel, their father lying still and silent in his own casket. A brain hemorrhage. His hands lay folded at the waist, those same eyes that had looked adoringly at his sons since the day they'd been born, forever closed. During the service, Frederik had cast Naomi a withering look of hatred. She hadn't subjected them to any further chapel visits since the business had died with their father. Instead, she'd switched to systematic neglect, leaving them to cook their own meals and keep the house while she worked an endless assortment of jobs. None of them had lasted long, for one reason or another. As a result, the boys had been forced to educate themselves, learning various facets of life and the world from the hundreds of books on their father's bookshelf. Frederik also read the many included embalming manuals, the entire encyclopedia, and even taught himself guitar using a dusty acoustic and lesson book he found in the basement. They'd watched various educational programs on PBS, one of only three channels their home antenna received. Their books exhausted and Naomi refusing to take them to the library, Frederik had resorted to sneaking her *Good Housekeeping* and *Ellery Queen* magazines when she'd passed out drunk after work, careful to place them back in the exact positions he'd found them in.

Frederik blinked the memories away. He was back in the present—downtown amid the throng of fans swarming the streets around the stadium. Tearing his gaze from the PSB's windows, he made his way several blocks to the Viking longboat replica located in the Medtronic plaza just outside the stadium. Scanning the more than seventeen thousand personalized paver bricks making up a majority of the ship's deck and surrounding area, he searched until he found a familiar one that read, "To Mother and Father—love, Frederik & Victor. Skol!" Having paid five hundred dollars for the dedication brick, Frederik had decided to add the addendum—the Viking warrior battle cry—to commemorate his family's Scandinavian heritage.

"We shall meet again," he said to himself, squatting to place a hand atop the brick. His words were lost amid the cacophony of conversations and cheers around him. The game was about to start, something he had no particular interest in, aside from the relative anonymity the crowd provided him. Removing the same burner he'd saved the Instagram post on, he checked over both shoulders before unlocking it and opening his Instagram app. Satisfied that he was in a place large and populated enough to confuse the police once they pinged the post's location, he brought up his saved draft and pressed the "post" checkmark. The throbber made its circular searching sign until the post appeared a moment later, the timestamp above it reading *A few seconds ago*. Smiling, he placed the burner and Polaroid into a discarded plastic bag he found on the ground, then jammed the bag into an overflowing trash can. If they came, good luck finding him.

CHAPTER 29

A fter calling the tipster back and verifying the information he'd given, Detective Randall asked the man to stop by the office on his way to the game to give a videotaped statement. The man agreed, but stated he'd only have a few minutes due to a tailgate he was organizing. In the meantime, Randall gave Tan the assignment of researching tax records on the former funeral home in question for the years following the bank sale. So far, she'd verified the two-story, forty-five hundred-square-foot Victorian-style home (located fifteen miles from downtown, just east of Lake Minnetonka and within the geographic area the task force suspected the killer lived) was owned by CMH Group, LLC. A county Property Appraiser's Office and official state corporation inquiry found little to no background on the company. A Google and Better Business Bureau search didn't produce any names of persons listed under the business, either. Randall had dealt with ghost corporations before, knowing that those in organized crime still used them as fronts for money laundering or other nefarious dealings. He had no evidence to believe that to be the case here, despite finding almost zilch on the owner of record. The post-COVID business world had been turned upside down, he knew, so its vagueness alone wasn't entirely suspicious.

The realtor stated that he'd shown the house to a man named Frederik Derring (the realtor had verified the man's ID prior to the showing). Randall conducted DVS, NCIC, and credit inquires for the name; twenty-seven such names came back, nationwide. Interpol came back with over a hundred matches, so he forwarded those to Whitlock for his agents to check. Two of the US-based Frederik Derrings lived in Minnesota. Randall immediately eliminated one of them due to the man being eighty-one years old and having had his driver's license revoked due to a failed vision test. The other man only had a suburban Minneapolis P.O box address listed, and no criminal record. His driver's license photo was a rough match, at best, due to their lack of a clear front-on shot of him. Strangely, it appeared that he'd never filed an IRS 1099 or a W-2. Furthermore, Randall didn't find any social media accounts that fit their subject. It being a Sunday, he knew they'd be a bit limited regarding the full government resources required to conduct a deeper dive into whatever CMH Group was. Likewise, they'd have to wait until tomorrow when the state agency that kept birth certificate information opened, unless they chose to initiate a time-consuming emergency subpoena. Frustrating, since criminals weren't bound by normal business hours. Still, moments after hanging up with the tipster, Randall wasted no time in dispatching a surveillance team to the house in case any of the half-dozen or so vehicles suspected in the PK cases showed up. They'd need a matching car, plate, or solid description of the suspect to be granted even a limited search warrant, he knew. So far, his idea about former family-style funeral homes had been based more on an educated hunch than the FBI's profile or any factual evidence. Suspicion wouldn't be enough. Losing a low-level case due to an illegal search was regrettable enough. But losing twenty-six kidnapping cases (and as many possible murder cases) to a savvy defense attorney poking the right holes in the case could levy a lifetime of sleepless nights on every member in the task force.

Twenty minutes later, Randall and Tan were introducing themselves to the tipster, a tall, sixtyish man with a fake tan and bleached teeth. Dressed in a purple zoot suit and a furry hat of horns, he looked anything but a realty professional. He must have recognized this because he removed the hat with a self-conscious smile as the detective pair led him into interview room one.

"Thank you for meeting with us, Mr. Keating," Randall said, reading over the man's background information. Tan had brought up his DVS and criminal history just prior to his arrival. Nothing more than a few parking tickets. After a brief introduction, Randall slid a photo pack across the table for Keating to look at. Along with their Frederik Derring's enlarged driver's license photo were five other vaguely similar photos of Caucasian men around the same age. "Do you recognize one of these men as the one you showed the house to?"

Keating inspected them closely, then pointed at the Frederik Derring photo. "This one, I think. But one of these other ones is like the billboard shot I saw. It was a long time ago, and I only saw him once. I was kind of in a rush to get out of there, too." He glanced at his watch. "Do you know how long this will take? My tailgate crew is waiting for me outside."

Randall ignored the man's question and switched tacks. "What can you tell us about the actual buyer...CMH Group, I believe?"

"I looked it up before I called the hotline. I have all my sales information on a Google Docs file, so I can bring it up on my phone. Realty can be twenty-four seven sometimes, but I'm sure you're familiar." He scrolled through his phone to refresh his memory. "Yep, here it is—CMH Group, LLC. Sole buyer. Corporations flip residential properties all the time, and it's common for one rep to see the house and another to handle the financials. Listed by Bank of Minnesota at six hundred twenty thousand, sold for five ten, all cash. Great deal, considering they got five acres of land with it." He handed his phone across the table for Randall to verify.

"Why so cheap?" Randall asked.

"Those types of funeral homes don't operate in this area anymore. Rarely anywhere in the country, so it was going to be someone's residence where they put their kids to bed and ate Thanksgiving dinner. Nothing devalues a property more than a home where hundreds of wakes were held in the living room and bodies were embalmed in the basement."

Randall couldn't argue there. "Still, someone could have demolished it and built on the land."

"This was after the housing bubble burst. Warren Buffett could barely get a loan back then. Cash buyers were scooping up cheap lakefront properties and homes in good neighborhoods, mostly. Even a steep discount would have been negated by the demo and rebuild, not to mention it's in a weird location. You wouldn't know it's there by driving along the main road."

"How could a property worth that much go unnoticed for so long, no matter what it used to be? The housing crash didn't last forever."

"The bank had thousands of other foreclosures to deal with that were easier to sell. And no one had any interest, so they sort of forgot about it."

"What made them remember?"

"The former owners left everything as-is when they skipped town. No one touched the place for years until a couple kids broke in on a dare and posted pictures and videos of the interior. Open coffins laying around, funeral clothes still hanging in the upstairs closets, even an embalming table and machine for that in the basement. After word leaked on what was found, the bank finally sent an inspector who confirmed it all. It got cleaned up, then I came in."

"Was any of the funerary equipment functioning when the house sold?" Tan asked.

"Lord, no. It'd been ten years since the utilities had been on. I imagine it would've cost a gem just to bring everything up to code if anyone wanted to run a functioning funeral home. Most the laws had changed, too. But the buyers didn't want to open a business, anyway."

"The man you showed the house to—this Frederik Derring— you said he claimed to have been raised in a similar type of funeral home?" Randall asked.

"Yeah, his father was a mortician. Or funeral director, what-ever they call them these days. Said that he and his twin brother grew up in a house just like it. Some town outside of Brainerd, can't remember the name."

Randall looked up from his notes and stared at the man. "He told you he had a twin?"

"Yes, identical. I remember because when he mentioned having a twin, I asked him which type, since I'm a twin, too. Mine's fraternal, though, since I have a sister."

"Was Frederik Derring present at the closing, or do your records state if he was involved with the actual sale?"

"No, he wasn't at the closing, only an attorney on behalf of the buyer. And the title company didn't list individual names, so I couldn't tell you if Mr. Derring was associated with the company or not." He shook his head. "If I had a dollar for every person who viewed a house without putting in an offer."

After jotting down the name of the attorney Keating had mentioned, Randall asked Tan if she had anything else she'd like to add. "I do," she said. "You mentioned the house had an existing embalming machine and table in the basement?"

"Yeah. Gave me the creeps just being down there. You swear you hear things."

"Do you know if they were removed prior to closing?"

"I believe they were still there. I do remember Mr. Derring

saying if he ever bought the place, he'd keep the table and machine. Something about them being conversation pieces."

Tan shot Randall a raised eyebrow look, then asked Keating, "That didn't strike you as strange?"

"No. As long as someone has proper ID, and isn't wearing a hockey mask and carrying a machete during a showing, I don't care what opinion they have of a house." He laughed at his own joke, then quickly regained his professional air.

"Anything else you can add about Mr. Derring?" Tan asked.

"Only that nothing about the place seemed to bother him. He wasn't even weirded out by the crematorium in the backyard. Said it'd be easy enough to remove down the road, if at all. I figured he was one of those weird rich people who do things just to be different. I can't remember the word for them."

"Eccentrics," Randall offered.

"Yeah, that's it," Keating said. "I see a lot of them in my business."

"We're familiar."

"I'm sure. Like I said on the phone, I forgot about the guy until I saw the billboard just now." He glanced at his watch again. "So…is that all?"

Randall said that was all for now and had just stood to shake the man's hand when a knock came at the door. Sergeant Fells stuck her head inside. Making a cutting motion across her neck, she held the door open while Randall thanked the man for his time, handed him his card, then passed him off to another detective to escort him back down to the building's lobby. Afterwards, Fells showed the detective duo something on her agency cellphone—an Instagram post timestamped 'A few minutes ago,' including two photos. The first depicted a photographed Polaroid of a redheaded woman closely resembling Nicolette Dunn, their abducted violinist. Appearing dead, with makeup and her dress's neckline partially covering an embalmer's stitch on the right side of her neck, her body was seated before a music stand and positioned as if playing her violin. The second photo was of the pad of an unknown person's right index finger, the arches, loops, and whorls clearly distinguishable in the photo's zoomed view.

"BCA just forwarded this to Whitlock and me a minute ago," Fells said. "They got a ping."

"Where from?" Randall asked, already recognizing the fingerprint pattern from twenty-four previous photos he'd seen.

Fells led them toward the windows near Randall's desk. "Somewhere out there..." she said, pointing at the crowded street below.

CHAPTER 30

When the game ended three hours later, the drunken crowd spilled out onto the plaza and streets surrounding the stadium to celebrate the home team's victory. Frederik was among them, blending in with his oversized purple jacket, matching cap, and face paint. The sunglasses gave him added confidence that, had the police decided to surveil the general area (he was certain that dozens of undercover detectives were planted in the crowd), he wouldn't be recognized. His various vehicles wouldn't be either, he judged, since their plates were fake and he'd switched several of them out over the past six months. He'd also painted them several times during their usage. The price for living in today's technological society. But he'd used that same technology in his favor, as he'd done today. Not since the Roman gladiators had humans congregated in such large numbers for sporting events. In a delicious bit of irony, it had been Law Enforcement Appreciation Day at the game.

As he made his way west along Washington Avenue toward the warehouse district, Frederik melted into a large group of purple-clad fans and continued walking until he reached the iconic Hewing Hotel. Looking up at the crowded rooftop bar, he promised to visit it again once this was all over, sipping a cocktail while he watched the picturesque downtown skyline. For now, he had a different celebration in mind. Turning left on Third Avenue, he passed beneath a freeway overpass until he came to a public parking garage. Climbing into the Miata's driver's seat, he pulled out of the space and waited patiently for the line of vehicles in front of him to exit before he drove through the clogged streets, making his way south along Hiawatha, then onto Cedar Avenue. Several minutes later, he arrived at a nondescript building on the corner of East 25th Street—Matt's Bar, original home of the famous Juicy Lucy burger. Situated in a quiet residential neighborhood, it had become one of his favorite haunts since moving to the Cities. With its wood-paneled walls and counter located near the constantly sizzling flattop, the beloved dive felt like home. After he'd taken his second victim (the figure skater) and posted her photo, he'd come here to relax himself. Years of troubling thoughts had disappeared as he'd chewed his food and sipped his Coke to the raucous local crowd around him.

Today, like each time he'd posted a victim's photo since, Frederik completed his tradition by driving a few miles west to Lakewood Cemetery. Overlooking both Lake Bde Maka Ska and Lake Harriet, with downtown in the distance, the sprawling 250-acre burial ground lay home to myriad stately crypts and thousands of tree-shaded tombstones. He turned down a cemetery road and wound his way several hundred yards until he reached a soaring monolith marker, his cue that the grave he sought was near. Parking, he walked down the hill until he came to a black granite headstone with two familiar names etched side-by-side on its glossy surface. He knelt on the leaf-strewn grass. "You'd be proud of me, Father," he said, placing a hand atop the name *YVES DERRING*. "I wish you could have seen even one of them. They're beautiful. You taught me well."

When he read the name beside his father's—*SARAH DERRING*—his throat thickened and his eyes grew misty. It happened every time he came here, no matter what the occasion. But especially so on celebration days. "I miss you more than you'll ever know," he said. He kissed his fingertips then pressed them against her name. It seemed cruel to him that the one woman he'd ever loved had been reduced to a simple etching in stone. If there was any solace in his heart, it was from the knowledge that if she were to look down upon him now, maternal pride would surely crease her smile. He was as sure of it now as he'd ever been. Thankful that his parents had bought plots in the large city cemetery instead of in their town's tiny one, Frederik delved into deep conversation. He talked to his parents in other places as well, but being so physically close to them made him feel especially connected to them. On several past graveside visits, he'd sworn he'd felt his mother's lips kiss his cheek, and his father's comforting hand upon his shoulder. But not today. Wherever they were, they kept a certain distance from him now. Not avoidance, but respect for his work, he felt. They'd know that he was almost finished, and how important it was for him to complete what he'd begun. Even from beyond the grave, they'd no doubt be aghast if they did anything to distract him from that goal.

During his visit, his mind drifted to the difficult time between their deaths, when he and Victor had been subjected to the increasing terrors of their stepmother. An especially troubling memory. Frederik tried to push it away, but the cloud he'd erected before the sun of his memory passed, and the painful image shined fully into his thoughts. A time when their father had been away on business, Frederik comforting his clearly terrified brother as their stepmother led them toward the chapel. Both boys knew what lay inside the casket. As they should have— both had helped their father prepare the body before his departure. A teenaged boy, killed in a farming accident. The boy's head had been severed by a combine, and Frederik had helped their father sew it back on. The body had been dressed with a high shirt collar to conceal the ghastly ring of stitches, but their stepmother had forced Frederik to fully unbutton it before ordering him to climb inside the casket with Victor...

He blinked the memory away then drove home, his spirit now soaring. Confident he hadn't been followed, he passed a city utility van parked at the junction of the main road and the wooded one leading to the house fifty yards down the lane. Two workers in reflective vests and hardhats stood knee-deep in a new trench, each of them shoveling dirt onto a growing pile. Frederik couldn't remember workers ever being present in that area before and thought back to the survey he'd studied when first moving into the house. The workers were in the easement, but he couldn't be sure what, if any, utility lines or pipes were buried there. Watching the workers in the Miata's rearview mirror, he crept along the wooded road toward the house, waiting to see if either of them looked up at his vehicle's plate. Neither of them did.

When the Miata turned left down the road toward the century-old, defunct funeral home, the pair of undercover detectives inside the borrowed city van observed it closely through the tinted windows. Using binoculars, they recorded the Minnesota tag number and conducted a DVS query on the registered owner's demographics—physical description, address, birthdate. Most everything except the name matched what Detectives Randall and Tan had listed for their person of interest: Frederik Derring. An NCIC search for the licensed individual found no criminal history, not even a parking ticket. It didn't take long to locate the man as currently living in nearby Eden Prairie; detectives confirmed he was at home and owned a similar Miata with the same plate number. The vehicle was located inside his garage, the engine cold. It's VIN matched sale records the man produced, and his wife and children vouched that he'd been home all day with them watching the football game. Satisfied, detectives left. Strange, however, that the man's license photo and that of Frederik Derring closely matched. And even more so that the man UC detectives had seen just now arriving at the former funeral home had had the same plate. He'd been wearing face paint, a hat, and sunglasses, but no other distinguishing descriptors had been confirmed other than him being a middle-aged white male. The Miata only had two seats (the passenger seat had clearly been unoccupied), with a small trunk the officers knew from experience could hold two small suitcases, or possibly an adult curled into a fetal position, but no more.

Sergeant Fells had given the two officers assigned to digging duty strict instructions to ignore any passing pedestrians or vehicles unless a serious felony was occurring. Following orders, the detectives on trench duty had allowed the Miata to turn without so much as giving it a glance. In the five hours they'd been out here digging and resting, the only pedestrians who'd passed by had been a female jogger pushing a baby stroller, and a teenager on a skateboard. A few dozen vehicles had driven by, but the only one that had turned down the road to the house had been the Miata. Knowing the road ended at the house, the surveillance officers inside the van waited ten minutes to ensure the driver hadn't made a wrong turn and came back out, or was delivering. Waiting also made sense since packing up the minute the vehicle had been spotted would look suspicious. After the ten minutes passed, they radioed Fells for direction.

"Standby," came Fells' static-filled reply. A pause, then their instructions: "Pack it up, fellas. Initiating a records warrant. 'Till then, we've got eyes in the sky."

As Frederik parked in the garage and made his way through the secure vestibule, a finger of suspicion teased along his spine.

He'd felt it before, most recently this past summer when he'd prepared to take his next victim, a barista from a local coffee shop. He'd listened to his gut then, abandoning his plan after noting a suspicious-looking vehicle with dark tinted windows parked down the street. Curious if his gut had been correct, he'd gone back later to check on the young woman, whom he no longer planned on taking. Conducting his own counter-surveillance, Frederik had observed a pair of civilian-clothed men later rolling their windows down and talking into lapel mics after the woman had gotten off work and driven away. An off-duty police detail, likely paid for by one of the young woman's family members in the police department, Frederik had assumed. He'd taken the bartender instead two days later. From then on, he'd reminded himself to always trust his gut.

Once safely inside the house, he immediately checked on Abby. She was right where he'd left her, asleep on her bed, or at least appearing so. Using another dummy Instagram account, he verified that his violinist post had been taken down. No worries, since its removal meant the police had gotten the message. Good.

He checked the property's official land survey and confirmed that no utilities ran along his property to the portion of road he'd seen the workers digging. His electric line ran a different direction, and the home used both a septic tank and a well system. He didn't have cable or natural gas, and the several other homes in the area didn't either, as far as he knew. Wishing to confirm his suspicions on the van, he called the city's off-hours emergency utilities line and called in as a motorist complaining about the workers creating a road hazard. They told him that none of the city or county utility companies were conducting emergency repairs in that area, and that those were the only ones performed on weekends and holidays. In addition, the state's department of transportation emergency line reported that no work at all was being done there, or was even scheduled to be.

Suspecting now that he was being surveilled by police, Frederik paced the main floor, pondering his next move as he discussed with several of the more conversational girls what he should do. Most helpful was the karate instructor and owner of a local studio who he'd spoken with about possible lessons two months ago. Appropriately, he'd placed her in his home gym at the back of the house. In a long forward barefoot stance, she held one fist cocked at her side and extended the other toward a broken board suspended from the ceiling by strings. Her eyes and half-open mouth expressed focused energy. Frederik was particularly fond of her pose, since he'd always wanted to take karate lessons as a kid, but more so because she'd given him the biggest run for his money. The black belt and mother of two had fought valiantly for her life after he'd attacked her inside the empty dojo.

"*In* The Art of War*, Sun Tzu says 'a skilled general will avoid the enemy when they are full of fight,'*" Frederik remembered her telling him when they first talked. He couldn't argue that point, since the police were hell-bent on stopping him. Still, he preferred a different maxim of Tzu's, one that echoed his own philosophy of the best defense being a good offense: "*Do not get in the way of an army that is homeward bound...*"

After much consideration, he decided he would take the girls downstairs and hide them all in the freezer until his instincts told him it was safe to bring them back. It would take him all night to remove them from their intricate placements, but he felt it necessary. He'd come too far to fail at this point. If the police came and asked to look around without a warrant, he would hide and ask Victor to help by allowing them to look around and hopefully eliminate the house from suspicion. He'd put up temporary wallpaper he'd saved, and clean up the scenes. As for the vehicles and support platforms in the garage, he'd move them around to the rear of the property and disguise them with tarps and fallen branches. A low-level attempt to conceal his involvement, one he knew may not work, but there wasn't a better alternative. He didn't want them in the house, of course, but worse was a search warrant, something he knew would be inevitable if they were refused entry. It would be an all-or-nothing proposition at that point.

He made two sandwiches and ate while watching Abby's sleeping form on the basement security monitor. Chewing thoughtfully, he allowed his mind to wander through the memories of how he'd come to possess each of the girls. It gave him comfort knowing that what he was about to do would help keep them safe. When he finished eating, he headed up to the main floor to begin when he paused at the same closed hallway door as earlier. He began to turn the knob when he stopped. Before, it had seemed necessary to enter and pay a visit. But not now. He had no appetite for entering the room and speaking without being spoken back to. Victor—increasingly moody lately—was likely to reach out to grasp his hand as he'd often done during their childhood. *I don't want a visit*, that grasping hand would mean. Another silent communication. Where his brother's mind had drifted since last night was anyone's guess.

The temperature up here was forty-three degrees, twelve points higher than the freezer he would place the girls in. Maybe it would be good for them to take a rest anyway. A warm front had arrived, and he'd agonized over the possibility of them getting sick. Their transitioning would still keep them healthy for a time, but it wouldn't last forever if they didn't stay cold. Proof of that was the figure skater, his logical starting point to place downstairs since she'd been up here the longest. Inspecting her, he noted purplish spots sprouting on her face and neck. Even more alarming was the fact that her left ear was dangerously close to falling off. He'd have to sew it back in place when he had a chance.

He worked his way from room to room and on both floors, telling them all how he loved them for their individual beauty, and how sorry he was to shut them away in the dark again. As he carried them down the elevator one at a time and deposited them in the freezer (he didn't bother covering them in plastic for now), his mind returned to the Carlson woman. He checked on her every hour, finding her either sleeping or sitting up in bed, staring at the wall. He wondered how long it would take her to change her mind about him. The fact that she'd resisted her purification bothered him only in that he'd responded poorly. Disgust filled him for taking things so far as to be accused of trying to rape her. *Rape.* The word alone caused his skin to crawl. He'd try again tomorrow once she rested, after he'd put the others safely away and removed the scenes. She'd seen a lot over the past few days. If things went his way, he hoped she'd see a lot more.

While the two undercover detectives toiled outside filling in the ditch, the two inside the van talked about the football game they'd missed earlier, and the chances the man responsible for plucking twenty-six women off the city's streets could be the one who'd just driven by them. They doubted it, since the task force had already followed hundreds of false leads over the past six months. The man in the Miata had clearly just returned from watching the game, probably at the stadium due to his face paint, team jacket and hat. Nothing in PK's profile mentioned him being a sports fan. Reports of the duplicate plate was enough to stop the vehicle should it be seen leaving the property, but DVS was known to screw up plates before. Still, they had a job to do, continuing to watch the driveway, grateful to not be outside digging in the half-frozen ground. With the ditch filled in and dusk looming, all four detectives waited for confirmation that a new aspect of the investigation—a camera-fitted drone hovering high above the home—had arrived. Its infrared night-vision camera was capable of registering the heat signature of any gas-

or battery-operated vehicle, or any animal larger than a mouse, that left the property.

Three miles away, a BCA agent sat inside a bureau sub-station with a state-of-the-art drone remote controller and monitor, his job to constantly monitor the house and immediately report any movement from it to undercover officers staged at points east, west, and south of the property. The woods were thickest behind the home, so to be safe Fells had taken the added step of deploying several camouflaged ground units just outside the acre-wide property line to cover that avenue. They'd considered doing the same with this home as they'd done with many others—knock and stalk. But Randall had lobbied against it. Posing as a door-to-door salesman or religious prophesier was safe enough in a heavily populated neighborhood. Any suspect living in such an area had experienced them before. But the home's isolated location, and the fact that PK had just posted a victim's photo several hours ago, prompted Randall to opine that that doing so with this home would appear extremely suspicious to any experienced criminal. Fells had agreed. They'd wait until they gained more evidence, all while constantly surveilling the home. No one involved wanted to pull the trigger too early, which was ironic since they finally had a decent target in their sights. As such, all undercover officers were given strict orders that, should a vehicle or pedestrian leave the property, they were to notify Sergeant Fells and Detective Randall immediately, then follow it to the end of the earth if necessary.

"Guess the realtor was right about him being a twin," Randall said, handing the teletyped birth certificate back to Tan. Having just read it over a dozen times, he shifted his gaze out his office window. The green roof was illuminated now—dusk had given way to full dark. The throngs of fans had long since dispersed, leaving the downtown streets eerily quiet. After conferring with Whitlock and Fells, he'd decided to request an emergency subpoena for the state agencies responsible for maintaining birth certificates and social security numbers. There wasn't any reason for the state to refuse a request for necessary law enforcement reasons, but Whitlock opted for this route since there was no telling if persons responsible would voluntarily disrupt their Sunday evening. They'd done similar things before, the task force having established an "express lane" of sorts with the case judge when it came to such matters. Time was running out. Tan, true to Randall's opinion that rookie detectives should handle important issues right away, had personally delivered the subpoena then returned the results twenty minutes ago.

"Born in Chatham, two hours north of here," she said, reading the certificate's information aloud more to herself than to Randall. "No flags from the local sheriff's office. Google was a no-go for any family, and no media stories under that name from what I've seen."

Randall chewed on that sentiment. "Too bad our guy grew up before the internet became a thing." No matter how many times he'd re-read Frederik Derring's birth certificate (paying particular attention to the portion listing him as a TWIN—IDENTICAL), he couldn't get it out of his head that not only might they now have two main suspects to worry about, but two who looked exactly the same. That was a twist he hadn't yet considered. Confounding matters worse was the real possibility that some of the abductions had been carried out solely by Frederik's twin.

"We need his brother's cert too," Randall said, looking around the busy office. Scores of task force members worked on computers, spoke on cellphones, and conferred amongst themselves. Fells and Whitlock stood near the victim board, going over something in a file the senior agent was holding.

"Too bad they don't list siblings' names on them," Tan added.

"We'll send a team up there in the morning to do a manual search if we have to," Randall said. But he knew even that could be a long shot since many rural counties kept iffy records. He'd often joked that some state jurisdictions probably kept records on stone tablets.

A deeper NCIC search for a Frederik Derring born on the birthdate DVS had for him turned up nothing. Likewise from a Social Security Administration query and a full credit report. He had no vehicles registered in his name or property owned, and he had no other known address other than the post office box they'd already investigated. Postal records showed it hadn't been accessed in over a year. A linked Interpol search came back *NO RECORD*. Assuming the man listed on the birth certificate was alive and residing on planet Earth—and his look-alike brother too—he'd somehow managed to become a living ghost.

CHAPTER 31

A t eight a.m. the following morning, Abby sat at the main floor kitchen table poking at her breakfast. Frederik sat across from her, watching her intently as he chewed a strip of crispy bacon. "You'll get skinny if you don't eat," he said flatly.

"Why does it matter? You're going to kill me anyway," she said, refusing to look up at him. She'd gotten to a place where she really didn't care what he said or did anymore, reaching a level of acceptance or apathy that only mildly surprised her. He'd gotten rid of the girls and their scenes during the night. She considered briefly that he'd become spooked and disposed of them. But she recalled the glint in his eyes when he'd let her out of the room an hour ago. Spooked, perhaps, but he'd never get rid of them, she decided. He'd just as soon die first.

Frederik popped the last piece of bacon in his mouth and drained the last of his coffee. "I wish you wouldn't think such dark thoughts. You're my guest, and guests should be made to feel welcome. Which reminds me, I wanted to get your opinion on your pose."

Now she did look up at him. "Are you serious? You want me to...pick how you'll *pose* me?"

He spread his hands and smiled. "Look at it as a joint venture. A few of the others chose for themselves as well."

For some reason, that disgusted her more than anything she'd seen or that had already happened to her. "You're sick."

"No..." he said, drawing out the word. "I am *not* sick. I know perfectly well what I'm doing."

"It's criminal," she said, spitting out the word before she could take it back. She noted how he sat back slightly in his chair when she said that. "The police will never stop looking for us," she continued. Her heart was pounding, but it comforted her knowing it was still beating at all. "When they find you, they'll kill you or put you in prison for life. Won't you let me go? I...I have things I need to do." After caring for Thomas Magnum, the secondary motivations that came immediately to mind did surprise her. If she died here and became posed like the rest of them, she'd never get to visit her doorman's sick wife. Abby had promised to do so over the weekend. Surely the woman would have heard about her disappearance by now, and would be further sickened, this time with worry. That made Abby's stomach churn with guilt. And she'd never see Derek again, or the girls from the clinic. Almost worse than that was the fact she'd never get to confront Hank. He would win if she died. If God Himself appeared before her now, she would swear on everything she'd ever loved that she'd withdraw any public acknowledgement of Hank's acts against her in exchange for a single private conversation with him. Hell, she'd stick the tube in her own jugular vein afterward, if that's what His Almighty wanted.

"Criminal, maybe," Frederik said after thinking about it. "But then again, many things are against the law. I'm sure you and your whore friends used to drink alcohol underage."

Her jaw dropped. "What did you say about my friends?"

"Did that touch a nerve?" he asked, tilting his head and sticking out his lower lip. "I'm sorry if that offended you. But it's true, at least for some of them, I'm sure. Letting pimply-faced young men do sordid things to them in dark dorm rooms littered with pizza boxes. None of you are pure. Not even my girls, at least until I made them that way before their transition-ing. Ask them yourself—they're happier now that they'll live with me forever."

Abby didn't try to hide her look of disgust. "That has to be the most twisted thing I've ever heard. And I've seen some twisted movies. But those are fake. You're for real. You're a sick fuck."

The elephant approached. She felt its heavy footfalls. It settled down on her chest, making it hard for her to breathe. But she forced herself to ignore it. She didn't have time to deal with it. From the hurt look on his face, she could tell she'd insulted him deeply. It felt terrifying and liberating at the same time, talking shit to the man who at any time could turn her into a death doll. That thought reminded her of the other girls. "Where are they, by the way?"

"They're taking a little siesta," he said, standing up and collecting both of their plates. He placed his in the sink then scraped off her untouched eggs and bacon into the trash. "For a bit, just to be safe." He came up behind her and gathered her hair in his hands. When one of his fingers brushed against her bare neck, her entire body stiffened. "I've been doing this for a long time, Abby. Part of me thinks I began doing it in my head as soon as my father passed away. He was a good man. Not just good—the best man I've ever known. What kind of relationship did you have with *your* father?"

Abby's skin began to crawl when he ran his fingers through her hair.

"My father died when I was seven," she said, her voice sounding mechanical even to her own ears. Her words seemed to come from somewhere else. The other side of the world, or outer space, perhaps.

"A stepfather then…?"

She didn't answer.

"Now, Abby," he said, gathering her hair in his hands again. He lifted it and bent to whisper into her ear. "You can never love me if you cannot trust me. Answer, please." She still didn't answer. She couldn't form the words even if she'd wanted to.

What happened next occurred so quickly that an involuntary cry escaped her. In a flash, he pulled the top of her chair backward, tipping her to the point where she would have crashed hard onto her back had he not caught the chair six inches from the floor. She'd mostly refused to look him in the eye before, having made excuses for not doing so or simply not caring if he got offended. But now she did meet them—or was forced to by some sheer sense of panic that he was going to do something hideous to her before she had a chance to prepare herself. Worse than making direct eye contact with him was the fact that she was doing so upside down, his scowl reversed into a crazed grin.

"Don't ever disrespect me by refusing to answer my questions," he said. His eyes bulged from their sockets. His nostrils flared. He'd always been a handsome man, in the strict physical sense. But now he resembled anything but a human. A monster had taken over where the man had once been. "You've been a guest in *my* home. *My* girls cook and do your laundry for you. And don't forget *me* cleaning your messy bucket. That takes caring. That takes devotion."

She somehow managed to swallow while being nearly upside down. "I'm…I'm sorry," she said. Tears formed in the corners of her eyes and threatened to spill sideways down her face, but she didn't want to cry for fear of appearing to beg for her life. If she'd been honest with him by telling him the things she had, she could damn well be honest with herself. "You scared me."

Almost as quickly as he'd tipped her backward, he righted her. The chair legs banged back down on the wood floor. In one smooth movement, he swung one of his legs across hers and planted himself on her lap. Taking her face in his hands, he brought his nose to within an inch of hers. He didn't seem angry anymore. The monster was gone, replaced by the man-thing that had been there before.

"I would never try to scare you, my love," he said, planting soft, healing kisses over her cheeks, nose and forehead. He finished by kissing both of her eyelids. For some reason, one she remembered from her darkest childhood days, that action did it. Hot, furious tears began to stream down her face. But it hadn't been the threat of physical pain or even death that had frightened her. It had been him forcing the image of her stepfather into her brain, of how he'd ended his interactions with her in that same healing, almost apologetic way, and her inability to focus her thoughts away from it. If the rape of her body had been terrible, this rape of her mind twenty years later was even worse.

"Let me make it up to you," he said, brushing away her tears. He stood her up and escorted her to the living room where he pointed a remote control at a speaker. Soon, classical music poured from it. Placing the remote down, he interlaced the fingers of one hand in hers and placed the other around her waist before leaning in close to her. She shied away at first, thinking he might try to kiss her, but when he extended their intertwined hands straight out to one side and faced that direction, Abby realized what was happening. Waiting for a certain place in the music, he began leading her in a waltz. Strauss, always one of her favorites. Until now.

They danced for what seemed an eternity. When the music finally stopped and he led her back downstairs, she considered what may happen next. Frederik seemed invigorated. His face was flushed, and Abby had felt different parts of him stiffening against her during the last part of their dance. That worried her. She could deal with the oddness of him insisting on eating meals together, and for the most part had become numb to the horror of what she'd seen in the embalming room. But a nascent fear

remained in her heart, a sleeping serpent in her consciousness—
he'd promised to try "purifying" her again. Soon, from what he'd
indicated. If what she remembered from listening to his
encounter with the violinist, she doubted very much the term
"purifying" applied in any form.

When they got to the bottom of the stairs, he said he needed
to use the bathroom. So did she. Apologizing for his lack of
chivalry, explaining that the coffee he'd drank had other ideas,
he told her to wait outside the open door while he went. He
unleashed a forceful torrent of urine, checking over his shoulder
several times to ensure she remained where he'd instructed her
to. When he was done, he lowered the seat then washed his
hands, taking the added step of tearing off some toilet paper to
dry the front of the sink. Balling it up then tossing the paper in
the trash, he exited and exhaled a relieved breath. "Whew—if
that wasn't like a cow pissing on a flat rock. Guess that means
my parts are still working." He motioned with his head while
extending a hand toward the bathroom's interior.

Abby brushed past him and stood momentarily staring at her
reflection in the mirror. Normally, she wouldn't bother trying to
close the door. In the several days she'd been here (she'd lost
exact count), she'd used the real toilet a dozen times at least.
And each time, he'd left the door wide open or propped his foot
in the doorway to keep it partially open. He'd been a gentleman
by not looking, although his earlier talk of trust had yet to result
in him letting her so much as wash her hands without him being
just around the corner. But a plan had bloomed in her mind
during their dance, when she'd looked dumbly up at their
extended hands. She'd been reminded of it then—the single
strand of the violinist's hair she'd plucked the night before—still
wrapped around her index finger. A stupid idea, more fantasy
than anything. Because she was going to die here. She was sure
of it now. But if that were the case, at least she could go into
death with a tiny part of someone who'd been normal. Maybe

he'd notice the hair on her finger while he washed and embalmed her. He'd peer curiously at it as she lay cold and stiff on the table, unwinding it from her finger and holding it to the light, his eyes dancing with wonder over why she'd done it. Or even when she'd done it. Perhaps in the elevator when they'd carried the violinist upstairs, or after, during those few moments he'd had his back turned to her.

During the dance, she'd remembered what Derek had said about his client who always took her hair with her after getting it cut—the crazy lady who was paranoid the CIA stole people's discarded hair to identify them by their DNA. Abby remembered laughing at it, and then they'd changed the subject from his work at the salon to something else entirely...

Her heart pounding harder than ever, Abby decided to take a risk. Turning confidently, she locked eyes with him before grasping the edge of the door and closing it softly. When the latch clicked, she stood there expecting him to open it and lecture her about trust or some other line of bullshit. Or become angry that she'd dared exercise some independence. But he didn't. She stood there breathing heavily, unsure if she should go through with it. She was sure he'd open the door while she performed her task. Enraged, he'd drag her screaming and kicking from the bathroom and savagely rape her. She wouldn't be able to fight him off this time. She'd already bitten him, and he wouldn't allow her to do anything similar again. Then, the table. Only, he'd make her suffer first. He'd promised that.

Come on, you scary-assed bitch, just do it and stop being a victim for once in your goddamned life...

She undid her pants and dropped them to her ankles, then plopped onto the seat. As she began to pee, she unwound the woman's hair from her finger. It had created an indentation in her skin, one she could only hope he didn't notice. He noticed everything. But she didn't have time to concern herself with what-ifs. Finishing, she pulled up her pants, flushed, then turned on the water. She opened the medicine cabinet and removed one of the pink Kleenex from the travel-sized pouch. Coiling the woman's hair inside one of the Kleenex, she plucked one of her own hairs then coiled that inside the tissue as well. Balling up the tissue, she went to toss it in the trash when a thought stopped her. No, not one of the tissues she and the other women had been given to use. He hadn't been this successful by being careless, and it made sense to her that he'd also be careful enough to check something they exclusively used. She spied the piece of toilet paper he'd just used to wipe the sink with and dug it out of the trash. Swapping out the hairs, she balled up both tissues then made sure to place them in the trash with her pink Kleenex on top. Quickly wetting her hands, she dried them, then closed the cabinet and shut off the faucet. She'd have to hurry; her inner clock told her she'd been in here longer than necessary. Her heart pounded so hard now that she was sure he could hear it through the door. She could. It was like a drum in her ears. *Boom-boom… boom-boom.* He'd be out there growing more suspicious by the second. If she discovered what she'd done, then—

The door tore open, and she jumped when she saw Frederik's face in the doorway. "You okay in there?" he asked, glancing around the bathroom. "I thought you'd fallen in."

Her heart stopped for a beat. Then for two. She wasn't sure if it would ever beat again. "I'm fine," she said, tears beginning to well in her eyes. Her heart resumed its pounding beat. "I'm just…embarrassed with you standing out here listening. I had to go…you know, number two…but then I couldn't anymore."

His eyes narrowed as he appeared to be deciding if she was hiding anything. When a tear trickled down her cheek, his expression softened. He came to her and cupped her face with both hands. "I'm sorry. Of course you were embarrassed. That's not something a woman wants to do with a man listening."

She nodded, feeling it would be best not to burst into total tears again. That could be construed as melodrama and could elicit suspicion. But the harder she tried to fight them, the harder it was to stop them. Despite her will to keep them away, they fell down her cheeks, hot and fuller than any tears she could ever remember spilling.

Don't do it! a voice inside her yelled. *Don't you let him see you crying ever again, not even when he brings you back in there and tries to fuck you...*

He was wiping away her tears and walking her back toward the bedroom. She steeled herself as he sat with her on the edge of the bed, stroking her hair and shushing her. "It's okay. You rest. I've got business to take care of upstairs. I'll leave you with the bucket if you need to go." He kissed the top of her head then left. He returned a moment later with the same water-filled blue bucket he'd given her to use during her extended time periods in here. Instead of the half roll of toilet paper he'd given her every time before, a full roll sat on the stick this time. He'd even formed a triangle with the first few sections of paper. Abby imagined him creating the homemade toilet on his garage work-bench, then wondered how many of the other women had also used it in this fashion. After setting the bucket down, Frederik patted the crude seat with one hand. To Abby, the gesture spoke more of him reminding her of her position rather than some false apology. She was his captive. He would kill her sooner or later. And as much as she'd hoped to do so, not even some pathetic attempt on her part to deliver to the world a piece of herself and the redhead was going to change that.

Keeping with his extreme sense of caution, Frederik vacuumed the entire house twice (careful to include the furniture and both the wood and tile surfaces too). He wiped down everything he was sure Abby and the other women had touched during their time here, plus a few other surfaces he thought they could have.

Per routine, he washed the dishes Abby had used, wiping them each with a towel until he was sure her prints didn't remain. Remembering something, he rooted through the basement bathroom trash can, systematically removing the handful of used pink tissues and placing them into a paper bag. Setting the bag beside the fireplace so that he wouldn't forget to burn it, he bleached down the bathroom, getting onto his hands and knees with a flashlight to search for loose hairs. Finding none that he'd missed, he noted the balled bit of toilet paper he'd used to wipe down the sink. Feeling he'd be bothered if he didn't properly empty the can while he was at it, he tossed it into a plastic trash bag, his intention being to add the bag of food scraps from upstairs to it before taking it to the main road receptacle. He'd been careful to burn sensitive trash, but he'd also been sensible enough to throw other trash out, understanding that the best way to avoid suspicion was to appear as normal as possible. Especially now if the police were, in fact, watching him.

But first things first. He placed a wax starter cube, several pieces of kindling, and a log in the iron fireplace. Lighting the cube, he waited several minutes for the fire to build properly before stuffing the vacuum bag and paper bag inside. He closed the squeaky iron door and stood watching the contents until they fully caught fire. Taking the plastic bag, he went upstairs and threw it in the kitchen bag containing wrappers and old foodstuffs, before tying it off and setting it by the back door. After he showered and changed, he placed it in the dumpster on the main road. Now, as his beloved mother used to say, everything was copacetic.

CHAPTER 32

Forty minutes later, a garbage truck made its scheduled stop at the beginning of a narrow, wooded road on the western edge of the city. The driver was accustomed to stopping here at this part of his route, grateful the owner of the home at the end of the private road had been gracious enough to place the bin here at the easement instead of at the home's wrought-iron gate. The driver had had this route for fifteen years. He remembered how the old owners had kept the bin just outside the home's fence, requiring him to either execute an awkward seven-point turn, or reverse along the narrow fifty-yard road, just to get out. Now, it was easy enough to stop the truck on the main road, operate the mechanical claw used to lift the green, ninety-six-gallon residential receptacle, and dump its contents into the truck's open bay before moving on.

The driver was acutely aware of the many different load amounts in each of the several hundred receptacles he dumped every day. He'd learned to guess the weight of a loaded bin's contents down to the pound. As he operated the claw and felt the shift of the truck as it first clamped, then lifted the bin, he played the guessing game he'd developed long ago to help pass the time. "Sixteen pounds," he said as the claw began the second of its three-step dumping process. But before it reached its third step—the jerky dunking of the contents into the overhead reservoir—a black sedan with darkly tinted windows flew in from behind him and screeched to a halt beside the truck's driver's door. A plainclothes cop (the driver figured as much, due to the man's shirt and tie, lanyard badge, and exposed firearm) jumped from the sedan's passenger seat and yelled for him to halt the dumping operation. Confused, the driver obeyed. Rolling down his window, he asked the cop what the matter was.

"Bring that bin back down," the cop ordered, pointing to the bin the driver had begun to dump. When the driver complied, the cop lifted the bin's lid with gloved hands and removed the sole garbage bag inside of it. After opening the trunk, he placed the bag into a larger, clear plastic bag, sealed it, then tossed it in. "Thanks," the cop said, closing the trunk and banging a hand on the side of the truck. Without another word, he climbed back into the passenger seat and the car he'd arrived in zoomed away.

BCA technician Pete Svenson was an hour into his eight a.m.–four p.m. shift monitoring the surveillance drone when a blinking red indicator appeared on his monitor. At the same time, a computer-generated Darth Vader voice came over the desk-mounted speakers, repeating the same message: "Motion detected…motion detected…motion detected…"

Svenson had used a computer app to select the alternate voice indicator, opting for his favorite movie character instead of the selection of drab monotoned voices the drone program came with. It was his first shift monitoring this particular surveillance drone. He'd replaced one of the midnight shift agents here in the Minnetonka PDP office, having first been briefed to immediately report any movement to or from the house, vehicular or pedestrian. PDP—the state bureau's Piloted

Drone Program—was relatively new to the agency. Due to the drones' one-hour battery life, several agents each had three drones they would switch from, with a new one assuming the surveillance before the other departed so as to maintain a constant visual. Seeking his helicopter pilot license, Svenson had been one of the first volunteers for the high-tech surveillance program. In his two years with the unit, his greatest claim to fame was helping to track a porch pirate ring plaguing suburban Minneapolis for months. He longed for serious action. So now, as his monitor blinked and Darth Vader repeated his throaty alert, Agent Svenson leaned excitedly toward the screen. A vehicle was moving slowly down the home's graded driveway. Due to the many overhanging tree limbs, it took a while for him to get a partial ID, but as the vehicle approached the wrought-iron gate, Svenson snatched his radio from the desk and pressed the transmit button. "D-6 to U-10, we've got movement. Blue Miata—white male, large build, no passengers."

He released the transmit button and waited for a response. Nothing. Goddamned UC guys were probably yapping on the phone with their wives or watching *SportsCenter* highlights on their laptops. In Svenson's opinion, the UCs had become over-reliant on the drones, falling into the same kind of complacency that had already bungled two of his cases since the program had first begun. Not wishing to repeat those instances, especially with this case, he decided to relay the information straight to the unit supervisor, someone widely known for his bad hearing. Switching channels, he raised his voice and enunciated slowly, nearly slipping by calling him by his unofficial moniker "10-9," police code for "please repeat."

"D-6 to D-1, we have vehicular movement exiting the property. Copy?"

A few seconds later, the supervisor responded: "10-9?"

Svenson rolled his eyes, then repeated the transmission.

"Copy, D-6," the supervisor finally acknowledged. "Maintain visual. UCs notified?"

"Negative. Failed to respond."

"Copy, I'll notify."

Svenson grabbed his controller from the table, a video game-like, hand-held device with a series of buttons and two miniature joysticks, then zeroed the drone's camera in on the opening driveway gate. Soon, the vehicle would clear it and travel the fifty-yard access road to the main surface street and likely get too far away for ground units to catch up to, assuming they didn't answer their radios in time. All the more important for him to keep an aerial visual and relay position and direction of travel to responding units. A chopper from the agency's flight unit was taking off should an extended pursuit be necessary. The various drones—much cheaper to operate and harder to detect—had been airborne since five p.m. the previous day, or almost eighteen hours ago, when Agent Whitlock and Sergeant Fells had agreed the long-abandoned, former funeral home Randall had found may be the best lead they'd had in months. Still a long shot, but a thousand other leads so far had barely amounted to a hill of beans.

As the Miata passed through the gate, Svenson angled the drone and zoomed the camera to better view the sportster's lone two bucket seats. "Confirmed no passengers, copy?"

"Copy. As long as he stays in the area, we'll stop him when he reaches his destination."

A backup drone arrived over the area. When its pilot was instructed to take over the aerial pursuit, thus relegating Svenson to remaining on the home surveillance, he got back on his mic. "D-6 to D-1, request permission to conduct pursuit." After several seconds of radio silence, and his full expectation that the supervisor would request a repeated transmission, Svenson was relieved to get an actual response.

"10-4, D-6, she's all yours."

Two minutes later, after Svenson landed his unit and took a backup to flight, he hovered it over the Miata to where another unit had trailed it moving south, then east on the freeway. The chopper arrived to assist the aerial part of the chase, although at a distance and high altitude. With a break in traffic, undercover detectives tailing it got the order to pull it over, first attempting to box it in. But the driver maneuvered out of it and shot ahead, racing several miles south until it became obvious where he was headed—Minneapolis/St. Paul International Airport. With a half-dozen unmarked cruisers chasing it, the Miata weaved through traffic before it took the airport exit and veered up the Terminal #1 hourly parking garage ramp. Due to FAA restricted airspace, the newly-arrived chopper pilot was ordered to stay out of the airport's no-fly zone, as was the drone. Still, several surveillance officers hurried on foot to monitor the skyway and Level T entry points into the terminal, as well as positioning several units at the garage exit. If the driver tried to quickly exit, they'd stop him. If he intended on taking a flight, they'd do their best to intercept him before he boarded. Should he somehow manage to board first, FBI agents would halt takeoff and conduct a person-by-person search of his plane. In the unlikely event his plane managed to take off after the boarding gate closed, they'd be waiting for him at his destination. Interpol would be contacted and an emergency detainer request made in the event the flight was international. No doubt, it had been a gamble not stopping him as soon as he'd exited the property. But many cases had been solved by following a suspect to a holdout or where evidence was located. Either way—and no matter where on Earth the man was headed—the task force would at least have an opportunity to positively identify him before deciding on their next course of action.

CHAPTER 33

Detectives Randall and Tan made it to the airport in twenty minutes, coordinating with Sergeant Fells to operate with the dozen plainclothes detectives already there. So far, no one fitting the Miata driver's general physical description had exited the parking garage into the terminal from either the skyway or Level T entrances. And even though the chopper had been forced to remain out of the airport's airspace, it had been helping to cover the garage's exit and perimeter with its high-resolution zoom camera. When a half hour had passed and the suspect hadn't been seen entering the terminal, or exiting the garage in his vehicle or on foot, Randall gave Whitlock an update. Unable to justify closing the garage to all traffic, they had to settle for systematically searching it while they stopped each exiting vehicle for general questioning, albeit five minutes after they'd arrived. They found the Miata soon enough, unoccupied in a space on the garage's third level, with all doors and trunk locked. A K-9 and cadaver dog sniffed the trunk's exterior; neither detected a person inside, alive or dead. With a search warrant already issued for the car due to the duplicate plate, a fifty-officer sweep of the entire garage found no persons hiding under vehicles or in common areas. Simultaneously, the car's trunk was searched. It was confirmed to be unoccupied. No prints or other evidence was found, either.

Hands on hips, Randall looked around the busy garage, avoiding the silent stares of Tan, Fells, and the scores of other task force members around him. "We're positive all those terminal entry points were covered?" he asked no one in particular.

"Yes," the UC supervisor said. "We were thirty seconds behind him. There's no way he made it into the terminal that fast from where he parked. Besides, our guys were already inside waiting for him."

"So he's somewhere else in the airport," Randall said, feeling a familiar frustration creep into him. Then, almost as quickly as he'd made that assertion, he shook his head. "No—he's not here. He switched vehicles. Fuck."

Fifteen minutes later, the drone pilot covering the home observed a beige sedan enter through the front gate. He couldn't make out the driver due to the darkly tinted windows, or the plate because of the overhead tree branches, but did verify that it drove up the driveway and parked inside the garage. He called it in immediately. Ten minutes later, he observed a black van exit the garage, come back down the driveway and exit the gate. The pilot only had a partial view the driver. "White male, age unknown, brown sweater. Copy?"

"Copy," came his supervisor's reply.

By the time the pilot maneuvered the drone behind the van and zeroed in to try reading the plate, bumper-to-bumper traffic on the freeway he'd just entered prevented that. The pilot didn't even attempt reading the front plate since that would have exposed the drone to the driver's line of sight. "Negative on the ID. Copy?"

"Copy. UCs will get it when traffic lightens up or when he parks. Follow and advise."

Detective Randall received the van update thirty seconds later. It didn't take him long to come to an even more frustrating conclusion. "However he did it, he had a plan for emergencies. It was him—PK, I'm positive."

Agent Whitlock had arrived at the airport after the search of the garage and Miata. Listening to Randall now, he nodded his agreement. As the rest of the assembled officers and techs packed up to head back to other assignments, he voiced what everyone else was already thinking. "He played us. He knew we were onto him."

Just then, Randall's cellphone rang. It was an update from Agent Teague. "Van is heading eastbound on 394. Possible Caucasian male."

"Tag?"

"Negative. We'll get it when traffic clears up, or when he stops."

"We're headed back to the office now," Randall said, making a rolling "let's go" motion to the others. "Don't stop it unless it's headed toward the airport, I want to see where it's headed. Set up a perimeter wherever the driver parks." Before hanging up, he asked Teague to meet them back at Homicide with his laptop in case the vehicle hadn't stopped yet. They could track it in real time. Since enough UC units were following it already, it didn't make sense for them to waste time wagon-training the vehicle. He and Tan would personally question the driver whenever and wherever he decided to stop, even if it was Alaska.

They rushed back to Homicide with lights and sirens. Agent Teague was waiting for them there and had just waved them over to where he sat with his laptop when he jabbed a finger at the screen. "He's exiting the freeway. Looks like he's headed uptown."

They all watched the chopper's bird's eye view of the van as it exited 35W and turned east on Lake Street. It continued another two miles until it turned into a parking lot and settled into the space closest to the building's front door. Shortly afterward, a side door on the van opened. Something odd happened then that caused Whitlock to openly question if perhaps the chopper had followed the wrong vehicle. It was Detective Tan who was the first to realize an important detail. "Is that who I think it is?" she said, leaning forward to squint at the screen.

Randall did the same. "I think so." He asked Teague to have the view focused. Teague obliged. Moments later, the screen expanded, exposing the business sign in the parking lot, then a closer view of the van's driver exiting the vehicle.

Whitlock leaned in closer too, peering hard at the screen. When he realized what Randall and Tan had, he turned to yell that they needed to respond to the location quick. But the detective duo was already running toward the door.

CHAPTER 34

Randall and Tan exited the elevator and ran full-speed into PSB's multi-leveled parking garage. Randall nearly slipped on a painter's drop cloth, knocking into an attendant stand with a "Wet Paint" sign on it. Not missing a beat, he jumped into his SUV's driver seat and Tan hopped in beside him. Tearing toward the garage's exit ramp, he activated the car's lights and siren.

"What about Sarge?" Tan asked, looking over her shoulder at the image of Fells and several other detectives standing in the parking lot, watching their vehicle pull away.

"She won't mind us ditching her," Randall said. "She hates being a passenger. Last winter she walked a mile in a snowstorm instead of riding shotgun in my cruiser." Looking both ways, he shot out of the garage and weaved his way through traffic, pausing at a red light. He nosed the SUV into the intersection and waited until it was clear before he sped through it. When his cellphone rang, he handed it to Tan and asked her to take the call. The caller ID read *FELLS*.

"Yes, Sarge?" Tan spoke into the phone. After listening to Fells speak, she uttered several "uh-huhs" and "yes ma'ams" before hanging up. "She asked if it really was who we thought it was. CMH Group? It's too big of a coincidence to be anything else. She said to go ahead and question him as soon as we get there, and to make it custodial. She'll stage down the block and set a perimeter."

Randall nodded. "Okay. I want you to start the questioning."

Tan stared at him, wide-eyed. "Are you sure?"

"Yes. He'll already be prepared for an experienced detective. No offense. But being green has its advantages—you'll come at him in a different way than I would, like last time. Just think things through logically and lead him the way they taught you during classroom. I'll take over if we need to cover anything you missed."

"Okay." She took a deep breath, then shot a surprised look down at his gray suit jacket sleeve. "Watch it—you got paint on your sleeve."

Recalling the black attendant stand with the wet paint sign he'd just knocked into, Randall lifted his right arm, noted a streak of black paint on the sleeve, then used that hand to steer. Despite the emergent situation, he didn't feel the need to ruin a perfectly good leather seat or the console. "Nice catch."

Tan sat back in her seat and focused on the traffic ahead of them. They were only five miles from their destination, but it felt like five hundred.

They parked down the block, opting to enter the office building without fanfare and surprise him. Since he'd just arrived himself, they doubted he'd be engaged in official business yet. It was 11:35 a.m., an odd time for most appointments of that nature to begin. If successful, they'd be able to get answers quickly enough and report to Fells. On the ride, they'd discussed the possibility of it all being a coincidence. But to Randall, the most experienced detective in the unit, and even

Tan, the most highly-touted candidate from a list of over two dozen, it wasn't.

Checking the van's windows to ensure it was unoccupied, Tan called the tag in and gave a general update to Fells, who'd just staged with the backup teams a block further down the street from where Randall had parked. Moments later, the tag info came back—they'd been right. Entering the building, they made their way down the chilly, dimly lit corridor to an office marked *Cromley Mental Health Services*, the same rented office they'd been to three days ago. Pausing to check several occupied offices they passed, and satisfied their occupants had legitimate business there, the detectives locked eyes and nodded a silent affirmation. Whatever the connection—probable cause on their side or not— they were sure one existed.

They stood to either the side of the closed door, their gun hands resting on their holstered pistols. Tan gave three sharp knocks on the door and announced, "Mr. Cromley?" When no immediate response came, she knocked again. Still nothing. Randall reached into his inner jacket pocket and activated a digital recording device. He nodded to Tan. Opting to take the initiative and not wishing to risk the chance that something detrimental was occurring inside, she cleared her throat and said loudly, "Mr. Cromley, it's Detective Tan and Detective Randall. May we speak with you?"

A moment later, a familiar voice came through the closed door. "Yes…please come in."

Randall pointed to himself, indicating for Tan to stay in position while he entered first. But as he reached for the knob, a familiar sensation came over him. It was happening again, that old impulse coming stronger now than it had during their clinic investigation. He swallowed hard and looked down at his shoes, then back up at Tan. He wanted badly to re-tie the laces, despite them being tied just fine. Or at least some old part of himself wanted to. It was crazy, because he was doing what the therapist had taught him, going over in his mind whenever the feeling came over him that he could plainly see they were tied, that there was no reason to submit to his old compulsion. To her credit, Tan appeared patient and calm. She stayed where she was against the wall, meeting his eye, giving an almost imperceptible nod of her head as if to tell him everything would be okay, he could do it. And then he *was* okay a second later. In that space of time when he'd overridden the compulsion, knowing he would have abided by his promise to report the incident had he succumbed to it, some unspoken bond seemed to have grown between him and Tan, albeit a small one. It had taken months and even a harrowing shootout to form one like that with Pappy; with Tan it had only taken three days and a few silent moments in a musty hallway.

Gathering himself, Randall gripped the doorknob and opened the door. The small windowless office was occupied only by Abby Carlson's counselor. The man sat hunched in his wheel-chair, his smallish hands folded meditatively atop his desk, as if he'd expected them. He was dressed in a brown sweater over a white button-down dress shirt, his blanket clutched around him. His glasses sat perched halfway down his nose.

"Detectives!" he said, his voice cheerful and his expression inviting. "What a surprise. When you knocked, I thought it was the cleaning lady. She knows I usually don't come in until noon on Mondays. I have to admit to hoping she'd leave if I didn't answer. I have a lot of work to do today." He smiled graciously, waving a hand to invite them in. They entered, with Tan following Randall's lead. They stood side-by-side in front of his desk, silent for a moment. Looking at him from this angle, with the man's hump still plainly evident and his severely curved spine even more obvious than before, Randall felt a pang of doubt over his hunch. Clearly this man had nothing to do with kidnapping women himself. True, he'd left the home Randall himself had deemed a possible connection to the crimes, despite

Randall having no sufficient proof to that effect. That fact only heightened the doubt already inside him. When the man motioned to the two chairs opposite the desk, both detectives sat down. The mood during their first visit here had been semi-formal and lukewarm due to them having considered him a mere witness. This time the mood was formal and chilly.

"We apologize for dropping by unannounced," Tan said. "But what we need to discuss is important. And serious. We'll ask that you postpone or re-schedule any appointments until we've finished speaking with you."

If the counselor was surprised by Tan's directness, he didn't show it. "My, that does sound serious. I do have two sessions this afternoon, but I'll ring my scheduling service and cancel them." He picked up his desk telephone and dialed a number. Audible to the detectives through the earpiece, the call's female recipient identified herself as a customer service rep of Pritchard Scheduling Service and asked what he needed. He asked her to please cancel his two afternoon appointments, then hung up. "Now, what was it you wished to discuss with me, Detectives?"

Tan paused. She hadn't had sufficient time to run the line of questioning over with Randall, or even to herself. It reminded her of cramming for a college exam, only a hundred times worse. *Remember the basics. He's not a witness anymore. And let him know this is going to be a custodial interview. Don't wait.* She removed a laminated card from her jacket pocket and read his Miranda warning to him. When she finished, she pocketed the card and asked him if he wished to still speak with them without an attorney present.

Without hesitating, he waved his hand. "I'd be glad to speak with you without my attorney present."

Tan didn't hesitate either; she decided to confront him right away. "Mr. Cromley, you were observed leaving a residence about twenty minutes ago in a black, wheelchair-accessible van located in the parking lot here. The home is in Minnetonka, along a wooded road at 438 Sand Hill Drive. Do you care to tell us what you were doing there?"

The counselor looked confused for a second. Quickly, his expression changed to one of sudden revelation. "You mean the house I own?"

Tan hadn't expected that response. When she looked at Randall, she could tell he hadn't either. "Is that your residence?"

"Yes."

"But your driver's license, vehicle registration, and business certification list a different address." As soon as the words left her mouth, she realized her mistake: that address was the very office building she and Randall now sat in. "Why would you list your office as your residence, sir?"

"In my line of work, I meet many troubled people. Most of them are well-intended, but some aren't. If my home address were to fall into the wrong person's hands—"

"That's understandable," she said. In a flash, she realized something else that had nagged at her for the past day. She and Randall had spoken of it—the old funeral home's listed owner of record. It was like finding a lost puzzle piece in the most obvious place you could have misplaced it. "The home's owner of record is CMH Group. That stands for Cromley Mental Health, doesn't it?"

The counselor smiled. "You're sharp." He leaned back, appearing to painfully adjust his malformed body within his blanket. He shivered as he did so, craning his small, stooped head to maintain eye contact with her.

Tan considered where to go from here. She'd been surprised that Randall had trusted her to conduct the interview at all, let alone keeping himself from interjecting. And to his credit, he'd kept his word by allowing her to work her way through it without taking over. She wanted to show him she could do it. But more than that, she wanted to show herself. "Are you counseling a man named Frederik Derring?" she asked him. No context.

Zero lead-in. It was a method she'd been taught that was high-risk or high-reward. Her heart began to pound, and her stomach turned queasy.

Instead of answering directly, he pointed to the bookcase in the corner. "Do you remember the book I told you about when you were here last?"

Both she and Randall looked that way. They exchanged frowns. "Yes. Why?" Tan said.

"If you recall, my condition is much like that of its protagonist, with the main difference being he could walk. I told you that I identify with the book's author for that reason. But there is another reason I didn't disclose. Not openly, anyway."

Tan's mind spun with this bit of new information. She prepared to motion to Randall and give him a look for help, but he stepped in on his own. "Mr. Cromley, we're aware of the patient-provider privilege. But Frederik Derring is now a suspect in over two dozen abductions and suspected murders. If you're providing him with mental health care, that privilege is waived. Legally, you're obligated to provide us details of any serious wrongdoing you're aware of him committing."

"Now I see why this is so serious. You'll forgive me for my secrecy, and my habit of lecturing. It's a product of my condition since I don't get out much. But I'll answer your question, since it's no longer necessary to hide my connection to him."

He paused, seeming to relish the moment. "Frederik Derring isn't my client. He's my brother."

CHAPTER 35

Detective Haag flipped the coin. "Tails," he called. When it clinked on the table, it spun several times before settling with tails facing up. Both he and Detective Pederson—one of the four MPD Homicide teams assigned to the PK task force—stared at the gleaming American eagle. "Tails never fails!" Haag rejoiced. They'd just gotten back to the department's property and evidence room, their given mission being a trash grab on their Minnetonka former funeral home of interest. They'd made it with just seconds to spare. Pederson had been riding shotgun and had rescued the single trash bag from the residential bin before the truck had dumped it. As they drove away, they'd argued over who's turn it was to pick through the trash and inventory any possible evidence. Thus the coin flip.

"Bullshit. It's fifty-fifty every time," Pederson said. "You got lucky again." He donned a pair of blue disposable latex gloves and dumped the bag's contents onto the back-lit, lipped tabletop. He'd lost their earlier coin flip too—Haag had called tails then as well—which had decided who drove and who would play dumpster diver.

"I wish I were lucky, but there's science behind it," Haag

said, leaning back in his chair with his hands folded behind his head. He watched with naked amusement as his partner sorted through the dripping, half-rotten foodstuffs. "The heads side of a coin has more material to it since the portrait is raised. If you flipped a hundred times, heads would land face-down fifty-two, maybe fifty-three times on average." He winked. "Science."

Pederson frowned in thought. "You can be a real dipshit sometimes, but that actually makes sense. I'll have to remember that." He continued sorting through the mostly food scraps but didn't find anything noteworthy. It had been the same result the previous half-dozen trash grabs he'd conducted. Lots of mess, little evidence. The few times he had found anything useful to an investigation, he'd wondered how criminals could be reckless enough to place weapons, traceable valuables, and in one case a severed head, in the trash. Even with kids in third-world countries owning smartphones, it was a wonder that an adult wrongdoer here in America would fail to perform a simple Google search on "Are the police allowed to take my discarded trash?"

Pederson moved on to the non-foodstuffs, consisting mostly of food wrappers, empty sanitizer containers, and a clump of dry toilet paper. Inspecting each item closely first with the naked eye, then with a magnifying glass attached to a moveable arm, he carefully turned the items over in his hands while looking for obvious evidence. He saved the clump of toilet paper for last, praying it didn't contain feces. Once, he'd found a perfectly round turd inside a similar clump of toilet paper. The guys had ribbed him for weeks afterward, stating that they were "giving him shit," or inventing various jokes involving the number two.

Carefully peeling away the paper's outer layer, then the second layer, Pederson frowned down at its contents. Two hairs, one red and one brown, lay coiled inside. Each about twelve inches long, they appeared human. It was the last thing he'd expected to see. "What the hell..." he began, then stopped when

a thought struck him. "Well, fuck me sideways. Mikey, get
Randall on the horn. Seems my luck is finally turning."

Detectives Tan and Randall sat staring at the man in the
wheelchair, neither of them able to utter a word. It was the counselor himself who broke the awkward silence by slapping his
hands together and uttering a good-natured laugh. "You'll
forgive me again. I do have quite the penchant for dramatics. It's
another byproduct of my condition, since I rarely get out except
for work or necessary appointments."

Randall leaned forward in his chair. "But the name Frederik
Derring isn't even close to yours."

The counselor smiled. "I was born Victor Derring. Yes, my
mother was a fan of Mr. Hugo too." He removed his glasses and
smoothed his hair backward from its previous side-combed style.
He stared at the detectives, waiting for them to understand what
he was doing.

It took a moment for Randall to get it, but when he realized
the striking facial similarity between the PK surveillance photos,
the DL photo, and the man sitting in front of him, his jaw
dropped. "You *are* Frederik's brother..." he said, nodding to
himself. Everything was coming to him now. "A set of twins
born on a Northern Minnesota farm. One born fully healthy, the
other born with..."

"Congenital scoliosis and severe microcephaly," the counselor finished for him. He placed his glasses back on his face and
fixed his hair the way he'd had it. "Both affect fewer than one
percent of male newborns. The sizeable hump you see is a
burden at times, which I conceal whenever I'm in public view.
Not for me, but for others' sake. Add the fact that identical twins
share 99% of the same DNA, and the odds of how we physically
present are about the same as a meteor crashing through the roof

and landing in your lap." He glanced at the ceiling. "Theoretically speaking, of course."

"When did you change your name?" Randall asked.

"Once we became of age, my brother and I began to drift apart emotionally. We were homeschooled and self-taught growing up. After spending every moment together for eighteen years, we wished to go our own ways. It was unsuccessful. Twins, especially the two of us, are unique. My brother can lead a relatively normal physical life, whereas I obviously have my limitations. Until we became teenagers, he was stronger mentally as well. But then he changed. Both of us did, but he became... darker, psychologically. A product of our childhood experiences, likely, but I don't make it a practice to diagnose family or friends, let alone myself."

"You understand that we'll need to verify your claim with the state."

"I'll save you the trouble." He struggled to reach into a desk drawer and flipped through a series of file folders. Finding the one he wanted and removing two documents, he handed them to Randall. The first was a birth certificate complete with a raised seal from the Minnesota Department of Health. The name "Victor Derring" was listed under the "Child" heading. Under the "Hospital" listing were the words "Home Birth." Finally, under the heading "Single or multiple birth" were the words "Twin Boys" and "Identical."

"There's nothing listed under 'Medical Conditions,'" Randall observed.

"The federal government leaves it up to the states to administer birth certificates as they see fit," Victor said. "Hospitals and counties record them differently. There are thousands of variations. Since my brother and I were born at home, whoever recorded ours may not have even known of my unique condition. As long as the census bureau receives basic statistics, they're happy." He folded his hands in his lap. "Frederik's certificate has identical information. But you two are the detectives, so I'm sure you've already verified that."

The second document was a laminated original Social Security card. It matched the name and number they'd already verified. "And CMH Group?" Randall asked, handing the documents back to him. "Part of it is on the plate beside your door. Except you omitted 'Group.'"

Victor moved his eyes toward the door. "A necessary omission. You'd be amazed at how intrusive LinkedIn and even Google can be. I chose a pseudonym for the same reason Erich Weisz likely did. The world may have come to know Harry Houdini, but the man behind the magician was wont to retain his relative anonymity."

Randall was tiring of the man's stagecraft. "Where is Frederik, sir? We've just told you what we suspect him of doing. Abby Carlson is the only one left alive as far as we know. She has friends, co-workers, and a cat who miss her. They're all she has."

Victor's face lit up with a sudden memory. "Thomas Magnum, that was her cat's name! I loved that show growing up. I always dreamed of being a private eye and driving a Ferrari."

Randall ignored the comment. "Help us find him, sir, and maybe we can salvage something out of this whole mess. We suspect he left your home this morning in a blue Miata, drove to the airport parking garage, then switched to a beige sedan. That vehicle was seen arriving back at your home shortly thereafter. Was it him?" Randall's blood was up. He'd arrived here believing that some sliver of a chance existed that PK had been inside the van when it had left the house. Not immediately stopping a suspect's car was one of the gambles of working kidnappings. If your hunch was right, you might save a life. If not, you may be left speaking with a victim's family, trying your best to avoid describing how their young son had been found dead in a ditch, or how their teenage daughter had been found full of flies in some alley, her underwear hanging from one ankle, and a city full of people who hadn't seen shit.

"No, it wasn't him," Victor said. "The Miata belongs to a close friend. I won't disclose his name to protect his privacy."

"One who drives a vehicle with a license plate assigned to someone else?" Randall asked pointedly.

Victor shrugged. "A DVS error, perhaps. Or my friend has run afoul of a traffic law and became frightened of the police, for good reason. Either way, it has nothing to do with me."

"And the beige sedan seen arriving at your home soon after?"

"A sick colleague of mine who I've allowed to convalesce at my home. I won't disclose their name, either, for the same reason."

"That's rather convenient, wouldn't you say?"

"I wasn't aware that having friends visit your home was a crime," Victor said. "As much as it may seem suspicious, it's the truth. I did volunteer my documents to you, and disclosed that Frederik is my brother. You would have found out eventually, but I've clearly saved you some trouble, now haven't I?" When neither detective immediately responded to that, he added, "I'm sorry, but my brother is elusive—a lone wolf, which is a bit of a misnomer since wolves are extremely social animals. With my condition, I go to bed very early. It's a big house, and I'm limited to what I see or hear from my bedroom. If you're looking for an admission that he resides there or has ever visited to my knowledge, I won't give it to you. He merely viewed the home for me three years ago."

"We can get a search warrant," Tan said, appearing to immediately regret saying it.

"If I'm not mistaken, the search of a law-abider's home is not legally permissible without probable cause. I'm no lawyer, but it seems that you don't have that."

"Will you give us permission to search your house?" Randall asked, cutting in.

Victor shook his head regrettably. "I'm sorry, but I draw the line at my home being intruded upon unnecessarily. I believe the Fourth Amendment covers that."

"That's your right," Randall said. He knew they were left with the decision of charging the man with aiding and abetting or not. Similar to other cases, the prospect was like Russian Roulette. Spin the chamber and snap it closed, then place the barrel against your head and squeeze the trigger. The odds that the hammer fell on an empty chamber were five in six. In the real game, you were left with brains against the wall if it didn't. But deciding to arrest a severely disabled professional in good standing with the community could not only jeopardize their legal case, but subject them and the entire department to a civil rights lawsuit for false arrest if he checked out. Randall remembered what Fells had told him about the city council's considered plan for the Homicide unit. Fallout from the recent riots had left the courts unsympathetic toward local law enforcement as well. The distasteful fact remained that they had zero evidence that Frederik Derring lived in the home, was currently present, or that any of the victims were anywhere on the property. They couldn't even say if he'd ever been there after the initial viewing, a fact by itself that was unlikely to grant them a search warrant. Their best case had been the Miata with its duplicate plates, but it wasn't at the home anymore, negating their need to search the home for it. But Randall's gut told him that Frederik was there, or had been recently. Perhaps the victims, too. One of the most frustrating aspects of law enforcement was that suspects—even guilty persons—had closely protected rights. Privately, he sometimes longed for the days of the Old West, when local lawmen had few bosses and often served instant justice with a pair of six-shooters or a length of rope.

He and Tan stood. Randall removed a business card and placed it on the desk. He'd done the same thing the first time they were here, but he couldn't think of anything else that would leave an impression. "Call us if you hear from him or know where to find him. You could help save an innocent woman's life."

Victor Derring picked the card up and tapped it against the desk. "If I do, you'll be the first to know."

CHAPTER 36

Sergeant Fells met them in the parking lot. Her face was a mix of hope and concern. "What's the word?"

Randall cast a glance back at the building he and Tan had just exited. "The counselor is Frederik's twin. He admitted to buying the home under his business acronym, but he insisted his brother doesn't live there or visit."

Fells's eyes narrowed. "What's your opinion?"

"Personally? He's arrogant as hell. Professionally speaking, he's definitely hiding something."

Fells looked at Tan, who nodded. "I agree. But we don't have any PC that he was driving the Miata, let alone that he was ever inside the house long enough to preserve and stage two dozen bodies."

Fells's cellphone rang. She conducted a short but animated conversation. When she hung up, her expression changed to one of relieved optimism. "That was Whit. They found something from the trash grab. Two hairs, both about a foot long."

"Female?"

"We won't know until BCA conducts a preliminary. No roots, from what Haag said. But the UCs haven't seen any females in or out of the house since they've sat on it, so it's promising."

"I doubt either Derring brother has ever had hair that long," Randall said.

"And what are the odds that hair from two separate decedents, or living females from years ago get thrown away at the same time?" Tan added.

"During a known criminal investigation," Fells finished. The three of them looked at one another, the implication already clear. "I'll notify the chief," she said, dialing a pre-programmed number on her phone. "He and I met with Ms. Dunn's mother last night at her ALF in Richfield. She's devastated, of course—Nicolette is her only child. Speaking of, make sure we get a hair sample from the mother; we'll have BCA run mitochondria on it. If I'm not mistaken, the violinist is the only redhead of the bunch."

"She is," Randall said, then added, "We'll get one from Abby's mother, too."

Fells frowned. "Why Abby's mother?"

"For some reason he went out of order not doing her first. I'd like to think she's somehow responsible for getting word to us that she's there." A second later, he slapped his thigh as a sudden realization hit him. "Her mother's deceased, I totally forgot. We can get an exhumation order if she wasn't cremated."

While Fells briefed the chief, Randall filled Tan in on the difference between mitochondria DNA and full DNA testing, namely how the former only compared DNA from a person's biological mother. It wasn't as conclusive as a full DNA test, but had helped get convictions before. He asked her to arrange for the elder Dunn's hair sample, and to verify if Abby's mother had been buried, and if so, where. "Absolutely," Tan said. Fifteen minutes later, she reported that Nicolette's mother had been notified and agreed to provide a hair sample; a detective team was headed there now to gather it. "And I got ahold of Abby's best friend, Derek. He said her mother was cremated, but that he knows about a lock of her hair Abby kept in her apartment after she died. I've got a team arranging for a warrant now."

"Perfect," Randall said, knowing that even the less definitive but quicker mitochondrial DNA testing would be enough to persuade the case judge to grant a broader search warrant before full DNA results could be available, providing at least one hair was a match.

The new warrant for Abby's apartment was granted, and the lock of hair recovered. An initial inspection at the BCA lab across the river quickly verified that the hairs found in the trash grab were human, and female. Everyone in the core task force group agreed that wouldn't be enough to be granted a search warrant. Since Abby couldn't be expected to remain alive for the one to two weeks it would take a full DNA test to be conducted, the decision was made to put all their effort into the mitochondria test for now. The BCA superintendent promised an unprecedented rush job, estimating a two-day test completion instead of the normal three to four. They'd work around the clock, activating every available agent and technician. Until it was finished and word came about the warrant, they'd surround the property on all sides and provide continuous air surveillance. If a fly entered or left the house, they'd know it.

CHAPTER 37

Victor parted the office lobby's micro blinds and watched the detectives' unmarked cruiser pull away from down the block. Even though they'd left, he knew they'd still be watching him. He'd arrived home after his first meeting with Detectives Randall and Tan assuming they'd uncovered more in the past week than they had in the past six months combined. He wondered what had tipped them off, what shred of evidence or witness had finally brought the details of his brother's deadly hobby to light. It would soon end for Frederik. That much was sure. The only question left to answer was when, and if he'd finish what he'd begun.

Using his wheelchair's joystick, Victor backed away from the window and motored back to his rented office. Looking around it, he sighed. This too would end soon. All a result of Frederik's reckless actions. Victor had forever been tied to him, and he had no doubt that tie would mean his own professional undoing. Even if he managed to keep his counseling certification, he'd never survive the public scrutiny. The press would hound him. Prospective clients would mistrust him. The brother of a kidnapper and killer may escape criminal prosecution and thus retain his ability to practice, but it was another thing for a patient to disclose their deepest secrets to him ever again. He glanced at the same book on the bookshelf he'd shown Abby and the police, a fantasy coming to him of traveling back in time to live his life in the tower, ringing the bell as he gazed down on Paris. It was a silly dream, he knew. Ironic too, in that he himself would have told a client with a similar dream to simply speak it aloud in order to realize it.

He wanted to sit here a while and take it all in a bit longer, but he didn't have time. Making a mental note to mail his most valued clients early Christmas cards before it was too late, Victor collected his briefcase, a stack of his most vital files, and the keys to the van. Motoring into the hallway, he chose not to look back. Better to remember the office as he'd last seen it, from behind his desk, and not like so many of his troubled clients, looking toward it.

"Done for the day?" a sixtysomething man he'd become familiar with asked from a rented office down the hall.

Victor paused at the open doorway and cast the man a meek smile. He started to say something, but his throat thickened to the point that he simply waved goodbye before pushing the assisted-open button and wheeling out the front door. In the parking lot, he pressed the "Open" button on his keyring fob, and the van's side door slid open, the electronic ramp unfolding outward to the pavement. Shivering against the cold wind, he gathered his blanket around him then slowly maneuvered the chair to the ramp's edge. He gave it enough forward power to safely nudge over the lip then advanced up the ramp. A well-practiced three-point turn later, he was positioned behind the steering wheel, his chair locked in place and his specialized seatbelt fastened. It had taken him several weeks to learn the wheel-mounted hand controls that operated the van's brake and accelerator, and over twenty hours of practice to combine their actions with driving through the course to become confident in his ability. When he'd finally passed his test and they'd delivered the van to the house, he'd felt like a kid on Christmas. At first, he'd struggled mightily to secure the chair and himself. But he'd done it. That had been important, since he would have to do it himself on most occasions. He'd been prouder taking his first independent drive on the freeway than he had graduating with his LMHC online degree. To his credit, Frederik had offered to drive him to clinicals on numerous occasions, stating he could fit the van with a removable normal driver's seat when needed. Victor had steadfastly refused. He was disabled, he'd said, not unable.

Pressing the "Close" button, Victor waited for the ramp to fold inward and the door to slide closed before pressing the brake and start engine steering wheel buttons. He slipped his right wrist into the wheel-mounted tri-pin grips and rotated the wheel to prepare to back out of the parking space. He knew the correct hand controls by heart, and without looking, he manipulated the correct ones to first reverse, then pull out onto Hennepin Avenue. He drove several miles, checking the rearview mirror every few blocks. An unmarked black sedan soon followed several car lengths behind him. A block further down the road, it turned right. Six blocks later, Victor checked the mirror again. This time, a white SUV with tinted windows traveled behind him in a different lane, the male driver wearing a jacket and baseball cap turned backward. Deciding to test his instinct, Victor turned left at the next light. The SUV turned left too. Victor made an immediate right, but the SUV kept straight. Victor pulled into a fast-food parking lot and turned around, pulling back out to reverse course. Soon after, the same black sedan he'd seen before along with a new sedan with tinted windows filed in behind him, each at different lengths and in different lanes. So, rolling surveillance, Victor determined. They likely had some sort of sky-based monitoring as well. No trouble, since he'd expected it anyway. Stopping at a red light, he glanced at the vehicle directly to his left and was unsure if that was one of them too since the driver had glanced his way. He needed to speak with Frederik. Removing his cellphone, he set it into the windshield-mounted holder then pressed an icon on the screen. Moments later, not waiting for Frederik to say anything, Victor said, "They know."

Frederik sighed. "Yes, I'm aware. The girls are safe, though."

"They'll find them," Victor said. "It may be days, or a week, even, but they'll come. And when they do—"

"Don't worry," Frederik said. "They may take them from me, but they'll never take you. We're brothers, and nothing can break our bond."

Victor turned left onto a different street. The same three vehicles he'd noticed so far turned with him. "They'll follow both of us no matter where we go," he said. "I've decided to quit my practice, effective immediately."

"Why?"

"What do you mean 'why?' The police know we're brothers; there wasn't any use avoiding it anymore. They accused me of harboring you in the house, for God's sake. The only reason they haven't already gotten a search warrant is because they don't have any proof that I'm sheltering you. You'll have to leave the house eventually."

"I'll slip out at night. Or on foot."

"They'll be planning for that, Freddie!" Victor yelled. "They do this for a living!" He wasn't accustomed to becoming excited. Or angry. But things had changed—quickly, and as far as he could tell, permanently.

"Calm down, Victor. You're working yourself up," Frederik said.

"How can you be calm right now?" Victor asked. He checked his mirrors again. "What will you do with the last one?"

"I still have three days to get her to come around. I want the timing right with her."

Victor laughed. "Three days? You might not have three *hours*. You need to display them while you can, the last one too, then burn them in the crematorium. Keeping them downstairs is doing nothing."

Frederik paused. "You can't ask me to burn them, Victor. If I have them all together for one day, it'll be enough."

"Okay, but then what?" Victor asked, turning onto the freeway toward home.

"We'll move. Get as far away as we can."

Victor swore under his breath. "You're not thinking rationally. You're too involved with this...thing. I'm almost home. We'll talk then."

Noticing one of the suspicious cars pass on his left, Victor pressed the same icon on his phone then focused on the road. He gripped the tri-pin until his knuckles turned white. His pulse quickened. Yes, he'd become upset, but what was he supposed to do? They'd be virtual prisoners for as long as it took the police to come knocking with a warrant. If he or Frederik didn't open the doors, they'd break them down, vestibules or not. Then Frederik's master plan, one he had proposed to Victor over a year before he'd begun collecting his girls, would fail unless he completed one final transition.

CHAPTER 38

He began on the second floor, with the stripper.

After speaking more with Victor once he got home and gaining a better idea of what the police may truly know, Frederik decided immediate action was necessary. Although alarming at first, the knowledge that detectives had returned to Victor's practice and confronted him shouldn't have surprised him. Frederik had kidnapped twenty-six women over a seven-month span, all from the Twin Cities and surrounding suburbs. It was a miracle he hadn't been caught yet. He wasn't sure if it was oversight on the police's part, his own brilliance, or luck. He figured it was a combination of all three.

He chose to re-position the stripper first for no other reason than her name had been Zelda—his favorite name of all the girls —despite him knowing it was a stage name. He'd been in the smoky downtown gentleman's club for an hour, sipping his drink and watching the action from a darkened corner when he first saw her. Dressed in clear platform heels and a white string bikini, the well-toned, short-haired brunette had sauntered on stage and begun her routine to a sultry R&B song. Frederik had been immediately enthralled. Twice while he watched her dance, other girls had come by and sat beside him, stroking his arm and plying him with promises of private room action. He'd shooed them away, unable to keep his eyes off the green-eyed former gymnast. That detail had come later when she'd approached him and engaged him in conversation. Now, after he fed her hardened, hooked left leg through the lower half of the pole and secured her upper body into the ground-stabilized support, he had both hands free to conncct the upper pole section. Positioning it first through the half-gripped fingers of her left hand, then into a pre-installed ceiling bracket, he stood back to check his work. Despite her appearing to swing around the pole as he desired, something was missing. Remembering, Frederik reached into a bag on the floor and removed two white tassels. Their selfadhesiveness long worn away, he dabbed a spot of glue onto their backs then pressed them onto her bare nipples.

He stretched his neck. It was sore again. He'd have to use the heating pad later, but time was ticking. Going off the list he'd made, he returned to the freezer and brought up the hairdresser and nurse, then sat the writer in front of her manual typewriter in the home office. After re-posing the glassblower with her blowpipe, block, and jacks, he took a break, making both himself and Victor lunch. When he was finished with the next batch of girls, hauling them up the elevator one at a time, he stood looking out a back window at the expansive yard. It was mid-afternoon now, the shadows on the lawn growing long. Still no sign of the police. They'd be working extra hard, no doubt, trying every angle to trip him up. He was sure he hadn't left anything for them to track him with, and figured they'd eventually gotten his description or finally traced one of his fake license plates from the many cameras throughout the city. By late afternoon he'd replaced all but two of the girls. He was tired, and his back hurt from the constant bending, re-adjusting, and lifting. While positioning the yoga instructor, he decided to stretch his muscles alongside her. Mimicking her downward dog pose, he placed his hands on the floor and arched his backside toward the ceiling for a full minute, tightening his core muscles and concentrating his breathing in the fashion she'd taught him during his lone private lesson with her. It worked.

Last came the zookeeper, appropriately. When he'd brought her home, Victor had suggested he use taxidermy animals in her exhibit, if for no other reason than to make her pose more authentic. But Frederik had refused. "Only a monster would kill an innocent animal for show," he'd said, disgusted with the idea. Instead, he'd bought inflatable versions of a monkey, lion, and giraffe for her display. Checking his notes, he positioned her back here in the enlarged mudroom since the windows looked out toward the heavily wooded backyard. He kept the blinds closed except for brief periods of time, for obvious reasons. After fastening the support stand around her waist and ensuring the heavy base would keep her upright, he stepped back to admire her. He remembered how she'd sat cuffed to the chair, weeping for her life as she'd watched the lifeguard's transitioning process.

"Tell me how you'd be," he'd whispered in her ear, promising to let her go if she told him.

"I...I would...I would want to be surrounded by my animals," the recent zoology graduate had said through her tears. Then, in graphic language that had surprised even Frederik, she'd volunteered to perform several self-degrading sex acts for him—some of which he'd never heard of before—if he let her go.

"You've already pleased me enough," he'd whispered in her ear, kissing it. When he'd produced the clear plastic bag and cinched it tight over her head, the woman had literally suffocated on her own screams. Because she'd been so sweet by agreeing to perform his special bedroom act he saved for the end of every session with the girls (offering for Victor to take a turn, although the man had declined), he'd given her a treat, albeit in death. A collection of live plants and flowers from a local nursery to place around her motif. She was thankful to have them, he knew. Her

frozen smile and appreciatively inclined head were proof.
Gazing now at her kneeling form, he felt a swell of relief that
he'd gone the extra mile for her. Her transitioning had been difficult due to an unexpected complication. He'd been forced to stop
halfway through due to a sudden water leak upstairs. When he
returned, she'd already stiffened. It had taken him hours to
massage her limbs to the point he could re-position them
correctly. He'd been exhausted and dripped with sweat, but he'd
succeeded. Relieved now that she had at least some version of
animals and foliage around her, he left and took a much-
needed nap.

When he awoke, it was eight a.m. Tuesday morning. He'd never
slept for that long before. Panicked that he'd missed the beginning of a police raid or an attempted escape, he checked on Abby
and verified with each layer of his home's security that all was
well. It was. Even Victor reported no issues, from what he could
tell during the night. After bathing and changing clothes, he let
Abby out to use a proper toilet and bathe also. He made breakfast and was pleased when she began to eat without prompt from
him. He'd been correct about the warm front—fifty-two degrees
during the girls' removal the day before. But it hadn't lasted
long, with the backyard thermometer now a tick above thirty.
Tomorrow would be even colder, said the weatherman, with
temps expected in the twenties. Soon, the inner-city lakes would
freeze over, the trees surrounding them bare and black, the land
whitewashed. The changing of the seasons, inevitable and
unyielding as always in this part of the country. He'd never
leave, unless forced to. As he sat with Abby, watching her
quietly eat, he decided tonight would be the night. He was rested,
and she seemed less fierce, less salty. She'd submit to him just
like all of them who'd gone through the purification process had,

going into death pure. Timing would dictate how long he had them all together, of course. He hadn't dared leave the house, per Victor's warning. His brother was younger by mere minutes and weaker, but his judgment at times was infallible.

Frederik sensed the police all around him. Surely, they would come. But after breakfast, when he pulled up a nail to peek through the heavy living room curtains, all he saw were trees. They looked like so many corpses themselves, cold and bare, their branches reaching toward the early-winter sky. He swore he heard them weeping.

CHAPTER 39

Special Agent Whitlock stood with his back to the photo-lined bulletin board, having chosen this place instead of the normal Homicide office conference room for dramatic effect. They'd just tried something new with the billboard, after all, and from all appearances it had produced a solid tip. Always willing to shake things up to inspire the troops, he'd also implemented a new meeting requirement from now on—they would all stand during its duration, however long that may be. He'd seen a battlefield commander in Iraq do something similar during a briefing, exposing himself and his entire corps of junior officers to one-hundred-degree heat in full sun instead of from beneath a tent. Inspiration from perspiration, had been the commander's message. Whitlock hadn't forgotten it. "James, what's the ETA on our lab results?" he asked Agent Teague.

The BCA liaison pressed his lips together. "Still looking like tomorrow, even with the expedite order."

Whitlock grunted. "Not good enough. He's spooked by now. Fells, what about surveillance?"

"No movement to or from the house since the counselor got home," she said.

"And our warrant?"

Detective Randall stood closer to the letter "D" on the board than any of the other assembled members, having nudged his way there as everyone had gathered around. He glanced at Abby Carlson's bright-eyed, smiling photo before answering. "We tried tickling the judge, but he's not ticklish yet."

Whitlock checked his watch—nine thirty a.m. "Everyone has a ticklish spot. Find his."

"On it."

The meeting continued for another half hour, after which everyone was dismissed with their marching orders. Before they returned to their desks or reported to their field assignments, Fells took Randall and Tan aside. The bags under her eyes foretold a story each of them knew too well—only several hours' sleep over the past forty-eight hours for any of them, most of that occurring at their desks or in the darkened conference room. "Any rabbits you have up your sleeve, Cal, feel free to pull them out," she said, giving him a frustrated look.

He jokingly raised his arm to look inside the cuff, then shrugged. "No rabbits, Sarge, but I'll keep my eye out for one."

From her position beside him, Tan said, "He did find some wet paint yesterday," then pointed out the streak of black paint on his jacket's lower sleeve.

Randall shrugged. "I guess I can bill the city when this is all over since it happened in the parking garage. Tan and I were running to my car and—" He stopped in mid-sentence, his eyes widening as a sudden thought came to him. "Shit, I just assumed."

"Assumed what?" Fells asked.

"Hold on a sec, let me check something."

Fells and Tan were left standing near the office desk watching as Randall ran to his cubicle across the open space. Moving his finger down a building phone directory taped to the wall, he stopped when he got to the listing labeled *MAINTE-NANCE SUPERVISOR*, then dialed the number from his desk landline. Five rings in, the echoey voice of a man picked up. "Maintenance, Ottman speaking."

Randall identified himself, then asked him about the painting project in the building's parking garage; specifically, the newly-painted black attendant desk on the garage's third level. "Yeah, what about it?" the supervisor asked.

"When was it done being painted?"

The man huffed. "How the hell should I know? I got people up my ass all day asking for stuff to get fixed. I just assign the jobs."

"It's important, sir. Please try to remember, or ask someone who knows. It could help our PK case."

"Shit...okay, um, let me ask Phil, he's the one who painted it." The supervisor put Randall on hold and came back on a minute later. In the meantime, Fells and Tan had made their way to his desk and stood staring at him, silent and inquisitive. "Phil says he painted it last Wednesday. Standard two coats."

"Is he sure it wasn't yesterday, Monday morning? I don't mean to pester him, but I need to be sure."

The supervisor sighed. "Hold on." He put Randall on hold again for a minute, then came back on the line. "Phil says he's sure it was Wednesday because that was the day his kid broke his leg at football practice. He said he'd just finished the second coat and put the wet paint sign up when his wife called him screaming bloody murder."

"But the sign and drop cloth were still there yesterday until almost noon," Randall said.

"Phil left early Wednesday for his kid. He just got back today. Chief's rule says wet paint signs get taken down by the person who puts them up to avoid accidents, so it would have been up until this morning when he came into work."

Thanking the supervisor, Randall hung up and leveled a sober look at Fells and Tan. "What was that about?" Fells asked.

Instead of answering directly, Randall posed a question to

Tan. "Friday, after we were notified about Abby's abduction, do you remember our interview here with the accomplice?"

"Sure. Why?"

"Was that before or after we spoke to Abby's counselor?"

She thought about it. "Before."

"Yes," he said, already knowing it in his mind but wanting second-party confirmation. "I put my jacket on for the interview to look more professional. When we parked in the business office lot, do you remember me looking inside the van's windows?"

"Yeah. You talked about the steering wheel controls, and both front seats being removed to accommodate an electric wheelchair. You even said a relative of yours once had a van like it."

"No—I mean yes, but that's not what I'm talking about. Was I on the driver's side or the passenger side?"

Tan thought about it, then said, "It had to be the driver's side, because when I looked through the window I was standing at, the steering wheel was on your side."

Randall mimed the action of shielding his eyes like he'd done that day. "I leaned in to get a better look inside the driver's window. My left elbow was on the glass, but my right—"

"—Was on the body," Tan finished. "Because the van didn't have windows in the back. I remember seeing you lean to your right to check the van's dash."

The two looked at each other for an extended moment of silence, until Fells asked, "Are you saying you got paint on your jacket Friday and not yesterday?"

"It had to be then. The only times I've worn it out of the office recently were Friday and yesterday. I'm positive it was fine from the cleaners a week ago since I checked that they didn't break a sleeve button like last time."

Tan held up a hand. "If the painter is correct, then the stain on your jacket couldn't have come from the stand. It would have had five full days to dry."

Randall nodded. "Then it had to be the van if it was freshly painted black. It's the only explanation. When the handicap designation and plate came back valid I didn't even bother checking the listed color on the registration."

"Don't beat yourself up over it," Fells said. "We've had a million details to sort through. It wouldn't have raised a flag until now anyway. But that's an awfully big coincidence for him to have it painted black the day *before* you first spoke with him. Most vehicles only get re-painted once in their lifetimes, if ever. Why would he do that?"

Without saying a word, Tan marched across the open cubicle area to the bulletin board and snatched Abby Carlson's information sheet down. Scanning it, she turned and held it up to them, her finger on a line they couldn't read from there. They didn't need to read it because Randall knew what she was referring to. "Because Abby Carlson was abducted in a *white* cargo van the day before," he said.

CHAPTER 40

An hour later, Detectives Randall and Tan exited the judge's courthouse office with disappointing news. Randall called Fells right away. "Judge still wasn't ticklish, Sarge. He said he would've approved the garage if the Miata had still been there, but even then the entire house would have been a mile away."

Fells swore through the phone. "What did he say about the hair evidence?"

"He said if the mitochondrial is a hit, he'll sign a warrant to search every inch of the place, and walk it over to me personally."

"Maternal match may not be enough to convict if a full DNA doesn't work. Wish those hairs had roots in them."

"But two dozen other bodies will be plenty enough," he said.

Four hours later, disaster struck. Construction workers digging up a water main on a busy street near BCA's St. Paul lab hit an underground natural gas line, knocking out the main electrical grid to that entire section of downtown. Agent Teague had been personally overseeing the hair testing, his instructions being to report immediately to Whitlock and Fells whenever the results were in. He called each of them with the news, stating the city estimated power wouldn't be restored until later that afternoon.

"Good God," Whitlock said. He'd remained at the PSB Homicide office, choosing it over his own FBI office since the main task force contingent had congregated there. "What about the generators?"

"I guess they're only routed for vital areas," Teague said.

"How much more vital can you get than a testing lab? Damned government…"

Not content to wait, the ranking federal agent for the entire task force made what he often referred to as a battlefield decision. "Fly the sample to our Chicago lab. I'll call in an emergency charter at MSP."

"The FBI lab there, sir?"

"Yes. Do it now. I'd rather waste an hour in travel time than waiting on a bunch of idiots playing pocket pool. The last outage we had there, they went six hours over their ETA."

"10-4," Teague said, then hung up.

One hour and forty-three minutes later, the untested remains of both sets of hairs in question were placed in a fire-proof safe then driven in an ambulance with lights and sirens from the darkened BCA building to Minneapolis-St. Paul International Airport. The safe was then loaded onto the chartered jet. Each of the potential victims' hairs had been partially degraded during initial testing, but enough samples remained for a one-time test at the FBI's Chicago lab, the closest one capable of performing such a test within a day. At 4:05 p.m. Central time, the remaining stages of mitochondria DNA testing began. If PK kept to his self-imposed time limit before killing his victims, Abby Carlson had a minimum of two days to live. But everyone attached to the case knew time was now warped. There was no telling when the killer—one who'd successfully evaded them for seven months—would play his last hand. In the meantime, a tactical search team had been assembled and placed on standby. They'd act immediately upon word of a warrant. Assuming one ever came.

CHAPTER 41

Darkness fell like a cold blanket across the land. One of several two-man ground surveillance units ringing the woods behind the former funeral home's property line sat side-by-side on folding camouflaged camper chairs. They themselves were dressed in cold-weather camo and matching ballistic vests. Along with their standard equipment and weapons, each had been issued night vision goggles and carbine scopes with the same technology. Every available resource had been thrown into the fire. Rumblings inside police headquarters had turned into wildfire rumors of an entire department disbandment. Folks were nervous, more so than they'd been in the riots several years before. A sick joke had begun circulating the department that went PK would hopefully post his final pic soon so everyone could go home and finally catch some "A-Z's."

One of the surveillance officers placed his night-vison goggles to his eyes and scanned the home's rear fence line, fifty yards distant.

"Anything?" asked his partner. He shivered, despite his thick coat, hat, and gloves.

"Nope," came the reply.

"This is bullshit, by the way."

"Yep."

"I told Sarge I'd go home sick if he put me here again tomorrow. This is two days straight."

"Sure."

"My PBA rep said there ain't shit they can do to me, even if I don't provide a doctor's note."

"Probably."

His partner turned to look at his darkened shape. "Can you ever say more than one word at a time?"

"Yep."

"Try."

"No."

"Why?"

"Because."

"Oh, for Pete's sake," said his partner, then turned to stare back into the darkness.

Inside the house, Frederik stood outside the closed hallway door, like he'd done so often since moving in. He rested his hand on the knob and began to turn it when Victor's voice called out to him. "I don't want to see them. It'll upset me."

Frederik removed his hand from the knob. "Just a quick visit?"

"No. Please. Not tonight."

"If not tonight, when?" Frederik asked. "The police may be here any time."

"Let them come, then," Victor said. "If they do, I'll remember what they looked like. Go enjoy yourself with the last one while you can."

Frederik sighed, then went into the kitchen to where the chef stood at the stove with oven mitts on her hands. The aroma of roasting beef and vegetables filled the chilly air on the first floor, about ten degrees higher than the upper twenties outside. Frederik had nailed all but one of the windows on each main level shut. This accomplished two things: it provided added security if the police decided to come, and it regulated the temperature of the upper floors. It was a bit warmer than he liked, since the girls needed freezing temps to avoid getting sick. But the medicine in their tissues, combined with the near-freezing temperature of the eight total rooms (and garage) they occupied, meant it could take days or even weeks for them to become significantly ill. He doubted he'd have that long anyway.

He'd dressed up for the occasion—his best suit, a wool scarf, and his favorite brogues. Abby would join him for supper, then a special night on the town, so to speak, one he'd created just for the two of them. Unlocking the latch in the firewood, Frederik pulled the hidden handle. The false wall slid along its concealed track, revealing the twin bedroom doors and freezer. The latter was empty now. He'd moved all the girls back where they belonged. They'd likely never return to the freezer, he knew, their fates now in the hands of whatever entity looked down from the heavens. Or looked up from below.

He knocked on Abby's door. "Ready?"

No response for a moment, then the door opened. Abby stood in the doorway, dressed in the expensive blue evening gown, heels, and glittery earrings he'd bought for her. Draped over one arm was a faux fur coat he'd given her to wear. It would be chilly for their night out, cold even compared to the basement's relative heat. If it got too bad, they could always come downstairs for a bit and warm themselves by the fire.

"You look stunning," Frederik said. He smiled wide, his dimples showing.

"Where are you taking me?" she asked, her eyes wary.

"Home," he said, putting out his arm for her to take. "Home."

CHAPTER 42

A bby walked on wobbly legs, her blue leather pumps fitting but digging into the backs of her ankles nonetheless. She was emotionally numb to the point she could barely stand. An inner sensibility willed her forward despite her innate womanly instinct warning of impending doom. Frederik had seemed increasingly desperate the past twenty-four hours. Irritable, even. He'd disappeared for long periods, showing up at odd hours to bring her food and something to drink. He'd stopped standing outside the bathroom when she went, opting instead to simply slide open the woodpile, then her door when she gave five loud knocks—their arranged sign to him that she had to use the bathroom. The bucket hadn't been here yesterday after she'd returned from breakfast, and hadn't appeared since. Even now, with him dressed up and the smile on his face, he seemed somehow sad. His expression reminded Abby of someone visiting a dying relative for the last time.

They took the stairs. The moment they exited onto the first floor, she felt an instant chill. It was at least thirty degrees colder up here than the basement. Her bedroom was unheated as well, but the radiant heat from the fireplace kept it and the other rooms downstairs at a manageable temperature.

Shivering, she donned her coat and followed his lead into the garage. He opened the back door of a red sedan and motioned for her to get in. She did, sliding in behind the young female driver, him getting in beside Abby. She knew the driver was dead, like all the women here. Abby kept her gaze politely forward to not upset him. She wasn't sure what he planned. This was strange, even for him.

Right away it became clear he meant to mimic driving her somewhere. He gave the driver an address then leaned back and put his arm around Abby's shoulders. "I made reservations," he said, appearing pleased with himself. "Fantastic place. I'm personal friends with the chef."

He removed his arm from around her shoulders and faced forward, remaining silent for several moments before he hopped back out and held the door open for her. "We're here," he said. He ushered her back in the house and past a collection of posed bodies in the main parlor that she'd already viewed, then past an open office door that she hadn't seen inside yet. A black-clad woman with frizzled black hair and dark eyeshadow sat at a felt-covered table. Tarot cards lay spread out before her, as well as a sign with the words "Olga the Oracle" in calligraphy, and a spooky night sky scene painted on the wall behind her.

Abby saw them, but she did not see them. Her legs were Jell-O, her skin belonging to someone else. Everything seemed slightly askew, as if the Earth had been tilted off its axis by some giant hand or a meteor. An electric charge filled the air. As Frederik led her from room to room, showing her familiar women and a few she hadn't seen before, she nodded politely each time he introduced her. "Pleasure to meet you," Abby said to a crouching woman holding a camera to one eye. Guiding Abby to sit with him on a settee facing the camera, Frederik pulled her in close to him for a pose. "Say cheese," he said. She tried to say the word, but nothing came out. Finally, Frederik said it for her. After they stood and passed by the photographer, Frederik held a hand to the corpse's ear and whispered regrettably, "I think she's camera-shy."

He escorted her into the dining room and pulled her chair out for her. She sat, heavily, and looked vacantly ahead while he first rummaged through the kitchen cabinets, then removed several pots from the oven. Moments later, he returned with a steaming plate of food for them both. "Eat," he said, serving her then sitting at the opposite end of the table.

"I can't," she mumbled. She picked up her fork and stabbed at the pile of roast beef and carrots. The mashed potatoes were covered in a savory-smelling gravy. Her stomach growled, but she knew if she ate anything she'd throw it back up.

"Try your best, even a few bites. You'll insult the chef again if you don't." He moved his eyes toward the kitchen and made a face.

So, she ate. Surprisingly, she didn't throw up. With each forkful, she became that much hungrier. Focused now on finishing the entire plate, she scooped forkful after forkful of food into her mouth, chewing madly while locking eyes with him. He ate slowly, almost cautiously, while he watched her. When she finished her food, she ran her finger across the plate several times to mop up the gravy. With a flourish she decided was the representation of all her emotions since she'd been here, she let the plate thud back onto the table, sat back in her chair, then let out a loud burp.

Frederik's jaw dropped. He stared at her, motionless. And then, as if some invisible force controlled him, his hands rose and began to slowly clap. "Bravo, my dear!" he said, beaming and looking toward the kitchen. "Did you hear that, Petra? She loved it!"

Next, Frederik took her into the game room for an after-dinner drink and a round of pool. The girls there were nice, too. He then walked her upstairs and took her into a darkened entertainment room where he sat her in one of two chairs he'd set out.

Standing beside her, he pointed a remote control at the wall and pressed a button. A moment later, a set of multi-colored spotlights illuminated a crudely made stage. At one end, a female African American rapper stood holding a diamond-studded microphone to her mouth. Her parted lips revealed a sparkling platinum grill. At stage center, a pole extended from floor to ceiling. A short-haired Caucasian woman in a white string bikini held onto the pole with one hand while curling a bent leg around it in mid-spin. After Frederik pushed another button on the remote control, a recent hip-hop song began pounding from hidden surround sound speakers. He began dancing in beat with the music, moving around the floor and motioning for Abby to join him in an impromptu dance session. Eyes wide, she remained frozen in her chair, unsure of what to do. Shrugging, Frederik raised one hand in the air as he pantomimed slapping an invisible dance partner's rear end. The pulsing anthem soon switched to a slower, old-school R&B jam. Approaching Abby, Frederik removed his wallet from his back pocket and fished out a wad of bills. He stuffed half of them into her hand and kept half for himself. "Go ahead," he said, indicating the stripper. "I don't mind. I think it's sexy for a woman to join in." He turned and approached the stage, gyrating his hips to the grooving music. His cocktail in one hand, he threw some of the bills in the air above the stripper's head. They rained down over her head and body, most of them coming to rest around her planted high heel. When one of the bills landed atop her shapely backside, he confidently stepped forward and tucked it into her string bikini bottoms. "Come on!" he whooped to Abby above the pounding music. He hooked a thumb toward the stripper, his face a picture of frat-boy exuberance. "She's super laid-back. I think she even does girls." He winked a prurient grin before showering the stripper with his remaining bills. Expelling a tired breath, he plopped down on the chair beside her.

Abby stared down at the wad of bills in her hand and did the only thing she could think of in the moment. She slammed them into Frederik's open hands and shot angrily to her feet. "I am *not* doing that!" she screamed in his face. She pointed a finger behind her, at the stage. "Those aren't real people!" she yelled. "They're corpses. You killed them. You killed them all. And you'll kill me, too. But I don't care anymore. Do it! Do it now! But I'm not going to play your sick fucking game with you for another second!"

Frederik sat back in his seat, his eyes wide and mouth agape. He could have been frozen like one of the girls, had his chest not been heaving. Then with his cat-like reflex, he was on his feet so fast she almost didn't see the motion. With one hand, he grabbed her by the hair and rotated his wrist. Just like that, she lost her balance and was on her butt being painfully dragged across the floor. "*YOU WILL NOT TALK BACK TO ME!*" he roared. He dragged her from the room into the hallway and headed for the stairs. Abby kicked and screamed, grabbing his hand with both of hers to try freeing herself from his iron grip. It wasn't any use. He was far too strong. And crazed. He'd been half-sane before at times. Tender even, on occasions. But not anymore. She'd crossed a final line, one that even she'd known the whole time she would have to cross at some point during this fucked-up situation. She was never going to sit still and let him kill her like a sheep gone to slaughter. He was definitely going to do it, but better to go out kicking and screaming. Maybe he could transition her like that.

CHAPTER 43

F our hundred miles away, just after seven p.m., an FBI tech ran down a hallway in the bureau's Chicago-based forensic laboratory toward the administration office. Bursting through the admin office door, the tech stood before the frowning supervisor. "It's finished," she said, holding out the paper out for the supervisor to read. "A match. Both of them."

Back in Minneapolis, while Sergeant Fells and Agent Whitlock coordinated the search team, Detectives Randall and Tan raced to the judge's house. They made it there in ten minutes. "Good evening, Detectives," he said, eyeing the paper Randall held out for him. "I take it you've got news for me."

The SWAT commander got the call two minutes later. Activated since yesterday and on twenty-four-hour standby, the fifteen-officer unit was backed up by a full contingent of FBI and BCA agents, and another twenty uniformed PD officers whose mission was to aid and support the tactical team in any way necessary. Special Agent Whitlock and the entire MPD brass had insisted on being present for the execution of the search warrant and possible arrest of Frederik Derring, should he be located inside the home. The state police and Hennepin County Sheriff's Office provided additional manpower, to include a helicopter and drones as they'd done before. The casual observer might guess the force assembled down the road and out of sight of the house was being sent to wage a small war. Indeed, to everyone involved in the largest criminal case any of them had ever been a part of, the force was every bit an organization set for warfare. The chief himself had arrived on scene and ordered that the house be torn apart board by board if necessary. He'd pay to have it re-built himself if necessary.

Marked cruisers blocked traffic in both directions of the main road and cut off access to areas behind the expansive property line. Teams were placed on high alert for anyone leaving the home through the woods on foot, and were cautious of possible tunnel endings. The helicopter and several drones arrived at a hover, their infrared cameras covering every inch of the grounds. In all, nearly a hundred heavily armed officers of all ranks, agencies, and classifications surrounded the property that each of them was convinced PK occupied.

War, indeed.

CHAPTER 44

A bby fought him the best she could, but he was ripping her hair from her scalp, and she felt herself slipping in and out of consciousness from her own hysterics. He dragged her down the stairs like a sack of potatoes, her hips and backside banging painfully on the risers as they went. They made it to the main level, through several rooms, the hallway, then down the basement stairs. At one point she felt her tailbone crack, and one of her hips felt like it had gotten knocked out of place. She was pretty sure a ligament in one of her knees had been torn when she'd tried to stand against his dragging force, and every muscle in her body felt severely bruised. More clumps of her hair were ripping out the further they went. But her immediate pain, and the fear that he was preparing to rape her, was quickly replaced by overwhelming dread as she realized he'd dragged her past her bedroom and straight toward the embalming room.

When he reached the table and bent to pick her up, she kicked and punched at him with every ounce of strength she had left. But he placed her in a half-nelson, the resulting loss of leverage taking away the effective use of one side of her body. His midsection was like iron against Abby's frantically twisting body. When he leaned over to open a drawer, she finally had enough room between them to reach up to claw at his face, but she could only reach his neck due to him stretching his head away from her further than should have been possible. She managed to twist halfway out of his grip, and very nearly escaped it altogether, but he grabbed the furry collar of her coat and yanked her back toward him as he removed something from the drawer.

A second later, he released the half-nelson and forcefully grabbed her head, twisting it to expose the side of her neck. Abby felt a prick then, like a bee sting, followed by a strange pressure, as if he were pressing some instrument into the soft flesh of her neck. She let out a gargled cry as she realized what he'd done. Confirming that, her vision began to blur. It would be over for her if she passed out, she knew. Fighting a sudden sleepiness, Abby yelled, her intention to force whatever he'd given her away through her shouts and screams, as if by sheer will she could reverse the drug that was already making her eyelids grow heavy and turning her limbs into lead weights.

There was a sudden movement from him, coinciding with her body lifting and rotating. The next thing she knew, she was staring lazily at the ceiling, the cold stainless-steel table beneath her and straps tightening across her limbs and torso. Her mouth drooped open as a distinct paralysis began to wash over her like a wave, beginning in her midsection and spreading outward. Even her jaw and tongue grew numb, like at the dentist when she was getting work done. She concentrated all her energy on making a final movement, anything to help her own cause, before the numbness overtook her. But all she could control was her right forefinger. It lifted once then fell still to the table.

Frederik disappeared from view momentarily, rummaging around in cabinets then fiddling with something on the floor. Unable to move her head, Abby shifted her eyes in that direction but only saw the back of him as he faced the counter. She heard him unfitting some sort of tool or device from a plastic tube, followed by him screwing another one on. There was a blurry image of him turning to stand beside her then, a scalpel, hooked tool, and weirdly-shaped tube in hand. She saw several items behind him now, specifically the machine on the floor with a hose snaking from it, and several jugs of pink solution atop the counter.

"I've never tried this on someone alive," he said, a second before her world went dark.

CHAPTER 45

Detective Randall wanted in. He wasn't SWAT certified, but he was the PD's lead detective on the case, and if it had meant walking over hot coals he would have still insisted on raising his hand to be on the follow-up team. To her credit, Tan volunteered too. "We've got plenty of folks going in," he told her. "You don't have to do this." They'd just arrived on scene and stood amid a crowd of swarming officers down the isolated road from the house.

"Neither do you," Tan said, donning her external ballistic vest.

He nodded, then slipped his own vest on. "Copy that. Be prepared if he doesn't let them take him alive. After they go in, wait for their direction, okay?"

"Got it," she said, locking eyes with him. She'd been a detective for less than a week, but already she'd seen more than most did in their first month.

In black-out mode, they surrounded the house on all sides and at a distance to avoid tipping the residents off. At the commander's order, the SWAT team marched down the road then stormed up the dilapidated home's front door and rammed it open. Immediately, they discovered a vestibule system and were forced to ram the interior door open as well. Simultaneous to the entry, separate squads cleared the garage and crematorium. It quickly became obvious that the latter hadn't been used in years and contained no persons or observable evidence. With the garage cleared, the two-woman, thirteen-man team spread out to first clear the home's two darkened main floors, then the basement. Night-vision goggles were lowered, ballistic shields were hoisted, and weapons of both lethal and less-lethal types went to ready.

They began clearing both floors simultaneously. No suspects or living victims so far. Twenty-five corpses were found, however—each of them female, dressed and positioned exactly as they'd been photographed in verified PK Instagram posts. With all but one of the rooms and spaces on the main level checked, two members stayed back to clear it while the rest headed for the basement. The room's door was locked. Two members bookended it, flattening themselves against the wall. One turned and kicked it in while the other covered. They entered and quickly cleared the mostly empty, dimly-lit space. One of the members radioed that they'd cleared it while his partner checked the room's only furnishing—a desk located at the far wall. Two flickering, battery-powered candles atop it illuminated several objects there, most notably a toothless human skull. The jawbones had grooved scratches in several places where the teeth should have been, and both eye sockets contained numerous tool marks. A dusty newspaper clipping sat beside the skull. The SWAT member flipped up his night-vision goggles and bent to read it. From the *Chatham Citizen*, and dated October 2, 1995, it first documented the mysterious disappearance of Naomi Derring, second wife of the late Yves Derring, the town's former funeral director. She'd gone missing just days after her twin stepsons had turned eighteen. Police had questioned them, but they'd claimed to know nothing. The article went on to detail how investigators had later found Naomi's headless body in a field the following day. No suspects had been named, no evidence found.

Also atop the table was a family portrait of a mother, father, and set of smiling identical twin boys. One of them had deep dimples in his cheeks, while the other had an obvious birth defect. The member bent closer to get a better look. What he saw made his eyes grow wide with alarm, causing him to fumble for his radio and utter a loud curse in the process.

CHAPTER 46

Moments before that, the other members tried the basement door. It was open. A team member with a ballistic shield led the way, all of them easing their way down the stairs single-file. It was mostly dark down here, with only a square of light coming from what appeared to be a kind of operating room at the basement's far end. A machine hummed loudly from inside of it, and due to the angle from the staircase only part of the room was visible. They reached the bottom of the stairs and crept toward the room, weapons up, and wary of a woodpile to their right that had been slid aside to reveal a hidden wall behind it. Three members peeled off to cover each of the doors there. Their angle to the room now better, the other ten members observed a young woman in a blue formal dress lying atop a stainless-steel table. She appeared dead, or unconscious. A several-inches-long bleeding incision was visible on the side of her neck, with one of the veins within raised above the skin's surface by a flat, hooked instrument.

Suddenly, a man appeared from out of view inside the room. Dressed in a suit minus the tie, and with the first several buttons of his untucked dress shirt undone, he appeared so distracted by the loud machine and the plastic tube he was stretching toward the woman's neck, that he failed to see the point man training his carbine on him from fifteen feet away.

"Police! Drop it and raise your hands in the air!" the point man yelled. Surprised, the man looked up at them, the device-topped tube still in his hand. "Drop it now, or I'll drop you!" the point man demanded, slipping his finger inside the trigger guard.

The man dropped the tube and raised both hands high above his head. When he did, the tube fell from his hand and the metal, L-shaped device attached to it clinked on the aged tile. "I give up," he said above the buzzing machine. "Don't shoot."

"Frederik Derring?" the commander asked, stepping forward with his own carbine trained on the man.

"Yes, I am he," the man said.

The commander reached into his vest pocket and removed an enlarged driver's license photo, as well as the best surveillance photo they had of their suspect, then made a quick comparison. They both matched the man in front of him. "Where's Victor?" he demanded. "There's no need to get your brother involved any more than he already is."

The man dropped his head and sighed. He dared to glance back briefly at the woman atop the table. When he turned his head back toward the tactical team, regret filled his eyes. "I'll tell you where he is. But know that my brother was powerless to stop me. None of this was his fault."

With Frederik's hands still raised above his head, two smaller hands emerged from inside his shirt and reached out to undo the remaining buttons of his dress shirt. The shirt and jacket both parted then to reveal an identical looking, fully-clothed one-third-sized version of Frederik. The smaller man appeared to have been pressing his tiny head and body against Frederik's chest, folding and positioning his limbs in such a way that the untucked shirt and jacket covering him had sufficiently hidden him; a baggy coat or loose clothing would have concealed him similarly. At first, it seemed the smaller man was somehow fastened there with a harness or some other device. But when Frederik removed his jacket and shirt then let them fall to the floor, it became clear there was no harness or other device holding the smaller man up.

Confused, the commander took another step forward, squinting unbelievingly at the image before him. "Victor Derring?" he said to himself, finally recognizing the smaller man. Just then, his radio squawked. It took hearing three repeated transmissions from the panicked caller for the commander to realize it was one of the members clearing the room upstairs.

"Bravo Six to Bravo One—they're one man! I say again, they're *one man!*"

When Frederik turned slowly to turn off the buzzing machine —against the commander's order not to move—it was obvious that Victor was fused to his brother's body. The connection began at Frederik's sternum and ended at his belly button, the attached skin between them visibly stretching with each pronounced movement of either man. Due to Victor's severely drooped yet independently-moving head, it occurred to the commander that it would have been possible for Victor to sufficiently breathe while in public if Frederik's undershirts provided ventilation. No doubt that would have caused the larger brother to overheat quickly, however. Had a blanket or other covering been draped over Frederik's upper body and sideways bent head, the resulting mass could have been attributed to Victor's hunched back and hump. It would not have been difficult for people— even the police during brief interactions—to believe his birth defect had produced them. Concealing Frederik's arms and legs would have been difficult under normal conditions. But Victor's constant use of a blanket, Frederik's folded legs and tucked arms while seated in a wheelchair, and common politeness from others would have combined to make it possible. The commander's mind spun as he considered these scenarios. Also, a mental health counselor would never have been able to get away with the trickery in a normal office setting, or if seen in public often. But using Zoom sessions, and with a fully-functioning brother to complete the physical necessities of life...

The SWAT members looked at one another, unsure of what to do. For an extended moment, it was as if they were all suspended in their own disbelief. Each of them watched in awe as Victor's malformed arms moved upward, the tiny hands first placing a pair of glasses on his face, then smoothing over a few strands of loose gray hair over his balding scalp. His clothed legs, previously folded, now unfolded to hang at the level of Frederik's knees.

"Here he is, gentlemen," Frederik said confidently. The team members finally rushed forward to cuff him then, but not before Frederik's hand reached that of Victor, their fingers interlacing in that mindless manner that had begun in the womb and wouldn't end until the grave.

EPILOGUE

Abby Carlson looked up from her spot on the lakeside bench and watched the man in the shirt and tie approach. "You're late, Detective," she said jokingly.

Randall checked his watch. "Two minutes, sorry. I'll buy you an ice cream cone to make it up."

She waved him off. "Just kidding. It gave me extra time to watch the sailboats before you got here. They're so peaceful."

"Yeah," he said, watching them cut across the lake. The downtown skyline was visible above the opposing shore's tree line. "I was serious about the ice cream, by the way."

Abby glanced over at the food shack. The smell of grilling burgers and hot dogs floated from it to their position twenty yards away. "Why not. It's a beautiful day for ice cream."

"Every day is a beautiful day for it," Randall said, leading her there. After they each got cones, they returned to the bench and sat down beside each other. After a minute of shared silence, and them licking their cones, he asked, "How are things?"

She sighed. "Better. I finally got the courage to see a counselor again. A woman this time. And in person."

Randall nodded. "I'm sure it's been tough on you. It has been for all of us, too. One of the SWAT guys developed PTSD and retired on disability."

"Really?"

"Yeah. Cops are human too."

Several moments later, a woman passed by on the paved walking path with ten dogs on leashes, struggling mightily to keep them all walking straight. Laughing, Abby removed her phone and took a picture of them. Turning serious again, she asked Randall, "Any idea where they went? I didn't want to know at first, but after two years I think I'm ready now."

Randall shook his head. "It's anyone's guess since the court didn't impose any travel limitations on them other than their agreement to leave Minnesota. I wish I could give you a better answer than that."

Abby took a frustrated bite of her ice cream and huffed. "Aiding and abetting. They didn't even serve Victor's full two years with his good behavior. Those poor women, and everything Frederik did to them…"

"Unfortunately, plea deals are an ugly reality with criminal cases. Even ones as heinous as this. But since there wasn't any precedent in this state forcing one conjoined twin into any continued incarceration because of their twin's crimes, the state's hands were tied."

"Yeah, but dropping so many murder charges over a technicality? It's just…wrong."

"I don't agree with the decision, either. You know that. But unfortunately, my opinion doesn't count. There was also the argument that Frederik could have harmed or killed his brother at any time if he'd told the police what was going on. Killing Victor would have killed him, too, but that's exactly how his lawyer won the argument. It basically would have been a murder-suicide to avoid prison. I'm sorry, Abby. It sucks every way you look at it."

She looked down at her cone and nodded her understanding.

"So, as long as they don't ever come back to Minnesota, they get to carry on with their lives anywhere they want with no restrictions. Even more reason for me never to leave the state, not even for vacation. It isn't fair for me to be the one feeling like a prisoner. But at least I love it here."

"Give it some time. You may feel different later. Maybe travel with a group of people if that would make you feel safer. But something tells me he's done with you. He had a certain look in his eye at Victor's trial—I can't explain it."

"Hmm," she said, absently touching the long scar on her neck. "I still think about them, you know. All the women I saw. They had lives, families. Part of the reason I went to another counselor was the guilt. Why was I the only one to make it out alive?"

"It's normal to feel that way, but try your best not to feel guilty for surviving, Abby. You played a huge part in us finding you in time. After attending all the women's funerals, I talked to a therapist, too. It helped. It also helped that Detective Tan and I got to give statements during the last state legislative hearing. They're considering a change to the law for criminal acts committed by one half of conjoined twins."

She spoke about never getting the chance to confront her stepfather—he'd died during her stay in the hospital following her abduction. "I guess I didn't need to do that after all," she said, her voice introspective. "Funny how what Victor taught me still works."

"Are you keeping busy?" Randall asked.

Abby sighed. "I'm at a different clinic now, and I still have my cat; he loves attention. And I joined an intramural softball league with Derek."

"That's great. Dating?"

"I saw someone for a bit after what happened, but not recently. I'm learning that I like my alone time." She paused. "I'm not sure if I'll ever have kids. Bringing a child into such a messed-up world almost scares me more than what happened to me."

"I can understand that," Randall said, brushing over bits of his own life. He still had his dog, Daisy, and only had four years to go until retirement. He was still in Homicide but felt a change to a less stressful unit may soon be in the works. Alicia and he had gone out on several more dates, but they'd decided it best to just remain friends. He'd gone on a Caribbean cruise the previous winter, his first. When he showed Abby photos he'd taken during an excursion when a monkey had sat on his head, she burst out laughing. He recounted a few recent cases, including the fact that the homeless man and accomplice in Abby's abduction had been found incompetent to stand trial last month. A team of court-ordered psychiatrists had discovered he'd been hypnotized by someone with mental health expertise and was manipulated into helping Frederik with not just Abby's abduction, but several others as well. The state was likely to drop his charges since they'd been unable to prove if Victor or any other specific person had been at fault.

After watching the sailboats for a bit and finishing their ice cream, they stood to leave. "Feel free to call if you need to talk," Randall said. "Hard to believe it's almost been two years already."

"I will," she said, facing him and smiling. It felt good to talk to him again. He'd been there moments after the SWAT team captured the twins and had even ripped his own tie off to hold against her bleeding neck wound. He'd also been there to answer her myriad questions before, during, and after the case. She felt a bond with him because of it, and even though she knew the two of them may never meet like this again or even talk as he'd offered, it was nice to know someone else out there knew how she felt about what happened.

They hugged and said goodbye. As she turned toward her

parked car, she looked down and noticed something. "Hey, your shoelace is untied."

Randall looked down at it, shrugged, then walked to his cruiser without bothering to tie it.

Nine thousand miles away, a man walked along a similar-looking body of water, although technically a harbor and not a lake. He'd arrived to this country a week ago, after hopscotching through parts of South America and Europe. He'd remained in the States following the trial but had discovered a distaste for many of his home country's other regions. Minnesota had always been his favorite, but he knew that to go back and get caught would mean a lengthy imprisonment due to his court agreement. So many painful memories from his old life, yet cherished ones as well.

He walked into a restaurant overlooking the sail-shaped opera house and sat at the bar. The beautiful weather and his buoyant mood called for a late-morning mimosa. Soon after he ordered, a friendly-looking young woman sat down beside him and ordered a Bloody Mary. "What part of America are you from?" she asked him.

"How can you tell?" he asked, turning to face her.

"I heard you ordering your drink as I was walking in. American accents are even stronger than our Australian ones, I think."

He laughed. "I'm not so sure about that."

"So says someone who doesn't realize he has an accent at all."

He executed a seated bow. "Touché."

Smiling, she extended her hand. "Connie Franklin."

He shook it. "Frederik. Frederik Hugo. Nice to meet you."

They made idle chit-chat then sat looking around in a moment of awkward silence. When their drinks arrived moments later, he paid for them both. "Thank you, but you didn't have to do that," she said, blushing.

"Don't mention it," he said, unbuttoning the top two buttons on his shirt. Even though winter was coming to this part of the world, he was getting warm. "To my new home," he said, raising his glass to hers. "May it be just as promising as my last." They clinked glasses.

"So, what do you do for a living?" she asked him, sipping her drink.

He smiled when she asked that, deep dimples creasing his handsome face. "I'll tell you if you tell me."

ACKNOWLEDGMENTS

Many people assisted with the creation of this book. Huge thanks goes to Jennifer Collins, my developmental editor, who once again lent a keen eye toward large-scale plot and characterization issues. Equal thanks goes to Jason Pettus, my longtime line editor. In addition to cutting and sculpting the text, he also offered added insight into broader story elements. Caryn Pine, my proofreader, provided valuable last-minute insight and finishing touches, and Jennifer Eaton created excellent interior formatting.

Special thanks goes to James K. Miller, a professional funeral director, who granted me a lengthy interview on his personal time. His expert knowledge in the field of mortuary science was vital to many of the book's technical issues. Thanks also goes to Cold Case Detective Ron Chalmers, of the Pinellas County Sheriff's Office. He took the time from work, family (and as my amateur adult ice hockey league teammate) to lend me in-depth insight into the aspects of a large-scale homicide investigation, an aspect of my former career I had not personally experienced. Appreciation of Robert Turner as well, for lending insight into law enforcement drones.

Numerous other people helped with this book as well. As usual, my longtime partner Andrea Honan offered valuable technical computer support, as well as heaps of patience, enthusiasm, and encouragement as I worked through multiple drafts. Her positive attitude and loving support were much needed and appreciated. My close family friend Bradley Wank offered professional advice on clinical psychotherapy, and many colleagues, friends, and family members assisted in various ways as well. Lastly, my birth state of Minnesota deserves its own recognition. I began writing there as a boy, and it shaped me in ways I'll probably never fully understand. In many ways, it is its own character in the book. I hope the story—and I— served it well.

The author asks the reader to please post an honest review at the online book retailers and social media accounts of their choice. It would help spread the word to others and is greatly appreciated.

Made in United States
Orlando, FL
20 December 2024

56139197R00224